Honour

ELIF SHAFAK

VIKING

an imprint of

PENGUIN BOOKS

VIKING

Published by the Penguin Group

Penguin Books Ltd, 80 Strand, London WC2R ORL, England

Penguin Group (USA) Inc., 375 Hudson Street, New York, New York 10014, USA

Penguin Group (Canada), 90 Eglinton Avenue East, Suite 700, Toronto, Ontario, Canada M4P 2Y3

(a division of Pearson Penguin Canada Inc.)

Penguin Ireland, 25 St Stephen's Green, Dublin 2, Ireland (a division of Penguin Books Ltd)

Penguin Group (Australia), 250 Camberwell Road,

Camberwell, Victoria 3124, Australia (a division of Pearson Australia Group Pty Ltd)

Penguin Books India Pvt Ltd, 11 Community Centre, Panchsheel Park, New Delhi – 110 017, India

Penguin Group (NZ), 67 Apollo Drive, Rosedale, Auckland 0632, New Zealand

(a division of Pearson New Zealand Ltd)

Penguin Books (South Africa) (Pty) Ltd, Block D, Rosebank Office Park,

181 Jan Smuts Avenue, Parktown North, Gauteng 2193, South Africa

Penguin Books Ltd, Registered Offices: 80 Strand, London WC2R ORL, England

www.penguin.com

First published 2012

001

Set in 12/14.75pt Bembo Book MT Std
Typeset by Jouve (UK), Milton Keynes
Printed in Great Britain by Clays Ltd, St Ives plc

A CIP catalogue record for this book is available from the British Library

ISBN: 978-0-670-92115-7

www.greenpenguin.co.uk

MIX
Paper from
responsible sources
FSC
www.fsc.org   FSC™ C018179

Penguin Books is committed to a sustainable
future for our business, our readers and our planet.
This book is made from Forest Stewardship
Council™ certified paper.

ALWAYS LEARNING

PEARSON

When I was seven years old, we lived in a green house. One of our neighbours, a talented tailor, would often beat his wife. In the evenings we listened to the shouts, the cries, the swearing. In the mornings we went on with our lives as usual. The entire neighbourhood pretended not to have heard, not to have seen.

This novel is dedicated to those who hear, those who see.

As long as he can remember he has had a sense of himself as prince of the house, and of his mother as his dubious promoter and anxious protector.

J. M. Coetzee, *Boyhood: Scenes from Provincial Life*

Esma

London, 12 September 1992

My mother died twice. I promised myself I would not let her story be forgotten, but I could never find the time or the will or the courage to write about it. That is, until recently. I don't think I'll ever become a real writer and that's quite all right now. I've reached an age at which I'm more at peace with my limitations and failures. But I had to tell the story, even if only to one person. I had to send it into some corner of the universe where it could float freely, away from us. I owed it to Mum, this freedom. And I had to finish it this year. Before he was released from prison.

In a few hours I'll take the sesame *halva* off the hob, let it cool by the sink and kiss my husband, pretending not to notice the worried look in his eyes. Then I'll leave the house with my twin daughters – seven years old, four minutes apart – and drive them to a birthday party. They'll quarrel on the way, and, for once, I'll not scold them. They'll wonder if there will be a clown at the party, or, better still, a magician.

'Like Harry Houdini,' I'll say.

'Harry who?'

'Who-deeny, she said, you silly!'

'Who's that, Mummy?'

That will hurt. A pain like a bee sting. Not much on the surface, but a growing burning within. I'll realize, as I have done on so many occasions before, that they don't know anything about their family history because I have told them so little. One day, when they're ready. When I'm ready.

After I have dropped off the girls, I'll chat for a while with the other mothers who have shown up. I'll remind the party host that one of my daughters is allergic to nuts, but, since it is difficult to tell the twins apart, it is better to keep an eye on both of them and make

I

sure neither gets any food with nuts, including the birthday cake. That is a bit unfair to my other daughter, but between siblings that does happen sometimes, the unfairness, I mean.

I'll then get back into my car, a red Austin Montego that my husband and I take turns driving. The journey from London to Shrewsbury is three and a half hours. I may have to make a pit stop just before Birmingham. I will keep the radio on – that will help to chase the ghosts away, the music.

There have been many times when I thought of killing him. I have made elaborate plans that involved guns, poison or, better yet, a flick-knife – a poetic justice, of sorts. I have also thought of forgiving him, fully and truly. In the end, I haven't achieved either.

★

When I arrive in Shrewsbury, I'll leave the car in front of the railway station and take the five-minute walk to the grimy prison building. I'll pace the street or lean against the wall across from the main entrance, waiting for him to come out. I don't know how long this will take. And I don't know how he'll react when he sees me. I haven't visited him for more than a year. I used to go regularly, but as the day of his release drew closer I just stopped.

At some point the massive door will open from inside and he'll walk out. He'll gaze up at the overcast sky, unused to seeing this vast expanse above his head after fourteen years of incarceration. I imagine him blinking at the daylight, like a creature of the dark. In the meantime, I'll stay put, counting up to ten or one hundred or three thousand. We won't embrace. We won't shake hands. A mutual nod and the thinnest of greetings in small, strangulated voices. Once we get to the station, he'll hop into the car. I'll be surprised to see how athletic he is. He's still a young man, after all.

Should he want to have a cigarette, I won't object, even though I hate the smell and don't let my husband smoke in the car or in the house. We'll drive across the English countryside, passing through quiet meadows and open fields. He'll inquire about my daughters. I'll tell him they're fine, growing fast. He'll smile, though he hasn't the slightest idea about parenthood. I won't ask him anything in return.

I will have brought a cassette along to play. The greatest hits of ABBA – all the songs that my mother used to hum while cooking or cleaning or sewing. 'Take a Chance on Me', 'Mamma Mia', 'Dancing Queen', 'The Name of the Game' . . . for she'll be watching us, I'm sure. Mothers don't go to heaven when they die. They get special permission from God to stay around a bit longer and watch over their children, no matter what has passed between them in their brief mortal lives.

Back in London, once we reach Barnsbury Square, I'll search for a parking space, grumbling to myself. It will start to rain – tiny crystal drops. Finally, we'll find a spot into which I'll squeeze the car after a dozen manoeuvres. I can deceive myself that I'm a good driver, until it comes to parking. I wonder if he'll scoff at me for being a typical woman driver. He would have done so once.

We'll walk together towards the house, the street quiet and bright behind and ahead of us. For a fleeting moment we'll compare our surroundings with our old home in Hackney, the house on Lavender Grove, marvelling at how different things seem now, and how time has moved forward, even when we couldn't.

Once inside, we'll take off our shoes and put on slippers – classic charcoal for him, a pair of my husband's, and for me burgundy slip-ons with pompoms. His face will crumple when he sees them. To put his mind at ease, I'll tell him they are a present from my daughters. He'll relax, now realizing that they are not *hers*. The resemblance is merely coincidental.

From the doorway he'll watch me make tea, which I'll serve without milk and with lots of sugar, that is, if gaol hasn't changed his habits. Then I'll take out the sesame *halva*. We'll sit together by the window, with porcelain cups and plates in our hands, like genteel strangers, watching it rain on the violas in my back garden. He'll compliment me on my cooking, saying how much he has missed sesame *halva*, though he'll politely decline another serving. I'll tell him I follow Mum's recipe to the letter, but it never turns out as good as hers. That will shut him up. We'll lock gazes, the silence heavy in the air. Then he'll excuse himself, saying that he feels tired and would like to rest, if that is all right. I'll show him to his room and close the door, slowly.

I'll leave him there. In a room in my house. Neither far away nor too close. I'll keep him confined within those four walls, between the hate and the love, none of which I can help but feel, for ever trapped in a box in my heart.

He is my brother.

He, a murderer.

Names Like Sugar Cubes

A Village near the River Euphrates, 1945

When Pembe was born, Naze was so sad she forgot about all she had suffered for the previous twenty-six hours, the blood oozing between her legs, and tried to get up and walk away. At least, that's what everyone said – everyone present in the delivery room on that blustery day.

As much as she might have wanted to leave, however, Naze could not go anywhere. To the surprise of the women in the room and her husband, Berzo, waiting in the courtyard, she was forced back into bed by a new wave of contractions. Three minutes later the head of a second baby appeared. Lots of hair, reddish skin, all wet and wrinkled. Another girl, only smaller.

This time Naze did not attempt to run away. She gave a wisp of a sigh, buried her head in the pillow and turned towards the open window, as if straining to hear fate's whisper in the wind, as mild as milk. If she listened attentively, she thought, she might hear an answer from the skies. After all, there must be a reason, a justification unbeknownst to her but surely obvious to Allah, as to why He had given them two more daughters when they already had six, and still not a single son.

Thus Naze pursed her lips like a folded hem, determined not to say a word until Allah had explained, fully and convincingly, the motive behind His actions. Even in sleep her mouth was clamped tight. During the next forty days and forty nights she did not speak a word. Not when she was cooking chickpeas with sheep's-tail fat, nor when she was giving her six other daughters baths in a large round tin bucket, nor even when she was making cheese with wild garlic and herbs, nor when her husband asked her what she would like to name the babies. She remained as silent as the graveyard by the hills where all her ancestors were buried and where she, too, would some day be laid to rest.

It was a rugged, remote Kurdish village with no roads, no electricity, no doctor, no school. Barely any news from the outside world permeated its sheath of seclusion. The aftermath of the Second World War, the atomic bomb . . . The villagers hadn't heard of any of this. And yet they were convinced that strange things happened in the universe, that is, beyond the shores of the Euphrates. The world being what it was, there was no point in wishing to discover it. Everything there had been, and everything there ever would be, was already present here and now. Human beings were ordained to be sedentary, like trees and boulders. Unless you happened to be one of these three: a wandering mystic who had lost his past, a fool who had lost his head or a *majnun* who had lost his beloved.

Dervishes, eccentrics and lovers aside, for the rest of the people nothing was astonishing, and everything was as it should be. Whatever took place in one corner was heard, at once, by everyone else. Secrets were a luxury only the rich could afford, and in this village, named Mala Çar Bayan, 'House of Four Winds', no one was rich.

The village elders were three small-statured, forlorn-looking men who spent most of their time in the sole tea house contemplating the mysteries of Divine Wisdom and the stupidities of politicians while they sipped tea out of glasses as thin as eggshells, as fragile as life. When they heard about Naze's oath of silence, they decided to pay her a visit.

'We came to warn you that you're about to commit sacrilege,' said the first man, who was so old the slightest breeze could have knocked him down.

'How can you expect Allah the Almighty to reveal His ways to you when He is known to have spoken only to prophets?' remarked the second man, who had but a few teeth left in his mouth. 'Surely there was no woman among them.'

The third man waved his hands, as stiff and gnarled as tree roots. 'Allah wants to hear you talk. If it had been any other way, He would have made you into a fish.'

Naze listened, now and then dabbing her eyes with the ends of her headscarf. For a moment, she imagined herself as a fish – a big, brown trout in the river, its fins glittering in the sun, its spots surrounded by pale haloes. Little did she know that her children and grandchildren would, at different times in their lives, feel attached to various kinds of fish, and an affinity with the kingdom under the water would run in the family for generations to come.

'Speak!' said the first old man. 'It's against nature for your kind to be quiet. What goes against nature goes against Allah's will.'

But still Naze said nothing.

When the honourable guests had left, she approached the cradle where the twins were sleeping. The shimmer from the lighted hearth painted the room a golden yellow, giving the babies' skins a soft glow, almost angelic. Her heart mellowed. She turned to her six daughters, who had lined up beside her, from the tallest to the shortest, and said, in a voice both hoarse and hollow: 'I know what I'll name them.'

'Tell us, Mama!' the girls exclaimed, delighted to hear her speak again.

Naze cleared her throat and said, with a note of defeat, 'This one will be Bext and the other, Bese.'

'Bext and Bese,' the girls echoed in unison.

'Yes, my children.'

Upon saying this, she smacked her lips, as if the names had left a distinct taste on her tongue, salty and sour. Bext and Bese in Kurdish, Kader and Yeter in Turkish, Destiny and Enough in every language possible. This would be her way of declaring to Allah that even though, like a good Muslim, she was resigned to her fate, she had had her fill of daughters and the next time she was pregnant, which she knew would be the last time because she was forty-one years old and past her prime now, He had to give her a son and nothing but a son.

That same evening, when their father came home, the girls rushed to give him the good news: 'Papa! Papa! Mama is talking.'

Pleased as he was to hear his wife speaking again, Berzo's face clouded over when he learned about the names she had chosen for the newborns. Shaking his head, he remained silent for few awkward minutes.

'Destiny and Enough,' he muttered finally, as though to himself.

'But you haven't named the babies, really. You've sent a petition to the skies.'

Naze stared down at her feet, studying the toe poking out of a hole in her woollen sock.

'Names hinting at resentful feelings might offend the Creator,' Berzo continued. 'Why draw His wrath upon us? Better stick to ordinary names and stay on the safe side.'

Thus saying, he announced that he had alternatives in mind: Pembe and Jamila – Pink and Beautiful. Names like sugar cubes that melted in your tea, sweet and yielding, with no sharp edges.

Though Berzo's decision was final, Naze's choices were not easily discarded. They would linger in everyone's memory, tied to the family tree like two flimsy kites caught in some branches. Thus the twins came to be known by both sets of names: Pembe Kader and Jamila Yeter – Pink Destiny and Enough Beauty. Who could tell that one of these names would some day be printed in newspapers all around the world?

Colours

A Village near the River Euphrates, 1953

Since she was a little girl, Pembe had adored dogs. She loved the way they could see into people's souls, even in deep sleep through closed eyes. Most grown-ups thought dogs did not understand much, but she believed that was not true. They understood everything. They were just forgiving.

There was one sheepdog in particular that she treasured. Droopy ears, long muzzle, a shaggy coat of black, white and tan. He was a good-natured creature that liked to chase butterflies and play catch with twigs, and ate almost everything. They called him Kitmir, but also Quto or Dodo. His name changed all the time.

One day, out of the blue, the animal started to act strangely, as if possessed by a mischievous *djinni*. When Pembe tried to pat him on his chest, he lunged at her with a growl and bit her hand. More than the shallow cut he caused, it was the change in the dog's character that was worrying. Lately there had been an outbreak of rabies in the region and the three village elders insisted that she go to a doctor, except there was none within sixty miles.

So it was that the girl Pembe, with her father, Berzo, took first a minibus, and then a bus, to the big city, Urfa. The thought of spending the day away from her twin, Jamila, sent a chill down her spine, but she was equally delighted to have her father all to herself. Berzo was a solidly built, broad-boned man with strong features and a large moustache, the hands of a peasant, and hair greying at the temples. His deep-set hazel eyes were kindly, and apart from the times when he displayed a temper, he had a calm disposition – even if it saddened him profoundly not to have a son to carry his name to the ends of the earth. Though a man of few words and fewer smiles, he communicated with his children better than his wife did. In return, his eight

9

daughters competed for his love, like chickens pecking at a handful of grain.

Travelling to the city was fun and exciting; waiting at the hospital was neither. Lined up in front of the doctor's door were twenty-three patients. Pembe knew the exact number because, unlike the other eight-year-old girls in her village, she and Jamila went to school – a decrepit, one-storey building in another village forty minutes' walk away – and could count. There was a stove in the middle of the classroom that spurted more smoke than heat. Younger children sat to one side of it, older children to the other. As the windows were rarely opened, the air inside was stale and as thick as sawdust.

Before starting school Pembe had taken it for granted that everyone in the world spoke Kurdish. Now she understood that wasn't the case. Some people didn't know Kurdish at all. Their teacher, for instance. He was a man with short-cut, thinning hair and a doleful look in his eyes, as if he missed the life he had left behind in Istanbul and resented having been sent to this forsaken place. He got upset when the students didn't understand what he was saying or made a joke in Kurdish at his expense. He had recently introduced a set of rules: whoever uttered a word in Kurdish would have to stand on one foot by the blackboard with their back turned to their classmates. Most students stayed there for a few minutes and were then pardoned on the condition that they didn't repeat the mistake; but from time to time someone was forgotten in the course of the day and had to spend hours in the same position. The rule had generated opposite reactions in the twins. While Jamila clammed up completely, refusing to speak any language whatsoever, Pembe tried hard to excel in Turkish, determined to learn the teacher's language and, through that, to reach his heart.

Meanwhile, their mother, Naze, didn't see the point in their going to such lengths to master words and numbers that would be of no use, since they would all get married before long. But her husband insisted that his daughters be educated.

'Every day they walk all that way back and forth. Their shoes are wearing out,' Naze grumbled. 'And what for?'

'So that they can read the constitution,' said Berzo.

'What's a constitution?' she asked suspiciously.

'The law, you ignorant woman! The big book! There are things that are allowed, things that are forbidden, and if you don't know the difference you're in deep trouble.'

Naze clucked her tongue, still not convinced. 'How's that going to help my daughters get married?'

'What do you know? If one day their husbands treat them badly, they won't have to put up with it. They can take their children and leave.'

'Oh, where will they go?'

Berzo hadn't thought about that. 'They can seek shelter in their father's home, of course.'

'Uh-hm, is that why they trudge so far every day and fill their minds with that stuff? So that they can return to the house where they were born?'

'Go and bring me tea,' Berzo snapped. 'You talk too much.'

'Perish the thought,' Naze murmured as she headed to the kitchen. 'No daughter of mine will abandon her husband. If she does, I'll beat the hell out of her, even if I'm dead by then. I'll come back as a ghost!'

That threat, empty and impetuous though it was, would become a prophecy. Even long after she had passed away, Naze would come back to haunt her daughters, some more than others. After all, she was a stubborn woman. She never forgot. And she never forgave – unlike dogs.

Now, as they waited at the hospital, Pembe gaped with her child's eyes at the men and women lined up in the corridor. Some were smoking, some eating the flat breads they had brought from home, some nursing wounds or wailing in pain. Over everything hung a heavy stench – of sweat, disinfectant and cough syrup.

As she observed the state of each patient, the girl felt a growing admiration for the doctor she had yet to meet. The man who could provide a cure for so many diseases must be an extraordinary person, she decided. A seer. A magus. An ageless wizard with miraculous fingers. By the time it was their turn, she was brimming with curiosity and eagerly followed her father into the doctor's room.

Inside, everything was white. Not like the suds that formed on the surface of the fountain when they washed their clothes. Not like the snow that piled up outside on a winter's night or like the whey they mixed with wild garlic to make cheese. It was a white she had never seen before – unyielding and unnatural. A white so cold it made her shiver. The chairs, the walls, the floor tiles, the examination table, even the cups and scalpels were awash with this no-colour. Never had it entered Pembe's mind that white could be so disconcerting, so distant, so dark.

What surprised her even more was that the doctor was a woman – but different from her mother, her aunts, her neighbours. Just as the room was swathed in an absence of colour, the doctor in front of her eyes had none of the female qualities with which Pembe was familiar. Underneath her long coat she sported a knee-length taupe skirt, stockings of the finest and softest wool, and leather boots. She wore glasses so square they gave her the appearance of a grumpy owl. Not that the child had ever seen a grumpy owl but surely this was what one must look like. How different she was from the women who worked in the fields from dawn to dusk, got wrinkles from squinting in the sun and bore children until they had enough sons. Here was a female who was used to having people, including men, hang on her every word. Even Berzo had taken off his cap and dropped his shoulders in her presence.

The doctor gave the father and daughter no more than a grudging glance. It was as if their mere existence tired – even saddened – her. They were clearly the last people she wanted to treat at the end of this arduous day. She did not talk to them much, letting the nurse ask the important questions. *What was the dog like? Was he foaming at the mouth? Did he act strangely when he saw water? Had he bitten anyone else in the village? Was he examined afterwards?* The nurse spoke very fast, as if there was a clock ticking somewhere and time was running short. Pembe was glad her mother had not come with them. Naze wouldn't have been able to follow the conversation, and would have made all the wrong assumptions, prickly with apprehension.

While the doctor wrote out a prescription, the nurse gave the child an injection in the stomach that sent her into a full-throated wail. She was still crying hard when they stepped out into the corridor, where the attention of the strangers worsened her distress. It was at that point that her father, with his head straight, shoulders erect – Berzo again – whispered in her ear that if she would be quiet and behave like the good girl that she was, he would take her to the cinema.

Pembe instantly fell silent, eyes glittering with expectation. The word 'cinema' sounded like a wrapped sweet: she didn't know what was inside, but she was sure it had to be something nice.

★

There were two theatres in the city. The larger one was used more by visiting politicians than by local performers and musicians. Before and after the elections crowds of men gathered there and fiery speeches were made, promises and propaganda circling the air like buzzing bees.

The second venue was far more modest but just as popular. It showed films of varying quality, thanks to the tastes of its owner, who preferred adventures to political tirades and paid smugglers large commissions to bring him new films, along with tobacco, tea and other contraband. Thus the people of Urfa had seen a number of John Wayne Westerns, *The Man from the Alamo* and *Julius Caesar*, as well as *The Gold Rush* and other films involving the funny little man with the dark moustache.

On this day there was a black-and-white Turkish film, which Pembe watched from the beginning to the end with her mouth slightly agape. The heroine was a poor, pretty girl in love with a boy who was very rich, very spoiled. But he changed. Such was the magic of love. While everyone – starting with the boy's parents – disparaged the young lovers and connived to separate them, they would meet secretly under a willow tree on the banks of a river. There they would hold hands and sing songs as sad as a sigh.

Pembe loved everything about the cinema – the ornate foyer, the heavy, draped curtains, the thick, welcoming darkness. She couldn't wait to tell Jamila about this new wonder. On the bus back home, she sang the film's theme song over and over.

Your name is carved on my destiny,
Your love flows in my veins
If you ever smile at someone else
I'd kill myself or grief would kill me first

As Pembe swayed her hips and fluttered her hands, the other passengers clapped and cheered. When finally she fell silent, more out of weariness than out of any sense of propriety, Berzo laughed, his eyes creasing around the edges.

'My talented girl,' he said, with a touch of pride in his voice.

Pembe buried her face in her father's broad chest, inhaling the lavender oil that perfumed his moustache. She didn't know it, but this would be one of the happiest moments of her life.

★

When they returned home, they found Jamila in a dreadful state – eyes swollen, face puffed up. All day she had waited by the window, fidgeting with her hair, chewing her bottom lip. Then, suddenly and without reason, she had unleashed a terrible cry. No matter how hard her mother and sisters tried to calm her down, she hadn't stopped wailing.

'When Jamila started to weep, what time was it?' Pembe queried.

Naze gave this some thought. 'Sometime in the afternoon, I suppose. Why are you asking?'

Pembe offered no answer. She had learned what she wanted to know. She and her twin, though miles apart, had cried out simultaneously at the moment of the injection. People said twins were two bodies with one soul. But they were more than that. They were one body, one soul. Destiny and Enough. When one closed her eyes, the other one went blind. If one hurt, the other bled. And when one of them had nightmares, it was the other's heart that pounded inside her chest.

That same evening, Pembe showed Jamila the dance steps she had seen in the film. Taking turns to mimic the heroine, they twirled, kissed and hugged like a couple in love, giggling.

'What's all this noise?'

It was Naze, her voice stiff with disdain. She had been winnowing rice on a flat tray.

Pembe's eyes widened with resentment. 'We were just dancing.'

'And why would you do that?' Naze retorted. 'Unless you two have decided to turn yourselves into harlots.'

Pembe didn't know what a harlot was but dared not ask. She felt a surge of resentment course through her – why couldn't her mother enjoy the songs as the passengers on the bus had done? Why were perfect strangers more tolerant than one's closest kin? She was still contemplating this question when she heard Jamila take a step forward, as if to own up to the guilt, and murmur, 'We're sorry, Mama. We won't do it again.'

Pembe glared at her twin, feeling betrayed.

'It's for your own good that I say what I say. If you laugh too much today, you'll be crying tomorrow. Better to feel bad now than soon after.'

'I don't understand why we can't laugh today and tomorrow and the next day,' Pembe remarked.

It was Jamila's turn to scowl now. Her sister's brazenness had not only taken her by surprise but also put her in an awkward position. She held her breath, fearing what would follow next: the rolling pin. Whenever one of the girls crossed a line, Naze smacked both of them with the thin wooden rod in her kitchen. Never on their faces – a girl's beauty was her dowry – but on their backs and bottoms. The girls found it strange that the instrument they so bitterly abhorred also made the fluffy pastries that they cherished.

Yet that evening Naze did not punish anyone. She scrunched up her nose, shook her head and looked away – as if she longed to be somewhere else. When she spoke again, her voice was calm. 'Modesty is a woman's only shield,' she said. 'Bear this in mind: if you lose that, you will be worth no more than a chipped kuruş.* This world is cruel. It won't take pity on you.'

In her mind's eye Pembe flipped a coin in the air and watched it land on her palm. There were always two sides, and two sides only.

* Small unit of Turkish currency.

Win or lose. Dignity or disgrace, and little consolation for those who got the wrong one.

It was all because women were made of the lightest cambric, Naze continued, whereas men were cut of thick, dark fabric. That is how God had tailored the two: one superior to the other. As to why He had done that, it wasn't up to human beings to question. What mattered was that the colour black didn't show stains, unlike the colour white, which revealed even the tiniest speck of dirt. By the same token, women who were sullied would be instantly noticed and separated from the rest, like husks removed from grains. Hence when a virgin gave herself to a man – even if he were the man whom she loved – she had everything to lose, while he had absolutely nothing to lose.

So it was that in the land where Pink Destiny and Enough Beauty were born, 'honour' was more than a word. It was also a name. You could call your child 'Honour', as long as it was a boy. Men had honour. Old men, middle-aged men, even schoolboys so young that they still smelled of their mothers' milk. Women did not have honour. Instead, they had shame. And, as everyone knew, Shame would be a rather poor name to bear.

As she listened, Pembe recalled the stark whiteness of the doctor's office. The discomfort that she had felt then returned – only now the feeling was magnified. She wondered about the other colours – periwinkle-blue, pistachio-green and hazelnut-brown – and the other fabrics – velvet, gabardine and brocade. There was such variety in this world, surely more than could be found on a tray of winnowed rice.

It would be one of the many ironies of Pembe's life that the things she hated to hear from Naze she would repeat to her daughter, Esma, word for word, years later, in England.

Askander . . . Askander . . .

A Village near the River Euphrates, 1962–7

Pembe was a woman of untenable thoughts and unfounded fears. This part of her personality wasn't something that had evolved over the years. Instead, she had turned superstitious abruptly, almost overnight: the night Iskender was born.

Pembe was seventeen years old when she became a mother – young, beautiful and apprehensive. There she was in a room bathed in a dusky light, staring at the cradle, as if she was still not convinced that this baby with his pink, fragile fingers, translucent skin and a blotchy purple mark on his button nose had defied all the odds and survived; that he would, from now on, be her child, hers alone. Here was a son – the son that her mother had craved, and prayed to have throughout her entire life.

Naze had had one more full-term pregnancy after Pink Destiny and Enough Beauty. It had to be a boy this time – there was no other possibility. Allah owed her this; *He was in her debt*, she said, even though she knew she was speaking utter blasphemy. It was a secret agreement between her and the Creator. After so many girls, He was going to make it up to her. Such was her conviction that she spent months knitting little blankets, socks and vests in a blue deeper than stormy nights, all of them designed for her perfect little boy. She wouldn't listen to anyone – not even to the midwife who examined her after her waters broke and told her, in a voice as quiet as the breeze, that the baby wasn't positioned right, and that they had better go to the city. There still was time. If they set off now they could be at the hospital before the contractions started.

'Nonsense,' Naze retorted, holding the midwife's eyes in her fiery stare.

Everything was fine. Everything was in His hands. She was

forty-nine years old and this would be her miracle child. She was going to give birth here in her own house, in her own bed, as she had done with each and every baby before, only this time it would be a boy.

It was a breech birth. The baby was too big and it was pointing the wrong way. The hours passed. Nobody counted how many, for it would bring bad luck. Besides, only Allah was the owner of time, the Divine Clockmaker. What was unbearably long for mere mortals was only the blink of an eye for Him. Thus the clock on the wall was covered with black velvet, just like all the mirrors in the house, each of which was a gate to the unknown.

'She cannot push any more,' said one of the women present.

'Then we'll have to do it for her,' said the midwife resolutely, but her eyes gave away the fear she was hiding.

The midwife put her hand straight through Naze until she felt the sleek, slippery baby squirm under her fingers. There was a faint heartbeat, like a sputtering candle that had reached its end. Gently but firmly, she tried to turn the baby inside the womb. Once. Twice. She was more relentless the third time, acting with a sense of urgency. The baby moved clockwise, but it was not enough. Its head pressed against the umbilical cord, dangerously stifling the amount of oxygen that went through it.

Naze had lost so much blood she was fading in and out, her cheeks the colour of winter. A choice had to be made. The midwife knew it would be either the mother or the baby. There was no way she could save them both. Her conscience was as silent as a moonless night, and just as dark. All at once, she made up her mind. She would pick the woman.

At that moment Naze, lying there with her eyes clamped shut, dancing with death, bleeding umbrage, lifted her head and yelled: 'No, you whore!'

It was a cry so shrill and forceful, it didn't sound as if it had come out of a human being. The woman in bed had turned into a wild animal, famished and feral, ready to attack anyone who stood in her way. She was running in a thick forest where the sun cast shimmering gold and ochre reflections on the leaves – free in a way she had never been before. Those within hearing distance suspected she had lost her mind. Only the mad could scream like that.

'Cut me, you bitch! Take him out,' Naze ordered and then laughed, as if she had already crossed a threshold beyond which everything was a joke. 'It's a boy, don't you see? My son is coming! You spiteful, jealous whore. Take a pair of scissors! Now! Cut my belly open and take my son out!'

Swarms of tiny flies whirred in the room, like vultures circling a prey. There was too much blood everywhere. Too much rage and resentment smeared on the carpets, the sheets, the walls. The air inside the room had become heavy, listless. The flies . . . if only the flies could be made to disappear.

Naze did not survive. Nor did the baby for long – the baby whose gender she had been wrong about the whole time. Her ninth infant, the child who killed her and then quietly passed away in her cot, was another girl.

So on that day in November 1962, as she lay awake in her maternity bed late into the wee hours, it was the thought that God could be so arbitrary that distressed Pembe. Here she was, only seventeen and already breastfeeding a son. She couldn't help suspecting that from somewhere in the heavens, under a watery light, her mother was watching her with envy. *Eight births, five miscarriages, one dead baby, and not one was a son . . . And here You are already giving a healthy boy to my hare-brained daughter. Why, Allah? Why?*

Naze's voice echoed in Pembe's ears until it became a ball of fury that rolled down to her chest and nestled in her stomach. Hard as she tried to fend off her anxieties, she ended up only building new ones. They drew circles in her mind, spinning like a pegtop, and suddenly there was nowhere to hide from the evil eye that was her late mother's gaze. Once she started paying attention to it, she noticed that gaze everywhere. It was in the grain and cashew nuts that she pounded in a stone mortar, turned into a paste and then consumed to enrich her milk. It was in the rivulets of rain that streamed down the windowpanes, in the almond oil that she applied to her hair at every bath, and in the thick, bubbly yoghurt soup that simmered on the stove.

'*Allah the Merciful, please make my mother shut her eyes in her grave and make my son grow up strong and healthy,*' Pembe prayed, rocking herself back and forth, as if it were she who needed to be put to sleep, not the baby.

★

The night Iskender was born, Pembe had a nightmare – as she had had many other times during her pregnancy. But this one felt so real that a part of her would never recover from it, never return from the liquid land of dreams.

She saw herself lying supine on an ornamental carpet, her eyes wide open, her belly swollen. Above her a few clouds slithered across the sky. It was hot, too hot. Then she realized the carpet was stretched over water, a rowdy river swirling under her weight. *How is it that I'm not sinking,* she thought to herself. Instead of an answer, the sky opened up and a pair of hands descended. Were they the hands of God? Or the hands of her late mother? She couldn't tell. They cut open her belly. There was no pain, only the horror of being aware of what was happening. Then the hands pulled out the baby. It was a plump little boy with eyes the colour of dark pebbles. Before Pembe could touch him, let alone cuddle him, the hands dropped the baby into the water. He floated away on a piece of driftwood, like the prophet Moses in his basket.

Pembe shared the nightmare with only one person, her eyes bright and burning as she spoke, as if she had a fever. Jamila listened, and, either because she truly believed in it or because she wanted to free her twin of the terror of Naze's ghost, she came up with an explanation.

'You must have been jinxed. Probably by a *djinni*.'

'A *djinni*,' Pembe echoed.

'Yes, sweetheart. The *djinn* love to take a nap on chairs and sofas, don't you know? Adult *djinn* can make a dash for it when they see a human coming, but infants are not so fast. And pregnant women are heavy, clumsy. You must have sat on a baby *djinni* and crushed it.'

'Oh, my God.'

Jamila twitched her nose as if she had caught a foul smell. 'My guess is the mother must have come for revenge and put a spell on you.'

'But what am I going to do?'

'Don't worry, there's always a way to appease a *djinni*, no matter how enraged,' said Jamila authoritatively.

And so, while Pembe was nursing her newborn, Jamila made her toss dry bread to a pack of stray dogs and rush away without looking back; throw a pinch of salt over her left shoulder and a pinch of sugar over her right; walk through newly ploughed fields and under spiderwebs; pour sacred rosewater into every cranny in the house, and wear an amulet round her neck for forty days. She thus hoped to cure Pembe of her fear of their late mother. Instead she opened the door to superstitions – a door Pembe had always known existed but through which she had never before ventured to go.

Meanwhile Iskender was growing. His skin the colour of warm sand, his hair dark and wavy and gleaming like stardust, his eyes brimming with mischief and his birthmark long gone, he smiled copiously, winning hearts. The more handsome her son grew, the more Pembe became terrified of things over which she had no control – earthquakes, landslides, floods, wildfires, contagious diseases, the wrath of Naze's ghost, the vengeance of a mother *djinni*. The world had always been an unsafe place, but suddenly the danger was too real, too close.

Such was Pembe's unease that she refused to give her son a name. It was a way of protecting him from Azrael, the Angel of Death. If the baby had no particular affiliation, she thought, Azrael would not be able to find him, even if he wished to. Thus the boy spent his first year on earth without a name, like an envelope with no address. As well as his second, third and fourth years. When they had to call him, they would say, 'Son!' or 'Hey, lad!'

Why didn't her husband, Adem, object to this nonsense? Why didn't he take control of the situation and name his heir like every other man did? There was something holding him back, something stronger than his quick temper and male pride, a secret between the two of them that empowered Pembe and weakened Adem, pushing him away from home towards an underground world in Istanbul, where he could gamble and be the king, even if only for one night.

Not until the boy had turned five did Adem take the reins in his hands and announce that this could not go on for ever. His son would soon start school, and if he did not have a name by then the other children would make sure he had the most ridiculous one imaginable. Grudgingly, Pembe complied but only on one condition. She would take the child to her native village and get her twin's and family's blessings. Once there, she would also consult with the three village elders, who, by now, were as old as Mount Ararat, but still dispensing sage advice.

★

'It was wise of you to come to us,' said the first village elder, who was so frail now that when a door slammed near by its vibration shook him to the core.

'It is also good that you did not insist on naming the baby yourself, like some mothers do nowadays,' remarked the second elder, who had only one tooth left in his mouth – a little pearl shining out like the first tooth of a toddler.

The third elder then spoke, but his voice was so low, his words so slurred, that no one understood what he said.

After a bit more discussion the elders reached a decision: a stranger would name the boy – someone who knew nothing about the family and, by extension, Naze's spectre.

With a borrowed confidence Pembe agreed to the plan. A few miles away there was a stream that ran low in winter and frantically high in spring. The peasants crossed the water in a makeshift boat attached to a wire that had been stretched between the two banks. The journey was unsafe, and every year a few passengers would fall into the river. It was decided that Pembe would wait where the boat landed and ask the first man who got across to name her son. The village elders, meanwhile, would hide behind the bushes and intervene should the need arise.

Thus Pembe and her son waited. She was attired in a crimson dress that reached below her ankles and a black lace shawl. He was wearing his only suit and looked like a miniature of a man. Time crept by and the child got bored. Pembe told stories to entertain him. One of those stories would stand out in his memory for ever.

'*When Nasreddin Hodja was a boy he was the apple of his mother's eye.*'

'Did she have apples in her eyes?' he asked.

'That's an expression, my sultan. It means she loved him very much. *The two of them lived in a nice cottage on the outskirts of the town.*'

'Where was the father?'

'He had gone off to war. Now listen. *One day his mother had to go to the bazaar. She said to him, "You should stay at home and watch the door. If you see a burglar trying to break in, start shouting at the top of your voice. That'll frighten him away. I'll be back before noon." So Nasreddin did as he was told, not taking his eyes from the door for even a moment.*'

'Didn't he have to pee?'

'He had a potty with him.'

'Wasn't he hungry?'

'His mother had left him food.'

'Pastries?'

'And sesame *halva*,' Pembe said, knowing her son well. '*After an hour, there was a knock at the door. It was Nasreddin's uncle, checking on how they were doing. He asked the boy where his mother was and said, "Well, go tell your mother to come home early and prepare lunch for us. My family will stop by for a visit."*'

'But he is watching the door!'

'Exactly. *Nasreddin was puzzled. His mother had advised him to do one thing and his uncle another. He didn't want to disobey either of them. So he pulled up the door, saddled it on his back and went to get his mother.*'

The boy chuckled but he quickly grew serious. 'I wouldn't do that. I would always choose my mother over my uncle.'

No sooner had he said this than they heard a noise. Somebody had crossed the stream and was walking towards them. To Pembe's – and the village elders' – surprise it turned out to be an old woman. She had a spectacularly aquiline nose, hollows under her wrinkled cheekbones and a set of crooked teeth. Her small, beady eyes constantly moved, refusing to settle anywhere.

Pembe told her that her son urgently needed a name and asked if she would kindly help, avoiding details like Naze's ghost or the village elders waiting behind the bush. The old woman didn't seem the least bit surprised. Leaning against her staff, she weighed something

23

up in her head, calm and compliant, as if a request of this kind was the most ordinary thing in the world.

'Mum, who is this?' the child asked.

'Hush, my lion. This nice lady here is going to give you a name.'

'But she's ugly.'

Pretending not to hear that, the woman took a step closer and scrutinized the boy. 'So you haven't found your name yet, I gather.'

The child raised his thin eyebrows, refusing to comment.

'All right, well, I'm thirsty,' she said, pointing to where the water-course had formed an inlet. 'Will you go and get me a cup of water?'

'I don't have a cup.'

'Use your palms, then,' the old woman insisted.

With a deepening frown the boy glanced at the woman, then at his mother, and then at the stranger again. 'No,' he said, a new edge to his voice. 'Why don't you go and get your own water? I'm not your servant.'

The woman tilted her head to one side, as if the words were a blow she had to dodge. 'He doesn't like to serve, does he? He only wants to be served.'

By now Pembe was convinced that they had picked the wrong person. To appease the situation she said in her most conciliatory tones, 'I'll go and get you water.'

But the woman didn't drink the water Pembe brought to her, cupped in the palms of her hands. Instead she *read* it.

'My daughter, this child will remain a boy for a long time and he will grow up only when he has reached mid-life. He will mature very late.'

Pembe gasped. She had the distinct impression that the woman was about to give away a secret, something she wasn't supposed to reveal.

'Some children are like the Euphrates, so fast, so rowdy. Their parents cannot catch up with them. I'm afraid your son will break your heart to pieces.'

The words fell between them like a stone hurled from out of nowhere.

'But that's not what I asked you,' Pembe said, a bit tensely. 'Have you thought of a name for him?'

'Yes, I have. There are two names that might suit him well, depending on what you expect. One is Saalim. Once upon a time there was such a sultan. He was a poet and a fine musician to boot. May your son, too, learn to appreciate beauty should he be given this name.'

'And the other?' Pembe held her breath with anticipation. Even the boy seemed interested in the conversation now.

'The second is the name of the great commander who always marched in front of his soldiers, fought like a tiger, won every battle, destroyed all his enemies, conquered land after land, united the East and the West, the sunrise and the sunset, and was still hungry for more. May your son, too, be invincible and strong-willed, and preside over other men should he be named after him.'

'This one is better,' said Pembe, her face brightening up.

'Well, then, you are done with me.'

With that, the old woman grabbed her staff, and started to walk away down the road with a surprisingly agile gait. It took Pembe a few seconds to collect her thoughts before she ran after her.

'But what is it?'

'What is what?' The woman turned and studied her – as if she had forgotten who she was.

'The name! You didn't tell me what it was.'

'Oh! It is Askander.'

'Askander . . . Askander . . .' Pembe repeated with delight.

When they returned to Istanbul the boy was registered at the office of the local registrar. Though several years late, with a lot of pleading and a substantial bribe, his existence was legally accounted for. The name written on his card when he started school was Iskender Toprak.

'A name worthy of a world leader,' Pembe said. By then she had learned who Alexander the Great was.

So it was that her first child, the apple of her eye, would become Askander in Kurdish and Iskender in Turkish. When the family immigrated to London, to the children and teachers in his school, he was Alex – and this was the name he would be known by in Shrewsbury Prison, by convicts and guards alike.

A Prince in the Tree

Istanbul, 1969

The spring when he was not yet seven, Iskender ran away from a man whom he had never seen before but had heard much about. Although the man was different from what he had imagined, this made him no less frightening. He had thick-rimmed glasses that slid down his nose, an unlit cigarette between his lips and a large leather bag that was rumoured to contain sharp instruments and a piece of skin from each of his victims.

At the sight of him, Iskender felt a bolt of fear shoot along his spine. He spilled the cranberry sherbet in his hand, red drops trickling on to his white shirt, like blood on snow. He tried to wipe off the stain, first with his bare hands, then with the hem of his cape. It was no use. His beautiful costume was ruined.

Stain or no stain, he was still a prince in his long silvery cape and his cap studded with sparkling beads, carrying a sceptre so polished it was almost translucent. Throughout the afternoon he had sat in a high chair like a nobleman inspecting his lands – though being a bit short for his age all chairs were high for him. To his left were four boys, older and taller but similarly attired. As if sizing them up for a fight, Iskender had studied them from head to toe and decided their costumes were not as impressive as his.

While the other princes gobbled sweets and cracked jokes, Iskender waited, jiggling his legs. How could they be so silly when they knew what was about to happen? His eyes strayed anxiously. There were many people in the room, but he was certain that none would come to his rescue, not even his mother, Pembe, especially not her. She had wept all morning, telling him how proud she was that her little boy was becoming a man. For that is what you became when you were circumcised: a man.

Iskender couldn't understand for the life of him how he would become a man with one cut of a knife. It was a riddle hard to solve. With less you became more. Nor could he fathom why he was told not to cry, though it was clear he would be hurt – while his mother could weep to her heart's content, though absolutely nothing was happening to her.

Out of the corner of his eye he watched the man with the leather bag, noticing a scar that ran from his left cheek to his jaw. Perhaps one of the boys on whom he had operated had given him the wound. For a minute he indulged the idea, imagining how, just when the man was about to circumcise him, he would free himself of the hands holding him down, snatch the blade and slash his tormentor's right cheek. Then he would help the other boys to their feet, and together they would dash for the door, victorious. But the fantasy faded away and the room came alive again – a blind *hafiz* reciting the Qur'an, a woman serving tea and almond paste, the guests chatting in hushed tones, and his most feared moment moving dangerously closer.

Slowly, Iskender slid down in his chair. His feet touched the floor, the carpet opening up beneath his weight. He took a step and held his breath, waiting for someone, anyone, to ask him where he was going, but no one did. He tiptoed past the double bed that had been placed in a corner – wrought-iron headboard, embroidered pillows, amulets against the evil eye and a satiny, cobalt-blue bedspread. Blue was Iskender's favourite colour. It was the colour for boys, which meant the sky was a boy. So were the rivers and lakes. And the oceans, though he had yet to see one.

Feeling lighter and bolder with each step, he sneaked through the back door. Once outside he began to run, picking up speed as he made his way across the garden, around the well, down the gravel road, past the neighbours' houses, up the hill. His costume was soiled but he didn't mind. Not any more.

Iskender thought of his mother's hands – combing her wavy, chestnut hair, making yoghurt in clay cups, caressing his cheeks, moulding figurines out of pastry dough. Until he reached the oak, he contemplated these images and nothing else.

It was an old tree that had roots running in four directions above the ground and branches extending towards the billowing clouds. His breath coming in gasps, he began to climb, fast and focused. Twice his hands slipped and he almost tumbled down, but each time he regained his balance. He had never been this high before and felt disappointed that there was no one to see his achievement. From up here the sky seemed so close he could almost touch it. Beneath a blanket of clouds, he sat with sweet satisfaction and pride, until he realized he did not know how to get down.

An hour later, a blackbird perched a few feet away. It was an exquisite creature with yellow rings around its eyes and touches of crimson, bright as rubies, on its wings. It chirped once, timid and frail but full of life. Had the bird come any closer, Iskender could have caught it between his palms and listened to its tiny heart beat against his skin. He could have sheltered the bird, loved and protected it, but in one swift movement he could also have broken its neck.

No sooner had this thought crossed his mind than he felt a pang of remorse. There were huge cauldrons in hell, bubbling away for those who nursed such sinful thoughts. His eyes watered. He had been confident that his mother would notice he had gone missing and send out a search party, yet no one was coming. He was going to die here, perish of cold or hunger. What would people say when they learned that he had died not because of illness or accident, like everyone else seemed to do, but because of cowardice?

Perhaps they had looked for him in all the wrong places and assumed he was gone. Perhaps they thought he had been attacked by wolves, not that there were any in the area. He imagined a terrible death savaged by the claws and teeth of ferocious animals. Would his mother be devastated or would she secretly rejoice at having one less mouth to feed?

Thinking about his mother's cooking made him realize how hungry he was. More urgently, he had to pee. Unable to contain himself any longer, he pulled down his trousers and held his willy, the cause of all his distress. He had barely started to relieve himself when he heard someone shout.

'Hey, he's up there! I've found him!'

In a few seconds a man appeared, then another, then ten more.

They stood by the tree, watching. Under their gaze, Iskender kept peeing as if his bladder had expanded to twice its usual size. Finally he pulled up his zipper and was considering asking for help to get down when he noticed that among the crowd was the man with the leather bag.

That was when the strangest thing happened: Iskender froze. His limbs went slack, his tongue went numb, and in place of his stomach was a rock. He could hear people beseeching him to get down, but he could not respond. He sat motionless, as if he had become a part of the tree. An acorn boy.

At first the onlookers below suspected he was playing dead, eager to get more attention. Only when they understood he wasn't pretending, that the child was somehow paralysed, did they start contemplating how to bring him down. A man began to climb but couldn't get as far as the lateral branch where Iskender was perched. Another tried his skill, with equal lack of success. Meanwhile, others were busy holding blankets for the boy to fall into or making lassoes, though no one knew exactly what to do with them. Nothing worked. Ladders were too short, ropes too thin, and the boy uncooperative.

Just then a voice cut through the air. 'What's he doing there?' Pembe shouted, as she scurried up the hill.

'He can't get down,' someone explained.

'Oh, can't he! He's a big boy.' Pembe was frowning at her son's stick-thin legs dangling over the branch. 'Get down here this minute!'

Like ice melting under the sun, Iskender felt his entire body thaw.

'Come down, you rascal! You've shamed your father. All the boys have been circumcised. You're the only one who acted like a baby.'

Try how he might, Iskender still couldn't shift his body. Instead he looked down and grinned. Perhaps if he made light of the situation, lighter it would become. It was a mistake. All the pressure that had been mounting inside his mother gushed into a stream of fury when she saw him grin.

'You spoiled brat! Come down this minute or I'll break your bones! Don't you want to be a man?'

Iskender gave this some thought. 'No,' he said finally.

'If you remain a boy you'll never have your own car.'

He shrugged. He would walk everywhere. Or take the bus.

'Nor your own house.'

Iskender attempted another shrug. He would live in a tent like he had seen gypsies do.

'Nor a pretty wife.'

A puzzled expression came over Iskender's face. He wanted to have a wife, someone who resembled his mother but never scolded him. He chewed his lip, brooding. After what seemed an endless wait, he dredged up the will and the strength to look down into her eyes – dark and green like two strands of ivy gently but firmly pulling him towards her.

'All right,' Pembe said, sighing. 'You win, I lose. You won't be circumcised. I'll not let anyone lay a hand on you.'

'Promise?'

'Promise, my sultan.'

Her voice was warm, reassuring. As she spoke, Iskender found his panic oozing away. He moved his fingers, then his toes, and managed to descend a few branches, to where a man was waiting on the highest rung of a ladder that had been propped up against the tree. When he was safely on the ground again, he ran to his mother, sobbing out loud.

'My son,' Pembe said, as if it needed to be verified. She hugged him so tightly he could feel her heart beating through her chest. '*Malamin*,★ my sultan.'

Iskender was happy to feel the earth beneath his feet, happier still to have been missed this much by his mother – and yet there was something suffocating about her embrace, sickly sweet. Her lips against the side of his neck, her breath, her clutch enclosed him like a coffin.

As if she had read his mind, Pembe grabbed the boy by the shoulders, pushing him back so that she could stare him in the eye, and slapped him hard. She said, 'Do not ever shame me again!'

★ 'My house, my abode' (Kurdish).

Half turning to the man with the leather bag, she added, 'Take him!'

Iskender's face went pale. He was more surprised than distraught. His mother had deceived him in front of everyone. And slapped him. He had never been hit by her before. The possibility had never even occurred to him. He tried hard to speak, but words had become like marbles, clogging his throat.

In the evening everyone commended Iskender for being brave during the circumcision. They said he hadn't shed a single tear. But he knew his performance had nothing to do with courage. Because he was still thinking about what his mother had done and why she had done it, he hadn't fretted over the operation. Never had it occurred to him that you could deceive the person you held dear. Until that day, he hadn't known that you could love someone with all your heart and yet be ready to hurt them. It was his first lesson in the complexity of love.

The Wish Fountain

A Place near the River Euphrates, 1977

Pembe was gone now, her mirror image, her reflection in still waters. She slept under a different sky and every so often sent Jamila letters and postcards with pictures of red, two-tiered buses and immense clock towers. When she came home for a visit, her clothes smelled differently, and felt soft to the touch. That was the part that struck Jamila the most: watching her sister open her suitcase, bringing in aromas, tastes and fabrics from foreign lands. Pembe had left with the unspoken assumption that everything would be as it was upon her return. But nothing had remained the same. Nor had she come back for good.

For years Pembe had been sending Jamila letters, telling her about her life in England. The children, too, jotted down a few lines every now and then, Yunus more than anyone else. Jamila kept these missives in a tin tea box under her bed, like hoarded treasure. She wrote back regularly, although she had less to tell, or so she believed. Recently she had asked Yunus if he had seen the Queen and, if so, what she looked like. He had responded,

The Queen lives in a palase. So big she gets lost in it. But they find her and put her on her throwne again. She wears a diferent dress every day, and a funnee hat. It has to be the same colour as the dress. Her hands are soft because she puts on glouves and lots of creamz, and she doesn't wash the dishes. I saw her picturse at school. She seems nice.

Jamila could not understand how the family had been on *that* island for so long but still not set eyes on the Queen, save in magazines and newspapers. Sometimes she doubted whether Pembe had ventured from the neighbourhood where she lived at all. If she always ended up confined between walls, what was the use of her travelling to a faraway country? Why couldn't human beings live and die where they were born? Jamila found big cities suffocating, and was daunted by the thought of unknown places – the buildings, the avenues, the crowds pressing on her chest, leaving her gasping for air.

In her letters, usually towards the last paragraph, Pembe would write, 'Are you angry at me, sister? Could you forgive me in your heart?' But she already knew what the answer would be. Jamila was not angry with her twin or with anyone else. And yet Jamila was also aware that the question had to be asked over and over, like a wound that needed to be dressed regularly.

They called her Kiz Ebe – the Virgin Midwife. They said she was the best midwife this impoverished Kurdish region had seen in a hundred years. Pregnant women felt relieved when she was in charge, as if her presence would ensure an easy labour, keeping Azrael at bay. Their husbands would bob their heads knowingly, and say, 'The Virgin Midwife is in command. Everything will go well. Thanks first to Allah, then to her.'

Such words amounted to nothing; they only deepened Jamila's fear of not living up to people's expectations. She knew she was good – as skilled as one could get before starting to decline from old age, poor eyesight or sheer bad luck. Like every midwife, she was aware of the danger of her name being uttered in the same breath as the name of God. When she heard the peasants speak such blasphemy, she would murmur to herself, *Tövbe, tövbe*.★ They didn't have to hear her; it was enough that God did. She had to make it clear to Him that she was not coveting His power, not competing with Him, the one and only life-giver.

Jamila knew what thin ice she was walking upon. You thought you were experienced and knowledgeable until you came across a delivery that filled you with dread, making you almost like a novice again. Every now and then something would go wrong, terribly wrong, despite her best efforts. At other times she couldn't make it to a labour in time and when she arrived would find that the mother had just

★ 'I take it back, I take it back.'

given birth on her own, sometimes even having cut the umbilical cord with a blunt blade and tied it with her hair. Jamila took these incidents as signs from God in which he was reminding her of her limitations.

They came from distant villages and forsaken parishes to fetch her. There were other midwives closer to their homes, but they sought her out. She was quite popular in this part of the world. There were dozens of girls who had been named after her – *Enough Beauty*.

'May she carry your name and be half as chaste as you,' prayed the fathers of the girls she brought into this world.

Jamila nodded, saying nothing, conscious of the insinuation. They would like their daughters to be modest and virtuous, and yet they wanted them to get married and have children in due course. Their daughters' names and dispositions might be similar to the midwife's, but their fates had better be different.

Approaching the window, a knitted shawl on her shoulders, a lamp in her hand, Jamila squinted into the dark. Under the deep mantle of the night, the valley was sleeping, bare and barren, bleary with tangled bushes and arid soil. She had always imagined a softness beneath this harsh landscape, which she likened to a rough man who hid a tender heart. Still, she didn't have to live on her own in so remote a place. She, too, could have gone. Somewhere. Anywhere. Not that she had the means or any relatives who were willing to help her start anew elsewhere. Already thirty-two, she was past her prime and beyond proper marriage age. It was too late for her to start a family. *A dry womb is like a melon gone bad: fine on the outside, desiccated inside, and good for nothing*, the peasants said about women like her.

Even so, she could marry a disabled or elderly man, just as she could agree to become someone's second wife – or third or fourth, though that was rare. Only the wife who had been married first was legal, of course, and could go to a hospital or courtroom or a tax register office and claim to be a married woman with legitimate children. But in this part of the country no one went to such places anyway, so long as you weren't in serious trouble or dying of an infection or out of your good mind, in which case what difference would it make whether you were the first wife or the fourth?

Her house – if house was the right word for this shack – was nestled in a hollow near a ravine in the outer reaches of Mala Çar Bayan. Down below one could see a cluster of rocks that resembled petrified giants from afar and glowed like rubies when the sun cast its rays on them. There were many legends about these rocks, and behind every legend a story of forbidden love. For centuries Christians and Muslims and Zoroastrians and Yazidis had lived here side by side, loved and died side by side. Their grandchildren, however, had long ago left for other lands. All but a handful of peasants remained in the area – and Jamila.

Deserted places that once teemed with life had a kind of sadness, a ghost grief, which floated in the breeze, seeping into every crevice. Perhaps that was why, after a while, the people of derelict landscapes resembled the places themselves: silent, subdued and sullen. But that was what lay on the surface, and with people, as with the earth, the surface was rarely the same as the core.

Underneath the layers of clothes that she wore to keep herself warm, there was another Jamila – young, pretty, jovial, with a laugh like the tinkling of glass upon glass. She rarely went out these days, hiding behind the practical woman who chopped wood, scythed the fields, drew water and made potions. At times she feared for her sanity. Perhaps this much loneliness had finally got to her, nibbling away at her mind little by little.

When the wind blew in from the faraway mountains, it carried with it the aromas of wild flowers, fresh herbs and blossoming shrubs. But at times it also brought a cloying smell of roasted meat that hovered over everything, clinging to her skin. There were smugglers and brigands in the area – wandering about the caves and precipices, never staying in any one place for more than a day. On moonless nights she could see their campfires twinkling in the dark like forlorn stars. The smells in the air altered depending on what they were eating and how close they came.

There were wolves too. Jamila could hear them during the day, late in the evening, deep in the night. They would snarl and growl, and sometimes yip in high-pitched barks or howl in tandem. Every so often they would appear on her doorstep, so close and furtive, sniffing her solitude. Then they would leave, their jaws set in a scowl, looking disappointed, as if they didn't find her inviting enough to feast upon. Jamila wasn't scared of them. The wolves were not her enemies, and, as for the bandits, they were interested in bigger rewards than her. Besides, Jamila took heart in her belief that danger always came from where it was least expected.

The smouldering heap in the fireplace stuttered to life when a twig caught fire. Jamila's face glimmered, even though the rest of the house was sunk in shadow. She suspected the peasants didn't love her, but they did respect her. Travelling on horse, donkey and mule, she was allowed to set foot in places no other woman could enter. She was often accompanied by people she knew, but also by complete strangers.

A man she had never seen before might knock on her door late at night, and plead, 'Come quickly, I beg you! My wife is giving birth in the village of so and so. We need to hurry. She's not doing well.'

He could be lying. There was always the possibility, however slight, of evil disguising itself. As she followed the man into the still of the night, Jamila was aware that he could kidnap, rape and kill her. She had to trust. Not him but Him. Yet it was also true that there were unwritten rules nobody in his right mind dared to violate. A midwife, someone who brought babies into this world, was semi-sacred. She dangled between the invisible world and the visible one, on a thread as delicate as a strand of spider's silk.

Feeding the flames in the fireplace with more wood, Jamila put the copper *cezve* on the fire. Water, sugar and coffee – all these items were in short supply. But families brought her presents all the time – henna, tea, biscuits, saffron, pistachios, peanuts, and tobacco smuggled from the other side of the frontier. Jamila knew that if she had received money, she would have been paid once and that would have been it. But if you were paid in trinkets, such giving went on for a lifetime.

She mixed the coffee carefully, gently. *Coffee was like love*, they said, *the more patient you were with it, the better it would taste*. But Jamila didn't know much about that. She had been in love once, and it had tasted sour and dark. Having scalded her tongue, she never spoke of it any more.

As she kept her eyes on the rising foam, she pricked her ears to sounds near and beyond. The valley was alive with spirits. There were creatures here no bigger than grains of rice, imperceptible to the naked eye but potent and perilous nevertheless. Birds tapped on the windows, insects bounced off the water in the buckets as if skittering across the surface of a lake. Everything had a language, she believed. The thunderstorm, the morning dew, the ants crawling in her sugar bowl . . . Sometimes she thought she understood what they said.

She loved nothing more than she loved being a midwife. It was her mission, her one fortune. So it was that in the fog, or scorching sun, or thirty inches of snow, any time during day or night, she was on call, waiting for the knock on her door. This nobody knew, but in her heart of hearts she was married already. Jamila was married to her destiny.

*

Outside the night wind rattled against the windowpanes. Jamila took the coffee off the flames and poured some into a small earthenware cup with a chipped handle. She drank it in slow sips. The fire was a bit like her life, smouldering within, not letting anyone come too close, precious moments burning into embers, like dying dreams.

Far away a bird cried out – an owl, which the locals called the mother of ruins. It hooted again, this time more boldly. Jamila sat there with her eyes clamped shut, her thoughts wavering. Despite the hardships, she remembered her childhood as a happy one. At times one of the twins would pretend to be the Mummy and the other the infant. Though older by three minutes, Pembe would always be the baby while Jamila would be the mother, trying to constrain, control and comfort her. She would rock her little one, singing lullabies, telling stories. Looking back on those games, Jamila was surprised to see how serious they had been.

She recalled how once her father, Berzo, took them to a town where they discovered a Wish Fountain. Women who longed to have babies, mothers-in-law who wanted to put a spell on their daughters-in-law, and virgins who yearned for well-to-do husbands came here, tossing coins into the water. When everyone had left, Pembe rolled up her hems, climbed into the fountain and collected the coins. Then they both ran, as fast as they could, shrieking with excitement, to the closest shop, where they bought boiled sweets and sticks of rock.

Much as Jamila enjoyed the adventure, she felt guilty afterwards. They were thieves. Worse. Stealing people's wishes was far more despicable than stealing their wallets.

'Don't be sentimental,' Pembe said, when Jamila revealed her worries. 'They had already let go of those coins and we pocketed them, that's all.'

'Yes, but there were prayers attached to them. If somebody had stolen your secret wish, you would be upset, no? I mean, I would.'

Pembe grinned. 'So what is *your* secret wish?'

Jamila faltered, feeling cornered. True, she wanted to get married some day – a wedding dress and a buttercream cake like those they made in the city would be wonderful – but it wasn't that important. She would love to have children, but was that because she really yearned for them, or because everyone told her she should? It would be nice to own a farmhouse and cultivate the land, but it was a fancy rather than a passion. As she thought harder, Jamila was glad that she was only a thief and not a visitor at the Wish Fountain. If she had been given a coin to make a wish, she might not have come up with one.

At her hesitation Pembe scoffed, her eyes aglow. 'I'm going to be a sailor and travel the world. Every week I'll wake up in a new harbour.'

Jamila had never felt more alone. She understood that as identical as they were in all respects, there was one vital difference: ambition. Pembe wanted to see the world beyond the River Euphrates. She had the nerve to pursue her heart, and not pay attention to what others thought about her. For a sinking moment it dawned on Jamila that she and her twin were bound to spend their lives apart.

Their father said identical twins were as blessed as they were damned. They were blessed because they would always have someone to count on. Yet they were also damned, because should one of them suffer despondency, they would be destined to suffer together and, therefore, twice as much. If that were the case, Jamila wondered, what was likely to cause them more pain – her sister's passions or her own apparent lack of them?

Memories

London, December 1977

As he took a handful of oatmeal biscuits off the conveyor belt and placed them inside the next tin box, Adem Toprak had a revelation: he could not remember his mother's face any more. He stopped for a moment, gooseflesh sweeping up and down his body – a pause that caused him to miss the next cluster of biscuits. Bilal, standing several feet down the assembly line, noticed the mistake and quietly covered it up. Had Adem realized what had happened, he would have given his friend a grateful nod, but in that moment he was still trying to recall what his mother used to look like.

There was a woman in the back of his mind, distant and hazy, as if she were standing in a fine mist. She was tall and slim, her face like marble, her pale eyes calm, concerned. A wedge of sunlight from a latticed window fell on the back of her head, leaving half her face in shadow. Her hair was coppery-brown, the colour of autumn leaves. But as the light dimmed, it changed to a shade so dark it appeared ink-black. Her lips were full and round. Perhaps not; Adem could not be sure. Perhaps she had thin lips that turned down at the corners. The woman seemed to change every second. Hers was a face sculpted out of melting wax.

Or perhaps he was confusing the memory of the woman who had borne him with the image of his wife. The long, wavy, chestnut hair that he now saw belonged to Pembe, not to his mother, Aisha. Had his wife become such an inseparable part of his existence that she eclipsed all his memories – even those from a time before they had met? He shifted his weight from one foot to another and closed his eyes.

Another recollection came. He and his mother were in an emerald-green field that overlooked a dam. He must have been eight. His

mother had let down her hair, which Istanbul's notorious *poyraz**
kept blowing about her face. Ahead of them, the sky was a generous
blue, flakes of gold, pewter and silver skittering across the faraway
hills. Of the dam's numerous gates only a few were open, and the lake
level was low. The boy felt dizzy as he watched the waters churning
beneath them. Any other day his mother would have warned him not
to get so close to the edge, but oddly not that day.

'Sheitan waits on the ledges to pull down whoever gets too close.'

That's why they fell all the time – toddlers who leaned over balcony railings, housewives who stepped on windowsills to clean the
windows, or chimney sweepers who clomped about near the eaves.
Sheitan would clutch their ankles with his claws and yank them
down into the emptiness below. Only cats survived because they had
nine lives and could afford to die eight times.

Hand in hand, they had walked down the hill, until they reached
the huge walls that sloped all the way down one side of the dam.
Aisha sighed at the top of the gully, her lips moving. She seemed to
have forgotten that the Evil One loomed close. Or perhaps not,
because, once he concentrated on what she was saying, the boy realized she was praying – to ward off misfortune, no doubt. He was
relieved, but only momentarily. What if the Devil were hiding somewhere behind the bushes, ready to push them into the void? With a
sudden impulse, he pulled his hand from his mother's and glanced
around until he was certain there was no one else there. When he
turned his head again, she wasn't by his side.

Bit by bit, second by second, he watched her fall.

*

Adem opened his eyes to find Bilal staring at him with something
akin to alarm on his face.

'What's going on, man?' Bilal asked over the clatter of the ma-
chines. 'You've missed more than a dozen batches.'

'Nothing.' Adem put his right hand to his heart and patted. 'I'm
fine.'

---

* The wind that blows from the north-east, often bringing rain.

40

Bilal's smile was slow but genuine. Nodding, he went back to his work, as did Adem. During the rest of the afternoon he managed to tackle every single biscuit. But those who knew him well could sense something was niggling him. Outside his control, beyond his power, an aching unease was crawling in the depths of his soul, sinister as a storm cloud.

He knew what it was: the fear of a cornered animal. He felt hounded, ground down, as if injected with a poison that didn't kill but slowed the prey. Wherever he turned he could see his predators' shadows. There was nowhere to escape – unless he left England for good. But he could not abscond, with his children and wife relying on him. And if he wanted to take his family with him, he would have to find money. A lot. He was stuck. The Chinese were aware of this too. That's why they didn't even bother to check on him every day. They knew they could find him whenever they wanted to – whenever he skipped a payment. But there was another reason why Adem couldn't go anywhere: Roxana.

★

Six weeks ago, Adem had woken one morning to a sensation of exhilaration and elevation so intense it was like soaring in a dream. The portents were there. The signs had never betrayed him before. His palms were itchy, his heart was beating faster than usual, his left eye twitching ever so slightly. Nothing bothersome. Just a faint tic that came and went, like a coded message from the skies. An ordinary day in other respects, but the feeling stayed with him. All afternoon everyone was polite to him and he was polite to everyone. It was a fine, sunny day, and the sky's reflection in the Thames was vivid and full of promise.

After sunset he went to the gambling den. One day soon, not long from now, he would stop doing this. He would break the habit, chop it off his body, as if he were pruning a sick branch from a healthy tree. Just as it was impossible for the tree to regrow the branch, he would never have the urge again. But not now. He wasn't ready to give it up quite yet. *For today it's all right*, he assured himself. *Today the signs are favourable.*

It was the basement of a double-fronted terraced house in Bethnal Green, resplendent with age. Inside it was a different world, though. There were five rooms: in each of them men played snooker or gathered around roulette, blackjack or poker tables. The air was thick with smoke. Those with more money or less fear were in the room at the back. From behind the tightly shut door one could hear the murmurs, the occasional gasps and grunts, and the rattle of the roulette wheel.

It was a place for men. The few women who minced around were already spoken for and therefore unapproachable. There were unwritten rules here that everyone obeyed. Indians, Pakistanis, Indonesians, Bangladeshis, Caribbeans, Iranians, Turks, Greeks, Italians . . . Everybody spoke English but swore, conspired and prayed in his mother tongue. The Lair, they called it. Run by a taciturn Chinese family who had lived in Vietnam for generations and been forced to leave after the war. Adem always felt uneasy next to them. The Chinese were not protective of each other like the Italians, nor were they temperamental like the Irish. There was always an unknown quality to their demeanour. A bit like the weather, they were prone to changing on a whim.

That evening Adem played blackjack and a few dice games, and then moved to the roulette wheel. He placed his first bet on black. It was an auspicious start. Next he did a combination bet. He won again, but the amount was not much. He switched to red and won thrice in a row, each time leaving his winnings from the previous bet on the current one. It was one of those magical moments when he could *feel* the roulette wheel. Just like him, the wheel lacked a solid memory. You could place the same bet over and over, and your chances of winning would still be the same. Roulette didn't observe any recognized patterns. So he played without memory, concentrating on every new bet as if it were his first and his last.

The men in the room gave him a thumbs-up, patted him on the shoulder and muttered words of encouragement. It was a remarkable feeling to be respected by strangers. To be admired and envied. He played another round, still triumphant. Now the crowd around the table had thickened. Fifteen minutes later he was still watching the ball spin around the wheel, still winning. The dealer asked for a break.

In need of fresh air Adem stepped out into the street. There was a tall, hulking Moroccan he knew from the factory, sitting by himself on the pavement.

'You're a lucky man,' remarked the Moroccan.

'*Kismet*. Not every day is like this.'

'Maybe Allah is testing you.' The man paused, giving him a cursory glance. 'You know what they say. *He who wants to ride a fast horse could break his back, but the horse has to gallop.*'

'What the hell does that mean?'

'I don't know but I like the sound of it.'

They laughed, their voices carrying in the night air.

'Here's a good one,' said Adem. '*One can flee to the end of the world but one cannot run away from his behind.*'

'Uh-hum.' The Moroccan was about to raise his glass when he noticed his companion's empty hands.

'I don't drink,' Adem said by way of explanation.

This elicited a chuckle from the other man. 'My, oh my. Look at you! You're hooked on gambling but when it comes to booze you turn into a pious Muslim.'

Adem's face closed down like a trap. He was not an addict. He could stop playing whenever he wanted. As for his reasons for not drinking, it was something he rarely talked about, especially with strangers. But tonight he made an exception. He said flatly, 'My father was a heavy drinker.'

No sooner had he returned to the basement than the lights went off. Another power-cut. The third this week. These days London was grey in the mornings with rainclouds, black in the evenings with shutdowns. *That candle shop in Hackney must be raking it in*, Adem thought. There was good money in wholesaling candles, a business that had become as vital as selling bread and milk.

Adem strained his eyes through the half-lit corridor, until he reached the room at the back. There were three Chinese at the table, sulking by a paraffin lamp – men of few words and impenetrable expressions. Adem knew it was time for him to leave. He had to be satisfied with what he had earned. He grabbed his jacket, tipped the dealer, and was about to walk out the door but then stopped.

Later on, whenever he recalled this moment, which he would do fairly often, he would think of the emergency handles on trains. He had never tried pulling one, but he knew if someone did, the train would come to a sudden halt. That night he had stopped as if there were such a handle attached to his back and someone had tugged and tugged on it.

A young woman had entered the room, like an apparition from the shadows. In the faint lamplight her sandy hair had an uncanny glow, curling below her ears, small and delicate. Leather miniskirt, white silk halter top, stiletto daggers on her feet. Every inch of her heart-shaped face sent out the message she was not pleased to be there, she'd rather be somewhere far away. He watched her sit next to one of the Chinese – a bald, portly man who acted as if he were the boss, and perhaps he was – and whisper in his ear. The man smiled a half-smile and caressed her thigh. Something tore inside Adem.

'So, you are still here. You want to play another round, my friend?'

This man had asked the question without raising his head or looking at anyone in particular. And yet Adem knew, as did all the people in the room, that the question was directed at him. He could feel the gaze of each person, but it was her eyes that pierced him – a pair of blue sapphires. He had never seen eyes that big, bright and blue. If his wife had met this woman, she would have feared the evil eye. For Pembe believed that if someone with such eyes stared at you, even for a moment, you had to run back home and burn salt on the stove.

Adem's face was aflame. He saw in that precise moment that he was about to commit the worst mistake in gambling, if not in life: to let yourself be provoked. But understanding this was one thing, accepting it quite another. With a tilt of his head, he answered, 'Yes, I'll play.'

He pulled it off again, though it was different this time. The energy around him had changed. He and the roulette wheel were two separate entities now, no longer in sync. Yet he didn't budge. He remained planted in his seat, watching the goddess watch the ball spin.

The lights came on. He took this as a good sign and continued to bet. He gained again and then again. The stakes were high. It was dangerous. It was insane. The Chinese tried to look unperturbed but their nervousness was beginning to show. Among the crowd Adem caught the eyes of the Moroccan, his brow furrowed in anguish. Shaking his head, the man mouthed, 'Enough, brother!'

But Adem couldn't quit. She was staring at him from the other end of the table, her lips like cherries, full and inviting, and he felt the possibility, a chance in a thousand but a chance nevertheless, of winning her heart if he kept on winning at roulette. Seconds later he heard someone call her and that's how he found out her name: Roxana.

Straight-up bet. He placed all his chips on the number fourteen. The ball spun counter to the wheel, like the two tides in his life, family and freedom, pulling him in opposite directions. A chorus of sighs rose from the onlookers – ripples of water reaching the shores. Now the ball made a jolt before finally landing in a slot. The wheel moved through another full turn. Her face lit up with amazement and appreciation, and something that he likened to admiration. He didn't need to look to know that he had won.

That was when one of the Chinese muttered under his breath, but in a loud-enough voice, 'Don't you have a family waitin', my friend? They must be worried for you. It's getting late.'

The hidden warning and the word *family* drew a thick curtain between him and the roulette, him and the room, him and her. Adem plunked the chips in a box, cashed them in and strode out. An acquaintance gave him a lift half of the way and he walked the remaining half.

There were piles of rubbish on the streets of East London; rotting waste was strewn everywhere, randomly scattered. The world had gone berserk. Everyone was on strike: firemen, miners, bakers, hospital workers, bin men. No one wanted to play the game any more. No one but the gamblers.

It was four in the morning when he reached the house on Lavender Grove. He smoked on the sofa, the cigarette turning to ash between his fingers, the pile of money warm and loyal next to him. Sixteen thousand, four hundred pounds. Since everyone was sound asleep, he couldn't tell his family about his victory. It would have to wait. He lay wide-eyed in the dusky living room, seized by a sense of loneliness so profound as to be insurmountable. He could hear the rasp of his wife's breathing. And his two sons, daughter, even the goldfish . . . All wrapped in a mysterious serenity.

This he had noticed while doing his military service back in Turkey. When more than three people slept in a narrow place, sooner or later their breaths would become synchronized. Perhaps it was God's way of telling us that if we could just let go of ourselves, we would all eventually be in step and there would be no more disputes. The thought was new to him and he enjoyed it for a while. But even if there was a harmony somewhere, he could not be part of it. It occurred to him, the way it had on other occasions, that he was a man just like any other, no better and no worse, but that he was failing the people he cared about. He wondered, for the umpteenth time, whether his own flesh and blood would be better off without him.

Unable to sleep, he left the flat at dawn. He carried the money with him, though he was aware that it was a foolish thing to do. Hackney was full of muggers and thieves who would not mind breaking his ribs for such a large sum. His walk changed to a lope, and he flinched and went cold each time a stranger approached him on the street.

At the United Biscuits Factory he was treated like a king. They had all heard. During the lunch-break his brother Tariq popped in to congratulate him – and to ask for a favour.

'You know how my wife is,' Tariq said, his voice dwindling to a confidential whisper. 'She's been nagging me for ever about the kitchen.'

Tariq had a theory about British kitchens: that they were deliberately made tiny and gloomy so that everyone would have to make do with takeaways. The architects were accomplices in the conspiracy, and so were the politicians, the councils and the unions, all duly bribed by the restaurant owners, and on and on went his diatribe.

Adem nodded amiably, even though he sensed his elder brother would borrow from him as much as he could, and, after spending a limited amount on his kitchen, would keep the rest in his savings account. Tariq was always hoarding and scrimping. It was hard to believe this was the same man who in his youth had generously supported his two brothers. When their father passed away, Tariq had worked hard, taking care of Adem and Khalil. Over the past years, however, he had become increasingly frugal, snipping toothpaste tubes to squeeze the last drop, clipping coupons from circulars, switching off the water heater, reusing the tea leaves, getting everything second-hand and forbidding his family to buy anything without asking him first, though when they did he always answered, 'There's no need.'

Drawing in his breath, Adem said, 'Do you ever think of our mother?'

On an ordinary day Adem could never have brought himself to speak like this. But now that his brother had asked him for a favour, he felt he had the upper hand. He deserved to hear a few memories in return for a handout. Yet the question was so unexpected that for a moment Tariq seemed at a loss as to how to answer it. A deep wrinkle formed between his brows, extending towards his forehead, where there were several white patches, a skin disease from childhood. When he spoke his voice sounded hard, gruff. 'Why would I do that? She was a good-for-nothing.'

Don't you want to know if she's alive, whether she had other children, how she's doing, whether she ever missed us? Adem wanted to ask and almost did. Instead, into the ensuing hollow of silence, he said thickly, 'I'll stop by your house tonight and bring you the money. Tell my sister-in-law she'll have her dream kitchen.'

After sunset, it occurred to him that if he gambled and won again, he would have twice the money he had now. Then he could lend money to Tariq, and to others, and wouldn't even have to ask for a penny back. Motivated by a noble cause, he went to the basement in Bethnal Green and saw the woman with blue eyes. Again he watched her watch the ball spin around the wheel. Again he played big. And he lost. Everything.

★★★

I had never stammered before in my life until that Tuesday. The 14th of November 1978. The day I decided to get myself a knife.

We were in the school canteen. Me and my mates. Blue plastic trays, shepherd's pie, jam roly-poly, metal jugs of water, the usual patter. One minute I was making jokes, the next I was tripping over words like a prat. It happened just that suddenly – so fast that everyone thought I was having them on.

We were talking about the next day's game. Chelsea were playing Moscow Dynamo. Arshad – a short, stocky Paki who dreamed of playing defence for Nottingham Forest – said he would bet his new Doc Martens that our boys in blue were going to win – a walk in the park, he said – but we all knew it was just bollocks.

Upset at not being taken seriously, Arshad turned to me with a twinkle in his eye and grinned, like he always did when he wanted something.

'Hey, you gonna give me that puddin'?'

I shook my head. 'Nn . . . not on yo . . . uuur . . . nn . . . neee . . . nelly! Fo . . . forr . . . gett . . . itt.'

He stopped and stared. Others did too, as though they were seeing me for the first time. Then someone mentioned this twat in another class who stuttered so badly nobody talked to him. Assuming I had been mocking him, they broke into laughter. I laughed too. But deep inside I felt a surge of panic. I pushed my tray towards Arshad and gestured with my head that he could have what was left. I'd lost my appetite.

When the break was over, I returned to the classroom in low spirits. How could I have developed a speech impediment, just like that? Nobody in my family stammered. Weren't these things supposed to be genetic? Maybe not. It could be a blip; a one-off. A temporary psych-out, like a bad trip. Maybe it would go away as suddenly as it had appeared. I had to find out. So I put my watch in my pocket and approached two girls to ask the time. But the only thing that came out of my mouth was a strangled sound.

The girls giggled. Airheads! They must have thought I had a crush on them. I turned away, my face burning. Out of the corner of my eye I could see my girlfriend watching my every move. When the history class started, Katie threw me a note.

Maggie, Christine, Hilary. If boy, Tom.

I crumpled the paper and slipped it into my pocket. Immediately, she hurled another ball. *What's up with you?*

I shrugged, meaning it was nothing important. But even if Katie got the message she didn't look convinced. So I wrote her back: *Tell you later!*

Throughout the entire class, I was worried sick the teacher would ask me something. I would become the butt of jokes for ever. Fortunately, there were no questions. As soon as the torture was over, I grabbed my rucksack and headed to the door. I decided to blow off the rest of my classes and go home early for once.

★

It was three thirty when I reached our house and rang the bell. As I waited for the door to open, my eyes slid to the name beside the doorbell:

ADEM TOPRAK

My sister, Esma, had written this in her flowery handwriting. Against her better judgement. 'We live here as well,' she grumbled. 'Why write only Dad's name?'

Esma was a frail girl but she always expressed herself with giant ideas: equal opportunity, social justice, women's rights . . . My friends thought she was either barmy or a Communist. If it were up to her she would have written instead:

THE TOPRAK FAMILY

Or else,

ADEM, PEMBE, ISKENDER, ESMA, YUNUS & THE GOLDFISH

Either way I didn't give a toss. I, myself, would have left the nameplate anonymous. That would have been more decent, more straightforward. It would be my way of saying nobody lived here. Not really. We didn't live in this flat, only sojourned. Home to us was no different than a one-star hotel where Mum washed the bed sheets instead of maids and where every morning the breakfast would be the same: white cheese, black olives, tea in small glasses – never with milk.

Arshad might some day play in League Division One, for all I knew. He could fill his pockets with pictures of the Queen and his car with gorgeous birds, but people like us would always be outsiders. We Topraks were only passers-by in this city – a half-Turkish, half-Kurdish family in the wrong end of London.

I rang the bell again. Not a peep. Where on earth was Mum? She couldn't be at the Crystal Scissors. She had quit her job days ago. I was the head of the family since Dad had gone off and I didn't want her to work any more. She cried a lot but didn't resist. She knew I had my reasons. People were gossiping. Where there's smoke, there's fire. So I told her to stay home. I had to put out the flames.

Nobody at school was aware of what was going on. And I wanted it to stay that way. School was school, home was home. Katie didn't know a thing either. Your girlfriend was your girl, your family was your family. Certain things had to be kept separate. Like water and oil.

It occurred to me that Mum might have gone to get the shopping or something. I had to have a word with her about that too. I took out my key, put it in the keyhole and turned it back and forth, but it didn't budge. The door was bolted. Suddenly I heard footsteps down the corridor.

'Who is it?' came my mother's voice.

'It's mm . . . me, MM . . . Mum.'

'Iskender, is it you?'

There was a trace of panic in her voice, as if something bad were about to happen. I heard a whisper, low and rapid, and I knew it wasn't my mother. My heart started to pound and I felt the air go out of me. I could neither move forward nor go backward, so I kept struggling with the key. This went on for another minute, maybe more, then the door opened.

My mother stood blocking the entrance. Her lips were curved up in a smile, but her eyes were oddly sharp. I noticed a strand of hair had come out of her ponytail and one of the buttons in her white blouse was in the wrong hole.

'Iskender, my son,' she said. 'You are home.'

I wondered what surprised her more – that I was home almost three hours early or that I was her son.

'Are you all right?' my mother asked. 'You don't seem well, my sultan.'

Don't call me that, I wanted to say. Don't call me anything. Instead I took off my shoes and pushed past, almost knocking her over. I went straight to my room, slammed the door and put a chair in front of it so that no one could get in. I climbed up on the bed, pulled the sheets over my head and concentrated on breathing – the way they had taught us in boxing class. Inhale. Exhale. Inhale . . .

Outside, there were secretive noises: the floorboards creaking, the wind blowing and a drizzle falling on the city. Amid the mixture of sounds, I could hear our front door opening and someone stepping outside, quiet as a mouse.

She used to love me more than anything – her first child, first son, roniya chavemin.* Everything was different now. Ruined. A tear rolled down my cheek. I slapped myself to stop it. But it didn't help. I slapped again, harder.

I listened to her feet coming down the corridor, soft and steady as heartbeats. She stopped by my door but didn't dare to knock. I could sense her movements, touch her guilt, smell her shame. We waited like that for God knows how long, listening to each other breathe, wondering what the other might be thinking. Then she was gone – as if she had nothing to say, no explanation owed, as if my opinion didn't count anyway, or my anger, or my pain. She walked away from me.

That's when I knew what Uncle Tariq had told me about my mother was true. That's when it occurred to me to buy the knife. Wooden handle, folding blade with a curved point. Illegal, of course. Nobody wanted to get into trouble with the Old Bill by selling a flick-knife, especially to a bloke like me. But I knew where to get one. I knew just the man.

I wasn't gonna hurt anyone. I only wanted to scare her – or him.

Iskender Toprak

* 'The light of my eye'.

Picnics in the Sun

Istanbul, 1954

Adem had spent his entire childhood torn between two fathers: his sober *baba* and his drunken *baba*. The two men lived in the same body, but they were as different from each other as night from day. So sharp was the contrast between them that Adem suspected the drink his father downed every evening to be some kind of magic potion. It didn't morph frogs into princes or dragons into witches, but it changed the man he loved into a stranger.

Baba (the Sober One) was a stoop-shouldered, talkative person who liked to spend time with his three sons (Tariq, Khalil and Adem), and had the habit of taking one of them with him wherever he went, a random lottery of love and care. The lucky boy would accompany his father to see his friends, on strolls along the Istiklal Avenue and, occasionally, to his workplace – a garage near Taksim Square where he was the head mechanic. Big cars with complicated names pulled in there either for repair or parts. Chevrolet Bel Air, Buick Roadmaster, Cadillac Fleetwood or the new Mercedes-Benz. Not every man in town could afford these models – their owners were mostly politicians, businessmen, casino patrons or football players. On the walls of the garage there were framed pictures in which the mechanics beamed next to their influential customers.

Sometimes Adem would escort Baba to the local tea house, where they would while away the day sipping *sahlep*,* linden or tea, and watching men of all ages play backgammon and draughts. Politics was a hot subject. That, football and the stories in the tabloids. With a general election coming up, the tea house was abuzz with fervent debates. The prime minister – the first democratically elected

* A winter drink made with milk, sugar and cinnamon.

leader in the country's history – claimed that his Democratic Party would win a landslide victory. Nobody could possibly guess that he would indeed get re-elected for another term, at the end of which he would be hanged by a military junta.

On such languid afternoons, Adem would imitate Baba (the Sober One), smacking his tongue on a sugar cube, holding the tea glass with his little finger raised in the air. There would be so much smoke around that when they returned home his hair would stink like an ashtray. Frowning ever so slightly, his mother, Aisha, would rush him to the bathroom. He wished she wouldn't do that. It made him feel grown-up to have the smell of tobacco in his hair. When he confessed this to his father one day, Baba laughed, and said, 'There are two things in this world that make a man out of a boy. The first is the love of a woman. The second is the hatred of another man.'

Baba (the Sober One) explained that those who knew only the former softened into wimps and those who knew only the latter hardened like rocks, but those who experienced both had what it took to become a Sword of Steel. As skilled artisans knew, the best way to solidify a metal was to heat it in fire and cool it in water. 'So it is with a man. You need to heat him in love, cool him in hatred,' concluded Baba, pausing for his lesson to sink in.

It worried Adem that he never had emotions this profound, but he kept such anxieties to himself. That same year he had his first asthma attack – a malady that would disappear in his teenage years, but never really abandon his body, chasing him throughout his life.

From time to time, Baba (the Sober One) would bring home leftovers from a slaughterhouse near by – chunks of meat, bones and entrails. On such occasions, he would borrow his manager's pick-up van, taking the family on a barbecue picnic. Adem and his two brothers would sit on the bed in the back, boasting about how many sausages or calves' feet they could eat in one sitting. Baba in the front, with his wife sitting next to him, would make jokes, and, if in an especially mellow mood, would roll down the window and sing. The songs would invariably be tearjerkers, but he rendered them so merrily no one could tell. Their van loaded with pots, pans and linen, their hearts light and gay, they would head to the hills over the

Bosporus. It troubled them that there was a cemetery in the vicinity. Yet there wasn't much they could do. So it was that since time immemorial the dead in Istanbul had resided in the greenest areas with the best views of the city.

Once there, the boys would look for a suitable spot in the shade. Before sitting, however, their mother would pray for the souls of the deceased, asking their permission to spend time on the land. Fortunately, the dead always answered in the affirmative. After a few seconds of waiting, Aisha would nod, and spread out the mats for everyone to sit on. Then she would light the portable stove, and set up everything needed to prepare the food. Meanwhile, the boys would romp happily about, destroying ant colonies, chasing crickets and playing zombies. As the smell of sizzling beef filled the air, Baba would clap his hands, indicating that the moment had come to open his first bottle of *raki*.

Sometimes he would start slowly and gradually pick up the pace. At other times, he would set off fast, downing three glasses in the time it would normally take him to finish one. But, one way or the other, by the end of the lunch he was always a few sheets to the wind.

No sooner had Baba emptied the first bottle than he would start to show telltale signs. He would scowl more often, cursing himself, and every few minutes would scold the boys over something so trivial nobody could remember what it was afterwards. Anything might annoy him: the food was too salty, the bread stale, the ice not cold enough. In order to soothe his nerves, he would open up a second bottle.

Towards the end of one picnic, as the sun was beginning to set and the seagulls were shrieking, time seemed to come to a halt, a sharp smell of anise hanging in the air. Baba added some water to his drink, watching the translucent liquid turn to a milky grey, as blurred as his thoughts. After a while, he rose awkwardly to his feet, his eyes solemn, his chin raised, and made a toast to the cemetery.

'You fellows are so damn lucky,' he said. 'No rent to pay, no petrol to buy, no mouths to feed. No wife nagging you. No boss reading you the riot act. You don't know how blessed you are.'

The graves listened, a low wind swirling the dead leaves to and fro.

'From dust we came,' Baba declared, 'and to dust we must return.'

On the way home, he insisted that the boys sit in the front with them. No matter how careful they were, stifling every gasp, watching their every word, something always happened, something dire enough to send their father into a lather. The potholes in the road, a missing traffic sign, a stray dog running in front of the van, the news on the radio. This new man, Khrushchev, didn't seem to know what he was doing; his brain addled by vodka, a vulgar drink that could not hold a candle to *raki*; Nasser expected too much of the Arabs, who spoke the same language but never listened to one another; and why didn't the Shah of Iran divorce this second wife of his, who obviously couldn't give him an heir?

'What a mess! What a shitty world!'

Baba (the Drunk One) cursed the municipality, the mayor, the politicians. For a few happy minutes his irritation was aimed at the world outside, sparing his family. Usually, someone in the van would do or say something to annoy him. One of the children would wriggle, hiccup, burp, fart or guffaw.

On this day Aisha begged him to drive more slowly.

'What in hell is wrong with you?' he inquired in a tone so composed it hardly matched the severity of the question. 'Can't I have a moment's peace? Hmm? Do you want me to explode? Is that what you want?'

Nobody answered. The boys stared at their scrubby knees, or at a fly that had flown in through the open window and now couldn't get out.

Baba raised his voice. 'I work my fingers to the bone. Every fucking day. Like a mule! Just so that you lot can eat. Am I the jackass of this family?'

Someone said *Estağfurullah** – a lame attempt at appeasement, considering what came next.

'You're vampires, all of you, sucking my blood.' He took his hands off the steering wheel to show his wrists, thin and sallow. 'Do I have more blood to feed you? Have you left me any?'

---

* Originally meaning 'Your health, your goodness', the word is now used to say, 'Of course not.'

'Please hold on to the wheel,' his wife whispered.

'Shut your damn mouth! I'm not going to learn how to drive from you.'

Adem could not help but feel sorry for Baba, who clearly was the victim, the sufferer. Guilt would gnaw at his every fibre. They had done it again. They had upset him, although he had warned them over and over. How Adem wanted to make it up to him, to kiss his hand and promise never to suck his blood again.

'Do I tell you how to cook lentils? Of course I don't. Because that's not my job. And driving isn't *your* job, woman! What do you know about cars?'

Another time he slammed on the brakes so hard that the van spun round as if on ice. They careered across the road straight into a flower-bed, escaping a ditch by only yards. Adem opened his eyes to a stillness he had never known before – the perfect silence that descends after an accident. He noticed, for the first time, the susurrus of the wind, the quills of light in the air. His brother Tariq was holding his elbow, his face twisted with pain, his lips curled around a moan that never came. Slowly, Baba opened his door and walked out, his upper lip bleeding. He circled the van and opened his wife's door.

'Get out!'

'Oh, please,' Aisha said, her face ashen.

'I said get out!'

Grabbing her by the arm, Baba dragged her towards the bonnet of the van, which had popped up when they came to a stop. He said, 'Since you know so much about cars, fix this.'

Not a single muscle moved on her face. Baba shoved her head down into the engine and stopped only when her forehead hit it with a thud.

'What? Can you not fix it?'

She mumbled, words so strangled neither Adem nor his brothers could make out their meaning. But they all heard Baba announce, 'Then zip your mouth and don't tell me how to drive.'

Together they pushed the van out of the flowerbed, the two boys and Baba. Tariq watched without a word, clutching his fractured arm. Their mother, too, waited on the verge, weeping. It was always the same. Every picnic would start with great hopes and end with someone crying or broken.

At night Adem would remind himself that it was his other *baba* who fumed and raged, just as it was his other *baba* who punched the steering wheel/the walls/the tables/the doors/the china cupboard, and, when that didn't help, beat them with his belt, and once kicked his wife in the groin, sending her flying down the stairs. It helped to remember that it wasn't the same man. Not that this lessened the pain or the fear, but it made it easier the next morning to go back to loving Baba (the Sober One).

A Scrap of Truth

London, December 1977

There was an artists' lounge backstage. Not that anybody called it that – only Roxana. She alone liked to think of the cold, cramped dressing room that smelled of cigarettes, talcum powder, perfume and sweat as an area for artists to rest before they went on stage. That didn't mean she thought of herself as an *artiste*, for she did not. When need be, she would use other words to describe her profession – *performer, danseuse, entertainer, exotic dancer*.

It was almost midnight now. In less than fifteen minutes it would be her turn to take the stage. As she scrutinized her costume, she sprinkled silver glitter on her chest. For the first act she was dressed as a samba dancer. A tiara with flamboyant purple feathers, a bikini top ornamented with rhinestones and sequins, silvery, metallic trousers and, underneath those, the skimpiest G-string – to be revealed at the end of the show. With practised ease, she opened the make-up set and arranged the cosmetic pads and brushes of varying sizes. It was an old, worn-out kit that had been used many times by many women. The sponge applicators had turned an unhealthy mushroom tone, the mascara brushes were caked with a thick, crusty substance, and some of the colours on the palette were gone, their pans staring at her like empty eye sockets. There was no more turquoise, for instance, nor platinum nor champagne – Roxana's favourite shades – so she went for amethyst. Again.

When she was finished with her face, she put on a frosted peach lipstick. Lastly, she pushed up her breasts and arranged them so that they looked bigger, plumper, inside the frilly bra. They never called them 'breasts' in England. What funny names they had instead – boobs, tits, wobblers, milky moos.

She had once danced in private for an elderly gentleman – a conservative MP who moonlighted as a fur merchant, so it was rumoured – and heard him say, 'Shake your jiggly wigglies for me, love.' It had taken her a few seconds to figure out exactly which parts of her body he was talking about.

Her English had improved remarkably over the years, although her accent was still strong, unyielding. At times, she stressed her *r*'s deliberately, stretched out her *u*'s, replaced *w*'s with *v*'s. Since she couldn't get rid of her accent, she made it even thicker, bolder, the way everyone in England expected a Russian to speak – for that's what Roxana told each new person she met, that she was from Russia.

In truth, she was from Bulgaria. But in England, even in London, where one heard so many languages and dialects on the street, people didn't know much about her motherland. The Balkans were a jigsaw puzzle with myriad pieces, each of which was equally unfamiliar, eccentric. If Roxana said she was from Bulgaria, they would nod tactfully and ask no more. But whenever she remarked she was born and bred in Russia, they would respond with a barrage of questions. It was intriguing, and somehow romantic, to be from the land of snow, vodka, caviar – and, oddly, KGB spies.

'Girls who aim highest end up falling down the furthest,' people always warned. But, even if that were true, even if she would stumble eventually, and even if her dream was destined to be shorter than a butterfly's breath, it would count for something to have made the attempt, wouldn't it? Roxana was her own creation. She had found herself a name (Roksana, Roxane or Roxie, as men interchangeably said), a nationality, a past, a future and a story to tell. The truth, her truth, was not hidden under layers upon layers, like a Victorian lady's petticoat. It consisted of the total of all the fabrications that made her what she was – a girl from a sleepy town in Bulgaria pretending to be Russian and dancing to Brazilian sambas in a striptease club in the heart of London.

★

Behind the stage, past the magenta curtains that had not been washed in ages, if ever, Roxana now stood ready, in full make-up. She peeked out and saw that the club was full. Another busy night. There were the regulars, a few new customers: the bachelors, the soon-to-be married, the recently divorced and the long-time husbands. Black, brown, and white. Young and old, but mostly middle aged.

Then she spotted him at the bar, drinking his soda slowly. The dark-haired Turkish man with the expression of infinite despair, who wore his apprehension like a moth-eaten jacket. She had first seen him in the gamblers' den, where she had been invited by one of the Chinese owners. That's where she had learned his name, Adem. She had watched him win a large sum at roulette and knew that any other man would have immediately gone out and blown every penny of that money. But he had come back the next day, played even bigger and lost all of it. One part of her despised him for his stupidity. Yet another part of her applauded his recklessness.

Since then he had turned up at every one of her shows, and each time invited her for a drink afterwards. He had been solicitous, asking her about her past, expecting to hear the gloomiest confessions. The only scrap of truth she let slip was about her father's drinking habit.

'Really,' Adem said. 'So your old man was just like mine, uh? Baba died of a swollen liver.'

That was when she winced, as if she had tripped over an unseen obstacle. She didn't want to learn this man's sad story. She didn't want to learn anyone's sad story. All she wanted was to make up her own stories, taking comfort in the knowledge that they were not, and never would be, real.

She would give him the cold shoulder, tell him to stay away from her. This might hurt his feelings, but it would be better for him – and his family. Perhaps then he would be faithful to his wife, although she doubted it. Men like him, once they started frequenting this place and fantasizing about the romantic escapades that life had denied them, did not go back to their homes until they experienced something memorably disastrous.

Big Oath
London, October 1977

Yunus was the only one of the Toprak children who had been born in England. His English was fluent, his Turkish halting, his Kurdish nil. He had auburn hair that curled at the ends, a few freckles across his cheeks and ears that stuck out, giving him a boyish charm. His head was slightly out of proportion to his body and a bit big for his age, *from too much thinking*, according to his mother. His eyes changed from moss-green to myrtle depending on the colour of the outfit he was wearing or his mood. He was named after the prophet Jonah, the fleeing prophet: the man who, upon learning that he was bound to inform the people about truths they weren't ready to hear, headed for the hills, hoping to dodge the mission God had for him; the man who ended up being swallowed by a whale and having to endure three dark days and three dark nights, alone and full of remorse.

Seven-year-old Yunus loved to listen to this story, his face alight with curiosity as he pictured the fish's stomach – dark, deep and damp. There was another reason why this ordeal interested him: just like the prophet himself, Yunus had a tendency to cut and run. When he didn't like it at school, he ran away, and when he didn't like it at home, he fled his family. At the slightest onset of boredom, he was on his feet, ready to take flight again. Despite Pembe's unrelenting efforts, he spent so much time outside, mastering the side streets and back alleys of Hackney, that he could give directions to cab drivers.

Pembe said she never understood how her children could be so different from one another, and Yunus *was* different. He was the introverted one. The philosopher. The dreamer. The hermit who lived in an imaginary cave of his own, finding riches in ordinary things, company in solitude, beauty everywhere. While Iskender and Esma begrudged other people their good fortune and quarrelled, each in their own way, with their circumstances, Yunus loathed no one and belonged to himself alone. Though everyone in the family felt they were an outsider, albeit for different reasons, Yunus seemed the most comfortable in his skin. When he retreated into his inner self such was his completeness that he didn't need any distraction. He could have lived in the belly of a fish and have been all right.

Pembe believed he had turned out this way because he hadn't had enough of either her womb or of her milk. Yunus was the only one of her children who had been born prematurely and who, upon refusing her breasts, had had to be fed formula. 'See the outcome? It's made him distant, unreachable,' she complained.

While Iskender craved to control the world, and Esma to change it once and for all, Yunus wanted to comprehend it. That was all.

★

Early in the autumn of 1977, Yunus was the first to notice that something was not right with his mother. She looked withdrawn, lost in thought. A few times she had forgotten to give him pocket money. And she also fed him less, not shoving as much food into his mouth, which is how Yunus knew something was definitely wrong. Pembe would never forget to feed him; even if it were the morning of the Apocalypse, she would make sure he went to heaven with his belly full.

Not that Yunus minded on his own account; it was always other people he was concerned about. Anyway he had found a way to make pocket money. And it was more than Pembe ever gave him.

There was a house on Moulins Road, several streets north-west of his school. A large detached Victorian building, solitary, abandoned and haunted by ghosts, according to the locals. It had a steep roof, a wrap-around porch and pointed arch windows. Yunus had discovered it on one of his many explorations in the neighbourhood. A group of young people were squatting there. Punks, anarchists, nihilists, pacifists, social dropouts and deviants of various views and many of no single affiliation . . . They were a colourful bunch, mostly in shades of red and black. Nobody in the Toprak family knew how Yunus had first made their acquaintance but the squatters liked him, the wise little boy that he was. They sent him on errands when they were knackered or simply unwilling to move. Bread, cheese, milk, ham, chocolate bars, tins of tobacco, Rizlas . . . Yunus had learned where to get the best deals for each item.

At times they also asked him to retrieve packages from a dour-faced Asian man who lived in a badly lit building, ten minutes' ride away by bike – a task that Yunus secretly dreaded, even though the man tipped him and didn't ask any questions. There was a disturbing stench in his place – of decay and sickness. The squatters' house, too, stank – sometimes even worse. And yet beneath the heavy odour that enwrapped everyone and everything, there were other aromas: of flowers, spices and leaves – lives in transition.

Inside the house there was a wooden staircase winding up three floors, so steep and rotten that it wobbled every time anyone went up or came down it. The internal walls of the ground and first floors had been knocked through, creating open spaces that were used as large bedrooms – even the bathtubs had been turned into beds. The second floor was called the *agora*. The squatters regularly met there, like the ancient Greeks in a city-state, to discuss, vote on and seal the decisions of the commune.

Most of the furniture in the house was reserved for the *agora*: lamps scavenged from second-hand shops, armchairs and dining chairs – no two of which matched – sofas with cigarette burns all over them. There was an ornate crimson oriental carpet. No one knew where it had come from. A little threadbare here and there but still in good shape, it was probably the most precious item in the entire squat. Piled all around were towers of books, magazines and fanzines, and a medley of coffee mugs, wine glasses, biscuits long gone stale, harmonicas and a broken cassette player that no one tried to repair . . . Everything belonged to all and not much belonged to anyone.

The number of residents changed from week to week. This Yunus discovered on his second visit, when he met new faces and learned that some of those he had met earlier had moved out.

'It is like a floating house,' a man explained, and gave a stoned grin. 'This is our ship and we're sailing to the Big Unknown. Along the way some passengers disembark, others hop on board.'

The man's hair was dyed canary yellow and spiked into shapes that resembled flames. It looked as if his head were on fire.

'Yeah, an ark,' said a young Irish woman with almond eyes, coal-black hair and a radiant smile. She turned to face the boy and introduced herself. 'Hi, I'm –'

But Yunus never heard her name. Not then, not later. He was busy staring at her lip ring, her pierced eyebrows, and the tattoos that covered her arms, shoulders and upper chest. Noticing his astonishment, she asked him to come closer and showed him every visible tattoo on her body, like an art collector showing off his collection to a party guest.

She had an archer on her left arm because it was her sign – Sagittarius. And because she didn't want the archer to feel alone and miserable, she had put an angel with a golden harp next to him. Starting from the nape of her neck, expanding towards both shoulders, was a large lotus flower, white and teal, the roots going all the way down her back. On her right arm was a pink rose in bloom, and underneath it a word: *Tobiko*.

'What's that?'

'Oh, it's a long story,' she said with a shrug.

'My sister says there's no such thing as a long story. There are only short stories and the ones we don't want to tell.'

'Uh-hum, that's cool. And what does your sister do?'

'She's gonna be a writer. She wants to write novels where nobody falls in love because love is for fools.'

The girl laughed. Then she told him the story of her tattoo. Once she'd had 'Toby' inscribed above her wrist, the name of her boyfriend. *He was in the music biz, always tanked.* But she loved him all the same. One day she told him she was pregnant, even though she wasn't: she just wanted to see what his reaction would be. Men went one way or the other when they heard such news. You never could tell. They changed – the kindest of them reacted heartlessly, while the most stand-offish turned docile, considerate, *totally Zen*.

'How did your boyfriend do?' Yunus asked.

'Oh, he went mental. He really lost it, the rat-arsed fecker!'

Toby's response was to question whether it was his baby. And, even if it was, he said, she still had to *sort out this mess*. And that was when she ditched him, strong as the urge had been not to. Erasing a tattoo was no small feat, and there would always be a scar. She wasn't against scars – they were part of life – but she didn't want *his* scar on her. So she went to a tattoo artist and had him turn Toby into Tobiko.

'Wow. And what does it mean?'

'Oh, it's a Japanese dish,' she explained. 'Flying-fish eggs.'

'Flying-fish eggs,' Yunus whispered, as if he didn't want to break the spell. In front of his eyes dozens of flying fish jumped out of the water and glided gracefully towards the setting sun. Yunus, the boy named after the prophet who had survived the belly of a whale, was in love.

From then on he appeared at the squatters' house at the slightest opportunity. They let him stay, even when there were no errands. He sat next to Tobiko, hanging on her every word, though he could rarely follow the conversation. *Unemployment, false consciousness, work-ers' rights, cultural hegemony* . . . If you remained outside the capitalist system, it was impossible to make any meaningful change inside it, he learned. But if you became part of that order, it would destroy your soul. *So how do you transform something from within but remain detached from it at the same time, mate?* Yunus pondered hard as he drank smoky tea and the occasional sip of wine, but no matter how high he floated he could not come up with an answer.

At night Yunus would dream of the squatters' house drifting in a sea so perfect it blended with the sky, where seagulls soared and swooped. He would see the squatters paddling in the water, loud and naked, like cheerful mermaids. Tobiko would be there, standing on a cliff, her long black hair fluttering in the wind as she waved at him, pure joy. Yunus would wave back, feel the sun on his face, dive deep into the blue and swim until his muscles ached.

In the morning he would wake in a wet bed.

*

There wasn't much cooking done at the squat, save for their speciality dish: chilli con carne. Mince, tinned tomatoes and bags of kidney beans. In lieu of dinner there were biscuits, chocolate bars, apples, bananas and supermarket pastries near their expiry date. If in the mood Tobiko would bake fairy cakes with whatever was available in the kitchen and add generous amounts of hashish to the mixture.

Hackney Council had long been trying to evict the squatters so that the house could be renovated and sold for a healthy profit. There was an ongoing war between the two groups. Most recently the LEB, having discovered that the squatters had figured out how to connect their electricity, had sent someone round to cut it off. Now there were candles and oil lamps on every floor, eerie shadows crawling across the walls. The toilet was repeatedly blocked, the stench often vile. Yunus could not understand why Tobiko continued to live there. If only he were older and had his own job and flat, he would ask her to live with him. But then she would probably bring the Captain with her and the Captain would have to invite the entire gang, because leaders needed people to lead, and thus everyone would end up in his place, which in a few weeks would be exactly like the squatters' house.

The man everybody called 'the Captain' was a rail-thin bloke with hair falling into his flint-grey eyes, teeth slightly stained from tobacco and a ring on every finger, including his thumbs. He had a penchant for saying aloud whatever came into his head. He loved to talk, his gravelly voice growing more passionate with each new point, his audience spellbound. The Captain was the first person to call Yunus a 'Muzzie'. The boy had never heard the word before and didn't like it at all.

'Don't worry,' said Tobiko, when Yunus shared his concern with her. 'Despite appearances, he's not a racist. Because how can he be a racist when he's anti-fascist, right?'

Yunus blinked.

'What I mean is, he likes to pigeonhole people, just to know where everybody stands. His mind works like that.'

'My sister, Esma, loves words too,' Yunus cut in, knowing it was a silly comment but saying it anyhow.

Tobiko smiled. 'The Captain doesn't love words. He makes love to them.'

Envy and despair must have shown on the boy's face, for suddenly

Tobiko pulled him towards her and kissed him on the forehead. 'Dar-lin', how I wish you were ten years older!'

'I will be,' Yunus said matter-of-factly, even though he had blushed up to his ears. 'In ten years.'

'Mind, in ten years' time I'll be a dried prune, old and wrinkled.' She ruffled his hair – a favourite gesture of hers that he hated, though he could never admit that to himself.

'I'll age fast,' Yunus ventured.

'Oh, I know you will. You're already the oldest little boy I've ever known.'

With that she kissed him again, this time on his lips, light and wet. He felt as if he were kissing rain.

'Don't you ever change,' Tobiko whispered. 'Don't let the greedy capitalist system get to you.'

'O-kay.'

'Give me your word. No . . . wait. Promise on something that matters to you.'

'How about the Qur'an?' asked Yunus timidly.

'Oh, yeah. That's brilliant.'

And there and then, his lips quivering, his heart hammering, seven-year-old Yunus made an oath to Allah that he would never ever let the capitalist system get anywhere near him, though he didn't have the foggiest idea what that could mean.

★★★

Shrewsbury Prison, 1990

Finally it has arrived. A poster of Harry Houdini. The man who could not be chained or shackled. Or imprisoned, for that matter. My idol. It's one of his earlier shots. Black and white, and many shades of grey. Houdini is young in the picture, a wiry magician with a wide forehead and stunning eyes. The sleeves of his tuxedo are rolled up, displaying half-a-dozen handcuffs around his wrists. Not a trace of fear on his face. Just a vague, pensive air to him. You would think he was surfacing from a dream.

I put it up on the wall. Trippy sees it and breaks into a grin. My cellmate's name is Patrick, but no one remembers that. Whenever he sees something that grabs his attention – which happens fairly often, even in a place as dull as this – he says, 'Man, that's trippy!' Hence the name.

Trippy is younger than me, a touch shorter. Sallow skin, hair receding at the top, dark brown eyes, heavily lashed. No matter what a con's age, his mother thinks he is a good boy corrupted by bad friends. Usually, that's bollocks. In Trippy's case it's true. Nice lad from Stafford, messed with some nasty pieces of work. The funny thing is those prats were able to beat the rap, but Trippy is banged up for ten years. That's how it is. Nothing happens to jackals. Only the ones who play at being a jackal get caught. I'm not saying we're any better. Passing yourself off as a jackal is worse than being one, sometimes.

This I have never told him, but Trippy's eyes remind me of Yunus's. He's the one I miss most. I've never been a true brother to him. I wasn't there when he needed me, too busy fighting the wrong battles.

Yunus is a big man now. A talented musician. So they say. He has been to see me only twice in twelve years. Esma still visits from time to time, though not lately. She comes to tell me how much she misses, pities and hates me, in that order. Not Yunus. He has cut and run, like he always did. Even Esma's sharpest words don't hurt as much as my little brother's absence. I would like him to forgive me. If he could find it in his heart, that is. Not because I expect him to love me. That's a pipe dream. I want him to forgive me for his own good. Anger is toxic – gives you cancer. People like me are used to it, but Yunus deserves better.

'Who is that man?' asks Trippy, pointing at the wall.

'He was a great magician. The best.'

'Really?'

'Yup, some of his tricks are still a mystery.'

'Could he make people disappear?'

'He could make bloody elephants disappear.'

'Wow, that's trippy!'

We spend the afternoon talking about Houdini, our heads filled with stories, and, in Trippy's case, with dope. I like to have my spliff every now and then. But that's about it. No pills, no smack. Never tried it, never will. I'm not going down that road. When I remind Trippy he has to quit, he puts his thumb in his mouth and makes a sucking noise: 'I'm not a baby.'

'Shut your gob!'

He grins like a naughty boy, the dope-head. But he doesn't push it. He knows he's the only one who can talk to me like that and he knows my limits.

Shortly after the evening roll call Martin appears with a short, stocky guard we've never seen before. The man has a dimple in his chin and hair so black I wonder if he dyes it.

'Officer Andrew McLaughlin has started today. We're visiting a few cells.'

Martin is going to retire soon and he wants to make sure we'll respect this young man who's here to replace him. There is an awkward silence, like we are all embarrassed and don't know what to say. Suddenly Martin's eyes land on the poster behind me.

'Whose idea was that?' he murmurs and without waiting for an answer he turns to me. 'Yours, wasn't it?'

Martin is a lousy actor. He has already seen this poster. If he hadn't approved, I'd never have got it. But now he acts as if he's seeing it for the first time. Just to show the new boy he might be retirement age but he still doesn't miss a trick. He says that all these years he's watched men put up all sorts of pictures on their walls – of their wives and family, religious icons, film stars, football players, cricket players, Playboy bunnies – but Houdini, that takes the biscuit.

'Maybe you're losing your mind,' Martin says with a chuckle.

'Maybe,' I say.

Officer McLaughlin approaches and sniffs the air around me, like a hunting dog on a trail. 'Or maybe he's planning to escape. Houdini was an escapologist.'

Where did that come from? The vein on my forehead throbs mildly. 'Why would I do that?'

'Yeah,' Martin asks, his eyes suddenly harder. 'Why would he do that?'

Then he turns to the new screw and explains. 'Alex has been here since '78. He has only two more years to go.'

'One year and ten months,' I correct him.

'Yeah,' Martin says and nods as if that sums up everything.

In Martin's face, as usual, there are two feelings competing – revulsion and respect. The former was there from day one and has never disappeared – contempt for a man who committed the worst crime

69

imaginable and screwed up the one life God gave him. The respect came much later, and most unexpectedly. We have a history together, Martin and I.

But Officer McLaughlin's face tells a different story. 'I think I know your case,' he says flatly. 'I remember reading about it and saying to myself how could anyone do that to his own mother.'

I realize we are the same age. Not only that. We are the same material. We might have frequented the same streets as teenagers, kissed the same girls. The strangest feeling seizes me – as if I'm looking in a skewed mirror. McLaughlin is the man I could have become had I followed a different path. And I'm the convict he might have turned into had he not managed to duck at the last minute.

'Fourteen years, eh? What a shame,' he says.

Martin coughs nervously. You don't remind a man of his crime in passing, like chatting about the weather. You do that only when push comes to shove. Usually no one reminds anyone of what went before. A man in gaol is a man incarcerated in the past anyway.

'Alex has turned a corner in the last few years,' Martin butts in, like a tourist guide. 'He's gone through some dark times and is now coming back.'

Dear old Martin. Such optimism. I've been through hell, true. But he knows and Trippy knows and I know and my mother's ghost knows that I'm still there.

I had an awful reputation. I suppose I still do. I easily went for a rib. It was hard to predict what would piss me off. Even I couldn't tell most of the time. When I was off key I got violent. My left punch was as strong as a brick, so they say. Sometimes I just burst out. The only other cons who would get like this were the junkies. When they craved goods and there was no supply, they lost their rag. But I'm no addict. And that makes me scarier, perhaps. This is my sober state of mind. I harmed myself. My head. Because I didn't like what was in there. I burned cigarettes inside my palms. They swelled, like puffy eyes. I slashed my legs. Lots of meat on a leg, the thighs, the knees, the ankles. Plenty of possibility. In Shrewsbury a razor is as precious as a ruby, but not as impossible to find.

'You two will get to know each other,' says Martin.

'Well, I'm sure we will,' says Officer McLaughlin.

Trippy is watching the tension build, uneasy. He knows what's happening. He's seen it before. Sometimes a screw takes against one of us and that's the end of the story. You get off to a bad start and it never gets any better.

The tourist guide makes another attempt at reconciliation. 'Alex is a boxer. He's our athlete. He earned a medal when he was at school.'

It is a funny thing to say in my defence and needless to say no one laughs. I want to thank Martin for backing me, but if I move my eyes away from the young officer, even for a second, I will leave myself open.

He has to see I'm no wimp. The last time I was one, it was over twenty years ago. I was a boy in a tree running away from circumcision. It didn't help. Since then I've never been weak. I've been wrong. Fucking wrong. But never weak. So I don't flinch, I don't blink, I keep staring into the eyes of this McLaughlin, who is staring into my eyes probably for the same bloody reasons.

Then they leave.

★

I wake up in the middle of the night with a start. At first I think my mother has visited me. But, hard as I try, I can't feel her presence. No rustle like a leaf falling, no soft glow like moonlight trapped. There is only Trippy, snoring, farting, grinding his teeth, fighting his demons.

I sit bolt upright on the bed and look around to find out what on earth could have woken me up. And then I see it. There on the floor is a paper. Somebody must have pushed it through the bars in the door. In the dimmest light penetrating from the corridor, I pick it up. It's a newspaper clipping. The Daily Express.

BOY KILLED HIS MOTHER FOR 'HONOUR', 2 DECEMBER 1978

A 16-year-old boy of Turkish/Kurdish origin stabbed his mother to death in Hackney in an act of honour killing. Iskender Toprak stabbed Pembe Toprak in front of the family home on Lavender Grove.

It is claimed that the 33-year-old mother of three had an extramarital affair. Neighbours said, though they remained married, Adem and Pembe Toprak no longer lived together. 'But when the father is absent like that the mother's honour is guarded by the eldest son, which in this case was Iskender,' said an eyewitness. The police are now investigating whether the teenager, who is still at large, acted alone or was used as a pawn by other family members to carry out a collective murder plan.

A spokeswoman for Scotland Yard told *The Times* that this case was neither the first nor would it be the last in the UK and Europe. She announced that at the moment they were investigating 150 deaths that could be linked to honour killings. 'Sadly the number could be higher since not all cases end up in the hands of the police,' she said. 'Family and neighbours know more than they tell. Those closest to the victims are the ones who suppress valuable information.'

'It is a growing cancer in modern society,' the spokeswoman added, 'given that in numerous communities the honour of the family is deemed to be more important than the happiness of its individuals.'

My hands shake so hard that the newspaper clipping flaps as though in a mighty wind. I'm dying for a cigarette. Or a drink. Something strong and simple. My father never knew this, but me and the boys used to have a cider or beer every now and then. Never whisky, though. That was another league. I had my first taste of it under this roof. You can find anything in gaol, if you know your way around.

I fold the paper in half, creasing the corners down into the middle. A square, two triangles, a rectangle . . . I make the corners meet, pull the triangles apart and there it is: a paper boat. I put it on the floor. There is no water to make it float. No gust to push the sails. You would think it was made of cement. It doesn't go anywhere. Like the pain in my chest.

Iskender Toprak

Esma

London, December 1977

We lived in Hackney, on a street called Lavender Grove. It was a constant disappointment to my mother that there were no lavender bushes around, only the name. She never stopped hoping to find some one day, in someone else's garden, or around a corner, a forgotten grove, a sea of purple.

I loved the neighbourhood. Afro hair salons, the Jamaican café, the Jewish baker's, the Algerian boy behind his fruit stall who pronounced my name in a funny way and always had a little present for me, the penniless musicians who lived around the corner and rehearsed every day with their windows open and introduced me, without knowing it, to Chopin; the artist who drew portraits in Ridley Road Market for ten bob, and once made mine for only a smile. All creeds and colours.

Before this house, there was a flat in Istanbul – the place where Iskender and I had spent the early years of our childhood but that now belonged to another time, another country. This was where our family had lived prior to our move to England in May 1970, shortly before Yunus was born. Like many expatriates, Mum, too, had a selective memory. Of the past she had left behind, she would reminisce mostly, if not solely, about the good things: the warm sunshine, the pyramids of spices in the market, the smell of seaweed in the wind. The native land remained immaculate, a Shangri-La, a potential shelter to return to, if not actually in life, at least in dreams.

My recollections, however, were of a mixed nature. Perhaps, of the past they share together, children never remember the same bits as their parents. Once in a while my mind ran back to the basement in that old house: the furniture upholstered in azure; the round, white, crocheted lace doilies on the coffee tables and kitchen shelves;

the colony of mould on the walls; the high windows that opened on to the street . . . The flat etched in my memory was a dimly lit place where a crackly radio was on all day long and a faint odour of decay lingered in the air. It was always dusk in there, morning or afternoon made little difference.

I was little when the place was *home* to me. I would sit cross-legged on the carpet in the living room and look up with my mouth half open at the windows near the ceiling. Through them I could see a frantic traffic of legs flowing left and right. People going to work, returning from shopping or out for a promenade.

Watching the feet of the passers-by and trying to guess what their lives were like was a favourite game of ours – a game with three players: me, Iskender and Mum. So, for instance, we would see a pair of shiny stilettos walking at a brisk, hurried pace, ankle straps neatly tied, heels clattering against the pavement. 'I think she's going to meet her fiancé,' Mum would say and then come up with an intriguing story of love and heartache. Iskender, too, was good at this game. He would spot a pair of worn-out, dirty moccasins and fabricate a story about how they belonged to a man who had been without a job for quite some time and was now so desperate he was going to rob the bank around the corner, where he would get shot by the security guard.

Though the basement did not get enough sunshine, it did receive plenty of rain. Drizzles were no threat, but whenever it rained more than two inches in the city the drains in the house overflowed, engulfing the back room in a messy, murky lake. Wooden ashtrays, spatulas, picture frames and bamboo baskets were good swimmers. Baking trays, chopping boards, teapots, and the pestle and mortar were hopeless. While the glass vase on the table would plummet fast, the plastic flowers in it would float. Then there was the backscratcher . . . I wished it, too, would sink, but it never did.

My parents had talked about moving out of the apartment, but, even if they had had the means and found a sunnier basement in this impoverished neighbourhood, there was no guarantee that it would endure Istanbul's infamous downpours any better. Perhaps over the years they had also developed an attachment to their flat. Dark and damp it may have been, but it was, nevertheless, home.

Istanbul . . . Deep in the slow, whirling memories the city's name stood out from the hundreds I had stored away throughout my life. I placed the word on my tongue, sucking on it slowly, eagerly, as if it were a boiled sweet. If London were a confection, it would be a butterscotch toffee – rich, intense and traditional. Istanbul, however, would be a chewy black-cherry liquorice – a mixture of conflicting tastes, capable of turning the sour into sweet and the sweet into sour.

★

My mother first started to work shortly after my father had gambled away two months' worth of wages. Suddenly, money was needed like never before. While Iskender was at school, Mum started to go to the houses of the rich, where she would take care of their toddlers, cook their food, clean their rooms, scour their saucepans, iron their clothes and occasionally offer a shoulder to cry on. I would be left in the care of a neighbour, an old woman with a sharp tongue and poor hearing, but otherwise nice.

In the evenings Mum would tell us, as if they were bedtime stories, about life in the villas where every child had his or her own room, and modern husbands invited their wives to have a drink with them. She had once seen a couple put jazzy music on a machine and dance – which had struck her as something of a shame, for they stepped on the carpet with their dusty shoes, confirming her belief that there was something queer about the wealthy. Otherwise why would anyone throw green olives into their drinks, ruin lush carpets and nibble yellow cheese cubes jabbed with toothpicks?

After working for several families, Mum found a full-time job. They were famous people, her employers. The woman was an actress and had just given birth to a girl. As for her husband, we never came to learn what exactly he did, but he was always busy and travelled frequently, that much we knew. My mother's job was to take care of the house and the baby, as well as the actress, who didn't seem to be coping well with the changes in her life. Colicky and moody, the baby constantly cried. But the new mother wept just as easily and sometimes even more. She was beautiful – almond eyes, jet-black hair, a shapely nose, slender hands with the thinnest veins. If her fans had seen her like this, they might have been disappointed, but Mum felt a rush of fondness for her in her shabby, despondent state.

By then the old lady who looked after me had fallen sick and Mum started taking me with her. While I played on my own, she would toil, and secretly sprinkle cardamom seeds around the actress's bed to protect her from the *djinn*. Then we would take a bus and a *dolmush*,* and go home, just as the sky hung low and dim above the city. A full month went by. Mum expected to get her wages any day, but there was no mention of it and she was too shy to ask.

One afternoon, while Mum was cooking and I was playing under the kitchen table, the woman's husband appeared. There was a faint, sour odour emanating from him – aftershave and whisky. His eyes were bloodshot but oddly amused. Unaware of my presence, he staggered towards Mum and grabbed her sides.

'Hush,' the man said, putting his finger to his lips. 'They're all sleeping.'

They're all sleeping. They won't see us. They're all sleeping. So we can sleep too. I'll buy you nice things. Shoes, bags, clothes, a pair of golden earrings . . . You're a good woman, a saint. Please have pity on me. My wife will never know. Neither will your husband. They're all sleeping. I'm not a bad man. But I am a man, like any other, and I have needs. My wife isn't a woman any more. She's changed since the baby, always weeping, whining. The entire city is sleeping.

My mother pushed the man against the wall; in his drunken state he offered little resistance. His hands dangled at his sides, his body slackened as if it were empty, like a soft toy. Yanking me with one hand, grabbing her handbag with the other, Mum stomped down the corridor, but then realized we didn't have enough money to go home.

'Sir . . .' she said. 'You haven't given me my wages.'

He was standing by the door, slightly teetering. 'You want money?' he asked, sounding surprised.

'It's my monthly –'

He cut in. 'You treat me like this and on top of that you want my money? What a bitch you are!'

* A minibus.

76

We marched out of the house. We took the bus, got off at our usual stop and decided to walk the rest of the way home. But Mum wasn't paying attention to where we were going. Step by step, we drifted away from main avenues into serpentine streets that seemed to lead nowhere. It was getting dark. We found ourselves by the seaside in an area where we had never before set foot. There were huge, black rocks along the shore, the waves crashing against them. We sat there, catching our breath, observing the splendour of the city and its indifference to us.

Noticing tiny seashells on the beach, I stood up to collect them. I was still lingering by the sea when I saw two men approach my mother. They were eating sunflower seeds, spitting the shells out, leaving a trail behind them like in the Hansel and Gretel story.

'Good evening, sister, you seem so sad,' said the first one. 'What's a woman like you doing here at this hour?'

'Yeah, you look like you need help,' said the other.

Mum didn't answer. She fumbled in her handbag for a handkerchief, still sniffing. A few hairpins, house keys, bills to pay, a handful of hazelnuts she had taken with her but forgotten to give me, a photo of her children, and a mirror in which she saw her melancholy, but no handkerchief.

'Do you have anywhere to go tonight? Why don't you join us?'

'We'll take care of you,' the other said sassily.

'I don't need your help,' Mum retorted, her voice tinted with irritation. Then she turned towards the shore, and yelled, 'Esma, come here, quickly!'

The men were surprised to see me, but they didn't back off. Instead they followed us silently. It was a game. Mum would resist. They would insist. Mum would resist. They would insist. Mum would surrender.

'Get away! Don't you see I'm a married woman?'

One of the men glanced nervously at her, but the other scoffed and rolled his eyes as if to say, So what?

Dark and misty, there were fewer and fewer pedestrians around, and the traffic was sparse. We hurried, careful to avoid the corners, where the moonlight etched grey outlines on the trees. We saw one or two women, strolling next to their husbands or brothers, enjoying the protection, the privilege. Ten minutes had gone by, or maybe more, when we came across an old man with a boy.

'*Selamun aleykum*. Are you all right?'

Not waiting for Mum to respond, I blurted out, 'We're lost.'

Tipping his head in a gentle nod, the old man smiled at me. 'And where is your home, my dear?'

Mum whispered a district, but out of courtesy she added that he shouldn't worry about us.

'Well, you're in luck. My grandson and I are going that way too.'

'No, we aren't,' objected the boy, who was slightly older than me.

The old man squeezed his grandson's shoulder. 'Sometimes the shortest way is to follow a friend's route.' Then he turned to the two men behind us and scowled so hard that they averted their eyes, suddenly embarrassed.

Thus we started our walk home – Mum, me, the old man and the boy. I inhaled the salty scent the wind brought from the sea, eternally grateful to the strangers who had so unexpectedly turned into companions of the road. When we reached our street, Mum asked the man the name of his grandson.

'Yunus,' he said with pride. 'He'll be circumcised next month, *inshallah*.'

'If God gives me another son,' Mum said, 'I shall remember you and name him Yunus, so that he can be as kind to strangers as you have been to me.'

★

Back in the basement flat, sitting under the windows now filled with a slate-coloured emptiness, my father was waiting, chain-smoking. The moment he heard our keys in the lock, he leaped to his feet. 'Where have you been?'

'We had to walk,' Mum said, and frowned at me. 'Esma, take your coat off and go back to your room.'

She pushed me towards the corridor, and closed the door so harshly it bounced open again and stood slightly ajar. 'I didn't have the money for the *dolmush*.'

'What do you mean you didn't have the money? How much did they give you?'

'Nothing. I'm not going to work for them again.'

'What the hell are you talking about?' my father asked, raising his voice a notch, but no more. 'I have debts, you know that.'

'They didn't pay me . . .'

For almost a full minute I didn't hear a sound. Then, as if surfacing from dark waters to grab a breath, my father inhaled loudly. 'You come home at this hour and you think I'm going to believe your lies. Where's the money, you whore?'

There was a backscratcher on the sofa. A mustard-yellow, cold tool made of a ram's horn. In the twinkling of an eye, he grabbed it and flung it at Mum, who was so distracted by his words that she failed to dodge it in time. The implement hit her on the side of her face with a thud, cutting her neck.

No, my father Adem Toprak did not beat his wife or his children. And yet on that night, and on other nights in the ensuing years, he would easily lose his temper and turn the air blue with words that were full of pus and bile; he would smash objects against the walls, all the while hating the entire world for pushing him to the edge, where he feared the shadow of his abusive father was waiting to tell him he might not, in the end, be that different from him.

A Box of Baklava

A Village near the River Euphrates, 1961

Born and bred in Istanbul, Adem only left the city for the first time when he was eighteen years old. Taking with him a suitcase full of clean underwear, lavender cologne and a box of *baklava*, he got on a bus and arrived twenty-four hours later, drained and disorientated, at a south-western town he knew not much about. From there he travelled in the back of a lorry to a village that bordered the northern tip of Syria. This was where his brother Khalil had been doing his military service for the past five months.

His face tanned from the winter sun, Khalil had lost some weight, but the greatest change was in his demeanour. His eyes had acquired a thoughtful gleam and he seemed unusually reticent, as if wearing a uniform had altered his character. Even as he gladly accepted the underwear and cologne, he seemed more pensive than merry. Adem examined him with curiosity, for he, too, would become a soldier in about a year. Military service being compulsory, he had decided to do it as soon as he left secondary school. University wasn't for him, and he couldn't afford it anyway. Upon coming back from the army, he would find a job, get married and have six children – three boys, three girls. This, in a nutshell, was the future he had envisaged for himself.

When visiting hours were over, Adem left his brother in his garrison and rode a donkey back to the nearby village. Frozen earth, the colour of porridge, stretched out as far as the eye could see. Nature was resilient here, unyielding. Only as he was observing the landscape did it occur to him that he had forgotten to give Khalil the box of *baklava*.

Kismet, he thought to himself. *Maybe it was for someone else.*

Upon arriving in the village Adem found the *muhtar* – the headman.

It was a lucky coincidence that his father had done business with him in the past. Though the two men hadn't seen each other in many years, they had kept in touch through common friends. And so, prior to his trip, Adem had sent a postcard to his father's acquaintance to notify him of his arrival. Worryingly, he had not had a reply.

'Postcard? What card?' yelled the headman when Adem knocked on his door. 'I didn't receive anything.'

He was a swarthy man, so tall that he had to stoop before walking in and out of doorways. A thick moustache curled upwards atop his lip, and his sideboards were slicked down with a substance that looked like oil.

'I . . . I'm sorry . . . then I'd better go,' said Adem.

'Where do you think you're going?'

'I . . . look, I –'

'No visitor has ever been unwelcome under this roof,' roared the headman.

Slowly, it dawned on Adem that the Kurdish man was not angry with him. Nor was he shouting. His voice was naturally loud and husky, and his Turkish so unpractised that it made him sound enraged even when he wasn't.

'Well, thank you. It's only for a night, really.'

'A night? You cannot leave so soon! There is a wedding in two days. You must join us. Otherwise the groom's family will be offended.'

How can they can be offended when they don't even know me, Adem wanted to ask. But the customs were different in this part of the country, and far more pronounced. Besides, he didn't have any reason to hurry back to Istanbul. It wasn't as if anyone there was desperate for him to return.

Weddings, joyful as they were, had long been a source of sadness for Adem, for they always reminded him of his mother, Aisha. Her name was not mentioned in their house any more; her photos had been destroyed as if she had never been. The lace she had tatted, the handkerchiefs she had embroidered, the necklaces that had once adorned her long neck, and the blouses, stockings and hairpins she had worn – all had been burned on a bonfire lit by Baba (the Drunk One).

So it was that Adem accepted the headman's offer and remained in the village, gorging himself on fresh butter, cream and honey. The next afternoon, the headman dozed off after lunch, his wife and daughters immersed themselves in polishing the copper utensils in the house, and his sons became caught up in a backgammon tournament. Adem had seen his brother in the morning. The second visit had been shorter, though no less sentimental. Again he had forgotten the *baklava*. Now, having no interest in backgammon and for want of anything better to do, he decided to go out for a walk.

He strolled through the village, observing the rickety houses, the cracks in the walls, the children with dirt under their fingernails, the ruts left by carts and caravans that had crossed this land, never to return. It was bare and bleak but oddly beguiling. He came across a pack of stray dogs basking in the dirt, and one of them, a large canine with a tawny coat and bloodshot eyes, showed its teeth. The other dogs followed suit, snarling and growling, their ears pinned back. Adem turned around and began to run, even though he knew it would prompt the pack to chase him. Panting, he scrambled down mud tracks without a sense of direction, until he arrived at a sod house with chickens and hens in the front garden. There was someone sitting on the garden wall – half-girl, half-woman – who, upon closer inspection, was sniggering at his panic. Adem dashed towards her, and entered the garden without permission, taking refuge in her self-confidence.

Only seconds later the dogs reached the garden and hemmed him in on every side. One came dangerously close, crouching. Just as it was about to attack, the girl clapped her hands and shouted, in a voice mixed with authority and amusement, words that Adem could not comprehend. The effect was magical. One by one the animals sat down, their heads low, their tails between their legs.

Adem stared at his saviour, annoyed at having been rescued by a girl, but deeply relieved. She had a dimple in her left cheek, and large, liquid eyes, evenly spaced, the colour of a bottomless lake. In her hand was some kind of pastry, which she eagerly went back to devouring. He had never seen a girl with such an appetite.

'You scared of dogs?' she asked.

He didn't respond.

'If they know that, they'll frighten you. Smart animals! My sister loves them.' She leaned forward as if revealing a secret. 'I don't.'

She spoke Turkish with a heavy accent. *An ignorant Kurdish girl*, he thought. *Probably lice-infested.* He shot a glance at her neatly plaited hair, chestnut-brown with glints of gold and amber. So strong was the urge to touch her plaits that he raised his hand, but then stopped it in mid-air.

'How is it that you know Turkish, when most people in the village don't?' he said.

'I went to school. All my sisters did. Father insisted.'

Adem's eyes scrutinized the house, inspecting the dresses, skirts and socks pegged to a line, drying. 'How many sisters do you have?'

'I'm the eighth girl in the family.'

'Wow. And no boys?'

Shaking her head, she changed the subject. 'Hey, would you like some? I made it.'

He took the piece of pastry she offered and sank his teeth into the rich, fluffy dough. He wasn't expecting it to be so good. The dogs looked up expectantly, wagging their tails. Under their reproachful eyes, the two ate in silence, not knowing how to keep the conversation going.

'I live in Istanbul,' Adem said, when he found his voice again.

'Really? Everybody says it's beautiful.'

'True,' Adem answered with a trace of pride. He decided he was beginning to like her. There was a lightness to her manner that he found fascinating, and the ease with which she spoke soothed him.

'May I ask you something?' she said suddenly, and went on without waiting for an answer. 'Is it true that the cobblestones of Istanbul are made of gold?'

What kind of a girl was this, Adem wondered – brave enough to confront a pack of wild dogs but so naive as to believe in such nonsense. Yet he was smitten by her charm, and heard himself say, 'Yes, they are. If you were to marry someone like me, you could come to Istanbul to see for yourself.'

She blushed. 'Why would I marry you?'

'Because I can take you far away.'

'I don't want to go afar. There is more than enough here.'

He was still considering how to respond when they heard a woman's voice coming from the house. She jumped to her feet and stood facing him, holding his eyes with the intensity of her stare. Then she turned to the dogs and, shaking a finger, shouted, 'Leave him alone.'

As soon as she disappeared, Adem began to inch his way out of the garden. The leader of the pack watched him intently, and, just as he passed by, it growled, giving him such a jolt that he dropped what remained of the pastry. Dismayed, he looked at the mushy mess on the ground, the sugar mingling with the soil.

There were no golden pavements in Istanbul. Or anywhere else in the world. No dreams to pursue. Such things existed solely in legends and fairy tales. The real world with its real people resembled a mixture of sugar and soil, and was, more or less, of the same taste. Didn't she know that?

★

The next day Adem attended the wedding, which was like nothing he had ever seen before. A courtyard filled to the brim with men of all ages sitting in a half-circle, a musician bashing away at his drum while another played the clarinet, children running around unattended, and women watching from the flat rooftops, their faces half covered, their hands hennaed. Adem noticed that the unmarried men were careful not to look upwards, and he did the same, keeping his eyes level.

Across from the entrance were the groom's father and the bride's father, sitting side by side but without exchanging a word. Depending on their rank or degree of proximity, relatives were positioned on either side. The bride and the groom were in the centre, where everybody could scrutinize them to their heart's content. The groom had been newly shaved, and he smiled often. It was impossible to know how the bride felt, for her face was hidden under a glittery, crimson veil. From time to time a woman tiptoed close, bringing her something to drink. Together they lifted her veil ever so slightly so that she could sip without spilling anything on to her clothes, and without being seen.

Adem was planning to sit in a quiet corner when the headman spotted him and bellowed, patting the seat beside him. 'City-boy, come next to me.'

So he did. He sat there good-humouredly, enjoying the celebration, until the man next to him pulled out his gun and began to fire it in the air. Immediately, others followed. The sound was deafening. One of the bullets hit the roof of a house near by and left a hole there, dust showering from the boards. Fearful of being shot, Adem glanced around in panic, and in the swirl of chaos he caught his breath at the sight of her, standing on a flat roof, looking at him, calm and composed, as if she were aware of being the only serene thing in a world out of control.

As soon as the shooting subsided Adem excused himself to look for a toilet, though what he really wanted was to find a way to talk to her. No sooner had he walked out of the main gate than he spotted her, sitting by a well, immersed in preparing a huge pot of yoghurt drink. When had she come down from the roof?

'It's good to see you again,' he said.

She gave him a cold glare. 'What are you talking about?'

It occurred to Adem that she was pretending not to have seen him before, for reasons of modesty and reserve that were, no doubt, required of a young woman in a place such as this. He decided to play along. 'I'm sorry, I shouldn't have intruded. You don't know me, of course. My name is Adem. May I learn yours?'

'And why should I tell you my name?' she snapped, her lips twisted in a scowl, a dimple in her right cheek.

Her eyes were different today, the same and yet altered, glowing with a condescending sparkle, or so it seemed to him. For a sinking moment he suspected she was making fun of him. He excused himself and ambled away.

When he returned, having taken a leak behind a bush and calmed somewhat, she was no longer by the well. The bride was leaving for her new house, mounted on an ivory horse that was pulled by a boy, so that she, too, would bear sons. The animal's mane was decorated with scarlet ribbons and evil-eye beads, its tail braided. While a group of children and a number of women followed the horse, ululating and clapping, the male guests prepared to sit down for the wedding dinner. Large, round, copper trays were carried inside by youngsters. As he strode back, Adem could smell the flat bread and meat. Upon entering the courtyard, he saw her again. She seemed in a hurry, carrying a crying toddler.

'Why are you angry at me?' he asked, blocking her way.

'What? Why should I be angry at you?' she said with a peal of laughter. Even the child in her arms seemed engrossed, suddenly quiet.

'Then why didn't you tell me your name?'

Tucking a lock of hair into her loosely tied scarf, she smiled. 'Because you didn't ask. But, since you are now, it's Jamila.'

He nodded, grateful.

'What about your name?'

'But I told you a minute ago,' he said in a throaty whisper.

A bemused look crossed her face. 'Maybe you talked to Pembe, my twin sister. When did you see her?'

As if prompted by the question, the shooting started again. The child broke into a wail, and Jamila had to rush her out of the courtyard. Adem stood there, feeling slightly dizzy but also relieved. A twin! Yes, that explained it all. The harsh demeanour, the frosty stare. That was not Jamila. Not *his* Jamila.

In the evening Adem stood by the window and watched the moonlight crest on the roofs, shedding silver streaks across the village. The house lights resembled glints of cigarette tips in the dark. He had missed Istanbul and was glad that he would be leaving soon. Yet what was he going to do without Jamila?

He went to see the headman, whom he found in his nightgown, smoking his pipe. There was an oil lamp beside him, which reflected shadows across the walls, creating hollows under his eyes. 'I want to give you this *baklava* and thank you for your hospitality and –'

'Ah, I cannot eat that. I wish I could,' the headman said wearily. 'Diabetes.'

Adem stared at the box in his hand. Maybe it was meant for someone else. He took a deep breath. He had planned to approach the matter indirectly, but now he could see there was no way to do that. 'Today at the wedding, I saw a girl.'

'A girl?'

Slowly, Adem watched the man's face as he raised his eyebrows, taking in the implication. *Oh, God! The boy thinks he has fallen in love.*

'Tell me about this girl,' the headman urged. 'What's her name?'

'Jamila,' Adem replied, feeling his face grow hot.

'Jamila . . . I don't know any Jamila.'

'Long brown hair. Big green eyes.'

Taking slow puffs from his water pipe, the headman shook his head. 'Nope. There's no such girl here.'

'She speaks Turkish.'

'Oh . . . I think I know who you mean. Berzo's girls. They all went to school. Are you referring to Enough Beauty?'

'Enough Beauty?'

'Yes, she and her twin, they were named twice. Pink Destiny and Enough Beauty,' said the headman, but offered no other explanation. 'Look, you're too young to know this, but a man's love is the reflection of his character.'

Adem listened, not knowing what to make of this.

'If the man is quarrelsome, his love is full of fights. If he is placid and kind, his love is a balm. Should he pity himself all the time, his love will crumble to dust. If he is a jolly chap, his love will abound with joy. Before losing your heart to a woman, you need to ask yourself what kind of love can you give her?'

'Well, I'm a good man,' Adem said.

'The only good man I know of was the prophet, may peace be upon him,' said the headman. 'Anyway, Berzo has too many girls. Custom requires that they marry the eldest one first. And Jamila is the youngest. However, I can see that it might be a perfect match. The family has gone through hardships. The mother, Naze, died in childbirth, poor woman. She so wanted to have a son. Berzo got married again. But the new wife has given him no children yet. And then the eldest girl, Hediye . . .'

'What happened?'

'That man is doomed, son. He might want to marry off the girls quickly. Jamila might not have to wait.'

Adem broke into a grin. There was a hope, after all, however slight.

'But don't forget they are poor,' the headman whispered. 'Your father and brothers might not approve of a Kurdish bride, a villager. On the other hand . . . your family doesn't have the best of reputations since your mother ran away with another man. Perhaps it's better for you to choose someone here, out of the way.'

All at once Adem's face darkened. He'd had no idea that the man knew about his family's shame. Words, like wandering tribes, were of no fixed address. They travelled far and wide, scattering over the earth.

A Love Like a Comet

A Place near the River Euphrates, December 1977

In the stillness of the night, Jamila was dozing by the fireplace, her head tilted to one side. Her left hand was dangling over the edge of the chair and her right hand was firmly clutching a letter. She had fallen asleep while reading it for the fifth time.

Her sleep was uncomfortable, full of demons. Colour had rushed into her cheekbones, and a light sheen of sweat gleamed on her face. In her dream she was in a town that looked both oddly familiar and unlike anywhere else in the world. A river ran through its centre, wide and unruly, with vessels of all sizes lapping at their moorings, bobbing up and down. Jamila found herself alone on the water-front, peeking inside one of the fishing boats. There was a gathering of people inside the cabin, their expressions sullen, their bodies pliant and viscous, as if made of wax. They were talking fervently about . . . *her*.

A half-moan, half-sigh, escaped Jamila's lips. One of the group – a man who strangely resembled Adem – noticed her and alerted the others. Furious and spiteful for no reason at all, they scampered off the boat and on to the dock, hunting for her. She sprinted away as fast as she could, passing through serpentine alleyways and cobbled squares, but soon she got tired, her feet heavier than cement blocks. She would wake up in a little while: when her pursuers finally cornered her in a blind alley, she would catapult herself, with all her might, out of the dream, panting. But at the moment she was still there, in the town of her nightmare.

The air in the hut felt musty, stale. The last log in the fireplace cracked and burst into flame, sending out a shower of golden sparks like dust from a magic wand. Outside in the valley a bird cried out. There were footsteps, but they were distant, indistinct. Jamila didn't hear them. Not yet. She was still running for dear life, having just turned the bend into the dead-end street.

Right now, Jamila's face looked older than that of a 32-year-old woman. There were wrinkles around her neck, twisty lines that resembled an arcane alphabet chiselled in wood. The truth was she had stopped feeling young years ago.

With a sudden jerk Jamila's body was pulled back and she woke up, the carved panel of the chair imprinted on her cheek. There was such a nasty pain in her left shoulder that she dared not move at first. Gently, she massaged her stiff limbs with one hand while still holding the letter with the other. For a moment she stared at the paper through empty eyes, as though she had forgotten what it was. But, unlike the boats in her dream, the letter was real. It was as real as the mountains that surrounded her and just as portentous. Jamila began to read it again.

Sister of mine,

Since I came to this island, where I have yet to see the sea, I have wished many times that you were by my side. But never as much as I do now. If you were here, I would put my head in your lap, and tell you that I am falling. Will you hold me?

Adem is no husband to me. He doesn't come home any more. He has found himself another woman. The children don't know it. I keep everything inside. Always. My heart is full of words unsaid, tears unshed. I don't blame him. I blame myself. It was the biggest mistake of our lives that I was his bride, instead of you. It's true, he never loved me the way he loved you. He is a man who has many regrets and no courage. I feel sorry for him.

How I wish we were children again, you and I. Stealing coins from wish fountains. If only we knew then what we know now.

Did I tell you what Adem once said to me? 'I wish I had a magic eraser,' he said. 'There are so many things I would like to change.' And, though he didn't confess this, I know he also meant us. I should have never married him. It wasn't in my hands, but I didn't try to prevent it. Not really. I so wanted to get out of the village. He was my ticket to other lands. Jamila, you must be upset at me, are you? I would be, if I were in your shoes.

Do you ever think of our sister Hediye? The other day I made halva for her soul. I distributed it to my neighbours. They were a bit surprised, not being familiar with our customs. It was a shame that we didn't mourn her the way we should have. Do you feel the same way?

Your loving half, Pembe

Jamila stood up, rubbing the calluses on the palms of her hands. She approached the window and peered into the night. She thought she had heard a sound, but upon listening more carefully, she doubted it. Sighing, she went back, put the kettle on the stove and began to make tea.

★

'There are so many stars in the sky tonight,' Adem had said. It was a bone-chilling evening in the year 1961.

Leaning closer, his eyes raking her face, Adem told her that some loves were like the brightest stars. They winked at human beings, filling hearts with hope and joy, even when the times were bad. Some other loves resembled the Milky Way, with the ghosts of their ancestors trailing behind in a pale stripe of afterglow.

'What about our love?' Jamila asked. 'Is that a star too?'

Adem flinched at the ease with which she embraced the word. He had been contemplating how to tell her that he loved her, but here she was saying it herself. She was brisker than him, and bolder. For him everything was happening too fast, leaving him dazzled and intimidated in equal measure. Yet there was no time to wait for time to catch up with them. No time to walk holding hands, no time to taste furtive kisses, no time to get to know each other.

His face wore a gallant smile as he said, 'Our love is a star with a huge double tail. Do you know what that is?'

Jamila had shaken her head.

'It's called a comet.'

'A comet . . . ' Still repeating the word, Jamila leaped to her feet, grabbed the sickle off the wall and hacked off a lock of her long hair.

'For me?' Adem asked, surprised.

'It will remind you of me. Always keep it with you.'

In her face were affection and concern, and something that he hadn't seen in anyone else: trust.

'I don't need to keep it with me; you'll be next to me all the time,' he said. But he put her gift in his pocket, as if he didn't believe his own words.

Years later, she would learn more about comets, about the ways they could crash into one another. Although Adem had probably been unaware of this at the time, she came to realize that, just like two comets, they had headed with amazing speed towards collision, trailing behind them the burden of promises unkept, dreams unfulfilled.

★

Jamila took the kettle off the fire and poured tea into a small glass. Before her first sip, she popped a sugar cube into her mouth and sucked on it broodingly. Then, with unnecessary force, she grabbed a pen, as many unused to writing tend to do. Unlike her twin, who wrote half in Turkish and half in Kurdish, she stuck to Kurdish only.

My dear Pembe, my flesh and blood, my other half, my endless longing,

I am never angry at you. Our lives are created by Allah, and Him alone.
These days I wake up with a heavy feeling. Something under way. I cannot sleep in my bed any more. I fall asleep on chairs. Nothing helps. I have nightmares. It will pass, of course. Nothing to worry you about.

Jamila put down the pen; her hand had gone slack, and her forehead was creased. She could hear people approaching from the north-west – three or four visitors, she guessed. She could detect the snap of twigs under their heavy boots, and the clatter of the pebbles that they sent down into the valley below.

They could be soldiers. They could be brigands. They could be anyone. Jamila glanced at the door. It was bolted, and the windows were closed with worm-eaten wooden panels. She put on her headscarf, took her rifle off the wall. There was nothing else she could do.

She wanted to finish the letter. She had to tell Pembe more about this gnawing feeling inside and warn her not to do anything careless or improper about her marriage. But had Pembe ever been cautious in her life? Her twin, that skinny girl who always asked impossible questions, and even wanted to know why tree roots were in the ground and not up in the air where they could drink rainwater instead – she had grown up but not changed.

Weighing it up in her heart, it also worried her that her sister had a face like an open book. Whatever Pembe felt, from the smallest delight to a hint of sorrow, she projected. If she could not hide the most uncomplicated emotions, how could she possibly conceal her indifference towards her marriage from everyone?

Outside, the footsteps drew closer until they stopped at her doorstep. There was the slightest tap, bashful but persistent. Jamila took a deep breath, muttered a quick prayer and opened the door.

There were three men with a couple of dogs at their heels. They were outlaws, she could see that. Splinters of ice clung to their moustaches like icicles dangling from eaves. One of them came forward. A heavily built man with deep-set eyes and a gold-capped tooth. She had seen him before: he was their leader.

'My wife,' the bandit said curtly. 'You must come with us.'

'When did the pain start?'

'Two hours, maybe more.'

Nodding, Jamila took her coat and her rifle, and followed them.

Later in the night she was in a derelict house with bullet holes in the door and a corrugated-iron roof overhead, her face covered in blood and sweat, her hands holding the strangest baby she had ever come across.

It was a girl or, more precisely, a girl and a half. She had a baby boy's body attached to her chest and abdomen. They had started their journey in their mother's womb as twins, but one of them had developed while the other had stopped halfway, as if he had feared the world to come and changed his mind. The undeveloped baby had remained joined to her twin.

'You must go to the city,' Jamila said. 'They'll have to perform surgery. The second body needs to be removed. Then your child will be all right.'

The smuggler stood transfixed, his eyes narrowed in a way that was neither disbelief nor acceptance. 'Is it an omen?'

Jamila was half expecting this question and she answered gently, 'It is not an omen. Such births are rare, but it happens. Some twins cannot separate.'

'There was a goat with five legs. Just like that,' he said, as though he hadn't heard a word of what she had said.

'This child of yours is special. She needs your love,' Jamila said, realizing how few words she could find to comfort this man of the mountains. 'If anyone tells you otherwise, that person is not your friend. Do you understand?'

The man looked away.

Yet when Jamila was back in her cottage, exhausted but still unable to sleep, she wondered if it had indeed been a sign. Not for the bandit and his family, but for her. She sat down and finished the letter to her sister.

I've just come back from a difficult birth. Conjoined twins. One dead, one alive. If you were here, you would ask: 'Why does He let this happen? It's unfair.' But this is not how I look at it. I surrender fully, unconditionally, I do my best to help my people.

My dear, we cannot erase the past. That's not in our hands. I am not, and I never was, upset at you or at Adem. Can you stop a gusty wind from blowing? Can you make the snow turn any colour other than white? We easily accept that we have no power over nature. But why don't we admit that we cannot change our fates? It's not that different. If Allah guided us on to separate paths, there must have been a reason for that. You have your life there; I have my life here. We have to accept. But I am worried about your marriage. Can't you try harder to make it work? For the sake of your children, you must.

You mention Hediye. How strange, I have been thinking about her too, lately more than ever.

Your loving sister, always,
Jamila

No Wisdom without Foolishness

A Village near the River Euphrates, 1961

In the afternoon, the call of the *muezzin* wafted through the small Kurdish village. Adem listened, a dreadful sensation growing in the pit of his stomach. Time trudged on agonizingly slowly, and yet also too hurriedly. He had postponed going back to Istanbul for a few days, but he couldn't delay his return any longer. He went to the mosque with the headman, and prayed for the first time since his mother had left home.

'Allah, my God, I know I don't pray often enough,' he whispered as he sat on the prayer rug. 'I didn't fast during the last Ramadan. Or the one before. But help me, please. Let Jamila's eyes see no other than me. Ever!'

'Are you all right, lad?' asked the headman when they walked out into the bright day. Despite the sun, the air felt chilly.

'I need to marry her.'

'Aren't you too young for that?'

'I'm old enough to get betrothed.'

'Yes, but you don't even have a job. You haven't done your military service. Why are you rushing?'

The day before Adem had gone to visit his brother Khalil in the barracks, and, with his help, had sent a telegram to Tariq in Istanbul.

BROTHER I MET A GIRL STOP SHE'S THE ONE STOP I KNOW I'M YOUNG STOP

BUT THIS IS GOD'S CALL STOP WILL MARRY HER STOP NEED YOUR BLESSING STOP

AND MONEY STOP

Adem didn't tell the headman any of this. Instead, he said, 'Because

I've found the girl I've been waiting for, and I'll die if I can't have her.'

'You need to talk to her father, then.'

'What if he says he doesn't want to see me?'

'Don't worry, I'll talk to Berzo for you. He won't eat you.'

'Why are you helping me?' Adem asked after a brief pause.

This elicited a chuckle from the headman. 'Because somebody should. You don't seem like you could do much without assistance.'

Getting a meeting with Jamila's father was easier than Adem had imagined; bringing the subject up, however, seemed impossible. Never a talkative person, Berzo had turned more taciturn after the death of his wife and his daughter Hediye. So when Adem visited Jamila's house with the headman by his side and the box of *baklava* under his arm, he found a sullen man, his eyebrows clamped down, his stare glassy.

'I came here to talk about your daughter,' Adem said, after they were served tea and dried figs. Then, remembering that the man had a great many, he added, 'Your daughter Jamila, I mean. Enough Beauty.'

'No call her that!' the man said in broken Turkish.

'Sorry . . .' Adem faltered.

Jamila's father let out a stream of words in Kurdish, which the headman translated curtly as 'He says only the girl's late mother can call her Enough.'

Adem felt a self-pity that bordered on despair. Thankfully, the headman intervened. 'This young man is an outsider, true. But he's an honest person and he comes from an honourable family. I know his father. Adem's intentions are pure. He would like to marry your daughter.'

Once again Jamila's father spoke in Kurdish; once again his words were partially translated: 'What kind of a marriage proposal is this? Where are your parents?'

'My mother is dead,' Adem lied. 'And Baba is ill.' At least that part was true. 'I've two brothers. The elder one, Tariq, is like a father to me. I've already sent him a telegram.'

Lapsing into an unwieldy silence, they sipped their teas, finished their figs. Finally, Jamila's father said, 'You cannot marry her. She's already spoken for.'

'What?' Adem blurted out. Why hadn't she told him? He turned to the headman, who averted his gaze.

Switching to broken Turkish again, Berzo went on, 'She's engaged to a relative. They marry next year.'

'But –'

'You want to marry a daughter of mine, take Pembe. They are same. You like one, you like the other.'

Adem shook his head, his eyes defiant. 'No, I want Jamila. She's the one in my heart. You give Pembe to your relative.' He was crossing a line but he couldn't help it.

Berzo slurped the last of his tea, smacking his lips with a little grunt. 'It cannot be. My last word.'

When the two of them were outside in the garden, Adem threw up his hands, bellowing at the headman. 'What's going on here? You owe me an explanation. What are you hiding from me?'

The headman took out his pouch and began to roll a cigarette. 'A year ago Jamila's elder sister Kamile was going to get married. Just before the wedding the two families got into a fight. I don't even remember what it was about, but it turned nasty. Berzo called off the wedding. The groom's family was so upset they kidnapped Jamila in retaliation.'

'What?' Adem rasped.

'They kept her somewhere for a few days. Then Berzo sent for them and gave his consent to Kamile's marriage. In return they brought Jamila back.'

'Did they . . . touch her . . . ?'

'Hmm, nobody knows for sure. They say they didn't lay a hand on her, but they're shifty and the girl never explained. Her father beat her several times but still not a word. A midwife examined her. She says Jamila has no hymen but some girls are born like this.'

Adem was shivering.

'The good news is that the family of Kamile's husband accepts the girl as a bride for an old relative. A widower. Her honour is saved.'

Gripped by a new realization, Adem glared. 'You knew about this all along.'

'A headman knows everything that takes place in his village.'

'Why didn't you tell me?'

'There still was a chance you could get her. And, if not, you had to find it out for yourself.'

Adem wasn't listening properly, blinded by fury. 'I thought you were my friend. A wise man!'

'Nobody is wise,' the headman said. 'We are all half-fool, half-wise. There is no wisdom without foolishness. And no pride without shame.'

But Adem was already storming away, almost running, as if he were being chased. Only this time there was no pack of stray dogs behind him. He found Jamila in the house of a neighbour, weaving a carpet with women of varying ages. When they saw him looking through the window, the women giggled and covered their faces. Instantly, Jamila leaped to her feet and dashed outside.

'What are you doing here? You're shaming me!' she said.

'Shame! Yes, exactly,' Adem snapped. 'The word I was looking for.'

'What are you talking about?'

'Well, you tell me. Apparently, there's some explaining that you need to do.'

All at once Jamila's stare hardened. 'All right, then, let's talk.'

They walked to the back of the house where recently someone had been making flat bread on the tandoor, and though the fire had gone out there were a few embers among the ash, still glowing. Around it there were patches of grass, strips of green, like a harbinger of spring.

'Your father says you may not be a virgin.' He hadn't meant to say it so bluntly, but that was how it came out.

'He told you that?' Jamila said, avoiding his eyes.

Adem had expected her to react more dramatically, protesting in the face of such insolence, crying her heart out. But she was oddly composed as she raised her head and looked at him.

'What about you?' she asked.

'What about me?'

'What did *you* say?'

He wasn't expecting this question. 'I want to know the truth!' he said.

'The truth is what you make of it.'

Rage rose like bile in his throat. 'Shut up. Stop fooling around with me.'

'But I wasn't,' Jamila said, a tired look on her pretty features. 'Will you love me the way I am?'

He said nothing. He wanted to say 'yes', but it just didn't reach his lips. As he glanced towards the mountains, he heard her mutter, before she marched away, 'Well, I suppose I won't be seeing the golden stones of Istanbul after all.'

That day in the Kurdish village Adem spent the rest of the afternoon on the move, quarrelling with himself. His feet crunching audibly upon a pile of dirt, he paced circles around a mound overlooking Jamila's house. He could see the garden where he had first run into her. It had been five days since he had come to this godforsaken village. In five days his life had changed so much he didn't think it would ever be the same again.

One part of him wanted, in fact was desperate, to go to Jamila's father and tell him that he didn't care. He loved her, and, as far as he could see, she loved him. That was all that mattered. Everything else was trivial. He would marry her and take her far away from here as promised.

Another part of him, however, was doubtful, disturbed. Jamila had not defended herself or sworn her chastity, and her silence was so unsettling. What if she was not a virgin? How could he live with this doubt for the rest of his life? What would his brother Tariq say when he learned that he had found himself a tainted wife – an exact replica of their mother?

Tariq! What was he going to tell him? By now he must have read the telegram. Even the thought of having to confront his eldest brother was enough to tie knots in Adem's stomach. He couldn't go back to Istanbul and say it was all a horrible misunderstanding. Hours later, when he entered the headman's house, he found him smoking a pipe, waiting.

'There you are, city boy! No village girl for you, uh?'

'That's not true. I haven't changed my mind,' Adem said resolutely. 'I do want to marry.'

'Really?' The headman's eyes glinted with appreciation. 'You surprise me, lad. I thought you wouldn't want Jamila.'

'And I don't,' Adem said, after a pause. 'I'll take the other one.'

'What?'

'The other twin. I'll have her.'

Deep down in his heart, beneath the boldness he had presented as his personality, Adem knew he should feel awful about the turn of events. Strangely, he didn't. In fact, he didn't feel anything at all. Would a splinter of wood suffer pain while being carried along by a roiling river? Would a feather experience anxiety as it was wafted on the winds? That's how it was with him on that day, and for many more to come.

★★★

Shrewsbury Prison, 1991

Trippy has had a bad day. There are bad days here and not-so-bad days – and then there are 'zoned-out days', when you feel like a wrecked car. Despite the name, the last are not the worst. A zoned-out day is a bit like one of those nights when you feel so zonked that you can't possibly sleep. At times like that you're in a vegetative state, and do nothing, think nothing. Numb as a turnip. On such days you're too depressed to know you're down in the dumps. Somebody takes care of you or nobody does. Either way you don't mind. And the not-so-bad days, as to be expected, are rather passable. It's the bad days that are the worst – the ones that get to you and damage your soul.

A calendar is a daft invention. If time flies, as they say, it does not do so with equal speed at every moment. If only there could be a way to assess each day of the week separately. Let's say, a not-so-bad day is marked in white and equals one point. Then a zoned-out day would be red and have two points. And a bad day would be black and have three points.

A man who has lived thirty bad days will age three times faster than a man who has lived a month full of not-so-bad days. Do the maths and then you'll know why some people get old faster. As for me, ever since I came here I've had so many bad days, one after the other, my calendar is swathed in black. It reminds me of the kohl my mother used to outline her eyes.

Trippy's wife has asked for a divorce. He knew and I knew and every man in this dump knew it was bound to happen, sooner or later, and yet we were all shocked and appalled. Not because there is anything shocking or appalling about it. Divorces and breakups are pretty ordinary in our neck of the woods. But we still were duly thunderstruck for Trippy's sake. When you hear the news that the wife has walked out on a friend, you don't say, 'Yeah, I knew all along that was bloody going to happen.' You'd make him feel like a dick-head. A public failure.

But if you say, 'Bummer, when did that happen? You just never know with women, do you', or something along those lines, then you'd share your mate's pain. He'd still be a loser but privately.

She used to bring Trippy custard tarts, which the screws would rarely allow him to have. She kept baking all the same. A slim woman with copper hair, chalky skin, freckles all over her arms and an expression of immense patience. An illusion, of course. Nobody is that patient.

Today she came to tell him in person. You've got to hand it to her. She could have sent a note or no note at all, like some wives do. But she came and explained, in her own way, and in her gruff smoker's voice delivered words that tasted like ash. She told him she had met someone, and how smashing he was with the children, who needed a male role model around, especially their son, now that he had turned five. She told him that the kids would come to visit Trippy, because he was their father and nothing could change that. Then she kissed him for the last time, left a custard tart and was gone. Bam!

I often wonder what it would feel like to have a wife. A woman who knows your weaknesses and your failures better than you do, all your dead spaces, and has the map of your soul drawn into her palm, and loves you all the same. Someone who plants in your heart a lifetime of things so pleasant yet so minute you don't realize how much you have come to depend on them until you lose them all. God knows how much I regret not knowing that.

But I don't regret that my son, Tom, calls another man dad. I would have made an awful role model anyway, a lamentable father. And a lamentable father is like a fishbone lodged in your throat. You're not exactly sure how you got stuck with it, but when you do get rid of it, something remains, a permanent scar no one can see from the outside but you always sense is there. Nobody needs that kind of rubbish.

I remember once asking my mother why she had married my father. It was the closest I could get to inquiring whether she loved him or not.

She turned and looked me in the face. The light from the window caught the flecks in her green eyes. Amber and gold. I saw how pretty she was. You don't normally notice your mother's beauty. But that day I saw it plain and clear. It made me uneasy. A strange fear gripped me at that moment, and I didn't like it.

'It was a different world back then,' she said. 'Nothing similar to your life here in London. You young people are so lucky.'

It wasn't the answer I wanted to hear. No handkerchiefs embroidered with each other's initials. No palpitations of sweet desire. There were no amorous promises whispered in the dark in my parents' past. Love was such a remote possibility that they didn't even pretend. My sister knew it. She was aware the three of us were here only because of duty, surrender and indifference, not because of love. That is why I was disobedient, she was rebellious, and Yunus was perceptive.

Esma and I used to talk all the time.

'You two chatter like a downpour,' Mum would say. 'Rain outside the house, rain inside!'

I must have told Esma things I had not shared with anyone else – not even with the boys or with Katie. I confided in her because she always had something interesting to say. She was good with words. But also because, deep in my heart, I knew she was the only one in our family who was enough of an insider to get the picture and enough of an outsider to fall out of the picture. I liked that – until the autumn of 1978. Something snapped in me then and could never be fixed again.

★

Trippy spends the rest of the afternoon dead silent. His face is the colour of days-old piss. He put on a brave show in the visitors' room. He told his wife that he understood, that he really did, and wished her the best in life. Nema problema! He thanked her for being so supportive and generous all these years. Then he signalled to the guard that the visit was over, walked her to the door and kissed her goodbye, joking that he would miss her custard tarts.

Now he's sitting with his back to the wall, his jaws clenched and eyes steeled. The reality has sunk in, and he thinks she's a cold-hearted bitch who stabbed him in the back. Human nature being what it is, we hate most those we love most.

'I've had enough of this,' Trippy says, moving his hand to and fro, as if pulling out an imaginary clump of weeds.

'It'll pass.'

'Bugger it. The hell it'll pass.'

I try a different approach. 'You always tell me there are tons of miserable people out there. Everyone's got shit.'

Trippy pays me no attention. 'I'm sure she has a bun in the oven,' he says. 'From that git.'

'How do you know?'

'I fucking know,' he shouts.

He springs to his feet and paces the floor. His eyes land on the Houdini poster. For a moment, I get the impression he's going to pull it down and rip it apart. But he doesn't. Instead, a crestfallen look washes over his face. Then he lurches forward and, with all his might, punches the wall.

The thud is loud, deep, sickening. Suddenly I remember a moment in time. My father and I. We were on the street, quarrelling. The flare in his nostrils, the glare in his eyes – or was I the angry one? Yes, I flipped my lid and rammed into the wall. I struck my head again and again. People came running, the club's bodyguard was mad as hell.

Trippy's next thump brings me to my senses. I try to intervene but he pushes me so hard I land on my back. Until I grab his arms and wind him down, he manages to hit the wall several more times.

'You keep doing that and you'll get all the screws here. You hear me?'

His knuckles are bleeding, and his breath comes out in short gasps. I hold his head between my elbows, and wait for the moment to pass.

'You don't need this,' I say.

'Like you know.'

'I know.'

'I need to take it out on something,' he protests.

'We should get you a punch bag, then.'

Trippy goes thin-lipped. I know what he's thinking. A bag is no good. Lifeless, dull, muted. He wants to feel the flesh under his knuckles, hear the bones crack. If he were a free man tonight, he would go to a bar, drink like a fish and get into a nice, heated fight. Being a weedy bloke, they would rough him up. But that would give him something to joke about the next day. Something to focus on.

Still holding him, I tilt back my head and look him in the eyes. 'Hit me.'

'What?' he asks, his voice breaking up.

'Shhh, keep it down . . . ' I say. 'I'm a trained boxer. You forget?'

I watch the confusion drain out of his face. 'You're nuts,' he says and laughs, but we both know that means yes.

A kind of frenzy takes hold of me. I strip off my T-shirt and toss it away. I take a deep breath and let it go. I work on my breath for a while, never holding it too long. Inhale, exhale, inhale, exhale . . .

Shoulders down, stomach out, I clench my hands and tighten up my muscles. You have to have space. Between you and the enemy, the fist and the internal organs, the individual and the society, the past and the present, the memories and the heart . . . in everything that you do or that happens to you in this life, you need space. The space will protect you. The trick in taking a hard punch is to know how to create extra space.

All the time Trippy is watching me with a raised eyebrow as he always does when confronted with something he doesn't understand.

'So what are you waiting for, scumbag?' I prompt him.

The first blow comes a little unsteadily, sideways. It must have hurt him more than it hurt me. I let out a long, low whistle.

'What?' Trippy asks, annoyed.

'Nothing,' I say, allowing a smirk to cross my face.

Trippy hates people smirking at him. He just can't help it. It makes his blood boil. In fact, no one in this joint is particularly fond of smirks.

My abdomen is hard from years of working out but the force of the next hit catches me off guard. I feel a sharp jab under my ribcage, which comes and goes. Trippy stops and stares at me, surprised by his own strength.

Another memory pops into my mind. I remember the day my mother took me to a hammam in Istanbul. I must have been six or so. The steam, the heat, the echoes, naked female bodies with their legs apart, a granny and her sagging tits. Terrified, I hurried out. Mum caught me, shook me hard. 'Where are you going?'

'I don't like it here.'

'Don't be silly. I don't call you sultan for nothing,' she said. 'Behave like a sultan or I'll call you a clown instead.'

Space. I need to have more space from her memory. It drives me insane.

I smirk again. 'Come on, clown! I'm fillin' my boots here!'

Trippy's next punches are stronger, concentrated. He's not a stocky man, but he's no wimp. He reminds me of a hunting dog – thin, lean, without an ounce of fat on its body, but stubborn, unrelenting.

We go on like this for a good while. At one point Trippy gets carried away and sends a blow that lands on my chin, but other than that he works on the same spot. Somewhere behind that muscle there is my appendix, sleeping, curled up like a worm – an unnecessary organ. Although no good for anything, it still managed to kill Houdini.

In a few minutes the iron doors at the end of the corridor fall open, the lights are turned on. Somebody in a cell near by sniggers as if enjoying the commotion, and three screws come running. They storm in, thinking we've been fighting. Trippy puts his arm around me to prove to them that that is not the case. We are good friends. He gives a proud smirk. That does it. The smirk. As I said, nobody around here likes that.

Before we know it, there is shouting, swearing, threatening and shoving, a theatre of authority, a spectacle of power, and too much light, sharp and piercing, projected on us. Trippy and I cower like bugs caught in the kitchen at night.

'Don't you get it? We weren't fighting,' Trippy screams his head off.

'What were you doing, then?' says one of them. 'Dancing?'

Trippy looks at me, momentarily confused, as if asking, 'Yeah, what were we doing? What on earth got into us?'

★

Next morning Officer Andrew McLaughlin comes by, his vanity following him like a hungry dog. He has got used to the job but not to me. He's read the reports of the night before and says we must have been on drugs, for no man in his right mind would start a fight just like that. On the pretext of searching for our stash, he orders his men to leave no stone unturned – the books, the blankets, photos of Trippy's children, my notebook, even the insides of our bed mats.

Trippy gnaws at the insides of his mouth to suppress a smile. We're both thinking the same thing. We are miraculously clean. If this search had been a few days ago, they would have found a few goodies. But that's all gone now. We have nothing to worry about.

Just when they seem to be leaving, Officer McLaughlin stops. He has something in his hand, and he asks, 'What is this?'

It's a postcard with a photo of a carousel in an amusement park. Wooden horses, lights in the background. There is no one in the image, only a red balloon floating away and the suggestion of an unseen force lurking about, perhaps the wind.

'I can't hear you!' McLaughlin says.

Neither Trippy nor I answer. Officer McLaughlin starts to read aloud, changing his voice to a mocking imitation of a woman's.

'Dear brother . . . or shall I not call you that any more? What can I call you, then? Askander? Iskender? Alex? Sultan? Murderer? Do you remember the carousel Mum took us to when we first arrived in London? Wasn't it something? Yunus wasn't born yet and God knows where Dad was. Just you, me and Mum.

I'll never forgive you for what you've done. You might rot in prison or burn in hell, but neither the Queen's nor God's punishment will ever wash off this sin in my eyes. In the courtroom, I'll not support you. Whatever Uncle Tariq says, I'll testify against you. As of today I am mourning two deaths: that of a mother, but also of a brother—

Esma

'Your sis is cool,' says Officer McLaughlin, putting his hand on his heart as if hurt. 'It's nice to see one member of your clan knows right from wrong.'

106

He doesn't look at anyone when he says this but as soon as he's done talking his eyes lock on mine. I reach out to take the postcard from him, but he swings it up in the air, playfully. 'Tut, tut.' He purses his mouth. 'First you gotta answer me: why were you making Trippy hit you?'

At my silence, Officer McLaughlin shrugs and examines his fingernails. 'All right. I'll leave you two for now,' he says finally. 'I'll take this lovely card with me, Alex. When you feel like telling the truth, you come and see me, and I'll give it back.'

I don't need to hold the postcard in my hand to see what it says. He doesn't know that I've memorized every single word on it. Every 'not', every comma, every 'Mum'.

As soon as Officer McLaughlin has gone, I sit back. My throat closes and my eyes water. Try as I might to stay still, stay sane, I'm losing it again. I slap myself. It doesn't work. I slap again. It's going to be a bad day, I can tell.

Iskender Toprak

Racism and Rice Pudding

London, December 1977

Since the day she was born as the seventh daughter of a woman who longed for a son, Pembe had come to see this world as a hotbed of favouritism and inequalities, some of which she accepted as unchangeable, *the ways of humans*. But never in her life had she been subjected to open hostility for being who she was. Until that day in early December 1977 – the day she met him.

There was only one client at the Crystal Scissors – the retired librarian who seemed in no hurry to be anywhere – and Pembe asked the owner, Rita, for a break to do some shopping. Yunus had been craving his favourite dessert – rice pudding with orange blossom – and she intended to surprise him that evening.

'Rita, is okay if I go for one hour?'

Rita was not only her boss but also a dear friend. A tall black woman with a huge bosom, chipped teeth, the biggest Afro in town and a smile as sunny as the summer skies, Rita always used to talk about the place where she had come from. *Jamaica.* To Pembe's ears, the name felt nutty and crunchy, like a roasted cashew.

'Go, darling,' said Rita. 'I'll take care of the librarian. I bet she wants to tell me all about her holiday in Italy.'

Pembe left the salon feeling light and heavy at the same time. Light, because she had a full hour all for herself. Heavy, because things had not been going well recently. Esma was always sulking, a book in her hand, going through another phase. Iskender was worse. He came home late every evening, and she was worried that he had befriended the wrong kind of people; and her husband . . . well, she didn't want to know what exactly he had got himself into this time, disappearing for weeks on end, bringing home smells from another woman, when he did appear.

Adem was a sad man. He often talked about his childhood, mentioning the same forlorn memories again and again, unable to let go. It was like one of those snacks that you knew were harmful but you couldn't stop munching on, even when full. Inadvertently, almost without realizing it, he would start to talk about the past. As for Pembe, trusting that time, or her prayers, would put things in their place, she carried on without an ounce of protest, reassuring herself that it was all for the best – or would some day turn out to be. To her the future was a land of promises. She had not been there yet, but she trusted it to be bright and beautiful. It was a place of infinite potential, a mosaic of shifting tiles, now in a seamless order, now in mild disarray, for ever re-creating itself.

To him the past was a shrine. Reliable, solid, unchanging and, above all, enduring. It provided insight into the beginning of everything; it gave him a sense of centre, coherence and continuity. He visited it devotedly and repeatedly, less out of need than out of a sense of duty – as if submitting to a higher will. Whereas Adem was religious about the past, Pembe was faithful about the future.

Unlike the morning's soft sun, the early-afternoon weather had turned nippy and windy. Pembe was wearing the buttoned-up grey coat that made her look older, and also like a wartime girl who had to keep careful track of every scant penny, which, in fact, was what she was doing. She did a quick shop at Tesco, buying the ingredients she needed. Just as she was passing by the bakery around the corner, she spotted chocolate eclairs in the window. Not large, thick and filled with whipped cream but small and glossy, the way she liked them.

Though she rarely gave in to temptation, she made a beeline for the eclairs and entered the shop, the bells behind the door jingling merrily. Inside was the baker – a corpulent woman with legs covered with varicose veins and eyebrows so thin as to be almost invisible – chatting fervently with an acquaintance. Meanwhile her assistant was serving the customers. A skinny man, no older than twenty, with beady, blue eyes, inflamed cheeks that pointed to overly sensitive skin and hair cropped so short it was hard to tell its colour. His forehead was covered with spots, and his knuckles and arms had several tattoos, including a large swastika.

As there was another customer – a well-dressed elderly woman – ahead of her, Pembe had to wait. A minute later the bells jingled again, and a middle-aged man walked in, but she barely glanced at him.

The old lady was quite picky and had a tendency to change her mind every few seconds. She wanted plain scones, three, well, maybe four, but how about some Eccles cakes, no, on second thoughts, she would like the fruit scones, please. The strawberry tarts looked worth considering too, but were they fresh and the pastry crisp, she wondered, because, if so, she might like to get the tarts instead of the scones, which were a bit too everyday. And on it went.

Each time she changed her mind the assistant put the item back on to the tray where it belonged and took the next cake in demand, showed it to her and waited for her approval. When she finally made up her mind, settling on a half-dozen iced buns, they began discussing how to wrap them – was it better to put them in a paper bag, which was light and easy, but could get torn on the way, or to place them in a box, which was safer, of course, except harder to carry. Raising his head from behind the glass case, the assistant gave the waiting customers the once-over, focusing on Pembe. She didn't notice the bitterness in the young man's stare, but the shopper behind her did.

Finally the old lady left, moving so slowly that even the bells didn't jingle as she opened the door. Now that it was her turn, Pembe nodded at the assistant, but he ignored her and went about organizing the pastries. Then he proceeded to arrange the metal trays, taking out the boxes, putting them back.

'Excuse me,' Pembe said, pointing at the chocolate eclairs. 'May I have this . . . two, please?'

'Wait your turn,' the assistant muttered, wiping a pair of tongs.

Baffled more by his tone than by what he had said, Pembe hesitated for a moment. It was then that the other customer interjected, 'It is her turn.'

It worked. Putting the tongs down, the assistant approached them, his eyes glued on Pembe. 'So what do *you* want?'

Now Pembe had never confronted a racist before and the idea that someone could hate another person because of their skin colour, religion or class was as alien to her as snow in August. Not that complete strangers had never mistreated or belittled her, but those instances were all due to temporary flare-ups, or so they had seemed, rather than preconceived judgements over which she had no control. She was aware of how different the Topraks were from their English neighbours, and yet Turks and Kurds were different from one another too, and some Kurds were completely unlike other Kurds. Even in her tiny village by the Euphrates every family had another story, and in every family no two children were ever the same. If Allah had wanted to create human beings alike, He surely would have done so. Pembe had no idea why He had introduced so much variety into His creation, but she trusted His intentions. Accepting people the way they were born was tantamount to respecting the divine scheme.

The truth was, she was quite tolerant when it came to inborn differences. What she couldn't adjust to were the variations introduced afterwards. A punk with hair as spiky as a hedgehog, a teenager with his eyebrows pierced, a singer with tattoos all over his body or Esma's passion for wearing trousers and braces – these were the things she found hard to digest. Her linear logic put her in a quandary at times. When she met a homosexual person, for instance, she wanted to understand if he had been born that way or had turned that way over time. If it was God's doing, it was okay; if it was that person's doing, she didn't approve of it. But since, in the end, everything was God's work and His alone, she could not nurse disparaging sentiments against anyone for too long.

So when the assistant asked her what she wanted, Pembe heard the question but not the tone of scorn underneath it. Duly, dutifully, she answered, 'I want this one and that one, please.'

The assistant stared off into the distance beyond and above her head, as if she were invisible to him. 'Don't they have names?' he asked.

Thinking that the man had not understood her, Pembe approached the pastry trays from the side and pointed again at the eclairs without realizing that the hem of her coat was brushing against the cinnamon rolls.

'Hey, don't touch those,' the assistant yelled. He picked up one of the rolls and inspected it. 'Nah, I can't sell these any more.'

'What?'

'Do you see this bit of fluff?' he grumbled. 'It's from your coat. You have to buy the whole tray now.'

'Fluff?' Pembe pouted her lips as if the unfamiliar word had left a sour taste in her mouth. 'No, no. I don't want the tray.' In her confusion she flipped her hands upwards, and one of her shopping bags knocked over a basket with rock cakes, sending them on to the floor.

The assistant shook his head. 'Whoa, you're a walking catastrophe.'

By now the commotion had drawn the owner's attention and she clomped towards them to see what was going on.

'This woman here ruined the rolls and spilled the cakes. I told her she has to buy them, but she doesn't get it.'

Pembe's cheeks turned red under the scrutiny of the owner.

'I don't think she even speaks English,' added the assistant.

'I speak,' Pembe snapped.

'Then surely you must have understood what you were told,' said the owner speaking slowly, and unnecessarily loudly, as if Pembe were deaf.

'But he says buy all tray. I don't have much money.'

Folding his arms across his chest, the assistant remarked, 'Then we'll have to ring the police.'

'No police, why?' Pembe was beginning to panic.

'Ahem.' The customer standing behind coughed theatrically. Now all heads turned towards him, the silent onlooker. 'I've been observing your eclair crisis,' he said. 'And I feel obliged to say a few words. If the law becomes involved, I'll be the sole witness here.'

'So?' said the assistant.

'So I'll tell them the other side of the story.'

'What other side?'

'That you've mistreated your customer and you haven't served her properly. You were slow, impolite, uncooperative, difficult, even aggressive.'

'Now, now, gentlemen,' said the owner, a placatory smile hovering over her lips, as she realized the situation was getting out of control. 'Let's not make a mountain out of a molehill. There's no harm done. No need to go to the police.'

Quietly, as if through water, Pembe turned towards the other customer, seeing him, really seeing him, for the first time. He was wearing a sepia corduroy jacket with leather elbow patches over a beige turtleneck sweater. He had a long face, a prominent nose and light brown hair that had a golden tint in the light and was receding at the sides. His eyes were kind, though a bit tired; they were the colour of stormy weather, grey and intense behind a pair of glasses that made him look like a university professor – or so she thought.

The assistant, too, was inspecting him, albeit resentfully. He hissed, 'Well, how can I help you, then?'

'First the lady,' the customer said. 'You haven't helped her yet.'

★

They left the bakery together – strangers united by happenstance. It seemed natural that they should walk together for a few minutes, reliving the experience, renewing their camaraderie. He insisted on carrying her bags, and that, too, seemed all right, though she would have never allowed it had they been in her neighbourhood.

They walked until they reached the nearby playground, which was empty, perhaps because of the blustery weather. By now the wind was so strong that here and there the leaves came whipping down as if caught in a whirlpool. However, for the first time since she had arrived in England, Pembe thought there was something enchanting about the weather – beyond the wind and the rain and the clouds, there loomed a kind of serenity she had got used to and come to love without realizing it. She grew pensive.

He was watching her out of the corner of his eye, noting how her face was free of cosmetics, and her hair, which had blown free of its headscarf, was the colour of autumn, bright chestnut with reddish streaks that were so subtle even she might not be aware of their presence. He found her full lips and single dimple very attractive but kept his thoughts to himself. Nature's lottery was bizarre. This woman, if she were to dress differently and carry herself differently, would turn many heads on the street. Yet perhaps it was better that her beauty was half concealed.

'That boy was mad,' Pembe said, still thinking about what had transpired in the pastry shop.

'He was not mad,' the man objected. 'He was a racist.'

She paused, taken aback. *Racists were people who didn't like the blacks – those who were against Rita.* 'I'm not black,' she said.

He laughed at the joke. And when he realized she wasn't joking, he stared at her in wonder. 'You don't have to be black for a racist to take against you. There are many kinds of racism, though they're all the same, if you ask me.'

She listened, trying to wade through his accent, which was quite different from anything she had heard since she arrived.

'There are whites who hate blacks,' he went on helpfully. 'Then there are whites who hate browns. To make matters more complicated some blacks hate browns and some browns hate blacks, not to mention those self-hating blacks, browns and whites, and the blacks, browns and whites who basically hate everybody. Then there's religion, of course, the big divide. Some Muslims hate all Jews and some Jews hate all Muslims. Oh, and there are some Christians who hate them all.'

'But why hate?' she asked.

More than the question, it was the way in which it was asked, the sheer simplicity and innocence of it, almost childlike, that startled him. She was completely earnest, he noticed. Rising unemployment, poverty, xenophobia, ideological clashes, the oil crisis . . . At that moment none of these was a sufficient answer to a question so plain and basic. And he, a veteran sceptic, a dedicated disbeliever, an all-time pessimist, a man who didn't trust the news or the newspapers and took everything with a pinch of salt, including his own truths, and harboured no hopes about humanity's future, repeated, as if through a distant echo, 'Mmmm, that's so true. But why hate?'

Later on, neither of them would remember who had come up with the idea to sit in the playground. Pembe told him, in her broken English, that she worked at a hairdresser's and had taken a short break to buy ingredients for a rice pudding. She hadn't been able to find hazelnuts, she said, like the ones she used back in Istanbul, and would have to make do with almonds instead. To her surprise, he listened sympathetically. She had never thought a man, any man, would show so much interest in cooking.

'So you're Turkish?' he asked.

It didn't occur to her to say she was Kurdish, for it never did. It always took her some time to reveal her Kurdishness, like an afterthought. So she nodded.

'*Lokumcu geldi hanim, leblebilerim var*,'[*] he said in a singsong voice.

She looked at him, her eyes wide with incomprehension. To her amazement, he laughed and said, 'I'm afraid that's about it. I only know a few words.'

'But how?'

'My grandmother was Greek,' he said. 'She was from Istanbul. She taught me one or two words. Oh, she loved that city.'

He didn't tell her that his grandmother had left Istanbul at the time of the late Ottoman Empire, married off to a Levantine merchant, and that, till the day she passed away, she had missed her neighbours and her home by the Bosporus. Instead he tried to recall more words common to Turkish and Greek: *cacik-caciki, avanak-avanakis, ispanak-spanaki, ciftetelli-tsifteteli* . . . His accent made her giggle, which she did by lowering her head and closing her mouth – the one universal gesture repeated by people who were uncomfortable with either their teeth or their happiness.

He observed her for what felt like a long moment, and said, 'I don't even know your name.'

Pembe brushed a few strands of hair out of her eyes, and, though she rarely mentioned her multiple names together, and never translated them into English, heard herself say, 'Pembe Kader. It means Pink Destiny.'

He didn't arch his eyebrows or chuckle the way she expected him to do. Instead he stared at her as if she had just revealed the saddest secret. He then said, 'Your name is poetry.'

Now Pembe knew the word 'poetry' in English. Yes, she did. She smiled. She smiled for the first time in a long while.

[*] Street vendor's cry: 'Lady, I have Turkish delight, chickpeas . . .'

Opening the bag from the bakery, she took out the chocolate eclairs, offered one to him and kept the other for herself. He, in turn, shared his fruit loaf. They ate, at first in silence, then with tentative words, such as 'if', 'perhaps', 'I'm not sure but . . .' Slowly, they spun a conversation around an exchange that had started with racism and rice pudding.

His name was Elias. Like her, it had been almost eight years since he had come to London. He liked the city, and had no problem with feeling like a foreigner because that is what he was in his heart: a stranger everywhere. As she listened to him, Pembe wished several times that her English was better. But you didn't need to be fluent in a language to be able to speak it, did you? With her husband they spoke the same language and yet they rarely communicated any longer, if they ever had.

'So you Greek?' she asked.

She didn't tell him what her brother-in-law Tariq thought about the Greeks, or all the negatives she had heard about them.

'Well, not exactly. I'm a quarter Greek, a quarter Lebanese, a quarter Iranian and a quarter Canadian.'

'But how?'

'Well, you see, my grandmother married a Lebanese and my mother was born. Then she met my father. His parents were Canadian citizens originally from Tehran. I was born in Beirut myself but raised in Montreal, and now I'm a Londoner. So, what does that make me?'

So many journeys, so many ruptures and fresh starts in unfamiliar places. Wasn't he frightened of bearing this much uncertainty around him? Pembe recalled how she had dreamed of becoming a sailor, travelling to faraway ports in seven continents, but that was long ago.

As if reading her doubts, he smiled and said, 'Hey, it's not that bad. Some people are from everywhere.'

He tore his gaze from the wedding ring that he had suddenly noticed. She, however, had not realized that there was a faint mark where his wedding ring used to be, the shadow of a wife who wasn't there any more, but who had not yet fully vanished.

'You work?' she asked.

'Yup, I'm a chef.'

At this, her face lit up. 'Really?'

'Yes,' he said. 'I bet I can make rice pudding just as good as you do.'

Pembe imagined him dicing onions or poking at some courgettes in a frying pan. The idea was so odd that she let out a giggle, and almost at once she grew quiet, worried about hurting his feelings. The men she knew would barely enter the kitchen to get a glass of water for themselves, which, now that she thought about it, was also how she had been raising her two sons, especially Iskender.

'Your wife lucky,' she said.

'My wife and I are separated,' Elias said, gesturing with his hands as if breaking a piece of bread.

Deftly, Pembe veered the conversation into another direction. 'What did your father say? He said it's okay you cook?'

It was a bizarre question, and yet it was the right question. His father had not spoken to Elias for years, he explained, his voice rising and falling, though later on in life they had made their peace. He said his interest in cooking had started when, as a boy, he was looking for things to raise his sister Cleo's spirits.

'Your sister was sick?' she asked.

'No, she was special.'

He said the children in the neighbourhood had another word for it: retarded. Born with severe Down's syndrome, she was physically and mentally disabled. While he went to a local school where he was in a class of gifted children, Cleo had to travel a long distance every day to attend a special institution outside town. She was often grumpy, stressed, throwing her toys around, pulling out her hair, eating soil. The only thing that soothed her, young Elias discovered, was good food. A freshly baked apple pie put a smile on her face, helping her to become her dear old self again. And so, little by little, he learned to prepare delicacies for Cleo. In time he realized it wasn't so much that he was helping his sister but that she was helping him to follow his heart.

When you kneaded bread, the earth seeped into your veins, solid and strong. When you grilled meat, the spirit of the animal spoke to you, and you had to learn to respect it. When you cleaned fish, you heard the gush of the water where it once swam, and you had to marinate it tenderly, so as to wash off the memory of the river from its fins. Pembe listened, mesmerized, missing many words, but, to her surprise, understanding him.

★

'Oh goodness . . . I have to go,' Pembe said, jumping to her feet, only now grasping how much time had gone by.

'Shall I help you with your bags back to the hairdresser's?'

'No, no . . .' she said firmly. 'I'll be fine.'

It flashed into her mind that one of the passers-by might see them together and tell someone else. People would gossip, and from there the word would reach her family's ears. She understood, with a plunging heart, that there was no way she could see this man again. Unaware of her thoughts, he produced a card out of his pocket.

ELIAS STEPHANOS ROBERT GROGAN
CHEF

She looked at the words, surprised to see he had so many names, like the countries in his background. On the back of the card was the name of the restaurant.

'If you come in the evenings, I won't be able to leave the kitchen. Lunch-times are no good either. But should you stop by after four o'clock, I'd be most happy to show you around, and cook for you.'

In return she gave him nothing. No paper. No address. No promise.

He leaned forward to kiss her cheek, which she responded to by pulling back, which confused and embarrassed him, which she was mortified to see, so she gave him her hand, which he missed because he was still thinking about why she hadn't let him kiss her on the cheek. In their mutual confusion, he ended up brushing her wrist and she patted his shoulder. The awkwardness of the moment would have made an onlooker laugh, but to them it was rather discomforting, so they backed away from each other, as if they had touched a live wire, and then as fast as they could they went their separate ways.

118

Beauty and the Beast

London, December 1977

It was Tobiko's birthday. Less than a year before the Topraks' lives went into a tailspin, seven-year-old Yunus was in the squatters' house, deep in the throes of love.

Tobiko had turned twenty. 'I'm a typical Sagittarius,' Yunus heard her say – though he had no idea if that was good or bad. Yunus himself was a Leo but that didn't mean anything to him either. The only thing that mattered was that the age gap between him and Tobiko had grown wider, his prospects of catching up with her now slimmer than ever.

So he sat there with a scowl, munching buttered popcorn out of a plastic bowl. He watched the squatters – bright and full of beans – hand gifts to the birthday girl: silver piercings, safety pins, a spiked collar, braided bracelets, a studded belt, ripped fishnet stockings and a pair of combat boots. There was a patchwork quilt with the words *Medicinal Marijuana* embroidered on the edge, several necklaces with signs, a poster of Patti Smith, books (*The Shining* by Stephen King, *South of No North* by Charles Bukowski), a police helmet (stolen from a police officer who had momentarily left it on a table at a local café), a poster that said *Boredom is Revolutionary* and a black T-shirt with a picture of a punk band – the Damned.

Yunus stayed away from the fuss, as he wanted to be the last to give Tobiko her present. There were two reasons for that. First, he hoped to be alone with her, even if for a few minutes. But also he was not sure whether she would like the gift he had chosen – a suspicion that had deepened after seeing the hotchpotch of things the others had given her.

Laden with doubts, the boy was still sulking in the corner when the Captain walked in, wearing the tightest jeans Yunus had ever seen, a leather jacket that seemed at least two sizes too small for him and biker's boots. He did not bring Tobiko a present. Only a wet kiss and a promise: 'Mine later, babe.'

For a brief moment and with a sinking heart, Yunus considered doing the same thing. He could get up and stride towards Tobiko in a slow, purposeful fashion, in his grey school trousers and the blue sweater, which Mum had knitted for him, and say, in a tone just as deep and mysterious, 'Mine later, babe.'

What would Tobiko do then? Would she smile at him the way she had at the Captain? Yunus didn't think so. He closed his eyes as he felt the nervousness bubble up in his stomach. His mother always warned him, 'Be careful with girls. Boys are simple, girls are not. They will play you like a *saz*.'* If that was the case, if Tobiko was playing him like an instrument, the tune coming out of Yunus that day was bleak and melancholy, slightly off key.

'Hey, mate, you want a puff?'

Yunus opened his eyes to see a young man with long, thick dreadlocks lying at his feet. His close-set eyes were glued on an invisible spot in the ceiling, and he was holding a newly lit spliff in his hand. On his arm there was a tattoo: *When the Rich Fight, it is the Poor Who Die*. The boy couldn't help thinking to himself that if his mother could see him, she would be appalled. *But how do they wash their hair?* Pembe would ask, and add uneasily, as a new realization came upon her, *They do wash their hair, don't they?*

Now, Yunus had sipped beer before and taken a puff from a discarded dog-end, but he had never come anywhere close to doing drugs. It was a highly controversial topic in the squatters' house. There were those (Black Panther supporters, radical feminists, Marxists, Trotskyites) who were strictly anti-drugs and looked down upon the people who used them; those (hippies and ex-hippies) who favoured certain drugs – cannabis – but not others; and then there were those (punks, nihilists, situationists) who snubbed weed in favour of pills and chemicals that gave you high energy, high anger. Yet it wasn't the ongoing disagreement in the house that had kept Yunus from drugs all this time. It was the fear of his mother's fury.

* A string instrument popular in Anatolia.

But now that he had been offered *just a puff*, the boy didn't see why he should reject it. Politely, he took the joint and inhaled so deeply that he immediately coughed it all out.

'Did they teach you this song at school?' the man-in-dreadlocks yawned before he began to chant, '*Roll, roll, roll a joint, gently down the line.*'

Yunus giggled and puffed.

'*Have a whiff from my spliff, blow your fucking mind.*'

Yunus puffed and giggled. Between the two of them they made so much noise that they caught the others' attention, including Tobiko's. She walked towards them with a sad and startled look.

'Don't do that, darlin',' she said, as she snatched the joint out of the boy's hand and put it between her own lips. 'Why're you trying to be like everyone else? You're different. That's what makes you special.'

At the playfulness of her gaze, the apprehension in her voice, Yunus swallowed hard. Instead of uttering the laconic words he had planned to say earlier, he blurted out: 'But I have a present for you.'

'Is that so?' Tobiko said, faking surprise. 'What is it, pet, may I ask?'

Yunus stood up, holding his head high and thrusting out his chest, like a soldier ready to take orders. He handed Tobiko the package he had been keeping all evening – gold box, gold tissue, gold ribbon.

Inside there was a musical snowglobe – pink, purple and perfect. Two figures – a princess and an ogre – stood in front of a charming castle, holding each other. She was wearing a splendid dress, while the hulky monster stood by her side in a shy, awkward manner. When you wound the key, they began to dance to a tinkling tune that sounded as if an ice-cream van was passing near by. As soon as he saw this and learned it was from a tale, 'Beauty and the Beast', Yunus recalled that Tobiko was very fond of a David Bowie song with the same title. If she enjoyed that, she might like this too.

In truth Yunus had at first planned to purchase a different snowglobe in which flakes of rice rained on a bride and groom as they kissed in front of a church, but then he doubted whether Tobiko would like it. She was against marriage, against religion, and for all he knew she could also be against throwing rice in the air like that. So he chose the other snowglobe – even though it was more expensive and drained him of his savings.

In his eyes Tobiko was no different from the princess, gorgeous and flawless, whereas he was a bit like the monster. He was the beast in his elegant costume leading her on to the dance floor – the unlikely hero in the story, not yet a man but with the potential to become one someday. The boy carried his childhood like a bad spell, hoping against hope for it to be broken soon.

The glaring naivety of the object caught Tobiko unprepared. Holding the snowglobe in her palms as if it were a baby bird, she glowed with pleasure. 'Oh, this is fantastic!'

Yunus beamed. He was going to marry her.

'What is *fan-tas-tic*?' the Captain asked from the other side of the room, but Tobiko didn't answer him.

Yunus's smile grew wider and wider – so big that it turned into a mantle that canopied the house, hiding the spider webs, the moths circling the candle flames, the termites in the wooden chairs, everything and anything that he wished to make disappear, including all potential rivals.

★

The evening flowed with music from the Clash, the Cockney Rejects and the Sex Pistols, and with a huge chocolate-banana-hashish birthday cake. There were no candles on the cake to blow out, but the brass and pewter lanterns nicked from a shop the same day provided the celebratory air needed.

By now Yunus had had more than a few sips of beer and several slices of the dubious cake. His head wasn't exactly swimming, but his stomach certainly was. Doing his best not to vomit, he sat back, his gaze panning the walls. There, in the flickering light, he noticed a picture he'd not seen before. A man with hefty shoulders, a protruding nose, salt-and-pepper beard and hair in need of combing. Since it was Tobiko's birthday, he assumed the man must have something to do with her. 'Is that your grandfather?' he asked, pointing at the photograph.

Before Tobiko could make out what he was talking about, let alone answer him, the man with the dreadlocks overheard the question and turned to the others, yelling mirthfully, 'Hey, the boy is asking if Karl Marx is her granddad!'

There followed a ripple of laughter. 'He's everyone's granddad,' someone remarked gleefully.

'And our granddad will change the world,' the Captain said, clearly amused.

Realizing he had said something stupid, Yunus blushed up to his ears. Yet he had to stand up to the Captain. So he asked, 'Isn't he a bit too old for that?'

'He's old and wise,' came the answer.

'And he's fat too,' Yunus insisted.

This elicited another collective chuckle, but the Captain turned serious, his eyes suddenly narrowed to slits. 'Shouldn't you be a bit more respectful, my friend? That man was on your side. He fought for the rights of people like you.'

'Was he Turkish?' Yunus asked despite himself.

The squatters laughed so hard, one of them fell off the sofa. Wiping the tears from their eyes, still chuckling, they listened, hungry for more.

'*People like you* means the have-nots,' explained the Captain.

'What is a have-not?' Yunus asked.

'The have-nots are the people who have been denied the right to have, so that the haves can have more than they should have.'

Yunus stood biting his bottom lip, frowning.

'No other species on earth is as arrogant and cruel and greedy as humans,' went on the Captain. 'The entire capitalist economy is built on the systematic exploitation of the have-nots by the haves. You, me, our little friend here, and his family, we are the Commoners! The Salt of the Earth! The Great Unwashed!'

'My mother is always cleaning the house,' said Yunus, this being the only objection he could think of to the last comment.

They laughed but it was different this time. There was a gentler edge to their laughter – a mixture of pity and sympathy.

Carried away by his own righteousness, the Captain, however, failed to notice that the mood among his audience had changed. 'Wake up to the truth, lad!' he said. 'People like your parents are being exploited all the time so that others can fill their pockets.'

Stifling a gasp, Yunus leaped to his feet, a bit unsteadily. 'My parents are not exploited and we are not unwashed. My brother is a boxer.'

It wasn't only pride that made him talk this way. Yunus had never thought of his family as *poor*. True, his mother sometimes complained about making ends meet. But at home no one referred to himself as *needy*, *deprived*, *low-class* or, for that matter, as a *have-not*.

Nobody laughed this time. Outside, the night darkened. Somewhere not that far away, under a faint light from the street lamps, Pembe was waiting in the kitchen by the window, sick with worry about where her younger son was, her body cloaked in thick silence and solitude, like a figurine in a snowglobe.

'Hey, I didn't mean to offend you,' the Captain said and chortled, so that his next words would not be taken as a reproach. 'I suppose you're too young.'

Summed up in those last few words was everything Yunus absolutely hated: his age, his incompatibility, the impossibility of love. He eased himself into a chair, depressed.

'Don't mind him,' Tobiko whispered. 'It's getting late. You should probably go.'

'Right, I'd better leave,' Yunus conceded, his face set in a frown, his stomach feeling funny again.

'Goodnight, babe.'

Yunus waved them goodbye, not by putting his right hand on his heart, the way his father and uncle had taught him, but by raising his first and second fingers in a V-sign, the way the squatters did. No sooner had he taken a step than the room began to spin. The lights dimmed into a soft, pearly glow and he slipped into some other realm. Without warning and in front of everyone present, the boy puked not on the floor but on the birthday dress of the woman he loved. 'Oh, no,' he whined before closing his eyes, acutely aware that now she would never love him.

That night the squatters carried Yunus home. They rang the doorbell and ran away seconds before a devastated Pembe opened the door and found her son happily snoring on the threshold.

A Fluffy Cardigan

London, 18 December 1977

Since the start of the term Katie Evans had had a crush on Iskender, almost despite herself. *Alex. Alexander. Whatever. Complete arsehole. Bloody full of himself. Always with his groupies, thinks he's a gang leader.* But he was a bit of a hunk, she had to admit, with his light olive complexion and those smouldering eyes. Finally, she summoned the courage to ask him if he would like to go out with her, to which Iskender replied with a curt, 'Okay.' He said on Sunday he had to help his mother in the morning and had boxing practice from eleven to two. He was free to meet her afterwards, *if she so wanted.*

Hours before the appointment Katie was in her room trying on one garment after another, sulking in front of the mirror. The mohair jumpers in colours so soft – fuchsia, peach, lavender, sea foam – that she had bought with her mother seemed ridiculously tacky. So were the Laura Ashley skirts, the A-line dresses and Mary-Jane shoes. She saw her wardrobe through Iskender's eyes and was appalled at how prim and *girly* everything was. After much frustration and fumbling, she settled on a casual look. A pair of jeans, plimsolls and a navy-blue sweatshirt. She combed her hair into a ponytail and applied only a little make-up, hoping that he would take her style as a sign of self-confidence or modesty or, better yet, both.

Katie arrived at the café five minutes early, having checked her outfit in every shop window along the way. Forty minutes later Iskender still hadn't shown up. Too proud to accept defeat just yet, she called the waiter and asked for another Coke. Initially, she had wanted to order a milkshake – strawberry and banana, her favourite. But upon second thought she had changed her mind, thinking it could be *girlish.*

Katie's second Coke was almost gone, as was her patience, when the door was thrust open and Iskender marched in, chewing gum and shouldering a gym bag, his hair still wet from the shower. She could see he had taken his time, combing his hair just so, in no rush for their meeting.

'How're you doin', love?' he said.

And that word, that simple, silly word *love*, propelled her fury out the window. A flush of colour crept into her cheeks.

'Been waiting long?'

'That's all right.'

His dark eyes took her in, inspecting her hair, her lips, the baggy top that hid the shape of her breasts. Why had she not dressed up more, he wondered.

'How did the boxing go?'

'Blindin',' Iskender said. 'My coach is fab. Tough as nails. He's an ex-Para, fought in Northern Ireland. This guy has seen some pretty horrific stuff.'

'Did he ever use a gun?'

Iskender scoffed. '*Did he ever use a gun?* He must have killed at least ten. Suffered wounds in beatings and blasts. This bloke learned boxing the hard way.'

Katie paled ever so slightly. Suddenly she was glad she wasn't wearing one of her fluffy jumpers.

'So, what're you havin'?' Iskender asked, pointing to her empty glass.

'I've had two Cokes. Wanna join me?'

'Nah, I hate Coke,' Iskender said. 'It makes me feel bloated. There's something dodgy about that secret bubbly formula. I like milkshakes better.'

Not a single muscle on Katie's face moved as she watched Iskender call the waiter and order two drinks – another Coke for her, and a milkshake for him, banana and strawberry. They nattered on about school and the kids who never washed, the teachers they couldn't stand. She was starting to enjoy herself when his face fell, suddenly grim. 'Katie, what're you doing here with me?'

Her gaze flickered for a moment before settling on him again. Could she confess to him that she had spent the night before cuddling her tape recorder in bed, listening, over and over, to the Bee Gees sing 'How Deep is Your Love'?

'Well, we're just . . . chatting –'

'Look, don't get me wrong. I think you're gorgeous, really, but we don't match, you and I. We both know that. I mean . . . I'm not the right bloke for you. My world is different.'

She chewed her bottom lip, on the verge of crying, as if something precious were being stolen from her. And because he rejected her so openly, because he thought they were incompatible, because he was so unreachable, winning his heart suddenly became the most important goal in her life. 'But you don't know me at all,' she said, treading a line between affection and confrontation.

'Oi, I didn't mean to upset you,' Iskender said, not looking sorry at all. It was a lovely surprise to see *stuck-up Katie Evans* so insecure and fragile, and, he now suspected, sweet on him. 'Tell you what? We got off to a bit of a bad start. Why don't we try again?' He leaned forward and held her hand. 'Hello, how do you do? My name is Iskender. You can call me Alex.'

Her lips slightly parted as she said, 'Nice to meet you.'

Before they left the place Iskender excused himself to visit the toilet. Halfway down the staircase he ran into a young scrawny man with a shaved head, beady blue eyes and spots all over his face. The man, who worked as an assistant at a local bakery, studied Iskender for a fleeting moment, a subtle spark behind his tight smile.

When Iskender entered the toilet there was a black man at the urinals, and he sashayed to a stall, whistling a cheery tune. He closed the door and paused, startled by what he saw. There, on the surface of the door, was a two-foot-high swastika and next to it a number of racist slogans and obscenities. Underneath, it said *White Power*. Some of the words had been scratched on the surface with a metal object, while the rest had been hastily sprayed. Iskender checked the painting. Whoever had done this, it hadn't been too long since he was around.

He quickly left the stall and nodded at the man, who was now washing his hands, looking intimidated. As he clambered back to Katie, he so wished he had been there a minute ago, while the perpetrator was still around.

★

They took a walk, which came as a relief to Katie, who had consumed three Cokes. Strolling without purpose, they passed by greengrocers, chemists and betting shops, the last of the sun trailing them. Though it was a blustery day and the sky was a bleak mantle, there were many people out and about, doing their business.

In Victoria Park they stood by the pond, watching the pigeons. The grass felt good beneath their weight, fresh and promising. He put his arm around her, pulling her close, kissed her. She liked the smell of him, the taste of his lips, and she liked that he didn't try to fumble under her clothes to cup her breasts, the way other boys did, in hopes of going further. She noticed the zeal in his voice, the dare in his eyes, the hunger in his soul.

They held hands, and sat on a bench and watched the pedestrians, whispering into each other's ears a frivolous remark about every single person who went past. *Bonkers. Old trout. Mugger.* A few people smiled at them, happy to see another young couple in love. Others averted their gaze.

'How about the bloke over there?' said Katie. 'Doesn't he look a bit dodgy?'

Iskender's eyes followed hers until he saw a lean, dark-haired man approaching them. Immediately, his back stiffened, his arms around her loosened.

'What? Do you know him?'

Wordlessly, Iskender turned his back to the road and pulled up his collar better to hide his face. The man, whom everybody called the Orator, strode by a few seconds later without so much as a glance at the couple on the bench.

'What's going on? Is he someone you don't want to see?' Katie asked.

'He's quite all right. But I'd rather he didn't see me with you.'

Katie was intrigued by the way Iskender closed up like a steel trap whenever he was asked a question he didn't want to answer, including queries about his family and childhood. There were sides to him that she couldn't grasp. He was a cool bloke, she thought, but prone to outbursts of fury. When they met the next time – and she knew there would be a next time – he would treat her better. Of this, she was certain.

Miracles

London, 24 December 1977

In a spacious, well-lit kitchen full of cooks and assistants, Elias, the owner and head chef of Cleo's, slouched over a massive range cooker upon which various pans sizzled away. Slowly, he stirred a thick, creamy mushroom sauce. It was almost ready, but not yet perfect. He always included a pinch of nutmeg before taking the pan off the heat. That was his little secret. And today everything had to be just right. It was, after all, Christmas Eve.

An Orthodox Christian by birth, an agnostic by choice, he loved the spirit of Christmas: the singing, the family get-togethers, the sharing, the giving, but especially the belief in miracles. That was the part he could relate to the best. As a boy his favourite saint had been Saint Andrew of Crete – not because the saint was far more pious and virtuous than the others, but because, unlike many of them, he himself was a walking miracle. Saint Andrew had been mute from birth, and remained so until the day when, only seven, he suddenly started to speak of truths too immense for his age. Young Elias had loved this story, taking an impish pleasure in imagining the shock on the faces of the people around the child when he uttered his first words. He rejoiced in the fact that the saint had gone down in history as a good orator as well as a hymnographer. If a mute boy could do that, life might perhaps not be as dismal as it sometimes seemed.

After putting the nutmeg into the pan, Elias gave the sauce one more stir and turned off the burner. His sous-chef appeared beside him and carefully emptied the sauce into a porcelain container, where it would cool before being poured on to fifty-five servings of beef fillet steak.

Elias checked his watch before starting to work on the next dish: spiced pear cake with maple pecan sauce. He never used metal utensils while preparing any of his recipes. That was another one of his secrets. Everything had to be wood. Metal was cold, polished and too perfect. It didn't connect, it only controlled. Whereas wood was clumsy and rough but sincere.

It was only seven hours until Christmas. And, as far as counting went, 1978 was only days away. Elias didn't have great expectations for the coming year. Well, only one. That it would not be as dreadful as the one coming to an end.

Those twelve months had been the toughest in his five decades of life. Elias had started the year with his career on the rise, an attractive wife, a spacious house in Islington and more business than he could handle at the restaurant. At the end of seven months, he was single and living in a tiny flat with barely any furniture. Aside from a few friends, he hardly socialized any more – reeling from the toll of a divorce for which he hadn't been prepared. Emotionally, he likened his state to a model train whose batteries had run out while climbing up a hill. Throughout the last phase of his marriage he had kept trying, pushing and faltering with an energy he no longer possessed, until he had swerved off the rails. The divorce had been ugly, neither of them acting like their usual selves. He had often found himself debating financial issues more than emotional ones, until finally he let go – of her, the alimony, the memories.

He had loved his wife, and in some ways he still did. With her lean figure, narrow shoulders, pale complexion, crisply British accent and scintillating ideas, Annabel was the reason he had moved to this country. Since she was *more English than the Queen* and umbilically attached to her family in Gloucestershire, and since his job was more flexible than hers – she was the founder of a pioneering women's legal centre – it had seemed natural that, after a brief honeymoon on Ibiza, they should settle in London.

While Elias had not objected to this plan at any stage, the move had not proved easy. London in the early seventies was far from a culinary paradise. There were only a handful of first-class restaurants; and new approaches to food, let alone cross-cultural cuisine, were regarded with undisguised suspicion. Indian cuisine was relatively popular, but its flavours were unlike the ones Elias wanted to introduce. Overall, he found English cuisine heavy and insular, and the customers resistant to fresh tastes – all of which he intended to address.

In the end, their marriage finished exactly the way it had started: with a sense of urgency and a need to challenge. Once the divorce papers were signed, all that was left for Elias from seven and a half years of married life was an aged, lazy Persian cat called Magnolia, albums with photos he no longer wanted to see and the bitterness in his memory and, at times, his dreams.

At midsummer, he received a phone call from his mother informing him that his father had suffered a second heart attack and, this time, not survived. Elias had been unaware of the first.

'He talked about you every day,' she said. 'Your pa respected you and what you've done over there. He was too proud to say it to your face.'

The line was so poor Elias could not be sure he was hearing her correctly. 'I'm coming home, Ma.'

'Not now, dear,' she said. 'You'll come to see me and Cleo when you're better and when I'm better. Right now, we're of no help to each other. Stay where you are and do what you need to do. Your pa would have preferred that.'

But even without her words, Elias knew he had already decided not to abandon London. He would work and work, devouring his past as hungrily, as tenaciously, as a caterpillar eats away every leaf in eyesight, and then he would wait for someone to pull him out of this cocoon, miraculously transformed. The only thing that remained unscathed throughout 1977 had been his business. The restaurant was thriving – he was planning to open a second one in Richmond – as if to compensate for all the chaos elsewhere.

By now Elias had got used to the pain. It had started as a tightening in his stomach and moved up into his ribcage, nestling in his chest, making it hard to laugh, sometimes even to breathe. His friends kept ringing, pressing him to start seeing people again. They left messages on his answering machine, arranged blind dates for him with women who either worshipped or despised themselves. The truth was, more and more so lately, Elias found himself looking for excuses to be alone. Loneliness, that dull feeling he had dreaded almost all his life, had now become palpable and physical, almost like a liquid. It rushed into his pores, drenching every blood vessel and tissue in his body, water penetrating a dry sponge. Strangely, he didn't find it that bad.

Pink Destiny – that's what she said her name was. Elias couldn't help noticing how vastly different she and Annabel were. If his ex-wife had met Pembe, she would smile knowingly, finding her simple and unsophisticated. Wasn't this what all men wished for deep in their hearts, she would say? An *uncomplicated* woman – someone who wouldn't question, nag, confront or criticize them. Even so, Annabel would add, it was a false fantasy, for there was no such thing as an uncomplicated woman. There were only those who were openly complicated and those who hid it.

Despite Annabel's needling at the back of his mind, Elias had been thinking about Pembe. At first he had hoped she would visit him, and they would talk about the things they liked, perhaps even cook for each other. *A friendly exchange. Nothing else.* He had taken extra care with his appearance, but as the weeks passed that hope had been replaced by the awareness that she would not come. Why should she? In all probability he had been living in his head for so long that his grip on what was real or possible had slipped.

Working soothed him, as it had always done. Tonight, in addition to the Christmas traffic in the restaurant, they would be catering two prestigious events. The entire staff had been running full steam ahead, and he was glad that no one had had the chance to ask him why he had included a last-minute item on the menu: rice pudding with orange blossom.

Half an hour later, while the steaks were still being marinated in a zesty sauce, one of the new assistants approached. 'Chef, you have a visitor.'

Elias raised his eyebrows, surfacing from his thoughts. 'Hmm?'

'Someone is asking for you.'

'Later,' Elias said. 'I can't even take a leak now.'

As Elias watched the assistant shrug and turn back, a doubt crept in. 'Wait a sec. It's not a woman with auburn hair?'

'What exactly is auburn hair, Chef . . . is it . . .?'

'Never mind,' Elias muttered, deciding to go to check for himself.

Years after that Christmas Eve, Elias would remember that moment – how he had marched out of the kitchen, wiping his hands on a towel, and halted as soon as he saw her, standing in the foyer, smoothing down her skirt beneath her knees as if she suddenly found it too short, a burgundy handbag tucked under her arm, a shadow of guilt on her face, still not believing she had gone there.

They sat at a table in the empty restaurant, which felt odd, while the team kept running around, which felt even odder. Every few minutes one of the assistants came to ask something, and each time Elias answered with a mixture of anxiety and calm.

'You go to kitchen,' Pembe said after a while.

'No, no, don't worry. I have plenty of time,' Elias lied.

Resolutely, she shook her head. 'You go but can I come too?'

'You sure?' he asked. 'It's a henhouse in there. With a hungry fox on the loose. Only two hours before dinner, they're all acting a little mad.'

She smiled, impervious. The hairdresser's had been closed today, and since her family didn't celebrate Christmas, she said, she had time on her hands. Besides, she liked henhouses. Still hesitating, Elias led her into the kitchen, where everyone was too busy to gawk at her. He gave her a uniform, and then, upon her request, gave her peppers to dice, parsley to chop, ginger to peel, and so on. Without a word, without a break, she worked.

Later, when the time came for Pembe to leave, Elias walked her to the door. They stood under a painting in which a chalky-white, naked woman stared at them with indifferent eyes – a reproduction of Ingres's *Grande Odalisque*. For different reasons, they both felt uneasy, averting their gazes from the painting, from each other.

'I owe you one,' he said, and when he realized she didn't understand, he added, 'Thank you.'

'I thank you,' she said. 'You helped other day.'

So fearful was he of saying or doing something wrong, of eschewing cultural norms, that he extended his hand for a firm shake. Ignoring the gesture, she approached and kissed him gently on the cheek.

★★★

This afternoon I went to see Officer Andrew McLaughlin to get my sister's postcard back, as he knew I would.

He makes me wait for thirty minutes, and it isn't because he has other business to attend to but because he wants me to remember who's the boss. Also waiting to see him is a new arrival, a fish out of water. Nervously shaking his leg, clutching some papers, he's here to file a complaint. One look at this bloke and you can see he's wet behind the ears – untested, untried, unhurt.

'Don't be daft,' I want to tell him. 'Save your breath.'

It's never a brilliant idea to snitch in prison, especially not in the first weeks, when everybody is watching you like vultures, and you don't yet know who is who. There are some big toes you don't dare step on, and, if you do, you'd better brace yourself.

There is a board on the wall across from me with posters and fliers about organ donation, methadone-replacement therapy, a group for the friends and families of prisoners, Hepatitis B and C, and the Samaritans' Prisoners Support Programme. To a free man all of this might suggest the sorrows of life inside. But that's not how I look at it. After more than ten years' bird, it is the external world that I dread.

I was eight and Esma was almost seven when we came to England and saw from the top of a red bus the Queen's Chiming Clock – that's what we called Big Ben. We learned the language fast, unlike our parents, particularly Mum. It wasn't the grammar that she didn't get. It's just that she didn't trust English in general. Not that she was more comfortable with Turkish. Or even her native Kurdish. Words caused trouble, she believed. They made people misunderstand one another. Nor did she trust those who depended on jargon, such as journalists, lawyers or writers. Mum liked songs, lullabies, recipes and prayer, where the words – if they mattered at all – were only secondary.

At home, with us children, my mother spoke a Turkish that was peppered with Kurdish words. We answered her in English and spoke only English amongst ourselves. I always suspected she understood more than she revealed.

Perhaps all immigrants shrink from a new language to some extent. Take the brick-thick Oxford English Dictionary and show a new arrival a couple of pages, ask about a few entries. Especially idioms and metaphors – they're the worst. Imagine trying to crack the meaning of 'kicking the bucket'. You learned the verb 'to kick' and you know what a damn bucket is, but, no matter how hard you try, it just doesn't sink in. Rhetoric is a bit like red tape. It makes you feel small, vulnerable.

My sister was different. Esma loved language. Duck to water. If someone used an expression she wasn't familiar with, she'd do anything to make it hers, like a collector who's found a rare coin. She adored words – their sounds, their hidden meanings. Mum was worried that her eyesight – and her options for marriage – would be ruined because of too much reading. As for me, I had no time for books. I had better luck with the slang: to me that had power, currency. That is, until the day I started to stammer.

I've changed here. Not overnight, but inch by inch. While I'm not exactly a 'trusted inmate', Martin gave me the privilege to use the library after hours. I read, research and reflect – the three big r's that can make life in prison a step closer to hell or heaven, depending on how you see it.

You'd imagine that everyone would hate a bloke like me. Only, strangely, it isn't the case. I receive letters, cards and gifts from places that are only dots on the map. There are boys who think I'm a hero. They don't have a clue about my life, but still. There are women who want to marry me, and cure me with their love. Sick in the head, that is.

Then there are the God Botherers, who want to 'work' on me. They come from all religions and no particular religion at all; I seem to have a quite broad appeal. Once in a while I even get some of that New Age bollocks. They send me leaflets, booklets, tapes. 'Let us help your injured soul by shedding the Light upon your darkest hours.' Pompous words! They pretend their message is for all humanity but are ready to burn at the stake anyone who doesn't go along with them. Still, they feel affection for the likes of me. They just can't get enough of us. So strong is their desire to correct sinners and score points in God's eyes. We're their tickets to heaven. We, the scumbags of the earth – the wicked, the fallen.

A journalist came to see me once: thin as a stick, but well dressed, short skirts, long sexy legs and all that. She visited me a few times, seemed to be on my side. 'Please rest assured, Alex, I only want to understand the story, and increase awareness in society by writing about it.'

How noble is that! Then she goes and pens the shittiest article. I was mucked around with as a child. It was all Mum's fault: as the elder son, I had been spoiled by her. 'This is a typical case of Middle Eastern patriarchal tradition,' blah, blah, blah. I was so irritated I never spoke to a journalist again. They're not really interested in the truth. All they want to do is to fit you into the story that's already in their minds.

There were also reports written, even a thesis at some university in London. And once there was this politician who used me as an example to smear all Muslim immigrants. 'This man is a prototype of the kind of immigrant who is clearly incompatible with the basic tenets of European civilization,' he said. To all these people, I'm invisible. So is my mother. We're just a means of furthering their own ends.

The door to the office opens and Officer McLaughlin's head pops out. 'Well, who do we have here?'

He moves aside and lets me in. The office has changed considerably. When Martin was here this was a different place, but then Martin was a different man. We all respected him.

McLaughlin sits at his desk and opens a file. My file, obviously. 'I see you were born in 1962,' he says. 'You and I are the same age, born in the same month. Can you believe it?'

Yunus is a Leo, Esma is a Virgo, I'm a Scorpio. And so is Officer McLaughlin.

'They say there are two different types of Scorpios, did you know that?' he goes on. 'Those who poison others and those who poison themselves.'

He stares at me, as if wondering whether I'm going to be the anomaly who falls into both categories.

'Here it says you were repeatedly put in solitary confinement. You got into too many fights. What a shit-stirrer! Let's see, you broke an inmate's nose, attacked a probation officer. Oh, you smashed another inmate's fingers. Four of them –' He pauses, taking the measure of me. 'Ouch, that must have hurt.'

My stomach clenches.

'How did you do that, Alex? Did you put his fingers on a hard surface and break them all at once or did you twist them one by one?'

I know what he's doing. He's reminding me of who I was – and still can be. My life here consists of two phases. At first, I was a pain in everyone's neck. There is no other way to put it. I was full of rage, resentment, totally lost. Then there was the second stage, which is, more or less, where I am today. Still angry and mad, but more at myself than at those around me.

'I crushed his hand with a concrete block,' I say.

'Right,' McLaughlin says, nodding as if he is appreciative. 'And the officer? What happened there?'

'I had a small beef with him.'

He asked for it. Pushed me hard to see how much he could get away with. Trying to make me bend over during strip search, calling me names, provoking me. I hid a razor in my toothbrush and slashed half his face. Later on he was sent to another gaol. I hear the scar hasn't healed.

'It says you've had seizures, epileptic fits, migraines, panic attacks, anxiety attacks, psychoses, suicide attempts . . . hmmm –' He stops: he's found something of interest. 'Speech impediment! Now what's that?'

'I stuttered,' I answer. 'For a while.'

It's gone, though not fully. When I get nervous I still trip over my tongue, but I'm not going to give him the pleasure of knowing that.

McLaughlin goes back to reading. 'Heavily medicated. Trazodone, Zimelidine, Lithium, Paxil, Valium, Xanax . . .'

Some had no effect at all; others seemed to work for a while, and some had so many side-effects I ended up worse than before. Lithium made me gain weight, Zimelidine caused a nausea so intense that I felt on the verge of vomiting my lungs out, and once Trazodone gave me a painful erection that didn't disappear for three days. I wonder if all that is in my file or if he's broken into my medical records, and, if so, whether that is legal.

Suddenly he sniggers at something he's read, his shoulders hopping. 'Oh, you don't eat meat!'

I nod.

Another laugh. 'Sorry, I can't help it. It's just that for a bully like you . . . I mean someone who's murdered his mother and has a systematic record of violence, it seems odd to worry about a few animals!'

When I fail to comment, an awkward silence falls over us.

'May I take my postcard now?'

'Sure,' he says, suddenly serious. 'As soon as you tell me why you made your mate hit you, you can have your bloody postcard back.'

'He was about to lose it big time. His wife asked for a divorce. He needed to hit someone.'

'And you, the Good Samaritan, offered your chest, is that so?'

He opens a drawer and takes out Esma's postcard. To my surprise, he doesn't play around but hands it right to me. Then he says, 'There are cuckoos who think Houdini died because of the blows to his stomach area. They claim one of the punches ripped his appendix.'

I don't say anything. No need to tell him I might be one of those cuckoos. If you hit the appendix repeatedly and with enough force, you might get a result. It's a matter of finding the right angle. At least it's worth a try. What do I have to lose? I'm experimenting with death.

'Alex, I have enough evidence to suggest that you were trying to meet your maker. That is, if you're a scorpion who has a tendency to poison himself.'

He's smarter than I thought. But I'm going to deny it all the same. 'Why would I want to kill myself? I'll soon be a free man.'

That is when Officer McLaughlin leans over his desk, looks me in the eye and utters the only right thing he's ever said. 'Alex, you and I both know you'll never be a free man. Even after you've been sprung from here, even when you're out there on the streets, you'll still be locked up in your guilt.'

Then he sits back. 'Just so that you know, Houdini's death had nothing to do with the blows he received. His appendix was already kaput.'

'Why are you telling me all this?'

''Cos it's a wise sailor who makes for port when a storm is coming.'

'What if there is no storm?' I say, standing on my feet. 'And you're making for port for nothing and missing the sunshine?'

It's a mistake, I know. I shouldn't be talking like that. But my ego is awake – if it had ever been asleep at all.

'Sit,' McLaughlin says.

I do. We wait in silence. A full minute goes by.

'You may leave now,' McLaughlin says.

As I head to the door, I hear him mutter, as if to himself, 'Why did you people come to England and bring us all your crap?'

In Britain the dislike of foreigners always catches me off guard. They don't always call you spic or greasy wop to your face, although there is that from time to time. Racism is not part of daily life, as it is in some other countries I hear about. It is subtle and always polished. It is not about your skin colour or your religion, really. It is about how civilized you are.

I walk back to my cell, greeting a few of the lads on the way. They are mostly local Englishmen under this roof, but there are also a few Hispanics, Russians, Bulgarians, Arabs, Africans. In every nation there are good eggs and bad eggs. That's my take. Some of the men have heads scrambled from drugs and fights. Mine might be quite mashed too. There's a lot of that, drugs. Some lags are only after getting wasted or getting into one another's pants. The poofs . . . it's harsh on them. When I first came here I didn't like any of the gangs and decided to form my own. It wasn't easy, but I pulled it off. We had strict unwritten rules that everyone obeyed. No tolerance for paedophiles and rapists. No fruits, diddlers, sickos among us. No smackies, no poppers, no snort.

Suddenly I couldn't front it any more. I was their leader but I left the gang because I had issues to resolve inside my head. I was heavily sedated, to prevent me from harming myself. On suicide watch twenty-four hours a day, seven days a week. For a long time I just sank – even lower than where I had been.

Then one night, my mother came to me. Her ghost. An apparition. Whatever you call it. I could smell her hair. It was that real. She stayed with me the entire night. Her face. Her eyes. I sobbed like never before. After that, I began to change and I'm a different man today. Maybe not better, but different. And that's a piece of information Officer McLaughlin will never find in my file.

★

When I enter the cell Trippy is sitting on his bunk under several blankets, his face ashen, his eyes closed. He seems totally spaced out. 'How did it go?' he asks.

'Brilliant! We didn't strangle each other.'

'Sweet,' he says and goes back to his stupor. He's been popping more and more pills since he got the news about the impending divorce.

For a moment I want to tell him to take it easy. But I can see that all he wants is to be left alone. I respect that. I go and lie down on my bunk, brooding.

There is a Bridge in the Other World, thinner than a strand of hair and more slippery than an eel. When the Day of Judgement arrives, every person will have to cross it alone. You'll hear the screams of the sinners as their skins are scorched and their bones boiled. If you're a sinner yourself, you'll fall into the blistering flames underneath. If you've done enough good in life, the animals you've sacrificed on Eid will wake from death and lead you safely to the other side. Who taught me this? It must have been Uncle Tariq, but I'm not sure.

I was seven years old when I stopped eating meat. Each Eid we would ask God's forgiveness for not being able to sacrifice an animal. The neighbours brought us meat, which was nice. But in our last year in Istanbul, Mum urged Father to buy a ram, and not just any ram, but a big one. We were going to England after all. Dad had found a job in a factory over there. God had opened a new door for us and we duly had to thank Him.

Father kept complaining about how expensive and unnecessary all this was. Still, one morning I woke up to a bleating coming from the garden, and there was a ram, grazing on thin grass. It was an impressive animal, with scarlet ribbons tied to its horns. They let me feed it and give it water. Mum and I applied henna on its post, which left scarlet patches. I spent the next two days by its side. It was my first and only pet.

Uncle Tariq said, 'Don't get too fond of that ram.'

'Why?' I asked.

He frowned. 'Didn't they tell you? It'll be slaughtered soon.'

Crying, I ran to Father. He seemed in a jolly mood and promised not to touch the animal. 'I have only one son,' Father said. 'I'll let you have the ram.'

God, I was over the moon. I felt proud to be a boy, not a weedy girl like Esma. The next day they sent me on errands and when I came back there was the ram's bloated body hanging from the tree.

I couldn't tell what hurt more: the death of my pet or my father's lie. Learning that Mum had been an accomplice? Or that I wasn't as favoured as I had thought? Mum put a smear of ram's blood on my forehead, kissed me, said I looked like a sultan and went to cook the meat. A pungent, sticky smell covered the house. In the evening, when they put the dish in front of me, I refused to eat it.

'Do you know how much that ram cost me?' Father asked. 'Do you have any idea, you ungrateful brat!'

At the time, I didn't what came over me but I do now. The anger. The adrenalin. The sensation of falling and rising at the same time. It hits you like a wave. Next thing you know you're standing on a crest and you can dare anyone, even your own father. I pushed the plate aside, more harshly than I had intended. The food spilled all over the table. Father blinked, not believing his eyes. Was I challenging his authority in front of my mother and sister? He went berserk. I had never seen him so enraged.

'Iskender, eat!' he shouted. 'I don't beat my children!'

Then I shrugged. That was the last straw. He pushed my head towards the puddle of meat. It was so unexpected that my chin hit the bottom of the plate and bounced back like a rubber ball. But my nose was still swimming in broth, heavy, oily. Mixed with my tears and my snot. I heard a slurp. It was coming from me. And that taste I have never forgotten. The taste of my weakness. Father kept pushing, his fingers tight around my neck. I chewed and chewed, lifting my head for air between gulps.

Finally he let me go. When I looked up, I saw he was ashamed of his reaction. He wasn't an abusive man, not in that way. I don't know what took possession of him that day. I don't think he knows either.

Mum ran to me, wiping my face. 'My lion, my sultan. Are you all right?'

I ignored my mother's hand on my forehead and glared at my father. Now there was resentment in his eyes but also a flash of misery. What were we doing to ourselves? Why were we always taking it out on each other?

Then and there I understood it was no good shaking in your shoes. If I displayed weakness, he would step on me. The whole bloody world would step on me. But if I were strong, really strong, no one could. Since then I have never been weak. At fault, yes. Entirely wrong. But not weak. Never. And since then I have not eaten meat.

Iskender Toprak

The Moustache

London, 1 January 1978

Five forty in the morning, and Adem was already awake. Lately he had begun to set the alarm clock at ungodly hours so that he could have some time to himself before Roxana woke. He liked to watch her while she was sleeping. Her face looked different then, less strained, no longer angry at him for who he was and what he couldn't become. Now, stripped of its peach-coloured lipstick, her mouth was smaller, without a hint of coldness; her hair spread out on the pillow like spun wool pointing in all directions, clutching around his heart.

Being in love with Roxana was like watching a boat pass by in the distance. Adem sat on the shore stock still, shielding his eyes from the sun. Under his gaze the ship kept moving. Not too fast, never in a hurry, an almost imperceptible farewell. He knew their days together were numbered. She was slipping away from him inch by inch, and the only thing he could do was to wait until she became a dot on the horizon. When she discovered that he had no money left, she would be done with him. He was aware of all this because she had made it clear from the start. *A woman has needs*, she was fond of saying. Roxana was always astoundingly, agonizingly forthright.

She had seen him lose at roulette, but she still believed he had money up his sleeve: savings in the bank, a loan that would be paid back or property in London. *Surely he must have something. He has been in this country for so long.* She expected Adem to reveal his hidden treasure any day now. Her expectations hadn't come out of thin air: he had done everything in his power to give her that impression.

The truth was, however, that a few days ago Adem had lost his job in the factory. His sloppiness had finally taken its toll. Now his only source of income was the money he had borrowed from friends; his

142

only asset, the house where his family lived. He had been given a mortgage six years ago, and had so far paid off only a quarter of it.

Sighing, Roxana turned in her sleep. Her face twisted, her nostrils slightly flared. 'No,' she said, and mumbled something incomprehensible. Then again, she repeated, 'No, no.'

Adem held his breath, trying to hear more. He wondered what she was dreaming about. Her body was here in bed with him but her soul was far away with another man. If so, was it someone she loved? He didn't know which would be worse: that she had never been in love and was incapable of opening her heart or that she had loved once and would never dedicate herself to anyone in the same way again.

Quietly, he got up from the bed. The blanket slid aside, revealing Roxana's bare thighs. She could sleep naked, winter or summer, utterly comfortable in her skin. He could never do that. Each time, he would take off his pyjamas before sex and instantly put them back on afterwards.

'Take your socks off in bed. You're like an old man!' Roxana complained.

He obeyed, though he didn't like it because he was always cold. The heating in the flat was poor. Old pipes in need of repair, leaking in places. But he dared not complain about it. Another thing Roxana didn't like was his moustache. 'Englishmen don't have them,' she often said. 'When're you gonna cut it? It makes you look like Stalin.'

Shuffling his feet in the dark, Adem went to the kitchen and turned on the light. The mess surprised him, even though he thought he had got used to it by now. Roxana hated housework and often reprimanded him for not giving her a hand. *You can't make me serve you. I'm not your wife, am I?*

She liked to say such things – insinuations as sharp as broken glass. Her bitterness was an inseparable part of her, almost vindictive. It wasn't really the harshness of her comments that he minded so much as the generalities she projected on to him. Every time Roxana lectured him, Adem had the impression that she was addressing all the men she had known. That hurt. Being part of a rogues' gallery, having no distinctive character in her eyes, made him feel like the temporary lover that he was. He wanted to be unique, her one and only. It didn't matter that there had been others before him. Well, it *did* matter, but at least if he could be assured that he was special it would lessen the discomfort. Roxana would laugh at such a thought. *I never said I was in love with you, did I?* Whenever he came close to talking about his feelings, something he had never done before, neither with his wife nor his children, she would wave her hand, as though to disperse some cigarette smoke that was bothering her.

Adem opened the cupboard, trying not to look at the sink, where a stack of dirty plates and mugs caked in mould swam in murky water. Managing to find a clean pot, he started to make Turkish coffee.

On the back burner on low heat, the coffee started to simmer, its slow boil strangely soothing. The kitchen was suffused with a pungent smell. Soon he sat at the table with a cup in his hand and drank it down in a few gulps. Still, he didn't feel fully awake. Still, he carried the night in him.

The day before he had gone to his younger son's school and waited outside, hiding in the shadows. *Like a criminal*, he thought to himself. When Yunus walked out with his friends, he had not called his name, his throat too tight. Similarly, a few times he had hung around a café called Aladdin's Cave in the hope of running into Iskender. Once he had spotted him in the distance, holding hands with a lean, blonde girl. He knew Iskender had an English girlfriend, but seeing them together, light and full of zest, had made him feel old, revealing the vigour he no longer possessed. In the months he hadn't been to the house his son had grown up so much! He was a young man, quite handsome. Much as he wanted to, he could not go and speak to him. People were looking. That was the hardest part. Meeting the eyes of friends and neighbours, making small talk all the while pretending not to notice what was on their minds. *A shameful man who abandoned his family for a dancer.*

Striding across the hall, he went to the bathroom, turned on the light and observed himself in the mirror. He frowned at his sunken eyes, the marks on his cheeks from old spots, the white streaks in his hair – how could his hair become hoary while his moustache was still black? He was going to trim his stubble, the way he had every morning for over fifteen years. But his right hand seemed to have another plan. With a sudden urge, he grabbed the razor.

When Adem came out of the bathroom, clean-shaven, he saw Roxana sitting up in bed, leafing through a women's magazine. He had only to glance at her to know that she had slept poorly and was not in the best mood.

'Do you have coffee for me?' she said, without looking up.

'Sure.' His voice sounded vaguely different when talking to her, like an echo of his own.

'My neck hurts again.'

He began to massage her neck, drawing widening circles above her shoulders, his hands settling momentarily on the small of her back. She let out a moan, her body relaxing as if in a foamy bath. He kept massaging, with more strength, until his fingertips met around her neck, accidentally at first, then with a purpose. It occurred to him, and not for the first time, that he could kill this woman. He said, 'I'll go make your coffee.'

'Wait.' She studied him intently. 'What have you done to your face?'

'Oh, my moustache,' he said. 'Do you like it?'

Even though Roxana nodded, she wished suddenly, and without quite knowing why, that he hadn't shaved it off, that he didn't love her this much and that everything could be different. A sad smile settled into the corner of her mouth, and all the bitterness seemed to bleed away from her.

Silent Surprise

London, 2 January 1978

Early in the afternoon, a golden glow illuminated the windows of the Crystal Scissors, where a bunch of Christmas decorations hung like ripe grapes, bathing the interior in a glittering light. Still reeling from a party the previous night, Rita was drinking her third cup of black coffee when the door opened and a middle-aged man walked in. His face was animated and bright, and he carried himself with a quiet confidence that could have been distancing, were it not for his warm smile.

Raising an eyebrow, Rita examined the stranger from head to toe. He didn't look like a representative for one of the shampoo companies or a petitioner trying to collect a few more signatures. Nor did he have the air of an inspector who had come to check the sanitary conditions at the salon. Well dressed and proper, he seemed a decent man – but one never knew these days.

'May I help you?' said Rita.

'Yes, please. I'd like to have a haircut.'

Rita let out a chuckle. 'I'm afraid we're not open yet. Not for another fifteen minutes and –'

'Oh, I can wait outside, no problem.'

'I was gonna say, this isn't a unisex salon. Why don't you try the barber around the corner?'

'Ah, I've been there before,' said Elias. 'That man should call himself a butcher, not a barber.'

'Well, I'm sure we can find you a good place,' Rita conceded, a hint of amusement in her voice.

'Just wondering,' he said in a sweeter tone, 'have you noticed lately how many salons have turned unisex?'

'Really?' asked Rita in mock amazement. She hadn't yet ruled out the option that he might be some sort of lunatic.

Working in the tiny room at the back, Pembe stopped cleaning the hairbrushes, and strained to hear who on earth Rita could be talking to. She thought she recognized the voice, but it couldn't possibly be *him*. Her heart leaping into her throat, she tiptoed into the salon. Such was her astonishment at seeing Elias chatting with her boss that she leaned against the wall, incapable of making another move.

Elias hadn't seen Pembe enter. 'I've kept my hair long for the past four years. I feel it's time for a change,' he was now saying.

'Uh-hmm, I always say to my customers, ladies, long hair is for women. That's the way the good Lord made it.'

By now Pembe was convinced that she had to intervene and shoo him away, but try as she might she couldn't think of a way to do it. Pursing her lips, and biting them raw, she continued to watch them.

'Then perhaps you'd consider helping me,' Elias said. 'I'm a chef, you see. Every day a customer complains about hair in his soup.'

Rita laughed. 'I'd love to help, darlin', but I'm waiting for my half-twelve appointment.'

'I do it,' Pembe butted in.

Both Rita and Elias turned aside and gaped at her, arms slightly akimbo, faces grim, as if they had forgotten who she was. Doing her best to sound casual, Pembe added, 'I cut his hair.'

It wouldn't be the first time. Though she had not trained as a hairdresser, Pembe had been observing Rita long enough to know the ropes. Cutting the hair of her children, especially of her sons, for many years had also taught her a few tricks.

'Well, that's settled, then,' Rita said with a dismissive shrug. She was about to add something else, but the door slammed open and her customer popped in. Rita walked towards the woman, her arms wide open. 'Margaret, how nice to see you.'

In the meantime, Pembe ushered Elias to a chair at the end of the room, where she whispered tensely, 'Why you here?'

'Sorry, I had to see you.'

'No, you don't!' she said, sounding like a petulant child. She put a smock around his neck, lined up the scissors on a plastic tray and began to wet his hair with a spray bottle.

Elias saw that Pembe was so vexed by his presence her hands were shaking. He felt such a strong urge to hold her and to apologize for upsetting her that he had to take a deep breath to control himself. He half regretted his bit of mischief. Nonetheless, the pleasure of having her this close outweighed the guilt. He watched her every move in the oval mirror on the wall. At her touch he closed his eyes, and when he opened them he saw that she, too, was observing him. Her next words, however, did not match the compassion in her stare: 'I cut your hair, but don't come more.'

'All right, don't worry. I promise, I won't come here again.'

Relieved, Pembe smiled for the first time. 'And how do I cut?'

'Now that, I dunno.' Elias had always kept his hair the same way and was only now beginning to realize he was not quite ready to change his style. But he said, 'Make me handsome, please, something nice.'

'You're nice already,' Pembe muttered in a voice so low it was a miracle he heard her.

Laughter broke out at the other end of the room. Rita and her customer were gossiping with gusto, engrossed in a world of their own.

'I need to ask you something.'

'What is it?' she replied apprehensively.

'Look, I . . . I'd like to get to know you better, and spend more time together. But if you'd rather I stay away from you, tell me.'

Pembe flinched. Her face paled a little, and after what seemed an eternity she mumbled, 'Don't stay away.'

Elias raised his right hand – the hand that was closer to the wall and therefore concealed from all eyes – and caught Pembe's right hand. It was the first time they had touched in a way that wasn't accidental, or a shy encounter, beset with guilt and panic. Like a falling man reaching out for a rope, he grabbed her hand and squeezed it so tightly it hurt. She didn't mind, for she felt the same – the intensity, the belatedness, the impossibility. Her hand grew as small as a sparrow in his.

They stood like that for another second until she pulled away. 'How I cut?'

'Make it like his, please,' Elias heard himself say.

Pembe followed his gaze to the nearby table, on which a magazine was open to a picture of a man at an awards ceremony – an athletic Hollywood star with porcelain teeth and suntanned skin. 'Like him? No! Yes? Sure?' She couldn't help the giggle that escaped her.

'Absolutely, I've always wanted to look like a celebrity.'

She took the magazine and studied the photo, even though she knew that he couldn't care less about the actor, that he was only buying time to be close to her. For the next half hour she toiled in silence, her brow furrowed in concentration. No more words were exchanged. Each time Rita stole a look at how they were doing, she saw only Pembe working and the strange customer reading one glossy magazine after another.

When she was finished Pembe took a mirror and showed him the back of his head. Elias heaved a sigh, trying not to be demoralized by the shortness of his hair and the sight of his nape. As she was taking off his smock, he asked, as if in passing, 'Do you like films, Pembe?'

'What?'

'I mean, cinema. Do you like to go?'

Pembe nodded, smiling. During the early years in England she had asked her children to take her to the cinema several times, which they had done, but language was always a barrier. She had found it difficult to follow the dialogue. 'Why you ask?' she said.

Now Elias approached, his eyes locked on hers. 'I've left something under the hairspray. Take a look at it, please.' Then he raised his voice to a merry pitch: 'Well, thank you very much. You've done a terrific job.'

From the other end of the salon Rita beamed, pleased to see another satisfied customer. While she and Elias exchanged pleasantries and he paid, Pembe stayed put, her eyes fixed on the can of hairspray. There was a ticket there – next Friday at four p.m. at a cinema in East Finchley. It was an old film. Black and white, and silent.

Disgrace

London, 5 January 1978

Tariq was the proud owner of a corner shop on Queensbridge Road. Six days a week, twelve hours a day, he sold sweets, snacks, toiletries, fizzy drinks, frozen food, cigarettes and sundries. He also had a stand where he displayed myriad newspapers and magazines, some of which made him frown each time his eyes slid over them – *Mayfair, Men Only, Fiesta, Knave, Penthouse, Club International*. There was too much indecency in this country; all this nakedness was no good. He couldn't understand for the life of him how some men found pleasure in these publications, and neither could he comprehend the women who posed in them. Didn't they have families – fathers, husbands or brothers? He kept the obscene material at the far end of the rack, under the tins of tuna and condensed milk, where their fans could still find them, but they would not bother innocent eyes.

Feeling hungry, Tariq checked the clock on the wall. It was only a quarter past eleven. His wife, Meral, brought him lunch in a tin pail every day at half past twelve – *kofta* with minted yoghurt, smoky aubergine purée, rice with garbanzo beans. A samovar would hiss in the background, ready to serve. For during an ordinary day, from morning till late in the night, Tariq guzzled around thirty glasses of tea, which he liked dark and plain, and with a sugar cube that he sucked on each time.

While he ate, Meral would make herself busy, mopping the floor, dusting the shelves and polishing the sign in the window that said *Oasis Mini Mar et*. He intended to fix the *k* but he never seemed to have the time to do so. Besides, the customers didn't seem to mind.

When the food was finished, Meral would take the empty pail and head home to finish her chores. Perhaps one day he would ask his wife to help him run the store, but he would never allow her to work in a distant place among strangers, the way Adem let Pembe. It just wasn't right. Unless there was a financial crisis, a woman should not have to look for a job.

Neither before nor after lunch did Tariq visit the local mosque, like some of the shopowners in the area. He was not a religious man – although those who saw him with his bushy beard and a rosary in his hand tended to assume the contrary. The beard he kept because it suited his face and also hid the pockmarks underneath. And the rosary was more out of habit than piousness. He had a collection of them at home – bright amber, light turquoise, coral pink, opaque onyx, jade green. Fast and steady, he fingered the beads, filling the shop with a constant clatter, which he didn't notice, over the drone of buses going past or cars screeching to a halt at the lights.

Of the three brothers, Tariq was the eldest, and had been the first to leave Istanbul to work abroad. Initially he was employed at a factory that produced machinery in a small town called Troisdorf in Germany. He had found the job taxing, the Germans unreachable and their language impossible. The Germans invited you to their country to work, not to mingle, and expected you to leave as soon as you were no longer needed. Adapting to their ways was like trying to embrace a hedgehog. There might be a secret tenderness, a gentle core underneath, but you couldn't pass the sharp needles to tap into it. The immigrant community could have helped him find his feet to feel less vulnerable, and thereby less resentful, but Tariq had never been skilful at making acquaintances, and the years in Germany were no exception.

Once, however, he befriended a Tunisian co-worker, and the man had taken him to Große Freiheit in the red-light district in Hamburg. Neon signs, music clubs, peals of laughter in all languages. Tariq was appalled to see women displaying their bodies like mannequins in shop windows. But their aloof expressions, the poise in their stare, were just as disturbing. They were not like the prostitutes in old Turkish films, buffeted and beaten by life.

'You like go in?' his friend asked in pidgin German, so he'd understand, pointing to an entryway decorated with blinking bulbs.

'What's in there?'

A smirk made its way across the man's face. 'What's in there?' he repeated in mock horror. 'Pussies, man. Blonde pussies.'

Tariq dropped his eyes, scowling at the stains on his boots. He mumbled a response so low it went unheard. 'I don't want to.'

His friend gave him a look of disdain. 'Up to you, man. If you can't do it, you can't do it.'

Tariq thought about hitting him, delivering a kick in the shins with his muddy boots, but the urge went away as swiftly as it had come. He watched the man whisk in through the door and out of sight, leaving him in the dimly lit street, where he could now hear a woman singing behind closed windows.

The same week at the factory Tariq learned from other workers that the man was telling everyone about how he had bottled out at the brothel, *saying he didn't feel 'up' to it*. People sniggered behind his back. Some suggested he could be a queer. Tariq was already planning to get married that same year, but the incident accelerated his plans. When he brought his bride from a town in Anatolia – a third cousin on his father's side – he asked Meral to visit the factory every day for the first month, so that they could all see he wasn't one of those queers, and shut their mouths.

*

At 12.25 the shop door swung open and Meral ambled in, her cheeks rosy from the wind. Today's menu was lentil soup, stuffed green peppers and *tulumba*.* She watched him eat for a while, taking pride in his appetite. Then she said, 'Pembe stopped by this morning.'

'What does she want?'

'She didn't ask directly but I think they're in need of money.'

'Money, money, money . . .' Tariq droned.

Tariq had once seen a film in which the hero turned into a gangster to save his younger brother from poverty, and to provide him with a better future than the one God had seen fit to give him. In the end, unexpectedly, the younger brother, who had now become a police

---

* Deep-fried dough soaked in syrup.

inspector, arrested the hero, even though he respected, loved and admired him, and was indebted to him for life.

But their own family story was not one of villains and heroes. Though he had done his best to help his two brothers keep their heads above water, wanting to believe that with some support they could change their destinies, Tariq knew that he was a limited man, and so were Adem and Khalil. His brothers had followed in his footsteps and become immigrant workers – one in Australia, the other in England. After a few years Tariq quit his job in Germany and went to England, where they said the weather was horrible but the people were polite.

Now, as Tariq dunked his bread in his soup, he inquired, 'Does Pembe know where he is?'

'She doesn't have a clue. But . . .' Meral paused, as she poured boiling water into the porcelain pot on the samovar. 'She knows that he's moved in with another woman.'

'Well, what do you expect, if she's not woman enough to keep her husband home . . .' Tariq said, leaving the sentence unfinished.

Adem should have never married *that* woman. There were better girls for him and yet, inexplicably, he had fallen for Pembe. Why her, and why so suddenly, Tariq had never understood. Not that he didn't see Pembe's beauty. But in his eyes this only added to her unreliability. Men were mistaken when they coveted attractive women. They could flirt with them in their bachelor days, but a spouse ought to have attributes other than good looks. From the very beginning he had opposed this marriage. But Adem had been alone in that godforsaken Kurdish village when he asked for Pembe's hand. Alone, and terribly young.

When their mother ran away with another man, Tariq had been sixteen years old, Khalil thirteen and Adem only eleven. In all the millions of homes in Istanbul mothers did their very best to keep their families together and children content, and yet their mother, only theirs, had walked out on them.

Not everyone would understand this, but their honour was all that some men had in this world. The rich could afford to lose and regain their reputation, buying influence as perfunctorily as ordering a new car or refurnishing their mansions, but for the rest of the world things were different. The less means a man had, the higher was the worth of his honour. The English didn't understand these ancient rules. Their wives could kiss other men, drink and dance with strangers, and they would look on smiling.

A man who had been cheated of the honour that was his due was a dead man. You could not walk on the street any more, unless you got used to staring at the pavement. You could not go to a tea house and play a round of backgammon or watch a football match in the beer house. Your shoulders would droop, your fists would be clenched, your eyes would sink into their cavities, and your entire being would be a listless mass, shrinking more and more with every rumour. No one would pay heed to you when you spoke; your word would be no more valuable than dried dung. The cigarette you offered would be left unsmoked, the coffee you drank bitter to the end. You would not be invited to weddings, circumcisions or engagements, lest you bring your ill luck with you. In your own corner and surrounded by disgrace, you would dry up like a desiccated fruit. Tariq knew this first hand because it had happened to his father. Baba hadn't died of cirrhosis. The alcohol may have sped things along, but in the end it was dishonour that had killed him. Adem and Khalil had been too young to understand this, but Tariq had seen it happen.

After Meral left, Tariq took a quiet moment to think. So far he had seen his brother's condition less as a vice and more as a calamity that had befallen him. Gambling was a sickness, the worst kind. But squandering your money on a dancer, a woman who was no different than the ones who posed in magazines, was worse. He had to have a serious talk with Adem, that is, if he could find him. When a man neglected his home to this extent, the rest of the family might easily go off the rails. To make sure this didn't happen, Tariq would have to keep a close eye on Pembe and the kids. They shared the same surname. If one of them was disgraced, shame would attach itself to him as the eldest Toprak. Their honour was his honour.

The Missing Piece

London, January 1978

The Phoenix Cinema had been founded in 1910. A modernist, tiled façade, a short flight of stairs to the foyer, Art Deco auditorium. It had served the nation by showing newsreels and escapist films throughout the war, but luckily remained unscathed by German bombs. Recently, after having been taken over by a small film distributor, the cinema had started to show obscure and art-house movies, although Hollywood classics were also occasionally on offer. But its location was so far from the centre that it was almost always empty.

Today there were only four in the audience – a young couple who seemed less interested in the movie than in inventing new kissing techniques, and a man who sat with his flat cap on and looked older than the cinema itself. The fourth was Elias, stiff and anxious, sitting somewhere in the middle, all by himself. It had been several minutes since the film had started, but he still kept glancing at the entrance. She hadn't come.

Elias watched the opening scene filled with apprehension. *A picture with a smile, and perhaps a tear*, it said on the screen. Despite himself Elias's face softened at the sight of Charlie Chaplin. He had always loved Chaplin – his humour interlaced with sorrow, his infinite humanity, those sad, soot-black eyes. Slowly, he found his tension leaking away and his mind drifting into the story of *The Kid*.

After a while Elias felt a slight movement at the end of the row, but he dared not turn to see who it was. Someone approached him in the dark and sat by his side, quiet as a shadow. His heart thumping behind his ribcage, Elias made out Pembe's face, beautiful and radiant, out of the corner of his eye. Her gaze was glued to the screen, her chest rising and falling.

I'm so glad you came, Elias wanted to say. *You know, I was so worried you were upset with me*. But he respected her silence and whispered not a word. Together they focused on the film.

Pembe watched *The Kid* with wide-open eyes, the look of surprise on her countenance deepening with each scene. When Chaplin found an abandoned baby in a rubbish bin, and raised him like his own son, she smiled with appreciation. When the child flung stones at the neighbours' windows so that the tramp – disguised as a glazier – could fix them and earn some money, she chuckled. When social services took the boy away, her eyes welled up with tears. And finally, as father and son were reunited, her face lit up with contentment, and a trace of something that Elias took to be melancholy. So absorbed did she seem in the film that he felt a twinge of resentment. What a funny thing it was to be jealous of Charlie Chaplin.

Elias observed her as she unpinned her hair, and then pinned it back. He caught a whiff of jasmine and rose, a heady, charming mixture. Only minutes before the film came to an end, he found the nerve to reach out for her fingers, feeling like a teenager on his first date. To his relief, she didn't move her hand away. They sat still – two sculptures carved out of the dark, both scared of making a move that would disrupt the tenderness of the moment.

When the lights came back on, it took them a few seconds to grow accustomed to real life. Quickly, he took out a notepad and wrote down the name of another cinema in another part of the town. 'Next week, same day, same time, will you come?'

'Yes,' she faltered.

Before he'd found a chance to say anything else, Pembe leaped to her feet and headed towards the exit, running away from him and everything that had taken place between them, or would have taken place, had they been different people. She held in her palm the name of the place they were to meet next time, grasping it tightly, as if it were the key to a magic world, a key she would use right now were it in her power to decide.

And so it began. They started to meet every Friday at the same time, and occasionally on other afternoons. They frequented the Phoenix more than any other place, but they also met at several other cinemas, all far-away from their homes, all unpopular. Since the films did not change quickly, they ended up watching *The Kid* twice. But they also went to *The King and I*, *The Thief of Baghdad*, *King Kong*, *The Passion of Joan of Arc*, *The Hunchback of Notre Dame* and *Ben-Hur*.

They viewed all these films not so much as stories from a bygone period as destinies still unfolding somewhere. Whichever film they went to see, it was always the same. She kept her eyes on the screen while he kept his eyes on her. Elias loved the way her expression altered with every new twist in the plot. He had the impression that he was meeting the numerous women dormant inside her, glimpsing sides of her character that were hidden from everyone, perhaps even from herself. Every so often, she also stared at him in the same way, as if keen to discover the depths of his soul. Elias shuddered, wondering what she really saw there, and whether she thought it was worth loving him.

In time he found out more things about her, pieces of a jigsaw puzzle that he would complete only long after she had gone. He came to learn that, despite her name, her favourite colour was amethyst. She loved singing old Kurdish love songs and had quite a fine voice. In addition to pork, which she didn't consume for religious reasons, she would never eat shrimps, snails, calamari or cranberries, all of which made her teeth clench, and yet she could suck on slices of lemon all day long. He also found out how young she was. Though the way she dressed and carried herself made her look older, she was, in fact, sixteen years his junior.

Slowly he was beginning to make sense of the situation. This unfathomable, almost enigmatic attraction that he felt for her, a woman so alien to the life he had led, was like a childhood memory coming back. For a reason unbeknownst to his conscious mind, but not to his heart, he felt the need to love and to protect her against the whole wide world. He'd had a taste of this emotion with the three women in his life: his sister, his mother and his ex-wife. Yet what he felt for Pembe was different from anything he had known before. She was his gateway to a world that, though more ambiguous and dangerous, also felt more real. It disturbed him enormously that it was an illicit love, but the possibility of losing her at any moment only added to his aching desire for her. She was the missing link in his life, the connection to his past, his ancestors, his Eastern side. Her love was one that made up for the lost pieces and the lost time.

Each time, shortly before the lights in the cinema came back on, they would move away from each other, and then go their separate ways. Thus they would never be seen together – or so they hoped.

She always strode out before him. He would linger behind, pacing inside the cinema, observing the posters on the walls, the litter on the floor, the sweets and the fizzy drinks, still thinking of the film, and of the light in her eyes, trying to get used to the emptiness she had left behind.

★★★

Shrewsbury Prison, 1991

In the middle of the night I wake with a start. It's dark in the cell except for the sickly yellow light creeping in from the corridor. They are supposed to have a calming effect on our nerves, these bulbs. Some shrink's idea. In fact, they make me want to puke.

The bed feels rough, like lying on blocks of cement. But that's not the reason why I've woken up at such an ungodly hour. Something is wrong, I can tell. I hold my breath and listen. The snoring, the farting, the moaning, the rustling, the clenching of teeth from the cells near by. People outside think that a prison is a terribly quiet place. It's not true. But tonight, despite the usual sounds, it feels strangely empty. Something is missing. Or else I'm losing my marbles.

My mother used to say that premonitions are God's whispers in a dark forest. From time to time, He would tell us to be careful, not to be friends with someone, not to push open certain doors, though we would never pay attention. But I'm not sure that's what's happening to me right now. A premonition is a sense that something bad is going to happen. What I feel is different. It's the kind of sorrow that hits you after something has already happened, and it's too late.

I prop myself up on my elbow, and prick up my ears. At first I suspect my mother's ghost has visited me, but I quickly realize she's not around tonight. My heart isn't pounding, which is what happens every time I sense her presence. No weird glow in one corner of the cell either, like freshly fallen snow. No soft rustling, as if from silk curtains. No scent of jasmine and rose. No smells of sesame halva. I'll never forget when that happened for the first time. It freaked me out like hell.

She used to visit me more often in the past. Then less and less frequently. Lately she doesn't appear at all any more. I dread that she'll never show up again. It's a stupid thought, but as long as she comes to see me there's a hope that she might forgive me.

At the beginning I was scared out of my wits. I couldn't go to sleep for fear that she would arrive in the midst of the night and strangle me. It took me a while to learn that ghosts don't do such things. You think they're after revenge. But they only want to understand. So they fix their empty gaze on you and wait for an explanation. They stare into your soul. They don't communicate. They don't ask. At least my mother doesn't. It's like a silent film, except in colour.

But tonight Mum hasn't dropped round. My alarm bells have nothing to do with her. What is it, then? I exhale. I inhale. Then I hold my breath. I listen, this time more carefully. Suddenly it hits me. Trippy isn't snoring. Nor is he twitching, tossing or talking in his sleep, which he always does, no matter how worn out or high. I get off my bed and approach him. His back is turned towards me. 'Trippy.'

No answer. He doesn't move. 'Patrick, you okay?'

I don't know why I call him by his real name, which I haven't done in years. But the word pops out. I fling the blanket off him. There is a foul smell. He looks strangely small, as if he has shrunk overnight. I shake him by the shoulders. He doesn't budge. I shake him harder. His feet dangle in a funny, clumsy way, like a broken puppet's. His arms are heavy, even though he is the skinniest bloke I know.

'Trippy, don't fuck about, mate! Stop it, man.'

I reach for his pulse. His neck is stiff and cold. 'Colder than a witch's tit,' he would say. There is no heartbeat. I prop his head against my arm and breathe into his mouth. The mouth that kissed his missus, and a few other women. The mouth that swore all the time, but also prayed. The mouth that ruined him, but was his saving grace. There is no reaction.

I start to laugh. Because it's ridiculous. The Angel of Death is either blind or has gone senile. Azrael should give up work. Doesn't God see that the henchman isn't doing his job properly? Why do the wrong people always die? I've been teaching Trippy how to use his fists. He was an awful student, slow on the uptake. But it was coming along. I've been making him hit me in the same place: on my abdomen. There are deadlier places on a man's body. Like the head, the neck, the Adam's apple, even the bridge of the nose. But if he hit me there it would look like a real brawl. Then Trippy would get in trouble. Punching me in the abdomen is less suspicious. Everyone knows I box for fun.

With the right force the abdomen is a fatal target. Internal bleeding. Pronounced dead in a few hours if left untreated. And there is no doubt in my mind that it would be left untreated.

Trippy didn't know all this, of course. It would be an accident. An inspector would come and scribble on his notepad. His secretary would type the report and leak it to the press. A tabloid would show interest: 'Honour-Killer Dies in Gaol'. Officer McLaughlin would cut out the clipping and place it in his file. They would talk about me, for a while. No one would feel sorrow. Then the case would be dropped. As clean as the plate from which a hungry man eats. Trippy would be off the hook and I would be gone. Free at last.

Houdini was just a reminder. Officer McLaughlin says there is no such thing, that it's just a cock-and-bull story, the magician didn't die of blows, as idiots like me tend to believe. But I don't care whether Houdini really died of this or that. Every time I see his poster I remember that it's possible to be punched to death. Then again, he reminds me of other things too. Sad things. It was because of Houdini that Uncle Tariq found out about my mother's lover and so did everyone else, including me.

I move Trippy to the side and sit next to him. Something cracks under me. I look to see what it is. I pick it up and start to chuckle again. 'You sad bastard.'

It's a syringe. When did he do that? Was it a mishap? Was it a golden shot? How is it that I didn't notice a thing? Did he wait until I had gone to sleep? I'm a log. I'm a bloody bag of shit. I sleep like a fat hedgehog in his winter nest. I'm disgusted at myself. I check the bed. The sheet is wet with pee, saliva and vomit. His body tried to flush out the poison. Then I notice Trippy's left fist, clenched hard, the joints on his fingers like spikes. I force the fingers open. There is a piece of paper. I approach the bars so that I can read it under the light from the corridor.

*Alex, brother. if you're reading this it means I've made the cut. You
wanted to go before me, didn't you? You prat. You think I didn't
know? But I was gonna help you. Honest to God I was. It's just I
couldn't take it no more. Don't get pissed off. I'll wait for you.
Whatever that is up there. I'll go and check it out. No more tricks.
No more Houdini. You were a good mate. When I see your ma I'm
gonna tell her that.*

Your friend Trippy

Tears roll down my cheeks. I slap my face. It doesn't help. I pull my
hair. With one hand, then with both. Harder. Harder. I can feel the skin
give way, the hair rip out. And all this time I'm making this sound like a
dog whimpering in the street. A car has hit me and run. My bones are
broken. Trippy has run over me.

I rise to my feet. My head is about to explode. Adrenalin is bringing
back a feeling I once knew well: anger. I thought I had left it at the
roadside. Two years ago I put it in a sack, tied it tight up and drowned it,
like an unwanted kitten. I promised myself to spend the rest of my life
trying, at least trying, to be a better man. But so much for trying. It's
found me again. It's followed me, sniffing its way back home. And here it
is, my old playmate Mr Anger. Loyal as ever.

I pull down the Houdini poster and rip it to pieces. I hurl my bed sheet
and blanket and pillow. I kick the walls, I pound the walls, I pounce upon
the walls, I hit my head against the walls.

Lights. Footsteps. Hassle. Someone enters the cell. 'What the hell?'

Others flock in. They push me to the floor, and keep my head down.
The lights are turned on. Too much light. My eyes hurt. Is that Officer
Andrew McLaughlin towering over me? What's he doing here? Night
shift? The man loves his job.

They're poking around, checking for Trippy's pulse. They find the
syringe. They see the note. One of them starts to read it aloud. Shit. I free
myself, catch them unawares. I jump to my feet. Before they know it I
seize the note.

'Hey . . .' a young screw exclaims, as if I have cheated in a game; and
he is pissed off.

Officer McLaughlin takes a step forward. 'Give me that.'

'It's mine.'

'Nothing is yours, you moron. Now give it to me.'

We stare at each other. Finally the moment has come. He can show me how much he hates me. And I can show him the feeling is mutual. No more pretending. No more fake attempts to be better men than we are. We are what we are. I put the note in my mouth.

'Oh, don't you even think about that,' Officer McLaughlin says. 'You've watched too many films, huh?'

I start to chew. Slowly. No need to hurry. They are all staring at me.

'Alex, you are gonna regret this so bad. I am giving you one last chance to save your arse. Stop it.'

Chew, chew, chew. Never knew paper tasted so chalky. I wonder if Trippy can see me. When we die do our souls leave our bodies right away and float up to the sky like a hot-air balloon? Or do they linger for a while? Did my mother's soul stay around and watch my hand pull out the knife that had stabbed her?

I swallow the note.

The first punch lands on my chin. I'm totally unprepared. My teeth bang against each other pretty hard. Officer McLaughlin knows where to hit. Not like poor Trippy. The other screws look away. They don't approve of it, I can see. They have wives, children. Good citizens. They want to sleep peacefully at night. Nobody wants blood on their hands. But they don't try to stop him either. Because that's the thing with bullies. Nobody says 'Enough!' to them. That's why bullies are who they are. And I should know, because I was, and still am, one of them.

★

My mother was a superstitious woman. In our house there were evil-eye beads everywhere. She put glass beads in my pockets, in my rucksack. Once I found one sewn into my leather jacket. We never whistled at night, never opened an umbrella indoors or trimmed our fingernails after sunset. Sometimes we wore our underwear inside out to ward off bad luck. At the dinner table we did not hand each other knives. Mum did everything in her power to protect me from others. But she forgot what was festering in me. Nothing can protect a man from what lies inside.

It was several weeks after my circumcision in Istanbul. The wound had healed, and I had started to play in the street again. It must have been autumn. I remember the trees shedding their leaves and the cakes of mud on the roads. There was a canal near our house. We never swam there. The water was fetid, smelly. People threw all sorts of things in it. Cans, bottles, boxes, plastics, leaflets with Communist propaganda. Once somebody found a gun on the bank.

On that day I was wandering along the canal, thinking about the gun. Who had owned it? A bank robber? Or an assassin? Had the police found him? I must have been completely absorbed in my thoughts. Otherwise I would have noticed them and changed my direction. Or hid behind a bush until they had gone. But instead I marched right into them. Three boys. A few years older than me.

'Look who's here? Little Red Riding Hood is out for a walk.'

'Iskender, where's your mama? She not with you?'

I shook my head.

'She's always calling you my sultan,' the first boy said. 'And all that Kurdish gibberish.'

'The Sultan of the Slums, he is!'

The first boy, who was standing in the middle and was obviously their leader, did not join in with the taunts. He was observing me. He looked concerned for me, even embarrassed by his friends' behaviour. I wrongly saw it as a sign, took a step towards him. My protector.

'Is it true you ran away from your circumcision?' the leader asked. 'You climbed a tree?'

I must have looked appalled. How did they know? Who had told them?

'Word gets around,' he said, as if he had read my mind.

'So what happened? Were you or were you not circumcised?'

'I was,' I said, and heard the weakness in my voice.

'He says he was,' the leader said. 'But can we trust him?'

They pushed me to the ground. They pulled down my trousers. I was shouting at the top of my voice.

'What is this? So small! Like an okra. No wonder he ran from his circumcision – a cut would have cost him a lot.'

'But he hasn't been properly circumcised,' said the leader. 'We should finish the job.'

Did he have a pocket-knife in his hand? Or was my mind playing tricks? I'm still not sure. All I remember is that I pissed myself.

'Oh, no. The sultan needs a good wash now,' said the leader.

They took off my trousers, and pants, and socks, and shoes. Then they threw them all into the canal. 'Go and fetch them. Or go home like this and let everyone see your okra.'

They left. But I didn't believe they were gone for good. I sat there, hugging my knees, rocking slowly, expecting them to come out from behind the bushes and attack me. I don't know how many hours went by. Darkness fell. It started to drizzle. I didn't mind.

My mother emerged from the shadows with two neighbours. She must have been looking for me everywhere. How did she know I was by the canal, the only place she had forbidden me to go on my own? She asked me nothing. She wrapped her shawl round me, took me home, washed me, combed my hair and put me into clean pyjamas.

'There,' she said. 'You look like a sultan again.'

Ten days later I had my own gang. Nothing spectacular. Just the five of us. But they were loyal to me to the bone. Gypsy kids nobody wanted to befriend. They were tough. They smoked. They collected everything: bottle caps, aluminium foil, aerosol cans. They didn't give a damn about anything.

We beat up two of the boys but didn't touch the leader. I wanted to make him sweat. Not knowing if or when I would strike. By then I had had my first serious quarrel with my father. The ram incident. I had promised myself never to be weak again and I was keeping my promise.

One Sunday morning our doorbell rang. My mother opened it. There was a woman at the door, weeping. She said the day before a gang of boys wearing masks had assaulted her son. They had thrown him into the filthy canal. He would have drowned were it not for a plank that had saved him. He didn't know how to swim. She said these boys, these gangsters, had forced her son to drink his own pee. She asked, and did not ask, whether my mother knew anything about it, because her son had not given her any names.

I heard Mum invite the woman into the kitchen, saying she was so sorry for her son. She offered her tea and a slice of cake. But the woman wanted none.

'Yesterday was my washing day,' Mum said. 'Iskender helped me take down the curtains and put them back afterwards. So you see, he was with me all day long. In case you were wondering, my son had nothing to do with this.'

'You're sure?'

'Absolutely.'

After the woman left, my mother walked into the living room, where I was sitting under the window, watching the shoes pass by. I expected her to tell me a thing or two. A slap on the wrist. A pinch on my ear, at least. But she only looked at me long and hard, and I think I saw a trace of pride in her eyes. Then she said, 'What would you like to eat for dinner, my sultan? Shall I make you lentil soup, the way you like it?'

We didn't talk about the boy I had assaulted. Neither then nor later.

Iskender Toprak

The Brave Fight

London, March 1978

Even before he arrived at the squat, Yunus knew something was wrong. As he approached the old building he noticed the windows on all three floors were boarded up with cartons, crates and corrugated boxes – some of which displayed anarchist symbols. The day before, the temperatures had dropped to below zero and now icicles dangled from the gutters like tears. There was a heavy silence in the air, an eerie tranquillity.

The night of Tobiko's birthday, the night he was carried home by the punks, Yunus had arrived home so late, and in such a state, that Pembe – by then crazy with worry and on the verge of ringing round the hospitals – grounded him for several weeks. Every morning she would walk him to school and every afternoon she would pick him up. But today she finally started to work her regular hours at the Crystal Scissors again and Yunus was once more a free agent. Though he had promised his mother to go home directly after school and though he never lied, Yunus found himself, almost against his will, pedalling towards the address he knew so well.

After parking his bicycle he lolloped up the narrow path to the house, careful not to slip. To his surprise, he found the entrance locked. In the many times he had been there he had never seen the door closed, let alone bolted from inside. The squatters always boasted that this was the only dwelling in London that needed no keys, no padlocks, because it was a house after all, and not a prison of private property like all the others.

There being no bell, Yunus knocked, first politely, but soon with growing alarm. Several minutes later he was pounding hard.

'Leave us alone!' somebody shouted from inside.

Yunus stopped, stunned. Could it be that the squatters did not want to see him any more? Was that why they had quarantined them-selves? Timidly but steadily, he started thumping again.

'Get away from us, you chauvinist!' roared someone else.

A female voice butted in, 'Fuck off! We're gonna fight!'

Now the boy was horrified. Much as he loved Tobiko, he was not ready to confront a houseful of seething squatters. His voice breaking, he shouted, 'But it's . . . it's me, Yunus here! May I please come in?'

There was a momentary lull, followed by a ripple of laughter. A few seconds later the door was pushed open a crack. A man stood at the entrance: he resembled Iggy Pop, as shirtless as the singer himself, exposing his bare, hairless chest. When he saw Yunus he beamed and hollered over his shoulder, 'False alarm, everyone! Coast is clear! It's the bairn!'

'Hello,' Yunus said. 'I was just cycling by and wanted to see how you lot were doing.'

'Never better! We're getting ready to kick some arse.'

'Whose arse?' Yunus asked quietly.

'Oh, the authorities,' Iggy Pop said in a fluster.

Authority – it was another one of those adult words Yunus had heard before but never quite understood. Once he had asked Tobiko what it meant, and in her urge to make a wisecrack she had told him, 'It is what fathers have in abundance, mothers never have, and boys like you are, by definition, denied until you're old enough.'

And a wide-eyed Yunus had asked, 'You mean it's a moustache?'

So when Iggy Pop uttered the same word, the boy had the impres-sion the squatters were getting ready to attack men with moustaches. Shell-shocked and unmoving, he stood there with a look of disbelief on his face.

Unaware of the boy's concerns, Iggy Pop poked his head out the door and glanced left and right to make sure there was no suspicious activity on the street. Then he yanked Yunus into the house, closed the door from behind, bolted it with a makeshift wooden bar, which was secured with nails and wire.

'What's going on?' Yunus asked, but the man had turned around and was already clomping up the stairs.

When the boy reached the second floor Yunus couldn't believe his eyes. All the squatters were gathered there, some making catapults out of thick rubber, some organizing truncheons, darts and blow-tubes, while others were preparing ammunition. Everyone seemed purposeful and intent, working feverishly under a cloud of agitation. The air was laced with the smoke of cigarettes, incense and weed. A pot of tea, or what seemed like it, sat on a small burner, puffing out steam with a low, tired whistle. To Yunus, even the pot was worked up into a frenzy.

The Captain was standing in the midst of the commotion, issuing commands like a Scout leader. It was the utter concentration on his weasel-like face that made the boy suspect there was an order to this chaos. One of the many things that crossed his mind at that moment was to get out of there immediately. But his need to see Tobiko out-weighed his discomfort. Where was she? Try as he might, he could not see her anywhere.

Yunus approached a punk – a youngish recruit with spiky hair and round glasses that magnified his eyes – whose nickname was Bogart.

'Hi there, what're you makin'?'

'Hello, Jonah! You want to give me a hand?'

Yunus shrugged. 'Okay, what do I need to do?'

'Pour this liquid into the bottles, is all.'

Thus the boy took the plastic funnel and began to fill wine bottles with turpentine, making Molotov cocktails. 'These smell funny,' Yunus remarked after a while. 'What're you goin' to do with them?'

'Hurl them at the authorities,' Bogart piped, matter-of-fact.

Yunus stiffened, a small twitch along his jawline. Why were the squatters so determined to hurl reeking bottles at men with mous-taches? And what could he do to spare his father? 'Are you going to attack all of the authorities?' he demanded.

'Nah! That's impossible. There are so many of them, bloody bas-tards. They breed like rats,' said Bogart, his prominent Adam's apple bobbing up and down. 'Damn them!'

'I'll be back,' Yunus said, as he rose to his feet. He had to do some thinking on his own.

In every room he entered Yunus found a similar uproar. It was no joke. The squatters were getting ready for a war. And then he saw her – Tobiko. She was sitting on a mat alone, her head bowed, eyes shut, deep in meditation. Yunus perched beside her, taking the opportunity to watch her unmistakable profile. Her black hair, her tattoos, her piercings. He tried to fathom how he, young and penniless as he was, could save her from the imminent battle.

'Is it you, wee one?' Tobiko asked in a low, beguiling voice.

Yunus felt himself reddening. 'How did you know?'

'I saw you coming, you twit.' Turning aside, she gave him a wink and a peck on the cheek. 'My, you look so serious. What's up, sweet?'

'I don't quite get what's going on here.'

'Oh, it's the council,' Tobiko said, her eyes glinting with scorn. 'They want to kick us out. Can you believe that? They sent an eviction notice that gave us a week to move out. That was nine days ago. We're expecting them at any moment, the bastards!'

'But why?'

'So that they can flog this property to fat cats like them.'

As it dawned on him that this had nothing to do with men who wore moustaches, Yunus felt relieved. Then he strained his ears, as though expecting to hear battering rams, police cars or ambulances surrounding the house. But there was only the wind out there – a sharp, chilly wind. Drawing in a slow breath, the boy inquired, 'Where will you go?'

'Nobody is going anywhere,' Tobiko remarked.

'But the house belongs to them, right?'

'No, it doesn't. Some houses are everyone's property. If you ask me, all houses ought to be like that.' Tobiko straightened her back, and continued in a voice as decided as her gaze. 'Their plan is to throw us out. And our plan is to fight back 'coz if you don't fight the system, you are the system.'

'Perhaps they'll change their minds,' Yunus offered. 'God is great.'

'God? God has another planet just like ours. There's another me there and another Jonah. They resemble us but they aren't us, because how could they be, when we're down here, right?'

The boy listened carefully but the words escaped him, like sand slipping through his fingers. He had never heard anyone question

Allah before, and for a reason he could not quite comprehend, he felt saddened. 'Mum says God loves us.'

'Love?' Tobiko choked, as if the word had stuck in her throat. 'Love is a fickle thing. Sorry to break the bad news: God has forgotten us.'

The boy's eyes grew small, then large again. He peered at his hands, mumbling something incomprehensible, as though reciting a prayer. Among the clutter of words and with some delay, Tobiko heard him say, like a distant echo, 'But I would never do that. I would never forget you.'

★

In the next hour the Captain drew the plan on a blackboard stolen from a school near by. Usually he was oddly sluggish, as if sedated, but as soon as he started his tirade he seemed to pulsate with energy. When the police raided the building, he said, they were all going to go up to the loft, where they had stored enough ammunition for a small army. The beds on the first floor and the tables on the second would be turned on their sides to be used as barricades. From behind the lines they would put up a fight so ferocious that the British media would be obliged to come and observe. As journalists sent pictures of resistance from the scene, young people around the world would question the brutality of Hackney Council. In the end the government, in its attempt to save face, would tell the council to back down, and the squatters would win the day.

'This is far out, man! This'll be our Paris Commune,' said Bogart, a lit joint dangling between his lips as he stood only a foot away from the Molotov cocktails.

'Well, the Commune ended pretty bloodily,' warned Iggy Pop.

Yunus knew that if the police raided the building at that moment and he was rounded up with the squatters, his mother would probably have a heart attack. He had to get out of there and he had to do it fast. If this was a war, it wasn't his war. Whatever the authority was, he didn't want to throw bottles and stones at it. Yet, feeling as he did, he still failed to move. Like a kitten in need of warmth, he stayed next to the woman he loved, preparing new ammunition, listening to revolutionary stories, eating hash popcorn and singing 'Rebel, Rebel'.

Fortunately for the boy, the clash that he feared did not take place that afternoon. It happened three days later, while Yunus was at school. Their preparations had been inadequate, and, though they put up a brave fight, in a matter of hours they were all arrested.

Most of the squatters would be released a day or two later, after a thorough-ish police check, and an ear bashing on proper manners and social conduct. The council, meanwhile, was swift to board up the house. The order to gut the house of everything inside wasn't long in coming.

The Amber Concubine

A Place near the River Euphrates, April 1978

Jamila swirled the pestle inside the mortar, grinding the saffron that was as red as a ruby. These were her last threads, and she didn't know when she would be able to get the next supply. Some other ingredients were also running low. Marjoram, tarragon, silverweed, devil's claw. She would have to make several trips to the mountains, including a visit to the smugglers. Yet lately she felt less and less like leaving her house, unless there was an emergency or a delivery, which amounted to the same thing, really.

All morning she had been in the cellar, working, contemplating. This was her sanctuary, her haven: this dim, dank, sixteen-by-fourteen-foot underground room with no windows and only a small trapdoor at the top of a set of steps. The entire place was lined with wooden shelves from floor to ceiling. On each shelf were jars, flasks, and bottles of various sizes and colours. Wild herbs, tree barks, fragrant oils, seeds, spices, minerals, snakeskins, animal horns, dried insects – hundreds of ingredients that she used for her potions and ointments. Four holes at different angles, narrower than the openings to mole tunnels, ventilated the hushed interior. Nonetheless, a distinct, earthy, pungent smell lingered in the air, although Jamila was no longer able to detect it. If a stranger went down there, however, he would become giddy, overwhelmed by the odour. But that wasn't likely to happen. No one else had ever been there, and no one else would ever be there in the future.

Each day, for the past fifteen years, Jamila had spent at least a good couple of hours in the cellar, preparing the concoctions that might be requested at a moment's notice with a knock on her door. She was the healer. The Virgin Midwife who spoke the language of birds, reptiles and insects. *A granddaughter of the Prophet Suleiman.* That's what the locals called her. That, too, was one reason why she had managed to survive on her own in the wilderness. They respected, feared and despised her. As a result, they left her alone. This woman who was no woman; a witch who paced the tightrope between two worlds.

When Jamila was in the cellar, she stepped outside of her body, becoming a conduit for an arcane energy that coursed through the universe, healing, mending, multiplying. There she gave birth to her own womb, and the womb expanded to cover the whole of the natural world around her, a cavern of warmth and compassion, in which she happily lost all sense of self. She could never tell whether it was night or day. Not that it mattered. She lived outside of the clock in a cycle of her own. Some days she worked there from dawn to dusk, preparing age-old recipes, experimenting with new ones. It never felt dull. Tiring yes, but not boring. Each flower, every mineral, held a divine secret implanted by God. People often missed the clues. They looked at mistletoe and saw a parasitic plant that grew on tree trunks, not the salve for blood circulation that it offered. Trust. That was what Jamila needed to achieve. When life forms trusted you, they yielded their secret. Not right away, but gradually. Then you knew which plant was right to heal which ailment. Everything in the universe, no matter how little or how insignificant, was meant to be an answer to something else. Where there was a problem, there was a solution, and often surprisingly near by. It was a matter of seeing. Jamila was a seer.

She was not interested in travelling to unfamiliar places, meeting strangers, discovering continents beyond the horizon. The world must be full of variety, but human beings were the same everywhere. It was enough watching the gas lamps in the hills below flickering at night. Allah had intended her to serve Him by unravelling the secrets of nature, so she believed it was her duty to stay where she was. She knew how to cure numerous illnesses, though there were a great many that were still a mystery. Underneath the long-sleeved, colourful gowns and ornamented vests that she wore, she always donned a *shalwar*, which helped her mount a horse when it was necessary. Night and day, she had to be ready for anything.

The locals had made up many stories about her. They said it must be the *djinn* who gave her the formulas for the remedies. Others believed she had sneaked into the Kaf Mountain. where no human beings were ever welcome, the abode of fairies, nymphs and sprites. Jamila shook her head in wonder when she heard such tall tales. In a region hungry for heroes, legends and miracles they expected her to embody all three. But Jamila knew she could only do what she could. Depending on the means of the person in need, she would haggle for her brews and balms, although often she gave them for free. With the little she earned she bought additional ingredients.

She also prepared poisons, though she would share those with fewer people. Poison was a gift from God. A divine blessing that often went unappreciated. You could see it as a curse or a cure, like almost all things in life. Nature was beyond good and bad. What could heal could make you sick. What could make you sick could heal. Jamila was convinced that the job of a poison-maker was no different from that of any other craftsman. Just like an artisan, she was responsible for the quality of her product and not for the way in which people made use of it. She sold poisons for field mice, shrews, rats, cockroaches and snakes. While she accepted that her products could be deadly, she always concluded that so was meat. Eating too much meat caused gout, an illness that could kill if it went untreated. But nobody stopped buying meat for that reason or went around arresting butchers.

Now, with her forehead glistening under the light from an oil lamp, Jamila put the mortar aside and took out a box. Small, square, mother of pearl. In it there was a stone. A most precious one. A diamond, as amber as honey, larger than a hazelnut. She held it between her fingers and inspected it. There were folks here in the valley who would slit one another's throats to have a gem this special. Fools! The diamond could never be possessed, only watched over. Every new proprietor was nothing but a temporary stopover on the diamond's extended journey. Jamila understood this and accepted it. The diamond was with her today, but tomorrow it could be elsewhere. In the meantime, Jamila used it to perfect her concoctions. Some stones exuded warmth, an inner light, and when she kept them inside a potion for a while, they yielded their soul, smoothing the edges, helping things to blend. She kept several jewels for this purpose, but the diamond was the best.

Since time immemorial the natives of Mesopotamia had called diamonds 'The Tears of Gods'. They believed they were made of the dust that fell from the stars above or from splinters that broke off from lightning bolts on stormy nights. Jamila had even heard some say that they were the crystallized drops of sweat shed every spring when Mother Earth and Father Sky made love. Wild imagination! People let their thoughts run amok when they came across things over which they had little control, as if by inventing stories they could make sense of all that was painfully confusing, including their brief stay in this world.

Compared to a diamond, human life was shorter than a summer rain. At the age of eighty, humans were old and frail, but a diamond was still considered an infant. Jamila guessed that between three and four hundred years must have passed since her stone had been mined, polished and faceted. Still young. It could live thousands of years, if not more.

When it came to greed for diamonds there wasn't much difference between the affluent and the poor, and really no end to it. He who had no prospect of owning a diamond coveted one. He who already had one yearned for more. Dishonesty, rapacity and cruelty – even at its young age, this diamond had already seen them all. It had a bloody history, like all rare diamonds. Merchants, wanderers, pilgrims, sailors, soldiers and spies had betrayed one another just to lay their hands on it. Maids had served their ladies with more respect, ladies had loved their husbands more devotedly, and husbands had felt more like a man with it under their roof. Ambiguities became certainties, flirtations developed into marriages, friends turned into foes, and foes turned into cohorts. Like a shaft of sunlight that reflected off pure white snow, the amber diamond rendered everything around it brighter, in the same way that sunlight seemed brighter when reflected off pure white snow; but it also carried darkness within. Jamila knew that a diamond of this splendour could exile a person from his own soul.

It was a gift from a *beg*. A man who was used to having people of all kinds bow in front of him, spreading terror and respect in equal measure. Jamila had saved his only son's life. Where doctors had seen no hope, she had toiled quietly, doggedly, bringing the boy back from Azrael's Kingdom, inch by inch, like pulling a sleigh out of broken ice. The first time the boy opened his eyes and spoke, the *beg* wept. Howled, in fact, like most men who were unused to crying did.

The *beg* offered her money. Jamila refused. Gold coins. A parcel of land. A honey-bee colony. A silk farm. Each time Jamila shook her head. She was about to walk away when he showed her the diamond. *The Amber Concubine*, he called it. She was drawn to it. Not to its worth but to the riddles it held inside. It was a stone of secrets, she could tell.

'They say it is cursed,' said the *beg*. 'It cannot be purchased, cannot be taken by force. It cannot be stolen. It can only be given from the heart, as a gift. That's how it came to me, and that's how I'm giving it to you.'

For a split second, Jamila felt as if she and the stone were connected in some deep and mysterious way beyond her understanding. Nonetheless, she declined. But the *beg* was a smart man. He understood that Jamila had been attracted by the gem and yet also repelled, worrying that if she had it with her, she would never be safe again. Part of the reason she had survived the attacks of thugs and robbers in the valley was because she had nothing worth stealing. The *beg* did not insist. But the same night he sent the diamond with a trusted messenger. Ever since then Jamila had played host to the Amber Concubine.

There were many odd things about human beings. They thought insects were disgusting but felt lucky when a ladybird landed on their fingers. They detested rats but loved squirrels. While they found vultures repulsive, they thought eagles impressive. They despised mosquitoes and flies, but were fond of fire-flies. Even though copper and iron were medicinally important, it was gold that they worshipped instead. They took no notice of the stones under their feet but went mad for polished gems.

It seemed to Jamila that in everything they did, human beings selected a few favourites to love and simply loathed the rest. Little did they understand that the things they disliked were just as essential for the Cycle of Life as the things they so treasured. In this world every creature was made to challenge, to change and to complete something else. A water mosquito was no less significant than a fire-fly, or brass than gold. That is how God, the Great Jeweller, had designed the universe.

A loud, sharp rap brought her attention back to her surroundings. Somebody was pounding on her door above. She jumped to her feet and put the diamond back into the box. How long had it been going on? She clambered up the stairs, her chest heaving. As soon as she lifted the trapdoor that opened into her living room, the clamour hit her like a slap.

'Open the door! Virgin Midwife, where are you?'

Putting her hands on two sides of the trapdoor, Jamila winched her body on to the upper floor. She closed the lid and pulled the carpet over it. Finally she grabbed her rifle. Thus prepared, she went to get the door.

She was surprised to see the smuggler whose wife she had attended the other day. The father of the one-and-a-half baby. She was about to ask how the baby was doing when she noticed the man behind him. He was carrying his companion on his back. Trails of blood. Thick, dark.

'Jamila . . . sister,' said the smuggler. 'You must help us.'

She understood. They had crossed the border into Syria, carrying goods. Tea, tobacco, silk, perhaps drugs. Things had not gone as they were supposed to. They had been ambushed. One of them had been shot. They could have left him there, but they hadn't. They had carried him all the way back. But the man had lost too much blood; his soul was already oozing away. She didn't need to take a closer look to know that he was dying.

'I'm afraid I can't help,' said Jamila. 'You need to go to a hospital.'

The smuggler sucked the ends of his moustache. He didn't look angry or upset, only impatient. 'You know we cannot take him there.'

Then, as if an agreement had been reached, they laid the wounded man on the sofa and left. Before he strode out, the smuggler said, 'If he dies, light a fire in your garden. We will see it and come back to bury him.'

★

His face was long and angular, his cheekbones high. Sullen-shouldered, gloomy of countenance, he was lanky, lean. Jamila tried to guess his age. He could have been in his late twenties but he could also have been past forty. With his cheeks drained of all colour and his fate creeping through his veins, he could have been of any age and no age at all.

She hoisted him up as gently as she could and put a pillow under his head, which felt oddly heavy and light at the same time. He made a throttled sound, muffled and inhuman, as if there were a lump in his chest, another bullet stuck in his throat. A trickle of blood seeped out of his nostril. Jamila had witnessed many hardships before and overcome quite a number of them, but nothing in her life had prepared her for the dread she felt now.

It would be kinder to kill him. A horse with a broken leg deserved to die with dignity. For him, a draught of hemlock would be enough. Good old plant. It was astonishing how many people mistook it for fennel and took their last breath without knowing why. The villagers called it 'Sheitan's Breath' but Jamila had a better name for it: 'Purple Haze'. If only she could make the man swallow the right amount, he would tumble into a lavender slumber, a final dream. Twice in her life she had come close to killing herself: after being brought back to her father by her kidnappers, still a virgin but for ever tainted; and on the day she learned Adem had asked for Pembe's hand. Each time, her determination to carry on, her fear of hell or simply the need to see the sun rise the next morning had compelled her to stay alive.

Jamila straightened her shoulders, determined not to permit herself to brood, strong as the urge was. She focused on the man's wounds. Deftly, she cut away his clothes, fully stripping him. The thinness of his body almost made her cry – the grime, the vulnerability, the bones sticking out. He had three major wounds: one in his leg, one in his shoulder, but it was the third that was critical. Close to the spine. Whoever had shot him had done so from behind.

Working the entire afternoon, the patient twice fainting from pain, Jamila took out two and a half bullets. The third, below his right knee, had shattered. She saw no reason to go too deep. If he survived this hell he could live with that much. She knew he would never be the same again. Like stones and diamonds, bullets, too, passed their soul into the bodies that they touched.

Long after the glow of sunset retreated from the skies, she dozed off in a chair by his side, her neck gone stiff. Tonight, like the night before, there was a bad feeling in her chest, knocking the air out of her.

It was his moaning that woke her up, his mouth closing and opening, like a fish out of the sea. She dabbed a handkerchief in water and wet his parched lips.

'More, please!'

'I'm sorry,' she said tenderly. 'This is all you can have now. I'll give you more later, I promise.'

He swore at her, slurring the words. His fever was high. He floated in and out of consciousness. She wondered if he was a decent man. Did it matter? Wouldn't she have tried to save him regardless? He must be married with children. If he died now, would anyone miss him?

Slowly, Jamila moved the carpet aside and opened the trapdoor. She had work to do in the cellar, a potion to prepare, this time for herself, something to help her restlessness. She stole a glance at the patient in bed. He wouldn't wake up for several hours. She pulled herself into the opening, and, once she had balanced her weight on the stairs, pulled the lid closed, holding it on her fingertips. There was no way she could put the carpet back, but at least the cover would remain closed. The man, if he woke up, would assume that she had gone out to cut wood. She let go. The lid sat back on its hinges with a thud.

Just at that moment, the smuggler opened his eyes. Through his blurred vision he surveyed the hut, his gaze moving from the neatly stacked woodpile to the rifle on the wall, until it finally came to rest on the trapdoor. An impenetrable look came over his features before he drifted back into a painful slumber.

Esma

London, April 1978

I closed the door and took a deep breath. It had become a habit lately, these midnight escapes. I locked myself in the bathroom after everyone went to sleep. I lit a candle, watching my face change with every flicker of the flame. I was not interested in observing the fifteen-year-old that I was. Instead I wanted to find out what was beneath the surface, connect with that other self I had yet to discover.

Most of the girls I knew had their own bedrooms and could keep their doors closed as they pleased. Not me. If I were to lock the door of the room I shared with my younger brother, my family would fear something terrible had happened to me. That is why I loved the bathroom – the only place where I could be alone with my thoughts and my body.

I took off my sweater and the flesh-coloured bra I hated with a vengeance. My breasts were pointy, with thin, blue veins, which I found repulsive. Two burdens to carry, as if I didn't have enough already. Just this morning one of the boys in my class had attempted to touch them, pretending to get a book from a shelf behind me. Noticing his intentions I was able to dodge him at the last minute. Right away, I heard a group of boys snigger. They had planned this together. They had talked about it. About *my* breasts. I felt sick.

Outside the rain was falling on Lavender Grove. As I looked from the window back to the mirror, I wondered, for the umpteenth time, what I would look like had I been born a boy instead. Grabbing a nut-brown eye pencil, I first thickened, then joined, my eyebrows. Next I began to draw a moustache above my lips. Not a thin, wispy bristle, but a big, bushy thing, curling over upwards. If Iskender saw me now, he would have shaken his head and said, 'Sis, you're off your trolley!' At times I felt like the odd one out, as if there had been a mistake in the celestial records that had caused me to end up here in this setting. I was struggling with being a Toprak while my true destiny awaited me elsewhere.

'Hello, this is my sister. She only likes losers,' Iskender said whenever he introduced me to someone, especially to a boy.

It never failed. The boy would then stay away from me. Not that I cared. Strange as it sounded when Iskender put it like that, he had a point. I found myself fatally drawn to the downtrodden, to the underdog. Even when I watched a football match, I so wanted the score to be a draw that I ended up supporting the losing team. The thought of how terrible the players must be feeling at that moment, crushed under the weight of their fans' disappointment and woe, was enough for my heart to go out to them.

'You side with snails. That's the problem,' Mum said. She believed there were two types of people in this world: the frog-allies and the snail-allies.

In the village where Mum had lived as a girl, the children used to catch frogs from a nearby stream. One day they captured the largest frog anyone had ever set eyes on. Someone brought a bowl from home and turned it over on the ugly animal, where it sat paralysed with fear. All day long kids came and tapped on the glass, leaning closer to see the frog better, excited and disgusted by its bulging eyes and scabby skin. Then one of the boys produced a snail out of his pocket and placed it under the overturned bowl. The frog immediately forgot about its distress, concentrating on its prey. In the meantime, the snail was inching its way along, hoping to break free of its prison, unaware of the danger. The frog leaped once, then twice, and caught the snail. Under the eyes of a dozen screaming kids, the frog ate the snail, a sticky, gluey slime oozing out of its mouth.

My mother said that that day all the children had backed the frog, clapping, cheering. 'But if you had been there, I bet you would have sided with the snail. Sometimes I worry about you.'

It was fine with me to be in the snail's camp – as long as I didn't have to keep up with those who lived at high speed, like some of the girls in my class. Our school was polarized. There were those like me, the *swots*, who ranged from ugly to ordinary at best, worked towards their O-levels and never got much attention save from the teachers. Then there were the *slags*. They couldn't care less about their classes and were so eager for their life to start that they didn't see the need to waste another minute on their education. The prettiest among them were the *Barbies*.

I would observe the Barbies, study their ways, as if dissecting a new species in biology class. They talked about nothing but boys, sharing meticulous information about which bloke fancied which girl. They kept detailed records of who went out with whom, curious as to whether they had done *it* yet, and, if so, how many times, and whether the bulge in so-and-so's belly was because she was pregnant, and whether she would have the baby or put it up for adoption. They constantly fell in and out of love, romantically and frantically, experiencing every single day as an emotional rollercoaster that left longing in their eyes and juicy gossip on their tongues.

Their favourite pastime was shopping en masse. At times their mothers or elder sisters took them to department stores to buy lingerie. While the former tried to convince them to get sports bras, they chose lacey ones – sexy and dainty. The next day at school they showed them to each other in the loo, peppering their conversation with exclamations. If something was good, it was 'brill' or 'ace' Otherwise, it was 'rubbish'. The same terms were applied to food, clothes, teachers, parents, even countries and world affairs.

The Barbies occasionally complained about their periods to their close and not-so-close friends, to their boyfriends, to their mothers, and some to their fathers – the thought of which was enough to make me flinch. I wondered, and it was almost a scientific inquiry, how these things could differ so much from one culture to another, let alone from one household to another. If I had spoken about my periods to my mother, she would have turned red with shame. Then she would have lectured me with words borrowed from Grandma Naze.

Would things have been otherwise had I attended the local school with other neighbourhood children? If the names of my classmates had been Aisha, Farah or Zeineb, instead of Tracey, Debbie or Clare, would I have fitted in more easily? Perhaps, but I didn't think so. I knew it looked pathetic, but the truth was I preferred doing homework or reading a good book to hanging around with my peers. Still, I was proud of my achievement, thanks to my primary-school teacher Mrs Powell. Poor woman! The gossip was that her only son had been excluded from school and had moved out of the family home, she knew not where. In her distress Mrs Powell had dedicated herself to helping children from disadvantaged backgrounds find their feet. I was one of them.

Pleased with my moustache, I set out to draw a goatee on my chin. Yes, it was Mrs Powell who had come to our house and talked to my parents, convincing them to send me to a better school. Not a private school, but a grammar. *After years of experience I can recognize a special child from miles away. In my professional opinion, Mr and Mrs Toprak, your daughter is able and talented.* Mrs Powell had also spoken to the governors of the new school – predominantly white, Christian, English, middle class – and, whatever it was she had told them, it worked. Though a snail by heart, I had made a frog's leap.

I wanted to be a writer, but not a female one. I had even decided on my pen-name. John Blake Ono – an amalgam that consisted of the names of my three favourite personalities, a poet, a writer and a performance artist: John Keats, William Blake and Yoko Ono.

I often wondered why female names were so different from male names, more whimsical and dreamlike, as if women were unreal, a figment of one's imagination. Male names embodied power, ability and authority, like Muzaffer, 'the Victorious One'; Faruq, 'One Who Distinguishes Truth from Falsehood'; or Husam al Din, 'the Sword of Faith'. Female names, however, reflected a delicate daintiness, like a porcelain vase. With names such as Nilüfer, 'Lotus Flower', or Gülseren, 'Spreading Roses', or Binnaz, 'A Thousand Blandishments', women were decorations for this world, pretty trimmings on the side, but not too essential.

J. B. Ono. A name for booksellers to mention in reverent tones. A bit mysterious and surely androgynous. A name in no need of a bra.

★

Having finished painting the goatee, I inspected my face. It was no use. Even when disguised as a man I was not much to look at. If only I had my father's slimness and my mother's eyes – green, large and slightly slanted. Instead I had all the wrong features combined, including my mother's short neck and my father's ordinary eyes. My nose was bulbous, my hair so curly it refused to be brushed down, and my forehead too wide. I had a mole on my chin, an ugly brown bump. Many times I had asked Mum to take me to a doctor to have it removed, but it was one of those things she never paid attention to. She was a beautiful woman – everyone said so. And my brothers were good-looking. It was unfair that in between the two sons, the beauty gene had gone on holiday, skipping me.

Yunus had an angelic face, although the glow of childhood was beginning to wear off. Iskender, too, was handsome, but in a different way. His was the sort of appeal that was smouldering and mean – *dirty gorgeous*, as the Barbies would say. I was aware that a number of my classmates fancied my dishy brother and that they had befriended me only for that reason. Iskender sometimes came to pick me up from school, sending tough-guy glances left and right that, to my wonderment, always worked.

'Wouldn't say no to that!' the girls whispered.

'He looks so like Michael Corleone in *The Godfather*. All he needs is a gun!'

'When was the last time you had an eye examination?' I grumbled, unable to see any resemblance between Iskender and Al Pacino. But even if they heard the sarcasm in my voice, they didn't pay any attention to me. They found my brother *irresistibly masculine*.

Since our father had moved out, Iskender had changed a lot – full of himself, crabby, peevish. Always hanging with his mates, and that needy girlfriend of his. Hitting his punch bag day and night, as if the world was teeming with invisible enemies. If this was what they called teenage angst, I didn't think I wanted to grow up.

We had been very close, me and my mother, but all that changed the moment my breasts started to bud and I had my first period. The only thing she was interested in now was my *virginity*. She was always preaching about the things I should never/ever/not even in my wildest dreams do. Not once had she told me about what was possible and permissible; her powers of communication were reserved solely for rules and prohibitions. My mother warned me about boys, saying they were after one thing and one thing only. At this age most boys were selfish, and pushy, and many would never grow out of it. Yet she didn't impose the same rules on my brothers. Yunus was still too little, perhaps, but with Iskender she was totally different, open. Iskender didn't need to be careful. He could just be himself. No holds barred.

What Mum didn't understand was that I was not the least bit interested in boys. I found them boring, shallow, *hormonal*. Had she not talked about the subject day and night, I wouldn't have given sex a second thought. After all, snails were hermaphrodites, having both female and male reproductive organs. Why couldn't human beings be like that? If only God had modelled us on snails, there would be less heartbreak and agony in this world.

Heart of Glass

A Place near the River Euphrates, April 1978

The patient in the bed was burning up. Jamila checked his temperature by putting her lips to his forehead, the way she did with babies. She laid a gentle hand on his wrist, taking his pulse. It was both weak and rapid. Heartbeats were like drums heard from afar, like sounds of war. The human body was a mystery. It loved to fight. Though most people didn't realize this, the body was a warrior, and far more resilient than the soul. But, like all great warriors, it had an unexpected weakness. It was frightened of the unknown. It needed to understand its enemy so as to be able to resist, strike, deter and pulverize it. If it didn't recognize what it was fighting against, it couldn't prevail. That was where Jamila came in. Since time had begun, healers like her helped patients to regain their strength so that they could get to know their illness. She didn't cure them so much as enable them to cure themselves.

As she soaked a towel in distilled vinegar and placed it upon the smuggler's forehead, Jamila couldn't help but wonder, with the briefest of hesitations, what kind of a man she was nursing. There was no question in her mind that everyone deserved to live, but did everyone deserve to be brought back from death? It was a dilemma she contemplated every so often, arriving at no definitive conclusion. Were human beings born virtuous, and then grow to be corrupt? Or were they furnished with the seeds of vice even at the time of their conception? The Qur'an said we were all created from *a clot of blood*. How much of our present selves had been implanted in that droplet, Jamila wanted to know. A pearl, though pure and perfect, grew out of a speck of dirt that had penetrated the oyster shell by coincidence, if indeed there was such a thing. Even a bad seed could change into something exquisite. Yet there were also times when a smidgen of evil generated only more of the same. Some of the babies she had brought into this world would turn into swindlers, liars, thieves, rapists, even killers. If she possessed a way to predict how each and every child would develop, would she choose not to deliver some of them? Could she leave an infant in his mother's womb, comfortably entombed, so as to prevent him from bringing woe and misery into the world?

Each time she took a newborn into her arms, Jamila admired its little toes, the rosebud mouth, the button nose, and felt confident that nothing but good could come from a creature this perfect. But every now and then she also sensed that some babies were different. Right from the beginning. Not necessarily more insensitive or spiteful, but different. The mothers, too, might have detected this, had their intuition not been screened by a curtain of love. Not her, though. Jamila could *see* things. She just didn't know what to do with them afterwards.

Hard though it was to believe, there had been midwives who had killed the babies they had brought into this world. That was how the story of Abraham went – the story Jamila and Pembe had heard from their father.

One sunny day Berzo had taken his eight daughters to visit a consecrated pool in Urfa. Naze was about to give birth again, despite her age, and the family had gone there to pray for a son. The clouds were buffeting across the vast, generous sky. People were everywhere, a soft murmur of voices, like the faint rustling of leaves. Overwhelmed by everything they saw, the girls huddled together, timid but thrilled. They fed the fish. On the way back their father had told them the legend behind the place. Berzo was a different man on that day, his eyes not yet hard, his smile genuine. It was before everything had gone terribly wrong.

King Nimrod was a man of endless ambitions and cruelties. One day, his chief stargazer informed him that when a boy named Abraham was born his reign would come to an end. Not ready to let go of the throne, Nimrod ordered all the midwives in his empire to murder every newborn boy. Rich or poor, there would be no exceptions. Thus the midwives set to work. They first helped mothers to deliver babies, and if they turned out to be boys, then and there, they would strangle them. But Abraham's mother managed to escape the brutality. She gave birth on her own, in a cave in the mountains – dark, damp but otherwise safe.

When Abraham came of age he stood up against the cruelty of Nimrod. The patriarch was infuriated. He instructed everyone, old and young, to gather driftwood for a bonfire so huge that it would go on burning for days on end. Then he had Abraham thrust into the flames. But a while later the prophet walked out of the fire, unhurt except for a strand of his hair that had turned white. In an instant, God had turned the flames into water and the red-hot embers of wood into fish. Thus was born the sacred pool of Urfa.

Despite everything, Jamila didn't resent her life. After Pembe and Adem got married, she convinced her father to let her remain single and assist the midwives in the region. He had agreed, thinking it was a temporary wish. She had persevered. Today her only regret was not being able to become a doctor. If the circumstances had been different, that would have been her aim. To work in a large, clean hospital and wear a white coat with a tag that said 'Doctor Jamila Yeter'. *Doctor Enough Beauty*.

*

Leaning a little closer, Jamila cut two onions into thick slices and placed the rings under the patient's feet, wrapping them with linen scarves. While the onions drew the fever from the head towards the lower parts of the body, she kept changing the wet towel on his brow every few minutes and did what she always did when there was nothing else to do: she prayed. By midnight the smuggler's temperature had dropped. Satisfied, Jamila fell asleep on the chair, tumbling into a disturbing dream.

She was in a city on fire, alone and heavily pregnant. She had to find a place to give birth but everywhere she turned there was turmoil. Buildings came crumbling down, people dashed left and right, dogs howled in fright. In the midst of the commotion Jamila saw a huge bed with thick carved posts and silky pillows. She lay there and gave birth to a baby girl. Someone inquired as to her daughter's name, and she said, 'I shall call her Pembe after my dead twin.'

Jamila woke up, her heart racing. She checked the smuggler's temperature. It was now nearly back to normal. He had made it. Outside, the day had broken. Rubbing her aching limbs, Jamila downed a glass of cold water and tried not to think about the dream. Quietly, she lit the stove and started to prepare breakfast. She heated a chunk of butter and cracked three eggs, adding a pinch of salt and some rosemary. Cooking had never been her strength. Mostly she was content with simple dishes, and, as she had no one to care for, she had never felt the need to refine her culinary skills.

'That smells good. What are you making?'

Jamila flinched, turning back. The smuggler was sitting up in bed, his hair unkempt, his stubble gold and brown. She said, 'Oh, it's just eggs.'

He gave a grunt that might have been appreciation and might not. 'And who on earth are you?'

'I'm Jamila, the midwife.'

His expression grew reproachful. 'Why am I here?'

'You were shot. It's a miracle that you survived. You've been here for a week now. Here, have some tea.'

He took a sip and spat it out. 'Yuck! What's this? It tastes like horse piss.'

'It's a cure,' she said, trying not to feel offended. 'You'd better drink it, and you'd better not spit in my house.'

'Sorry,' he said in a coarse whisper. 'I guess I have to thank you for saving my life.'

'You should thank Allah, He's the one who saves lives.'

He pulled a face at the thought, and was silent for a while. 'Hey, midwife, do you have a cigarette?'

'You shouldn't smoke,' Jamila said.

'Please,' he said. 'Only a puff.'

Struggling through a range of emotions, Jamila produced a pouch of tobacco and some papers. As she began to roll a cigarette, he observed her hands, rough, red and chapped, sore from being washed thousands of times in cold water, the palms callused from chopping wood.

'You're a strange woman,' he said.

'So they say.'

'How can you live here on your own? You need a man to protect you.'

'Does your wife have a man to protect her now? I bet she's as lonely as I am. Some women are married and alone. Some, like me, are merely alone.'

The smuggler grinned, a half-humorous glint in his eyes. 'I can marry you. My wife wouldn't mind. She'd be happy to have company.'

Jamila lit the cigarette, took a drag and blew out the smoke. She passed it to him, unwillingly, ignoring his hand brushing her fingertips ever so slightly. 'That's very generous of you, but I'm happy the way I am.'

He gave her a judgemental look but made no comment. Then he spoke again, smoke streaming out of his nostrils, his voice trailing off, 'There were four of us crossing the border. Did they tell you what happened to the other man?'

Jamila shook her head, not sure she wanted to hear this.

'He stepped on a landmine. That's the worst, believe me. I'm not afraid of being shot or going to prison, only of landmines. It won't happen to me, though. I'll be buried intact. All my organs with me. No missing parts.' Not knowing how to respond, she asked, 'Do you have any children?'

'Three boys. One more on the way. He'll be a boy, *inshallah*.'

'Any daughters?'

'Yeah, four of them.' He bent forward, coughing up phlegm, his face twisted in pain. 'I must go back. They need me.'

'Well, they need you strong and healthy, not weak and wounded. You should get some rest first. Then you may leave.'

'I've heard people talking about you. They say you have a *djinni* husband who visits you on moonless nights. He's the one who provides you with the secret cures, right?'

Jamila took out a round copper tray from the cupboard, on which she placed flat bread, tea and the pan with the sizzling eggs. Carefully, she carried it to him. 'A *djinni* husband . . .' She smiled despite herself. 'I'm afraid I'm just an ordinary human being, and my life is more boring than you think.'

As soon as she uttered these words she regretted them. It was better for her if the man thought she was an extraordinary creature, a woman like no other. She should not show him, or anyone else, her imperfections, her vulnerability, her humanness. If they knew you carried a heart of glass, they would break it.

A Boy Made of Wax

London, May 1978

On the day the squatters were arrested, Tobiko, too, was taken into custody, but, unlike the others, she vanished shortly after being released. No one knew where she had gone. Worried, Yunus knocked on the door next to the squat. An old man opened it a crack and peeped from behind the security chain.

'Sorry to disturb you, sir. I'm looking for my friend, a girl with black hair and tattoos. She used to live in the house over there.'

'You mean where all the loonies live?'

'Uh-hmmm,' Yunus said hesitantly.

'Don't know any girl with black hair and tattoos. I hope they've bloody gone for good,' he said. 'And good riddance too.' The door was slammed shut.

Yunus decided to search the town on his own. Pedalling his bicycle along street after street, running after every woman who even remotely resembled Tobiko, he looked round markets and supermarkets, launderettes and off-licences, but he still couldn't find her.

So on that day in early May when he turned the corner of Kingsland Road, just steps away from the Rio Cinema, his mind everywhere and nowhere, it was Tobiko he was hoping to find. His drowsy eyes fell upon a couple who were standing in front of a flower stall, their backs turned to him, choosing a pot of flowers. He didn't know what it was about the couple that drew him in, but somehow he couldn't take his eyes off them.

The man reached out and touched her wrist, caressing lightly, lovingly. Her slender body was tilted into him, as if at any moment she would put her head on his shoulder. Suddenly, Yunus felt an uncanny discomfort in his gut, a rushing in his ears. The familiarity of the woman's chestnut hair, the jade dress with capped sleeves and golden buttons, the shape of her waist and the gentle, graceful sweep of her arm . . . The boy's heart fluttered. His face went ashen, his lips became taut.

The man pulled the woman towards him and whispered something in her ear, touching her neck with his lips, a quick, short brush, perhaps an accident, innocent and unintended, a bashful exchange, after which she half turned and smiled, exposing a dimple in her right cheek.

Mum.

The boy turned his bike around, pedalling fast. Under the layer of shock and panic that had fallen upon him, he was thinking, or some part of his brain was thinking, that he had never seen his mother like this before. The woman he had just watched was Mum, and yet so unlike her. There was an aura of happiness about her, as bright as the flowers she was buying.

That evening Yunus came home looking like a boy made of wax — pale, insipid. Iskender and Esma teased him no end, saying he resembled one of the figures in Madame Tussauds. Pembe was worried that he might have stomach flu and tried to make him drink peppermint tea. But Yunus rejected their pleasantries, ignored the banter and insisted on going to sleep early.

That night he wet his bed.

Haroun the Smuggler

A Place near the River Euphrates, May 1978

That day, late in the afternoon, Jamila went out to collect some wood. On the way back she sat on a rock, brooding. Tucked into her belt was a letter, which she took out and stared at through empty eyes, as though she had forgotten what it was. But, unlike the monsters in her dreams, the paper was real. It was as real as the mountains that surrounded her and just as portentous. She began to read it again.

Jamila my dear sister,

Throughout all these years I must have sent you hundreds of letters. There were good days and bad days. But this has been the most difficult letter to write. Sister, I've met someone. Please don't frown. Please don't judge me. Give me a chance to explain, though I'm not sure I understand it myself. I cannot confide in anyone but you. Nobody knows. I'm scared witless. But I'm also full of joy and hope. How can this be?

All this time I was convinced that my heart was dry. Like a piece of leather left in the sun for too long. Incapable of loving anyone, except you and my children. But never a man, I believed. When I met him, it was as if I had always known him. I couldn't put a word to this feeling. I tried hard to keep him out of my mind. I failed.

He's a cook. Like you, he knows the language of herbs and spices. Outside on the streets of London the young demonstrate. Everybody is furious at something, but not him. He says only patient people can cook. He is a man of many lands and many names, but no native soil. Perhaps he carries his hometown on his back, like an ageless turtle.

I know you must be appalled. I know what you're going to tell me: it's shaming. Mama's ghost will haunt me for ever. Papa's too. 'I'd rather see the corpse of a daughter of mine in the Euphrates than have her bring me disgrace.' That's what he said after Hediye ran away, remember?

Tell me, if you teach someone the alphabet, how can you stop him from reading? When one has tasted the elixir of love, how can she not thirst for it? Once you have seen yourself through your beloved's eyes, you're not the same person any longer. I was blind all this time, and now that my eyes are open, I'm afraid of the light. But I don't want to live like a mole. Not any more.

My dear, do not forgive me if you don't find it in your heart to do so. But please love me. Now and always. I'll do the same too. For ever and ever . . .

Your adoring twin, Pembe

She must be drained, Jamila deduced. There was something debilitating about love, an obscure force that robbed you of your senses and strength. Adem might not care, but everyone else would rush to malign Pembe – friends and neighbours, relatives both here and there. Even if she managed to get an easy divorce, would this cook agree to marry her soon enough to silence the rumours – this man with a portable homeland, no sense of the past? He was an outsider, a Christian in all likelihood, which made matters worse. The more Jamila thought about it, the more she realized the impossibility of it all. She needed to get her sister out of London, out of harm's way. She had to protect Pembe from gossip and slander, and, if need be, from herself.

Thoughts racing through her mind, she reached her hut and walked in with a batch of dry sticks on her back. She put down her load by the fireplace, taking quick breaths. Out of the corner of her eye she noticed that the smuggler had left the sofa, after several weeks in her care, finally able to stand on his feet. She turned halfway towards him, smiling. That was when she noticed the rifle in his hand.

'You strike me as being a secretive woman,' he said, pointing the weapon at her. 'What are you hiding, I wonder.'

'How can I have anything? I'm a midwife. I'm not even paid money.'

For a fleeting moment he seemed convinced, but then he said, 'Well, we'll see. Take me to the cellar first.'

'What?' Jamila faltered. *How did he know about the cellar?* 'But there's nothing there. Just old trinkets.'

'Old trinkets are good,' he said. The veins on his temples were swollen, his eyes bloodshot. 'Come on, show me the way.'

Her body, unused to receiving orders from anyone, grew taut, resistant.

'Move or I'll blow your head off and feed you to the dogs,' he hissed. 'Then I'll go to the cellar all the same.'

She slid the carpet aside, opened the trapdoor and took a step back so he could see what was down below.

'No,' he said. 'We're going together. You first. But wait . . .'

He threw her a rope and made her tie her hands together in the front, loose enough for her to be able to use them, but so tight that she wouldn't be able to open the knot easily.

'I can't climb down like this.'

'Oh, you're a smart woman. You'll figure it out.'

Balancing her weight with great difficulty, grasping the highest rung, Jamila inched her way down the ladder, step by step. He followed. She could sense he was in pain, his wounds still sore. Yet his greed was stronger.

'Ugh, what's this stink?' he said, bending forward as if about to retch.

For the first time in many years Jamila noticed the smell – spicy and tangy, all pervasive.

'Well, well, what have you made yourself here?' he exclaimed, looking around. He took a jar of mustard seeds and shook it suspiciously. 'I knew it. You're a witch. So tell me what treasures are you hiding?'

'Nothing. Herbs and medicines, as you can see. I prepare potions. One of them has healed you, remember?'

'I thought you said only Allah could heal,' he retorted. 'And, you know what, you were right. It was none other than God. He always saves me. Men who haven't gone through half of what I have are dead. In their graves. But I'm alive. I always survive.'

He jabbed at her with the end of the rifle. She lost her balance, almost falling. 'I'm curious about how you taste,' he said, as he took a step closer and eyed her hips, her breasts. 'So you've never known a man. Poor thing. Maybe after this I should give you a ride, *Virgin Midwife.*'

Half turning his back to her, he started to search the table. He poured out the contents of bottles, sniffed at jars, emptied containers and smashed a few things carelessly. Jamila's mind was spinning. The Amber Concubine was there on the shelf, in its mother-of-pearl box. 'Let's go upstairs,' she said, her voice tense with the effort of concealing her unease.

'What's upstairs?'

'I'll cook for you, I'll wash your feet.'

The words cut the air like a knife. The smuggler stopped, his eyes searching. 'Do you think I'm stupid?'

She panicked. 'No, of course not. You're a clever man.'

'Why are you buttering me up? Why the change of heart? You should be hating me,' he said and then added, 'Where are you looking?'

Jamila realized her mistake. In her confusion, she had been glancing repeatedly towards the shelves behind him. His eyes followed hers. It didn't take him long to find the box. 'O-hhh, you filthy sorceress! Look at this beauty! It must be worth a fortune. Where did you steal this from?'

'It was a gift,' Jamila replied wearily.

'Oh, yes? You expect me to believe that?' he asked, as he pocketed the diamond. 'Come on, turn around. We're going up now. You first. And no tricks.'

As soon as Jamila made a move towards the stairs, he knocked her down with the end of his rifle. She lurched forward, her forehead hitting the iron rung, her body no longer hers, the world the colour of blood.

Hours later she woke up. Her head was spinning, her stomach churning, and the pain in her temples so excruciating she didn't dare to open her eyes. For a few minutes she moaned on the floor like a blind kitten. Then slowly, very slowly, she stood up, waiting for her eyes to adjust to the dimness.

She found a blade and cut the rope around her wrists. The entire cellar was in disarray, as if it had been plundered by an army. She saw the mother-of-pearl box on the table. She hadn't had a chance to tell the smuggler about the legend. The diamond was cursed. It could only be given or received as a gift. It could not be confiscated, it could not be taken by force and it could not be sold.

She climbed up, wincing with every step. When she reached the upper floor, she saw that the main door was open, the valley silent, airless. Suddenly everything seemed intimidating. The land that had nurtured and protected her all these years now teemed with scorpions, snakes, poisonous plants, vicious intruders . . . traps that God had set for her. She started to cry, listening to herself wail as if overhearing a stranger, sobbing hard the way someone would who had forgotten how to cry and was only now beginning to remember. The rest of the day passed by agonizingly slowly. She didn't venture out. She didn't pray. She didn't eat. Nursing a cup of water on her lap, she sat on the sofa, numb to everything.

Then she heard sounds. Men. Horses. Dogs. She wiped her eyes with the palms of her hands, the calluses on her fingers hard against her skin. He must be coming back with his friends, she thought. What else could he want? Her body? Her life? She couldn't find her rifle. He had taken that too. She grabbed a dagger but her hands were trembling so hard she knew she'd never have the strength to use it. So she put it back and went to the door, determined to face her fate.

Out of the dusk came four riders. Only one of them jumped off his horse and approached her, his boots squishing as if walking in thick mud. Jamila recognized the chief of the smugglers. The man whose wife had given birth to the one-and-a-half baby; the same man who had left the wounded smuggler with her and caused her this misery.

'Jamila . . . sister. May I come in?'

Wordlessly, she moved aside, letting him pass.

He saw the bruise on her forehead, the puffy eyes. 'I'm not going to stay long. We've already caused you much pain. I came to apologize for what happened. He did not deserve your kindness.'

She knew she should say something, but the words didn't reach her lips.

'I brought you things,' he said. 'My gifts to you.'

Out of the pocket of his *shalwar* he produced two drawstring pouches in silk, one red, the other black. He reached out for her hands and held them for a moment while staring into her eyes. Then he put the red bundle on her left palm, on her right palm the black.

Finally finding her voice, she inquired, 'Where is he now?'

'He won't give you any more trouble, trust me.'

'What was his name? I don't even know his name.'

'His name was Haroun,' he said before he strode away back to his horse. 'That's what we wrote on his stone.'

It took a moment for the words to register, and when they did she gave a gasp. Aghast, she opened the red bundle. Inside was the Amber Concubine, dazzling. Jamila then untied the second bundle. In it was a pair of ears. Sad, bloody. It was only then that she realized the two bundles were cut out of the same cloth, one having turned black with blood. In the end, though he had skirted the landmines, Haroun the smuggler was still buried with some parts missing.

On an impulse, Jamila dashed after the chief. For a second she feared he had vanished, another ghost in her life. But then she spotted the four horses down the rutted path. 'Wait for me!' Jamila choked.

He pulled on his reins, and his men followed suit.

When she reached them, she hesitated, at a loss for words. Tucking a strand of hair behind her ear, she arranged her scarf. She pleaded, 'I need your help, please.'

'Tell me.'

'I want to go to my sister in England. She's in trouble. She needs me.'

The men exchanged stares.

'I don't have a passport or money. Nothing. It has to be your way, illegal.' Jamila opened her fist. 'But I have the Amber Concubine and I'm allowed to give her to whomever I choose. And I choose you. You'll be a rich man and she won't bring you bad luck, trust me.'

'You want to give me the diamond in return for arranging a trip abroad.'

'That's correct.'

The chief smuggler furrowed his eyebrows, pulling the ends of his moustache, brooding. 'That's not easy. It's not like crossing the border to Syria.'

'I've heard there are men who arrange such things. I cannot find them, but you can. Remember Ahmad's younger son? Didn't he go like that? Which country was it? Switzerland? They hid him in a lorry, right? He made it somehow.'

Once she'd begun, the words gushed out of her like a river. She spoke from the depths of her soul with urgency and fervour, guided by a need she did not recognize, and possibly could not control.

He watched her, unmoving. In his deep-set eyes she saw several emotions at once: concern, understanding, loss and a secret admiration. 'I'll do what I can. If God wants it to happen, it will happen.'

Dazed, cold, shaking, she raised her hands and opened her palms, the diamond catching the last rays of the setting sun. 'Take her. May Allah bless you.'

He turned his face away, as if talking to the wind now, and said, thickly, 'Keep it. You deserve it, Jamila.'

Then, with a faint nod and without a further word, he kicked the sides of his horse. His men followed. She watched them gallop away, the dust from the hooves surrounding her like a haunting memory.

★★★

Shrewsbury Prison, 1991

When I arrive back from solitary, there is someone new in Trippy's bunk. So soon. I guess I half expected they would give it a bit of time, but Shrewsbury is jam-packed. And every day there are new arrivals. The prison system reminds me of the factory where Dad used to work. Like biscuits on a conveyor belt, cons keep coming. The screws arrange them, store them, lock them up. Cluster after cluster. This place is filled to the top. There is no room to mourn anyone.

At first glance, my cellmate seems okay, pretty harmless. I don't ask him what he's in for and he doesn't volunteer it. Those things you don't raise. A wiry little man, he has a high forehead, angular jaw, chiselled face. His hair catches the overhead light, and for a split second I am struck by the kindness of his expression.

Bowing slightly, he says, 'My name is Zeeshan.'

He pauses, as if expecting me to introduce myself. I cross my arms and frown at him, zipping my lips.

Then he says, 'Zeeshan happy to meet you.'

What a ridiculous thing to say. His English is a shambles. I'm guessing he's around forty. Far Eastern, brown, middle height. He tries to make small talk but I'm having none of it. Better to draw the line right away. Any other man in his shoes would instantly give up on me. He'd be worrying about how much of what he'd heard about me was true and whether he can sleep safely tonight. And every night for the next few months. But Zeeshan seems at ease. After enough playing mute, I decide to give him something to chew over.

'The man who slept in that bed has died,' I say.

'Oh, I hear,' Zeeshan says. 'Also hear you good friends. Must be hard for you. Very, very sorry. Accept my apologies.'

'You mean condolences?'

'Right.'

I draw a blank. Compassion always catches me off guard. I never know quite what to do with it. 'Now, I don't care who you are or what your name is,' I say. 'I'll tell you the rules around here. The sooner you learn them the better for you. Rule number one: don't ever invade my space. Rule number two: don't step on my toes. Rule number three: don't get on my nerves. Clear?'

He blinks in confusion. His small, slanted eyes dart from me to the wall, and from the wall back to me. 'Zeeshan clear,' he says.

'Good!'

Soon we hear the sounds. It's time for the morning unlocking. Cell doors crack open on each side. We keep our silence, waiting to be counted, pushed, shoved and patted down.

Officer McLaughlin appears. A bandage on his left ear. He and I exchange hard stares. He hasn't forgiven me for wolfing down Trippy's letter, and I haven't forgiven him for winding me up. He hasn't forgiven me for biting his ear, and I haven't forgiven him for sending me to solitary. We're even and back to square one. Except sharper now.

'Oi, I'm watchin' you,' Officer McLaughlin says. 'One more mistake and I'll be having you.'

I gnaw the insides of my mouth and say nothing. I take deep breaths to steady myself. He's standing so close I can see the wisps of hair in his nostrils. It's a nice distance, this one. I can easily butt his nose with a thrust of my forehead. Perfect angle. Pity, I let it go.

When we're alone again, Zeeshan stares at me, full of curiosity. 'Why he angry to you?'

''Cos he's a mouse pretending to be a man.'

Zeeshan laughs as if it's the best joke he's heard. 'Mouse-man, I like that.' Then he turns thoughtful. 'There are also fish-men, bird-men, snake-men, elephant-men. Very few human-men in this world.'

I have no idea what he's talking about. There's something weird about this bloke but I just can't nail it. He isn't put off easily and that smile of his gets on my wick. I'm about to tell him to wipe it off his face when he says, 'It not easy to fight always?'

'What?' I say, processing his question. 'Are you asking me if it's hard to have to fight all the time?'

'Yes, yes. I ask you. Fighting, fighting, not tired?'

I stare at him, stumped. He doesn't seem to be off his trolley. He sounds frank, genuinely inquiring. 'Where are you from?' I ask.

'Oooh,' he pauses, as if I've posed an impossible riddle. 'First time I was born in Brunei.'

'Where the hell's that?'

He looks offended. 'Brunei Darussalam. Island of Borneo. We a British Colony. Then Brunei is independent.'

'Well, the Queen's servants have done a rather poor job in teaching you English, then.'

'I learn English,' Zeeshan says, ignoring my snarky remark. 'I learn new things every day. Zeeshan good student.'

I scoff. I still haven't decided if he's just annoying or plain barmy. 'You said, the first time I was born, what does that mean?' I ask.

He beams, exposing all his teeth – small, narrow, mottled, like wild rice.

'First time born in Brunei,' Zeeshan repeats. 'Second time born in whole world. So I'm from everywhere. The world is my home.'

Suddenly the penny drops. 'Oh, bugger you. Don't tell me, you're one of those religious crusaders. Are you a God Botherer?'

'A what?'

'Question: are you a member of a cult or something?'

Again he doesn't get it, and for a second he looks frightened.

''Cos I'm telling you I'm not having anyone preach me the righteous path. Sick and tired of all that rubbish. You'd better get off your soap box.'

'Soap box,' he echoes, totally lost.

'What I mean is, are you a fanatic?'

'Fanatic!!' Zeeshan's face brightens, happy to finally recognize a word. But then his expression gets serious. 'Fanatic says, everybody wrong, I am right. Zeeshan says, everybody right, I am wrong. How possible me fanatic?'

'O-kay.' I can accept that. But then I am seized by a new thought. 'If you say you are from everywhere, then what's your religion?'

'My religion is love,' he says.

I roll my eyes. 'Never heard of that.'

For a moment, he looks affronted. 'Ear hears what it can hear. Lots of sounds in this world, we don't hear.'

'So are you Buddhist, Jewish, Muslim, Christian . . . what are you?'

'Ay, ay, ay,' he says, as if I have stepped on his foot. 'You ask are you this, are you that?' He pounds on his chest. 'All universe is in one person.'

'And that person is you?'

'That person is you,' he says, stressing the last word.

Okay, that's it for me. The fun is over. Now he's rubbing me up the wrong way. I don't like self-righteous people who think they have an answer to everything. 'The universe, huh? I'll tell you what's in there. Aggression, brutality, corruption, terrorism . . .' Then I add, 'Murder.'

'Uh-hmm,' says Zeeshan, as if he has never heard of any of these before. He closes his eyes, and for a second I have the impression he's going to sleep. But he soon starts to speak, his voice bright. 'You look at nature. You see animals kill animals. Big insects eat small insects. Wolf eats sheep. Oh so much blood. But in nature also animals protect animals. Fish swim together. Birds fly in flocks.'

'That's because there are sharks and hawks everywhere. If you stay together there's a better chance of survival.'

'Creatures care very much for creatures.'

'Yeah, nice bullshit.'

He opens his eyes. 'Zeeshan no bullshit.'

'Well, I'm sorry to break the bad news. Nature is all about war. Same here under this roof. Same everywhere. It's a rat race.'

He leans forward and squints at me as if seeing through me. 'Harmony everywhere . . .' he says, pronouncing the word 'harmony' like 'how many'. He then goes on: 'Same here. But main question is, is there harmony inside you?'

These last words I hear as 'How many inside you?' Perhaps it's the right question after all. I have no idea how many Iskenders I harbour within my soul.

'All right,' I say. 'If it all boils down to bloody harmony, if the bad and the good balance each other, then everyone can do as they please. What difference does it make?'

'Nooo, not like that. You can't do whatever you want. You only do what God puts in you. I have elements. You have elements. Zeeshan mostly water. You, maybe fire? Yes, I think you fire. If there is no harmony inside, that person always angry. Always fight, always pity. Sharp tongue like arrow. Universe is jungle, you say. In big jungle, I make my own garden.'

'What bleedin' garden are you talkin' 'bout?'

'Dear friend,' says Zeeshan, as if writing me a letter. 'Anger is tiger. You see the tiger and you think, oh what great animal, I want a tiger. But you cannot tame him. No one can. The tiger will eat you.

'Forget angry tigers, we don't learn anything from them. We learn from humans. When you meet different person, another name, another religion, that's all good. We learn from difference, not from sameness.

'Ego is like vulture. Wild bird. Vulture says, fly with me, you become strong man. But that's lie. It's trick. If your ego strong you are weak. If ego weak, you strong.'

He speaks slowly but surely. He picks his words carefully, as if they were glass flowers. When he finishes, I say, 'There's only one thing I'm wondering . . .'

'What is it?'

'Why didn't they put you in the loonies' wing?'

'What's that?'

I rotate my index finger around my ear. He recognizes the universal gesture for insanity. He laughs, a happy laugh. 'Yes, yes, true. They say Zeeshan a bit crazy in the head.'

★

That day the police came to Katie's house, I ran out the back door. I was lucky. I nicked a bike, cycled out of Hackney as far as I could go, then I hitchhiked. Two French students gave me a lift. Their accents thicker than a plank. Gay as a picnic basket, both of them. I had never met a homosexual couple before, and didn't like the idea at all, but was in no position to judge them. They saw my distress, sensed trouble, didn't ask anything. They bought me lunch, offered cigarettes, made me listen to some odd music.

They dropped me in Warwick. Before they left we smoked grass outside the castle. I remember us laughing our heads off, but I don't recall what the joke was, if there was one. Then they headed north.

Suddenly I was on my own. Four days later I was arrested – they caught me sleeping rough in one of the parks. By that time I was gasping for food. I was so worn out it was almost a relief. During the interrogation, I was calm, cooperative. They didn't tell me she was dead. Not for a while. I was confident that her injury was nothing big. It was only a stab, close to her right shoulder. How bad could it be? Then an officer came in and said, 'Don't you know? You killed her.'

Gobsmacked, I said, 'What d'you mean?'

'You killed your own mum, you sick bastard. How are you going to worm your way out of that?'

I didn't believe it. I thought it was a hoax to make me talk. One of those old copper's tricks. But they took a newspaper and put it in front of me. The same clipping Officer McLaughlin had filed, probably. That's when I learned Mum was dead.

During the trial, I was numb. I froze, just as I had in the tree the day I was circumcised. The press. The photographers. There were people with placards against me outside the courtroom, complete strangers. There were people supporting me, again strangers. In the crowd I saw Esma's face, like a white mask. Then I saw my brother, Yunus. His eyes wide open, uncomprehending. That was when I couldn't breathe. My lungs wouldn't yield air. I collapsed, wheezing like an old man on a respirator. They thought it was an asthma attack. The doctor was kind. He examined me, found nothing. Then I got the shrink. Horrible man, full of shit. I threw an ashtray at his head, sadly it missed the wanker.

But the very first night I was in the nick I slumped on my bunk and stared at the ceiling. For a good hour. I wondered if the shrink could be right. Did I have issues that went deep? Was I out of my tiny mind?

'He's not insane,' the prosecutor had declared in court. 'This young man is in his right mind. He deserves full punishment.'

Next night, again not a wink of sleep. In my experience the worse you sleep the crankier you end up. And so it went. Those early years felt like one long nightmare. And I was a nightmare to others. I gave them a hard time. Much later, one midnight, I remember it well. It was raining outside. Big storm, thunder, lightning and all. Then the rain stopped but the silence felt worse. It was then that I had the strangest feeling. It was as if my mother was here with me. She wasn't upset or vexed. She was beyond such things.

I started to sob. I cried, my chest heaving, hurting. All the tears that I couldn't shed all my life bled away from me.

★

After spending two weeks with Zeeshan I go against one of my own rules. I ask him, 'What are you in for? A man like you.'

His face falls. 'Oh, they say Zeeshan made terrible crime. No proof. But there is this gentleman. Court listened to him because he comes from famous surname. He say he saw me take handbag and harm old lady. She in hospital, coma.'

'You assaulted an old woman for money?'

'Zeeshan did no such thing,' he says. 'When lady opens her eyes she will tell the truth. I wait. I pray.'

'Okay, let me see if I've got this right. So you're telling me you're in for a crime you haven't committed? You expect me to believe that crap?'

He gives me this queer look, as if wondering how to break the news. Then he says, 'Since the day police come my house, I am thinking why did this happen? Nothing happens for nothing. God has purpose, what is it? I ask but no answer. But now I understand.'

'What're you going on about?'

'Listen, I didn't know why God put me in gaol. I said, why, why. But then I meet you. And I am not sad any more.'

'If you don't stop this gibberish I'm gonna make you really sad.'

He doesn't look the least bit intimidated. 'Now I understand why Zeeshan here. Thanks to you.' He pauses, sighing. 'It be easier if you had come to me, of course. But no, you didn't. So I had to come to you. So Zeeshan becomes prisoner. All for a purpose.'

'That's crap. Are you telling me that you're innocent of any crime but some cosmic force sent you here for me?'

'Yes, now you correct.' He beams, happy as a child with a new balloon.

The man is mad as a hatter. And he's getting worse every day, unless he's doing it deliberately. It suddenly hits me. I grab him by the collar and push him against the wall.

'Did Officer McLaughlin put you in here with me? Is this his idea of teaching me a lesson? You wanna drive me nuts, right? Is that the plan?'

He screws his face up as if I have already punched him. 'I tell you God send me here. You say, McLaughlin. Your McLaughlin small, God is big.'

I let him go and rub my temples – the beginning of a headache. 'How old are you?' I ask.

He lowers his eyes, shyly. 'Sixty-seven.'

'No kidding.'

'It's true.'

'You don't look sixty-seven.'

'Thank you,' he says. 'Zeeshan looks at himself.'

'You mean, looks after himself.'

'Yes, yes, looks after.'

Again he starts to talk crap. 'I came to you,' he says. 'I was of no use lately and God brought me here because God doesn't like laziness. We should all work very hard.'

'What work?'

'Mystics say –'

'What's that?'

'Mystic someone who looks inside heart, thinks all people connected. Differences only on the outside, skin and clothes and passports. But human heart always the same. Everywhere.'

'Here we go again. Another load of bollocks.'

He smiles either because he doesn't know what bollocks are or because he means to ignore me.

'Mystics believe when we die and wake up, God asks four questions. How did you spend your time, hmm? Where did you get your money from, hmm? How you spent youth, hmm? And fourth question, very important: what did you do with the knowledge I gave you? You understand?'

'No.'

'I have knowledge,' he says. 'I am a teacher –'

'I remember you telling me you were a student.'

'Every teacher is student.'

'Oh, give me a break.'

'I am a teacher,' he repeats calmly, 'and I came here to share my knowledge with you.'

I have seen all kinds of men inside. Among screws and my fellow prisoners alike. Psychos, loonies, the saddest, the weakest and the meanest, sometimes all together in the same person. But there never was and never will be anyone in Shrewsbury like Zeeshan. Born in Brunei, bred in the world. I don't know what to do with him.

Iskender Toprak

Esma

London, May 1978

Uncle Tariq and Auntie Meral came for a visit with their four children. After dinner we all gathered around the TV, watching *Coronation Street* while drinking tea and munching on fruit. There was little talk in the room apart from the occasional remarks addressed to the characters on the screen. Everyone was curious to see what would happen now that Suzie had managed to seduce Steve and Gail had caught them in an intimate situation. Uncle Tariq didn't think the affair would last long. Aunt Meral agreed, but nobody took her seriously because she always missed the point. I had to translate the key scenes for her because she didn't have enough English to follow the plot. Sometimes I added a few things of my own to strengthen the storyline.

After the guests had left and everyone had gone to sleep, I was in the bathroom again, observing myself in the mirror, when a knock at the door yanked me from my reverie.

'Busy!' I said through the keyhole.

Another knock, timid but persistent. Annoyed, I opened the door. It was Yunus standing there in his Peter Pan pyjamas. 'Oh, my goodness. What have you done to yourself?' he exclaimed.

Only now did I remember I had a goatee on my face. The best defence being a good offence, I retorted, 'What are you doing here at this hour?'

'I need to pee.'

I switched to Turkish as I noticed the bed sheet tucked under his arm. 'You sure you need to pee? It looks like you've already taken care of that.'

My brother's eyes flickered away. There was a brief silence as we each waited for the other one to say something, anything.

'All right,' I conceded. 'Just a sec, okay?'

I closed the door, turned the lights on, put out the candle and inspected my face one more time in the mirror. Then I poked out my head. 'Tell you what? Why don't you leave the bed sheet here? I'll take care of it.'

After a moment's hesitation, Yunus gave me a shy smile and handed over his guilt. I filled the basin with soapy water and soaked the sheet. I expected him to go back to his room, but he preferred to wait, peeking in through the half-open door. 'Sister, are you done?'

'Almost. It's not easy in the sink, you know,' I said lackadaisically. 'Why do you keep wetting your bed?'

Yunus was silent.

'Oh, don't worry. I'm not going to tell anyone.'

To my surprise he didn't seem relieved. Quite the opposite: his face darkened, his lip quivered. I took a step towards him, smiling at his big, innocent eyes and jutting ears, the boy I had always loved.

'Sorry, little'un. I didn't mean to offend.'

'I'm not offended. It's just I've a lot on my mind these days.'

'Like what?'

'I can't tell you,' he said. 'It's a secret.'

'Secrets are tricky. You want to get it off your chest but as soon as you do the word gets around. Like King Midas, uh?'

'Who is that?'

So I told him the story of the king whose ears were so large that he had to hide them under his hat. His barber, the only person who knew of this, had promised not to tell anyone. Yet the urge to share was so strong, he confided in a reed, the most harmless being he could think of. Then someone made a flute out of the reed, played it in a concert and the secret floated into the air. In a matter of days everyone knew that the king had the ears of a donkey.

'You mean, I shouldn't tell anyone,' said Yunus.

'Well, if it's anything important, I'd say just keep it to yourself. You can't trust anyone. Not even a reed.'

I half expected him to laugh but he didn't. Instead, he dolefully stared at me before turning his back and disappearing down the corridor.

'Good night, *canim*,'* I murmured, even though I knew he couldn't hear me.

As I stood there, my hands still soapy, I felt my chest tighten. A sneaking suspicion rose inside me. While I was dreaming of becoming a boy and contemplating all sorts of other mysteries, things were happening under my nose that I didn't see. Later on I would recall that moment, realizing it was the point at which ordinary life as I had known it fractured and we all began to slip, one after another, into some other realm, where too much happened too fast. I have since wondered if things would have been different had I acted otherwise that night. Had I let my brother share with me the secret that was eating him up inside, perhaps, just perhaps, I might have woken up earlier and been able to warn my mother before everything took a quick turn for the worst.

* 'My darling'.

The Slap

London, June 1978

On this particular Saturday, Iskender did not go boxing. Nor did he meet Katie. He and his mates had other plans. He left the house shortly after nine in the morning. A warm wind whisked his face, and the world seemed to open before him, making him feel alive, ready for anything. Pulling up the collar of his jacket, he maintained a steady pace. He believed the way a man walked said a great deal about him – his drawbacks, his wits, his courage reflected in his gait. Iskender trod with a slight forward thrust, his shoulders straight and his chin raised, as if sizing up the passers-by for a fight.

The boys were waiting for him in Aladdin's Cave. The four of them. Slouched over a plastic table towards the back. As he approached them, Iskender nodded in their direction. They returned the gesture. He noticed the respect in their eyes – the kind of respect that his father had never seen from anyone, including his gambling cronies, except perhaps on the days he won.

'Hiya,' Iskender said to no one in particular. 'Where's Arshad?'

'He's not here yet,' said Faarid, a short, soft-spoken Moroccan.

'Maybe he bloody wimped out,' said Aziz with a grin that displayed his gappy teeth. 'After this week I don't blame him.'

It had been a tense summer. Every day there was talk about another incident somewhere. Men were intimidated on the streets, women called names, children spat at. At nights bricks were hurled into the houses of immigrants; the washing on their lines was cut to pieces or dog turds were put through their letterboxes. But the worst had happened six days ago.

On the eleventh of June, early in the morning, a group of skinheads had gathered at the top of Brick Lane. By midday their numbers had swollen. They kept coming – on foot, by bike, car and van, some from as far as Putney. Then the march began, the chant was taken up, 'The National Front is a White Man's front.' Oddly, the police were nowhere to be seen – even when the protesters started to attack the shops of immigrants, shouting 'Kill the Black Bastards', smashing windscreens and windows, harming private property.

Faarid said, 'Did you hear what the coppers said afterwards? A spontaneous outbreak, they called it.'

'It sucks,' said Iskender distractedly.

The conversation was interrupted by Aladdin, the owner of the place – a lopsided, broad-boned man in his mid fifties, with one leg shorter than the other. Always had a kind word for everyone. He approached the boys with a smile but shook hands only with Iskender. He asked him how school was going and how his mother was doing, and how his uncle's shop was doing in these hard times. Questions that Iskender answered respectfully but curtly.

'So what are you gonna eat?' said Aladdin finally. 'Your friends waited for you to order.'

Iskender was pleased to hear that. 'We've a guest coming. We'll order when he's here.'

They watched Aladdin limp away. Iskender turned to Aziz, resuming the conversation. 'Anything else?'

'Oh, yeah, a boy was beaten up yesterday. A Bengali. They found him bleeding steps away from Arshad's house. That makes four in a month!'

Iskender chewed the insides of his mouth, his face crumpling like a mask.

'You know what drives me mad?' ventured Sonny. 'These racist buggers say they're not racists. *We are realists*. Bollocks! It's bad enough that they're racists. They don't need to be liars on top of that!'

His name was Salvatore, though everyone called him Sonny. His family had moved to Hackney from a village in Sicily. He spoke English so quickly and with an accent so strong that all too often half the things he said were lost on others.

'So when is this bloke coming? The famous Chinwagger!'

It was Chico who asked this, his fingers drumming on the menu. His father was Moroccan, his mother Spanish.

'Don't call him that,' said Aziz. 'Respect the man. Call him the Orator.'

'Same difference. You know what they say. The fool talks, the wise man listens! And this bloke always talks. So you do the maths!'

Iskender sat back with a frown and clasped his hands, a gesture that altered the tone around the table from jovial patter to a more sober exchange. 'He'll be here in half an hour. I thought it'd be nice if we met early and had a discussion. Things aren't rolling right. We'd be fools not to see the writing on the wall.'

Chico lowered his gaze. The others nodded, solemn and keyed up.

'They wanna kick us out of this bloody country,' Iskender said. 'You, me, him . . . Arabs, Turks, Italians, Jamaicans, Lebanese, Pakistanis . . . Are we just gonna sit and joke about it? Like fuckin' ducks at the funfair. That's what our parents want us to do. Smile and wait to be shot. But we're no ducks, are we?'

'Of course not,' Chico said.

'Look, I've heard this bloke speak before. He's good, really good. Let him come and say what he has to say. If you don't like him, you don't like him. That's the end of it. But at least he's no duck, we all know that.'

Just then the door opened and Arshad walked in, his hands thrust in his pockets. When Iskender saw the girl following his friend, his face changed. 'What the hell is she doin' here?'

'Hey, don't blame me, man. I tried to stop her . . .' Arshad said.

Iskender stared daggers at Esma. 'Go back home.'

'No, I want to listen too,' she said.

The boys watched the row with guarded smiles.

'Sis, I'm tired of your pigheadedness,' Iskender said. 'I'm not going to argue with you.'

'Well, don't argue, then.'

'You're getting on my nerves. This isn't stuff for girls!'

'Why not? Do you think those skinheads bully only men? You're damn wrong. They attack women too. And girls. If I'm good enough to be a victim, I'm good enough to fight back.'

'She's got a point,' said Aziz.

Heartened by the support, Esma pleaded, 'Oh, come on, *abi*, please.'

Iskender shook his head, albeit less forcefully this time. 'All right, but I don't wanna hear anything from you. Not a peep.'

'Yup. I'll sit here like a corpse,' she said, trying not to let the joy show in her face, but then added mirthfully, 'I'm dying to see what this bloke looks like. I'm sure I'll recognize him right away.'

That assumption, however, turned out to be wrong. When the Orator walked into the now half-full café, no one in the gang but Iskender identified him. The others had expected a sturdy, impressive person of an indeterminate age, wearing half-traditional, half-exotic garments, his hair flowing in every direction, his eyes sparkling like emeralds. So when a gaunt man in his mid twenties with ordinary features and faded jeans entered, they didn't give him a second glance, until he approached and greeted them.

'Oh, please have a seat,' said Iskender. He briefly introduced everyone, leaving Esma out.

Food was ordered. *Hummus, babaganoush, kebabs, falafel* . . . Iskender filled the guest's plate, which turned out to be pointless, for the man ate like a bird. His poor appetite slowed everyone down – even Sonny, who was always hungry, had to stop eating.

Then, while they were having their tea, the Orator began to preach. His voice was thin but it rose in waves, pausing every few minutes and picking up again, as if he were reading from an invisible pamphlet. He talked about the stages of late capitalism, and how close humanity had come to the Judgement Day. *We are all looking down the cliff. We'll see the fall of this regime.* The youth today were being doped so that they wouldn't question the system. Politicians everywhere were manipulating half of the drug traffic in the world. All ideologies were inventions to keep the young people in a constant daze. The fake 'isms' were the new drugs, sleeping pills for the masses.

'My aunt is a feminist,' said Sonny, slightly nervous from not having eaten enough. 'Her hair is shorter than mine and she always wears trousers.'

'Feminism to us is like a snowman in the Sahara,' commented the Orator. 'There is no need for it. And do you know why?'

'Because it makes women ugly. They don't even shave their legs any more, disgusting,' said Sonny.

The boys suppressed a chuckle while Esma rolled her eyes. Iskender was the only one staring at the Orator. Their eyes met with a mutual understanding, a shared sense of being above boyish reactions.

'I'd say, our friend here is right because feminism *does* make women look unnatural,' the Orator said. 'But that's a result, not a reason. Whereas I am asking why is it irrelevant for people like us?'

'Because it's *their* problem,' Iskender answered. 'It's a Western thing.'

Carrying a trayful of tea, Aladdin overheard the last words, his eyebrows arching suspiciously. For a second Iskender had a hunch Aladdin knew about this Orator and didn't like him. *Blokes like that are sowing bad seeds in the community. What's he doing here, putting things into the lads' heads?* As if he had sensed Aladdin's dislike, the Orator fell silent and did not speak a word until the drinks were served and they were again left alone.

'Exactly. Feminism is *their* answer to *their* problems,' the Orator continued, a glint of appreciation in his eyes. 'But it's a lame solution. Can you dry up a lake with a sponge? That's how effective feminists are. If Westerners have no family values and no respect for women, a bunch of activists screaming their heads off on the streets isn't going to change anything.'

Esma gave a snort. Out of the corner of his eye Iskender sent her a cold, menacing glance. 'Sorry,' she silently mouthed.

'Behave,' Iskender mouthed back.

If the Orator had noticed their peaceful exchange, he pretended not to. 'In the West people are confused. They confuse happiness with freedom and freedom with promiscuity. Whereas we respect our mothers, sisters and wives. We don't force them to dress up like Barbie dolls. It's a whole industry. Cosmetics, fashion, shoe designers. Have you ever heard of anorexia nervosa?'

The boys shook their heads.

'It's an obsession with body image. Women who suffer from it are on a diet all the time. They make themselves vomit after they eat. Every year dozens of women in Europe and the States are hospitalized because of this illness. Some die. Their hearts fail. But they still think they are fat.

'Brothers, don't forget that in the meantime, babies in Asia, Africa and the Middle East are dying of hunger. They cannot find a piece of bread to nibble. Never seen a sweet in their lives. While the women in the West puke up chocolate-brandy cakes in posh restaurants, people in the Third World are starving.

'It's no coincidence that the two major industries in the West are the machine of war and the machine of beauty. With the machine of war they attack, imprison, torture and kill. But the machine of beauty is no less evil. All those glittery dresses, fashion magazines, androgynous men and butch women. Everything is blurred. The machine of beauty is controlling your minds.'

A sense of awe canopied the table. Stifling a gasp, Esma examined her fingernails. She wished Iskender could make light of the situation. Pat the man on the back, tell him to take it easy, make them all laugh. He could if he wanted to. He had it in him. That kind of boldness, that kind of lightness, she thought. And yet, when she raised her head, the expression she found on her brother's face was nothing like what she had hoped for. 'Alex, can we please get some more tea?' Esma asked. 'All this talk is making me thirsty.'

The Orator checked his watch. 'Time for me to leave. It was nice to meet you.' As he stood up, he turned to Iskender. 'Why does she call you Alex?'

'Don't mind her. She's my sister . . . Everybody calls me that. You know, it's short for . . .'

'Alex is not short for Iskender,' the Orator inveighed. 'Think about it again, brother. Are we going to have to change our names so that the Brits can pronounce them more easily? What else will we have to give up? It should be the other way round. Make everyone learn your full name and say it with respect.'

With that he left, leaving an awkward silence in his wake.

Iskender jumped to his feet, nervous. 'I'll walk Esma home and come back.'

'Hey, I don't want to leave yet.'

But he had already reached the door. 'Chop, chop. Now!'

Esma complied, grumbling. As soon as they were outside on the street, she exclaimed: 'Bloody hell, I didn't like that bloke. Mr Uppity on his high horse.'

'You might not like him but he's a fighter.'

'He's harsh.'

'When the reality is harsh you too need to be.'

'Come on, he's just a macho tosser. He didn't even look at my face.'

'That's because he respected you, you twat! Would you prefer men ogling your legs? Is that what you want?'

'Oh, what's wrong with you?' she said, throwing her hands up. 'Relax! All this nonsense is going to your head.'

'Watch your mouth, Esma.'

'Yeah, I'm so scared!'

'You heard me. You're not coming to our meetings any more. I can't keep an eye on you all the time.'

'Who says you have to keep an eye on me?' she snapped. 'I can take care of myself, thank you very much. It's all Mum's fault. She raised you like this. *Malamin, berhamin.** And now you think you're the Sultan of Hackney!'

'Shut up.'

Esma didn't notice the change in his tone, the clenching of his fists, until it was too late. She was too carried away by her own voice. 'We were a team, you and me. It was fun. We used to laugh. Nothing's fun now. Look at you – look how seriously you're taking yourself.'

Iskender grabbed her by the shoulder and pushed her against a wall. 'People are being beaten up on the streets. An old man was knocked unconscious by stones just last week. What fun are you talking about?'

'Oh, so you're the big hero. Save us, please.'

The slap. It came suddenly, as if from out of nowhere. Esma held her cheek, too shocked to move.

'You stay away from this,' he said, without looking at her. 'I warn you.'

She watched him strut back to the café, hurrying. Once she thought she knew her elder brother like the back of her hand, but no longer. He had always protected her from others. Yet now, for the first time, Esma felt as if she had to protect herself from him.

---

* 'My abode, my lion.'

218

A Big, Brown Trout

London, July 1978

When Yunus ran into Tobiko after weeks of desperate searching, he was overcome with a mixture of relief and dread. Relief at having found her, when he had almost given up hope, but also a harrowing fear of losing her again. He clung to her like a clam to its shell.

She had changed somewhat, gained a bit of weight. Her hair, dark and shiny like a black pebble in rain, was still long, but the ends were now dyed an incandescent green. She had replaced the silver piercing on her bottom lip with a sparkling stud. On each earlobe she wore half-a-dozen crimson hearts, as tiny and bright as droplets of blood. Yunus counted them, noticing, once again, how small her ears were and how very pretty.

Tight-lipped, Tobiko refused to explain where she had been all this time or why she had failed to leave a note. *Here and there. Needed a change of air, pet.* Yunus was annoyed to learn where she was staying: in a three-bedroom maisonette with the Captain and his mother. A few others from the squat were also there.

The Captain's mother, Mrs Powell, was a retired teacher, a widow. In reality, she had little tolerance for the group under her roof, but she had agreed to host them for a while in the hope of spending more time with her only son. She had moved into the bedroom upstairs with her TV and hot-water bottle, leaving the rest of the flat to the punks. She seldom ventured out of her room, having all her meals there, pretending not to notice the incessant commotion or the smell of weed coming from downstairs.

The first time Yunus visited the punks in that flat, he sat on the sofa next to Tobiko, small and smiling.

'It's a temporary solution,' said the Captain by way of explanation. 'Until we go back to our old place. We're gonna bring everyone together again.'

'We're getting our house back and this time nobody's gonna kick us out. We've learned our lesson,' said Bogart, a cigarette between his lips, and a guitar with only two strings in his hand. 'We'll kick their arses.'

There was someone new with them who had no hair except for a mop on top, which he had dyed different shades of orange. He was nicknamed Mr Filch because he didn't believe in the need to pay for anything – books, LPs, food, underwear. Once he lifted a pair of Doc Martens, carrying a boot inside each sleeve of his gabardine coat. Now, sitting back with a grin, Mr Filch interjected, 'Yeah, you're like cats. Licking your wounds.'

Yunus listened to their blather, glad to have them in his life again, oddly soothed by their unconventional ways. Noticing his happiness, Bogart remarked, 'The kid is like a cat too.'

'And you're his cosy little basket,' the Captain said to Tobiko with a wink.

Tobiko laughed but only a little, so as not to offend Yunus. To change the subject, she turned to Bogart and asked, 'What was that you were playing?'

'Oh, it's a song I composed. You know I was thinking the squat raid was our Bloody Sunday. Sort of. So I made this song. It's called Bloody Tuesday.'

Needing no further incentive, Bogart began to sing. The melody was terrible, the lyrics even worse.

I'm on the edge, I'm on the dole,
Like a stone I tumbled into this hole,
This hole, this hole, this hole, this hole.
The Old Bill don't ring before they haul,
Bloody Tuesday, worst day of all.
Rise against the system! It has no soul!
No soul, no soul, no soul, no soul.

Iggy Pop – wearing an Afghan waistcoat and a buff-coloured T-shirt so short that it barely covered his nipples – plugged his ears with his fingers. 'Ow, can't you shut your bleedin' gob!'

'What?' Bogart exclaimed, stopping halfway.

'It's shite, man,' said Iggy Pop.

'It wasn't even a Tuesday,' said Tobiko. 'It was Wednesday when they raided.'

Bogart frowned. 'Says who?'

Yunus listened, half amused, half worried, knowing how easily they could move from childish merriment to outright war when they were stoned, slamming the doors, shouting and swearing, at one another or at themselves.

'What do you lot know? You knob-heads,' scoffed Bogart. He paused for a moment, scowling at Tobiko. 'You don't flipping remember what you had for breakfast.'

'Let's ask Yunus,' suggested Tobiko. 'He's neutral.'

'Neutral my arse,' the Captain objected. 'He's so soft on you, say snow is black, and he'd totally agree.'

Blushing profusely but feigning ignorance, Yunus knew he had to say something – a remark interesting enough to distract them. So he announced, 'I want to have a tattoo.'

Bogart chuckled. 'Whoa! This lad is cool!'

'We'll do it,' said Iggy Pop. 'No problem. I'm the best tattoo artist in town.'

'Darlin', won't your mam get upset?' Tobiko asked tenderly.

Yunus had already thought about this. 'Well, she will if she sees it. But if you put it somewhere on my back, she won't know.'

'Clever boy,' said Mr Filch.

'I'll go and fetch the set,' said Iggy Pop, rubbing his hands together.

'And I need to have a pee,' said Yunus quietly.

Upstairs, there were two doors, one on each side of the corridor. After a brief hesitation, Yunus opened the one on the left. He was surprised to see a woman sitting in bed in a mauve nightgown, munching from a box of Ritz crackers, watching the new episode of *The South Bank Show*. Her hair was a bird's nest and she must have been crying, as there were streaks of mascara on her cheeks. She looked slightly bonkers.

'Sorry, ma'am.'

Yunus was about to close the door when the woman murmured without taking her eyes off the screen, 'Are they recruiting you?'

The boy stopped in his tracks, not sure if the words had been addressed to him. 'Pardon?'

'Are they recruiting you?' the woman repeated. 'Will you be the youngest delinquent in England?'

'No,' Yunus replied, alarmed.

'That's good,' she said, still talking to the TV. 'All my life I've worked with children, but I can't help my own son.'

Now Yunus looked at the woman more carefully, recognizing Mrs Powell, the teacher who had come to see his parents about his sister's education. He also saw how much she resembled the Captain – wide forehead, long nose with round tip, slightly protruding flint-grey eyes.

'When my son was your age he was so adorable,' she went on. 'Children are delightful when they're babies, but then they start to walk and break everything, and when they grow up they hate you!'

Mrs Powell turned towards Yunus, her gaze a searchlight. There were dark bags under her eyes. She looked tired, in need of a good sleep. 'What do you call your mother, darling?'

'I . . . I call her "Mum",' said Yunus.

'Well, tell her she's a lucky woman. My son calls me "The System". He thinks I'm a bourgeois buffoon!' She sighed. 'Do you think he's right?'

'Oh, no,' Yunus said, perturbed. He remembered having promised Tobiko a while ago that he would never let the system get anywhere near him. Yet he didn't take to his heels. 'I think you're a beautiful lady, Mrs Powell. You just have to see yourself in sunshine.'

The woman stood stunned for a moment before she broke into a chuckle. A husky croak, but when she looked again there was a new sparkle in her eyes. 'That's the sweetest thing I've heard lately.'

'Cheers, ma'am.'

When Yunus returned to the living room, he found Tobiko sitting by the window, looking at a bird in the garden, its feathers iridescent in the afternoon sun. She had two mugs of hot chocolate ready. As they sipped their drinks, Yunus ventured, 'May I ask you something?'

'Sure, pet.'

'About secrets,' he said nervously. 'My sister says you should never share them with anyone. Not even a reed.'

Tobiko studied him curiously. 'I'm not sure what you're talking about.'

'I suppose I'm trying to ask . . . If there is a person you love and that person has a secret that nobody knows and it's a bit embarrassing . . . but you find it out. Do you think you should tell her that or not?'

'Wow, that's a tough one. I think you'd better keep shtoom, then.'

And with those words Tobiko placed her head on the boy's shoulder, carefully, not with her full weight. Yunus's heart pulsed in the hollow of his throat. He wished the moment could go on for ever. But soon the Captain and the others returned, carrying a box of needles and tattoo designs.

'All rightie. Let's get to work,' said Iggy Pop. 'Look, this could hurt a bit. Is that okay?'

Yunus nodded, biting his lip.

'And what kind of tattoo would you like? A word? A symbol?'

'Can you make me a whale, please?' asked Yunus. 'Like the one that swallowed the prophet.'

When the tattoo was finished, it looked more like a big, brown trout – the fish that Grandma Naze had, in another life, in a bygone world, wished to become.

Head of the Family

London, September 1978

Iskender's fourth encounter with the Orator was different from all their previous ones. The man had wanted to see him alone and somewhere other than Aladdin's Cave. They had agreed to meet in Victoria Park.

Entering the park through Royal Gate, Iskender strode resolutely towards the Victoria Fountain. He slowed down when he spotted the Orator standing with his back to a horse-chestnut tree, a satchel by his side, his hands in his pockets, his face pensive but otherwise inscrutable. From the way he looked it was hard to tell whether he had been waiting a long time or had just arrived. Today he wore thin-rimmed glasses that accentuated the square shape of his face. He had brown pointed shoes, a loose faded jacket and the kind of jeans only a mother would buy for her son, Iskender thought to himself.

'Heyya,' Iskender said, raising his hand to salute.

The Orator smiled faintly. 'Come, let's take a walk.'

Though he wasn't exactly in the mood, Iskender agreed. 'Sure.'

The sun was shining in a clear sky. Near by, the lake was serene, a carpet of jade-green with a pale mist hanging above the opposite shore. There were parents and children tossing bread pellets to the ducks. There were a few people out jogging. One couple on the grass seemed deep in the throes of passion. Iskender noticed the Orator avert his gaze, the thinnest wrinkle forming on his forehead. Finally, tired of walking, they found an empty bench where they could sit and talk in private.

'You strike me as someone with solid friendships,' said the Orator.

'Yeah, my friends are cool,' Iskender said brightly.

'Are you their leader?'

Iskender hesitated. He never referred to himself in that way.

'That's all right,' said the Orator, reading his mind. 'It's good that you're in charge but that you don't act like it. That's noble.'

'Thanks,' Iskender said. No one had called him noble before, and he could not help but feel a glow of pride.

'Your mates are decent enough but they're still boys, really. Long way to go. You're different. Far more mature. How has that come about?'

'My father isn't around,' Iskender heard himself saying. 'I had to grow up at top-speed, if you know what I mean.'

The Orator nodded. 'Well, that explains it.'

Iskender felt a warm sense of worth, almost liquid, a new thrill in his veins. He had not realized this before, even though it had been in front of his eyes the entire time. He had grown up fast. 'I'm the eldest, you see. I've a younger brother and sister.'

'I remember your sister,' said the Orator. There was an edge to his voice.

'Yeah, sorry she was a bit rude that time you met.'

'That's all right. Don't blame her. She's young. Her mind's in a jumble. The things she picks up from other girls, the magazines she reads, and there is TV, of course. A bombardment of propaganda.'

Iskender chewed his lip, listening.

'It's harder for women, that's the thing. There are too many distractions to divert them from the right path. All the glitter of the fashion world, then there's the search for rich husbands, smart furniture. It never ends.'

'Right,' Iskender said.

'If you don't mind my asking, why is your father not around?'

Iskender's jaw moved silently for a second, as though he were swallowing the first answer that came to mind. He felt uneasy, under scrutiny. Was this a test? Did the man know about his father? Was he checking to see whether Iskender trusted him? If it was a test, he didn't like it. 'He's got another life, is all,' he said curtly.

'I see.'

'How is it you don't reveal the slightest thing about yourself but expect everyone else to unveil themselves to you?'

The Orator smiled, a quick glimmer of sarcasm. 'That's what I like about you. You've got a lot of balls. If you don't like someone's attitude, you don't put up with it. You're a risk-taker by nature. No one messes around with you.'

'That's correct,' Iskender said. 'No bollocks.'

'Well, I respect that. I suppose, just like you, I don't like to open up. But, now that you've asked, I will.'

Iskender's face softened a touch. He felt a bit embarrassed about his momentary outburst.

'My father, Khalid, was born in Egypt and came to Birmingham in 1951. He taught himself English while working night shifts. *If you don't work hard, you'll end up as nothing.* That was his biggest fear, you know. Becoming a nothing! He changed his clothes, his food, his habits, but the accent remained. He married an English woman and I was born. They're nice people. Don't get me wrong. The trouble is they're so caught up in this world, they forgot the next. They have no faith. I feel sorry for them.'

A young woman whizzed by on roller skates, wearing shorts and a baseball jacket, both purple. Iskender stared at her legs before going back to what he was planning to say. 'Yeah, but at the end of the day, they are your parents.'

'And I love them but that doesn't mean I respect them. They are quite different things, love and respect. If your parents slip up, you've got to stand up against them.'

'My father –' said Iskender, not quite knowing where he was going with this. 'As we grew up he was never around. Then he left the house. Just like that. It's been almost a year.' He was trying to make light of the subject, but he couldn't hide the tremor in his voice.

Pushing back his glasses, the Orator studied Iskender. 'So you are the head of the family now. It must be tough. You've got to be strong. It's good that you're into boxing. But you also need moral fortitude.'

'I see what you mean,' Iskender said, slightly unsure whether he did.

The Orator opened his satchel and took out two booklets. 'Take these. When you've read them, let's talk again. Tell me what you like in each. And feel free to say what you *don't* like.'

'Esma loves books. I'm not much of a reader myself.'

'Well, that has to change, then.' He did not look bossy when he uttered this, merely purposeful. 'The mind needs ideas the way a car needs fuel to run. And ideas come from books, largely.'

'Yeah, I guess you're right.'

'By the way, keep them to yourself, will you?'

'You can trust me,' said Iskender, and was about to say more when his eyes slid to his watch. 'Oh, no. Gotta go!'

The Orator clicked his tongue against his teeth, a hint of betrayal creeping into his gaze. 'A girl?'

'Yup.'

'English?'

'Yup.'

'Why not one of ours?'

The question had taken Iskender by surprise. He had always thought of the differences between Katie and him as a matter of clashing personalities, never anything beyond that. Besides, the Orator himself was English through and through, wasn't he? When Iskender spoke again, his tone dripped with irritation, 'I dunno. It just happened.'

'Uh-hum. Is she a good girl?'

'She's all right,' Iskender said, even though he didn't really know what he meant by that.

'Well, go, then. Don't make her wait. I'll pray that He may guide you in the right direction.'

'Thanks, see you around,' Iskender muttered, pretending not to be annoyed by the man's intrusiveness.

The Debt

London, 30 September 1978

Late in the afternoon on Saturday, Iskender popped into Tariq's shop, the collar of his jacket turned up. His uncle stood up to greet him, a proud smile on his face. The boy had changed a lot over the course of this year; he was already taller than his father, and much fitter, stronger. The thinnest moustache traced the curve of his upper lip, and his eyes were shining with the fervour of his youth.

'Look who is here, my favourite nephew!'

Iskender gave a faint smile. 'How're you doing, Uncle?'

'Never better,' Tariq said. 'To what do I owe the pleasure?'

'I'm gonna meet a few friends in the neighbourhood, and I thought I should visit you first.'

The boy spoke a hybrid of Turkish and English slang. Though he did not have a terrible accent, his vocabulary was so limited he often used the same words to mean different things. As he stood listening, Tariq thought about sending him to live in Istanbul for a while – perhaps for good. Or, better yet, he would talk to Pembe and bring over a fiancée for him, a modest girl from an Anatolian village.

'How's school going? Do you enjoy your classes? Are the teachers treating you well?'

'School is fine,' replied Iskender offhandedly.

'And how about boxing?'

'I've an upcoming match,' Iskender said. 'But Mum doesn't approve.'

'Well, I can't blame her. She's worried that you might get hurt.'

Iskender remained silent for a moment, listening to the steady clatter of rosary beads. 'Uncle, a friend of mine is in trouble.'

'Uh, and this friend of yours came to you for advice, eh?'

'Yeah, I'm like a big brother to the boys. That's why he came to me.'

'And what exactly is your friend's problem?'

'He needs money.'

Tariq suppressed a sigh. 'How much cash are we talking about?'

When Iskender mentioned the amount Tariq stroked his beard, asking, 'Why would a young boy need that much?'

A shadow of concern crossed Iskender's face, a furtive look, but when he spoke his voice was unperturbed. 'It seems like his girlfriend got pregnant. The money is for the clinic.'

Tariq sucked at his teeth. 'This girlfriend –' He paused. 'Is she English English?'

'Why, yes, of course,' said Iskender.

That was a relief, that the girl was not one of the neighbourhood, or from another immigrant community. There would be no families involved, no fathers or big brothers with a vendetta. Tariq exhaled, deeply, as if releasing all the questions he had decided not to ask. Conscious of the boy watching him, he stood up and walked towards the safe, which he kept at the back of the shop.

When he came back there were banknotes in his hands. He put them in front of Iskender, who for a moment felt the need to glance away, uneasy. 'Tell your friend that you'll help him,' Tariq said.

'Thank you, Uncle.'

'But also let him know that this will be the last time you're cleaning up his mess. Your friend needs to get a hold of himself. Otherwise he's in for deeper troubles. You send him my regards and make sure he understands.'

'Don't worry. I'll make sure he gets the message,' Iskender said, as he put the banknotes in his pocket and headed to the door. Then he stopped. 'Uncle?'

'Hmm? Was there anything else?' Tariq squinted, suddenly suspicious that the boy might be the sort of trouble a few banknotes couldn't solve.

'Nothing else. Just wanted to say you're like a father to me.'

At which Tariq's face softened. 'Any time, son. I'm always here for you.'

Iskender gave the smallest of nods, suddenly serious. 'Some day soon I'll pay you back. You'll see.'

The Man from Beyond

London, October 1978

On Friday, when Meral entered the shop at her usual time, she found her husband absorbed in a phone conversation. Tariq had thrust his chin forward and was pulling at his beard, the way he always did when he was about to lose his temper. Whoever was on the other end of the line seemed to be doing most of the talking. Quietly, Meral swished past him, heading towards the back of the shop, where she opened her tin pail and began to set out her husband's lunch. Today she had cooked *manti*,* putting more chilli peppers into the yoghurt-and-butter sauce than usual, and she was worried that he might not like it.

Once she had set the table, Meral grabbed a damp towel and began to dust the shelves, the golden bracelets on her wrists clattering jauntily. She inspected the tins of meat and baked beans, the bottles of brown sauce, the tubs of coleslaw and potato salad, the jars of pickled onions – food she had never tasted.

'Who buys such things?' she had once asked her husband.

'Modern wives,' Tariq had replied. 'They don't have time to cook. All day long they work. In the evening they pop in, buy some tinned tuna, mix it with salad cream and call it supper.'

Meral wondered what kind of women they were. What types of families did they come from? Even the women on the cover of the men's magazines didn't surprise her as much as these wives who were not-wives. The girls in the magazines must have been either deceived or paid a fortune to pose in their birthday suits. They were fallen; may God help them to find the right path. But the modern wives were by no means victims. They earned money, drove cars, dressed

---

* Dumplings with spiced meat.

smartly, and some even had children; yet they would not even stuff green peppers for their husbands.

Deep inside, Meral suspected that her sister-in-law, too, had that attitude in her. Hidden, of course, nothing in the open. There was an independent streak in Pembe that she couldn't quite put her finger on – an undertow of unruliness in a sea of calm. But then Pembe's husband was no good. He hadn't shown up in ten months, and had not exactly been around before then. Her husband wasn't like that at all.

'Wife,' Tariq yelled, still holding the receiver in his hand.

'What is it?'

Tilting his head to the side, Tariq gestured towards the door. Three customers had just walked in. Two boys and a girl. So young. *Probably the same age as my elder daughter*, Meral thought. One of the boys had silver piercings on his eyebrows, and a lump of orange hair on top of his head, like a nest built by some exotic bird. The other boy was tall and lanky, and wore no shirt under his Afghan waistcoat, exposing his hairless chest. As for the girl, she had raven hair, skin as pale as flour, torn stockings and tattoos on every bit of flesh you could see.

Meral closed her eyes for a moment, as if she hoped that the youngsters would be gone when she reopened them.

'I bet she won't serve us,' the girl muttered.

'Oh, no! Did we scare you, lady?' the shirtless boy asked, leaning over the counter, half accusing, half amused.

Meral caught the smell of the young man's breath: it was tinged with beer and tobacco. Inadvertently, she took a step back. Out of the corner of her eye she checked on her husband. Tariq was still on the phone and it didn't seem like he would be getting off any time soon.

'Yes, what you want?' Meral asked guardedly.

How many times had she asked her husband to put in extra security in the shop, but he had refused on the grounds that it was too expensive. The only weapon that Meral could think of now, should the need arise, was a rod with a net that they used to take down items stored on the upper shelves.

'You got ginger ale, lady?' asked the orange-haired boy.

Raising her chin as if ready for a blow, Meral said, 'No gingah isle.'

Her voice was feeble, insecure. Having no idea what they were talking about, she had found it safer to reject the possibility straight away. But in the meantime the shirtless boy had discovered the fridge, where they kept the fizzy drinks. 'Oi, lady, you got loads of it here. Why did you say "no"?'

'Maybe she's planning to guzzle it all herself,' the orange-haired boy offered, scrunching up his nose.

'Don't be silly,' interjected the girl. Pointing at the shelves behind the counter, she then said, 'May I have a pack of marshmallows, please?'

Meral's gaze raked the merchandise in bewilderment. *What on earth does the girl want?* She grabbed the chocolate buttons, the liquorice bootlaces, the jelly babies, while the punks exclaimed in unison, 'No, not those,' until she found the requested item.

Their prattle was cut off by Tariq's booming voice. Clasping his hands behind his back, fingering his rosary beads, he approached them. 'Welcome,' he said, and turned to his wife. In his politest English, he asked her, 'So, what do we have here?'

'Mashmolluuu,' explained Meral, as she placed the pack on the counter with a loud thud.

Tariq nodded. '*Tamam, ben hallederim.*'★

Reluctantly, Meral went back to her dusting, but she was soon surprised by the sight of the orange-haired boy lifting two nougat bars. After a brief hesitation, she decided to pretend that she hadn't noticed, as long as the boy did not go on to steal anything of more substantial value. She watched her husband engage in merry banter with his customers. In addition to the ginger ale and the marshmallows the punks bought a pack of cigarettes, matches and a bag of Twiglets. They left the shop, waving goodbye to Meral, who couldn't help but wave back.

'Look at them,' Meral grumbled to her husband as soon as they were alone.

★ 'Okay, I'll do the rest.'

Tariq shrugged. 'What can you do – they are young and hot-blooded.'

They are young and English, Meral thought. If one of their children dressed up like that, her husband would have a fit. She, at least, was consistent. At home, on the street or in the shop, she was the same person everywhere. She didn't understand how on earth someone could pierce their skin or go around with torn clothes held together with safety pins. Meral was not going to pretend that she approved of their ways just because they were *customers*.

Oblivious to his wife's thoughts, Tariq tucked into his lunch while standing. 'Oh, this is quite spicy.'

'Why don't you sit and eat slowly?'

'No time. I need to leave.'

'What do you mean? I cannot wait here. I have soup on the hob.'

'The girls are at home. They'll take care of that,' Tariq said, still chewing. 'Wife, this is urgent. I hit a snag with the distributors. If I don't solve this today, we won't have anything to sell tomorrow. No milk, no butter, no eggs. Even the bread won't be delivered.'

This elicited a sigh from her. She asked, 'And where are you going?'

'Oh, to the other end of bloody London.'

★

Tariq took the bus as he deeply disliked the tube. It made him uneasy to travel underground. When we die we end up beneath the soil, but what was the point of going there while still alive?

He wasn't at all familiar with the part of South-West London to which he was travelling. It was a long way away and the bus was slow, but at least the drivers weren't on strike again. Smouldering with resentment at having to go to such lengths to solve what he regarded as a simple misunderstanding, he planned the conversation he would have with the manager. The man on the phone had accused him of not having a contract with them any longer. Idiot! Tariq took out a folded piece of paper from his inner pocket and checked it. They would be ashamed when he shoved the contract in front of their noses. Perhaps, to make it up to him, they would come up with a special discount. In any case, he had to clear up this mix-up right away.

He was a self-made man, and he wasn't going to let some chinless bureaucrat ruin years of sweat, blood and tears.

Two changes of bus and what felt like hours later, Tariq got off at Brixton. Though the afternoon was chilly, a bright sun had come out, as unexpected as a surprise party. There were people on Coldharbour Lane, enjoying the warmth while it lasted. Tariq observed the English children, their button noses red, their skins pallid, and their clothes always too light. Turkish mothers would swathe their babies and toddlers in cardigan after cardigan, and place a knitted blanket on top of them before taking them outside. English mothers, however, made do with a pair of shorts and a thin anorak. Sometimes the children didn't even wear socks. Why didn't they freeze? For the life of him, Tariq couldn't understand how the ability to deal with the cold could be cultural.

He would have liked to stop by a café and have some tea, but it wasn't in his budget. He was the only one in the entire Toprak family who had the wisdom and the willpower to save for a rainy day. Khalil was wrapped up in himself. He had his own life in Australia and never asked them if they needed anything. As for Adem, he was hopeless. He gambled, and whatever he won he handed to that Russian dancer everybody was gossiping about but whom Tariq had still not seen.

Doggedly, Tariq ambled past a cobbler's, a religious bookstore, a down-at-heel-looking charity shop, and rows of identical red-brick houses. Unlike the main road there were no pedestrians here, and the place looked deserted. Even the cinema had an eerie air to it, like a relic from another century. It was so old, this city. Full of traces of the past. Once Tariq had found pieces of shrapnel when he had dug out the flowerbeds in his garden.

He wondered how Meral was doing back at the shop. She would have to learn English fast if she was going to help him in there. Perhaps he should get her a pocket dictionary and make sure she memorized at least five words every day. All these years his wife had survived in England by speaking only Turkish in her small world and it had not been a problem. But now he saw clearly that Meral had to do better than that. After all, Tariq was not getting any younger, and he was now taking care of two families – his and his brother's.

Yet it wasn't only because of her poor English that Meral was so terrible with customers. She was too stiff and judgemental, and didn't know how to wait on other people. Odd though it was, this woman who had waited on others her entire life – her husband, her children, her relatives and her neighbours – could not bring herself to serve strangers. While he, who had never tended anyone at home or any-where else, was good with the clientele.

The sun had again disappeared under thick, grey clouds. A storm was coming. Tariq quickened his steps, having finally reached his destination.

★

The meeting was tense. Tariq was not allowed to see the manager, who had some *important business to attend to*. Disappointed, Tariq showed the deputy his contract, and they showed him a clause that said that the company could ask for certain changes, and even ter-minate the agreement without advance notification. Tariq threatened to find an alternative supplier, to which they responded with an 'as you wish'.

Twenty minutes later he stomped out of the building, feeling down but not defeated. He would have to ask around a bit, consult with other shopkeepers in Hackney and contact another company. The only problem was that he liked to advise others, not to get advice from them. He had a reputation to uphold. Tariq slowed down as he approached the cinema and inspected the poster on the wall outside.

THE MAN FROM BEYOND

HARRY HOUDINI

Though not a fan of cinema, Tariq was interested in the life of the great magician. A man who could break free while hanging upside down in a tank full of water, chained by his ankles and wrists, was a man who merited some attention. So he entered the foyer and took a look around. There was a board on the wall with several photos and reviews. Perusing these, he was disappointed to learn that it was an old silent movie. Black and white no doubt. Did people still come to see such things?

As if in response, the doors at the entrance of the auditorium opened and an English couple walked out. The film had come to an end, and the few members of the audience were leaving. Behind the couple Tariq caught sight of a woman. She was wending her way towards the exit, her eyes glued to the ground.

Inadvertently, Tariq stepped forward as if to apprehend his sister-in-law. He was about to call her name, ask what she was doing here on her own and offer to go back with her, when he noticed a middle-aged man approaching Pembe. He grabbed her elbow, murmured something inaudible and gave her a piece of paper, which she accepted with a smile and swiftly put in her pocket.

Behind them, Tariq stood perplexed, his mind roaming wildly, his eyes darting back and forth, under a poster that read: NOTHING ON EARTH CAN HOLD HOUDINI A PRISONER.

The Decision

London, October 1978

On Saturday morning, when Iskender approached the café where he
was to meet Katie, he was astonished to see Tariq standing outside,
pacing up and down, tugging hard at his beard.

'Uncle, what you doin' here?'

'Waiting for you. I stopped by Aladdin's Cave and your friends
told me you might be here.'

Uncle Tariq had left the shop during opening hours to search for him?
Iskender felt his stomach twist in a knot. 'Is everything all right?'

'We need to have a talk. Man to man.'

'Is this about the money you gave me the other day?'

'Oh, just shut up and listen to me.'

'But I've got to see someone now.'

'Never mind about that,' Tariq said, his voice coming out as a
croak.

Only then did Iskender realize how tense his uncle was, how profusely he was perspiring in his sweater, as if the day were scorching
hot. They sat on a nearby garden wall, surrounded by an awkward
silence. Tariq lit a cigarette. Iskender wondered if Katie could see
them from where she was sitting inside the café, and what he would
say to her if she came out to ask what on earth was going on.

'My son,' Tariq said. 'I've some bad news for you.'

'Yeah, I figured.'

Tariq drew unsteadily on his cigarette, smoke curling in and out of
his nostrils, and said, in the quietest voice, 'It's about your mother.'

*

When Iskender entered the café, his lips were pursed, his eyes hard,
his face as pale as a ghost. He marched towards Katie, who was

waiting at their usual table, about to finish a scone and halfway through her second strawberry and banana milkshake.

'Late again,' Katie said with a sigh.

'Sorry.'

'I've got used to it, you know. But I was hoping today would be different. I thought, for once, you'd care about someone other than you.'

Iskender took her hand and kissed her fingertips. 'Why're you so grumpy?'

'Why? As if you don't know why.' Katie paused, as if on the verge of saying something else, but then she started to cry.

Iskender fished a wad of money out of his pocket and placed it into her palm. 'This should help a bit.'

When she didn't make a comment, he added, 'I got it from my uncle. Never had a chance to give it to you because you didn't want to see me.'

'Well, I told you I had to think this over. On my own.'

'So?'

'So put that money back,' Katie snapped and pulled away as if she had touched a red-hot coal.

'What do you mean?'

'I've changed my mind, Alex.'

'You've done what?'

'Don't give me that look. It's just . . . I'm not going to do it. I'm having this baby.'

'Are you out of your fuckin' mind?' Iskender exclaimed. Then he dropped his voice. 'You're only sixteen. Your mother will have a heart attack.'

'It's all right. She already knows.'

'You must be kidding!' Gripped with a new suspicion, Iskender hissed, 'Oh, I see. She's the one who's brainwashed you.'

'That's not true! Why do you always get so worked up when I mention her?'

'Because we've talked this through. We made a decision! Together! I went to my uncle, got the money. I found the clinic. I made an appointment. Twice! You kept postponing. Finally we agreed to go ahead. And now the princess says she's changed her mind.'

Katie started to cry again. But it felt different this time, devoid of self-pity. A tear dropped into her milkshake, leaving a salty drop on the pink surface. 'This is a child of love. He has a right to be born.'

'That's bollocks, Katie Evans.'

'No, it is not,' she protested. 'I already feel connected to it . . . him . . . or her, whatever. I'm already three months gone.'

'What? Why didn't you tell me?'

'I didn't know myself,' she said fiercely. 'But it doesn't matter. When our baby is born, I want you to come to live with me and my mother.'

Iskender arched his brows. 'You really believe in this crap, don't you? You've gone barmy!'

Katie pushed back her chair with a loud scrape, and in a shrill voice full of hurt, and almost unrecognizable, she said, 'I'm not gonna sit here and let you talk to me like that. I'm outta here.'

'Where the hell are you going?'

'Home. To lie down. Mum says I shouldn't tire myself too much.'

Iskender slammed the table, the bang so loud a few customers glanced up at them. But Katie didn't seem intimidated. 'Tell you what, why don't you calm down and think of some names? Have a couple ready for boys and girls.'

Taking a deep breath, Iskender sat still, his head in his hands, his stomach twisting again. He didn't look up. He could sense the waiter watching this little drama unfold, wondering what he would do now that his girlfriend had stormed out. Right now, he neither wanted to see his friends nor to go home. He bit into what remained of Katie's scone, brushing off the crumbs that fell on his lap. He wished he could just as easily get Uncle Tariq's awful insinuation out of his head, leaving no trace of it behind. Feeling self-conscious, he took out one of the booklets that the Orator had given him a while ago, which he had been carrying inside his jacket pocket but never opened. He tried to wade through the verbose sentences, the words sliding by in a jumble of letters. Soon he gave up and called the waiter to order more food than he could possibly eat. After all, he had money.

Mother

London, October 1978

Yunus cycled along Richmond Road, the wind tossing the soft curls in his hair. He wore a starched white shirt, buttoned up so tightly that his neck had turned an alarming pink. He did not undo a single button, for he believed that he looked more handsome like this. Besides, the style went well with his leather jacket, which though big for him was the coolest thing he had ever worn. His cheeks burned with shame as he thought about how he had got hold of it.

Earlier that morning, Yunus had rolled out of bed with a mission. In the dim light that washed the corridor, he tiptoed to his brother's room. Iskender had had a boxing match the night before and come home late, tired out. He was snoring lightly, curled up in a ball, his head under his pillow. The jacket his mother had bought him for his last birthday was tossed on a chair, its leather so dark and sleek that it shone like black ice. The walls were covered in posters. *Star Wars*, Muhammad Ali in the ring, Bruce Lee's *The Way of the Dragon*, Superman flying over Manhattan, James Dean riding a motorcycle, a Union Jack, Kenny Burns confronting Frank Stapleton in Arsenal v. Nottingham Forest.

As Yunus glanced around, he felt a pang of envy he didn't know he had in him. Iskender had his own world in here, sports gear, trainers and, most of all, freedom. Nobody meddled in his life. He came home at irregular hours, left whenever he pleased, and seemed to owe no one an explanation. It wasn't fair, and Yunus knew he wasn't the only one who thought so.

With a newly found stealth, Yunus put his arms into the leather jacket, feeling both discomfited and thrilled. Discomfited because he was taking something that belonged to his brother, and, even though he would return it that evening, it was still theft. He also felt thrilled, if not actually a few inches taller, as he assured himself that Tobiko would like him better this way. The jacket was cool, all the rage. Tobiko would surely see that he was not a little boy any more.

Just then Iskender turned in bed, his head sliding from under the pillow. Yunus held his breath, unmoving. He waited until he was sure his brother was sound asleep again. He remembered the days when Daddy would scold and punish Iskender for every little wrongdoing, but those were long past. Now, Iskender seemed to think he was in charge, always hot under the collar and impossible to reach. If only Mum would stand up to him and make him accept that she was the boss, but she was too distracted and distant.

The secret. Hard as he tried Yunus could not bring himself to hate the man he had seen with Mum. Who was he? How could he make her smile like that when no one else could? Would he try to take her away? But he couldn't ask. He couldn't tell. No one.

As he cycled fast and forcefully in his jacket, Yunus decided he would never get married. It was too messy, too painful. Why did so many people get hitched when so few wanted, really wanted, to remain so? Yunus liked living in communes better. The only thing he didn't like about them was the dirt and the dust. Otherwise, he was convinced that squatting resulted in greater happiness. When he grew up, instead of starting a family, he would start a squat with Tobiko. They would have lots of friends and plenty of food in the fridge, and if they had babies, they would raise them all together.

Chaining his bike to a wooden fence, Yunus made his way towards the house that belonged to the Captain's mother. To his surprise he found the door ajar. He checked the rooms on the ground floor, the kitchen and the bathroom. The punks were nowhere to be seen. Perhaps they had gone out to buy a few things or to scavenge furniture from the local skips. It was quiet except for the sounds of a dripping tap and some creaking pipes. Yunus decided to wait in the living room, flicking through a pile of grubby handouts, comic books and flyers – one with the photo of a youth smashing a shop window. Underneath the picture it said:

The State is waging social war against its subjects.
You know why? Because that is its function.
That's what it means to be a State.

Resist the State's Ideological Apparatuses.
Resist their compulsory happiness.

Yunus didn't know what Ideological Apparatuses were, but he had an idea about what 'the State' was: a woman with a large bosom, magnetic personality and impressive bouffant. Whenever Mum wished to praise a woman for her strength and skills, did she not say *Devlet gibi kadin*?★ What he didn't get was why on earth the punks would be upset with such women and *their apparatuses*.

The boy was still inspecting the flyer when he was startled by a blast of music. Almost simultaneously he realized two things: that the noise was coming from upstairs and that it was the sort of catchy pop song the squatters loathed with a vengeance. The punks would never listen to that kind of music. It must be Mrs Powell, he assumed. But that, too, was odd. Remembering how despondent the woman had seemed when they had met, he couldn't picture the same person listening to such a cheerful song.

Curious, Yunus climbed the stairs, now detecting a slightly out-of-tune female voice accompanying the lyrics. He stopped in front of the bedroom and knocked on the door. He waited, knocked again. Getting no answer, he peeked in.

There, in the middle of the room was Tobiko, her eyes half closed, her hands clutching a hairbrush, her entire body twisting and twirling as she sang and danced. She had moved the furniture aside to create more space. The curtains were shut tight against the day, penetrated only by splinters of sunlight. In this dim setting she looked lean and tall, and totally unlike herself.

Yunus stood rooted to the spot, gawking at the punk priestess he loved. After what felt like an eternity, the song reached the end. *Take a chance on me* . . . Tobiko chanted into her bristly microphone, falling on her knees, shaking her head while her hand drew spirals in the air, a mixture of Swedish pop with Indian dancing. No sooner had the melody subsided than she opened her eyes, aware of a presence in

★ 'She is a woman who is a state unto herself.'

the room. She turned towards the door and gasped. 'Oh, Yunus! You scared the hell out of me.'

'I'm sorry,' Yunus mumbled. 'Didn't mean to.'

Tobiko rose, a little unsteadily, attempted a smile, diffident, almost bashful. She placed the hairbrush on the dressing table, turned off the cassette player and opened the curtains, blinking at the light. 'What're you doin' here?'

'I came to see you. Found the door open,' said Yunus. 'What were you listening to?'

'Oh, I was just killing time. Mrs Powell has lots of this sort of pap,' she said, tailing off.

'Where is she?'

'Doctor's appointment. She won't be back till three.' Tobiko dropped her voice to a whisper. 'I think she's seeing a shrink.'

'Really? She was very sad,' said Yunus pensively, but was immediately distracted by another thought. 'The music you were playing, it was ABBA, right?'

'How do you know?'

'Mum likes it too,' said Yunus, beaming.

'Well, I don't, really. Not my cup of tea. It's too cheesy. Don't you think?'

Yunus regarded Tobiko with tender amazement. For the first time since the day they had met, he caught a glimpse of the little girl inside her. He wasn't the only one, he realized, who was trying to appear older and tougher than he actually was.

Unaware of his thoughts Tobiko said, 'You've got yourself a nice jacket there.'

'Thanks,' Yunus said, but didn't let the subject drop. 'Do you think you could play that song again and teach me what you were doing?'

Tobiko smiled puckishly. 'You wanna dance with me, petal?'

Though he blushed up to his ears Yunus didn't backtrack. 'Yeah, why not?'

'All right,' Tobiko conceded. 'But since you've made such an effort, I'd better put on something nice too.'

Together they opened the wardrobe and were astonished to find it crammed to overflowing with clothes and accessories, shoes and posh hats.

'This lady must be spending all her money on clothes,' said Tobiko.

'She has nothing in black,' Yunus remarked.

But Tobiko, the woman who wore nothing but punk fashion, didn't seem to mind. She looked admiringly at a mauve scarf, a champagne-beige skirt, a lilac blouse. There was an evening gown with sparkling sequins, a jacket trimmed with brown fox, a fur coat that would reach down to her ankles, soft to the touch.

Tobiko took out a hanger with a long vintage dress on it, satin and taffeta, a purple so pale that it was almost white. It had a nipped-in waist and the thinnest amethyst straps, decorated with a hundred gems.

'You'd look pretty in that,' Yunus said.

Tobiko shook her head as if she found the idea preposterous. Yet when she spoke, she said, 'Can you leave me alone for a few minutes? Don't come back till I call you.'

Yunus waited in the corridor for an eternity. When he was invited back into the room, there was another woman there, someone who had Tobiko's eyes and her tattoos, but other than that nothing in common with her. She had let down her hair and got rid of her make-up. The black lipstick was replaced by pink and the smoky eye-shadow was gone. Instead of torn fishnet stockings she wore flesh-coloured tights. Gold platform shoes, diamond drop earrings, a bashful smile on her face, a whiff of perfume in the air, enchanting.

Yunus let out a whistle in the way Iskender had taught him. 'You look . . .' He dithered, realizing no word was powerful enough to describe what he was seeing. So he ventured, 'You look like the State.'

Tobiko laughed. 'I am the State,' she said, opening her arms wide.

Then she grabbed two hairbrushes, one for herself, one for Yunus. She turned on the cassette player and, as the music began, they sashayed on stage, hand in hand, all smiles. Thousands had come to listen to them tonight. All tickets had been sold out weeks before; many more were waiting outside the concert hall. Light as a feather, cool in his leather jacket, Yunus played the piano, the guitar, the drums, the saxophone. She sang and danced, flapping her skirts. At each refrain they stood back to back, leaning against each other. The audience went crazy.

When the music was over and they were both panting on the floor, Tobiko put her arms around Yunus. 'The other day you were asking me about secrets. Well, our love for ABBA will be our secret. Promise me you can keep it.'

That afternoon Yunus learned things about Tobiko he had never imagined could be true. Still clad in her ABBA dress, she smoked a joint and confessed to him that she hadn't ditched Toby, her ex-boyfriend. It had been the other way round. He had left her, just like that, shattering her heart to pieces. Then she had met the Captain, but she didn't love him, though she couldn't let him go either. She had been bolder in the past, but with every passing day she was becoming more dependent, clingy. She said it was all because she had an incurable Electra complex. She equated the men she loved with her father, and still competed with her mother. Then she showed Yunus a short poem entitled 'Mother'. But, just as Yunus had begun to read it, they heard footsteps downstairs. Mrs Powell had returned.

Tobiko panicked. 'Oh, no, shit!'

'Don't worry,' Yunus said. 'I'll go and distract her while you change.' Then he put the poem in the pocket of his jacket and scrambled downstairs.

★

In the evening, at the dinner table, Iskender shot one menacing glance after another at Yunus, but refused to ask where his jacket had been all day. After supper he announced he was going out for a walk. He would go to see the boys, and play snooker for a while. He needed that – to collect his thoughts. Despite his mother's objection, he left, paying her no attention. Since the talk he had had with his uncle, he had been treating his mother frostily, though he had still not confronted her.

The evening was crisp, nippy. Iskender pulled up the collar of his jacket and thrust his hands in his pockets. There was something in his pocket, a piece of paper. He took it out and read it by the next street-lamp.

With a simple swoop of his hand, Iskender crumpled the paper and tossed it into a rubbish bin. Somebody was playing games with him. All night long he tried to figure out who it could be, and, when he couldn't, returned to the last two lines of the message, which went round and round in his head:

Mother lies, Mother deceives,
She is not who she says she is.

★★★

Shrewsbury Prison, 1991

Slow day. Painfully sluggish. Work in the laundry until 11.30. Return for lunch. Read a book in the afternoon, listen to Zeeshan blabber on about love and harmony. At four o'clock we are all locked up. Half an hour later Officer McLaughlin appears.

'It seems like you're gonna have a visitor soon,' he says.

'Who is it?'

'Why don't you see "it" for yourself.'

I've only ever had visits from Esma, and even she stopped coming this year. But I'm surprised that Officer McLaughlin has approved this. Given my recent track record he could have vetoed it straight away. I spend the rest of the evening brooding like a bird on a nest. Then it finally dawns on me. Officer McLaughlin knows that whoever it is that's coming to see me could throw me off balance. He's relying on that. I have a protective shell round myself no one gets through, but there are a few people who can shatter my nerves. Only a few. They can get through my armour the way a ghost walks through walls.

'You worried,' says Zeeshan.

Regardless of whether it's a question or a statement, I don't deny it.

'Yeah, it's bloody stressful not knowing who's gonna come to see me tomorrow.'

Zeeshan says, 'We never know what comes tomorrow but we always start new day, hopeful.'

I'm not in the mood to listen to his nonsense. So I lie on my bunk and shut myself off from the outside world. It feels like another bad day. I've had many of those in my life. But there is one day that was worse than them all: the morning after.

246

The morning after committing a crime you awake from a bottomless night. Somewhere in your brain there is a signal, a red light flashing. You try to ignore it. There is a chance, however slight, that it was all a dream. You hold on to that chance, like a falling man who grabs at the first rope he sees. A minute goes by. An hour. You lose count of time. Until, suddenly, it hits you. The rope is not tied to anything, and its end is loose. You tumble into reality head first.

There I was on Lavender Grove, a knife in my hand. I heard the screams. Shrill, unending. Somebody was howling. Oddly, it sounded like my mother. But it couldn't have been her, for she was lying on the ground, bleeding. Echoes growing inside my brain. I looked at my left hand. My stronger hand. But it had gone slack, as if it had been attached to my body only temporarily and now belonged to someone else. I tossed the knife under a parked car. If I could, I would have thrown away my hand.

I began to run. My jacket was splattered with blood. I can't explain why nobody stopped me, but they didn't. I darted down alleyways, through back gardens, without the slightest idea where I was going. I must have crossed streets, bumped into people, frightened dogs. I don't remember. The next half-hour is blank. But I remember finding a phonebox.

I rang Uncle Tariq. I told him what I had done. There was an awkward silence. I thought he hadn't heard me. So I repeated myself. I told him I had punished Mum for her illicit affair. From now on she'd never do such a thing again. I said her wound wasn't too bad but it would take some time to heal. I had stabbed her once on the right side of her chest. That would show her how grave her sin was. It would give her time to think about her mistake, to repent. And the man would be scared out of his wits. He would leave us alone. Our family's honour was cleansed.

'What have you done, son?' His voice sounded strangled. 'This is terrible.'

I was taken aback. 'Bb . . . but . . . wee . . . ttt . . . alk . . . ed ab . . . ab . . . ou . . . ttt . . . this.'

'Surely we did not,' my uncle said.

The man who had told me everything and then impressed upon me, over and over again, that I had to do something and do it soon, had vanished into thin air. I was stunned.

'Iskender, son, you have to turn yourself in. I'll tell the police this is exactly what I told you when you rang me. You cannot run from the law!'

Suddenly I had the strangest suspicion that Uncle Tariq had rehearsed this moment. Had he been waiting for this? Preparing his speeches. What he would tell me on the phone, what he would share with the Old Bill, what he would declare in court . . . He was prepared for it all.

'Son, are you there? Tell me where you are.'

I hung up. I took off my jacket and dumped it in a rubbish bin. Then I went to Katie's house on Albion Drive. I had walked her home many times but I had never gone inside. I rang the bell. To my relief it was she who opened the door.

'Alex, what a surprise,' she said. A smile bloomed on her face. 'Oh, sweetie, I knew you were going to come.'

Katie ushered me in. She said her mother would be thrilled to learn I had decided to come to live with them. She hugged me, her belly hard and round between us. She didn't look four months pregnant to me. More like she had swallowed a ball.

I asked Katie to show me the bathroom. I washed my hands. The me in the mirror was no different than the one I had seen on other days. I half expected there to be something unusual in my face, in my eyes. But there wasn't. I washed my hands again, scrubbing hard. The soap smelled of roses. I opened the cupboard and found some bleach. On the bottle there was a pretty housewife, her smile whiter than clouds. I poured the bleach on my hands. There were cuts in my palms. It hurt like hell. I kept scrubbing. There was something under my fingernails. Dirt? Paint? Blood? It just wouldn't wash off.

Katie came in to ask if everything was all right. She hugged me, checking the couple in the mirror. Me, her, our baby. She took it in with pride. I noticed she had the same smile as the bleach lady's. A sense of achievement.

She turned off the water. 'You're clean enough for me, love.'

We went into the living room. Katie's mum was sitting in an armchair by the window, waiting. She was wearing a wrap-dress. One of those silky things you see on TV. Royal blue. You could see her breasts. She had *freckles all across her chest, like specks of nutmeg. Her hair was freshly combed. Her lips painted red. Her head could have dined out in a posh restaurant, but the rest of her seemed in a domestic mood. I tried to concentrate on her face. I tried not to glance below her head.*

Mrs Evans offered me tea in bone-china cups. Warm fruit scones. We ate in silence. There were framed photos on the walls. Dozens of them. I saw Katie's father in some of them. He didn't strike me as the kind of man who would stray.

Mrs Evans was watching my every move. I had a feeling she was checking under my fingernails. I hid my hands.

'Alex, my daughter tells me you want to name the baby Maggie if it's a girl and Tom if it's a boy.'

I turned to Katie. She avoided my eyes.

'Yeah, I guess.'

Afterwards Mrs Evans asked me if I believed I would make a responsible father. I said I didn't know but that I would do my best.

'Sometimes one's best is just not good enough,' she said.

It sounded like something she'd heard on TV. Or like something someone had told her in the past. She said she would help us – a temporary scheme, of course – until we got on our feet. She would do this for her grandchild. The first. She smiled. Her teeth were pearly-white and perfect.

At night Katie told me we had to sleep in separate rooms. I would have to take the sofa in the living room. She said it was just for now. Soon we would get married and then we would have the same bed. For ever.

She brought me clean sheets, a pillowcase. Slowly, she pulled up her sweater. Her breasts were swollen, her nipples dark rings. I could see the veins – blue, big, jutted. She asked me to put my ear on her belly. I didn't hear anything for a while. Then I felt a movement, like someone stretching from a deep sleep. One, two, four times. It was like magic.
I wondered if Mum had made Dad listen to her belly when she was pregnant with me.

I pushed Katie away. I said, 'Sorry, I need to sleep.'

'Of course, darling.'

When she left me alone, I stretched out, looking around. Net curtains, cushions with flower designs, swirling wallpaper, an ornate vase on the mantelpiece, a grandfather clock. I thought I would never sleep but as soon as my head hit the pillow I was dead to the world. I woke up at dawn. Katie was standing by my side. Her face pale, her eyes wide open.

'Alex,' she said. 'There are two policemen at the door.'

I got up and held her head between my palms. I kissed her. Her mouth tasted salty. The taste of panic.

'They're asking for you.'

We shuffled out into the corridor. Katie's mum was standing by the door in her nightgown. There were traces of cream on her face. Her lower lip quivered. She pulled her daughter close, as if I had a contagious disease. I saw the lights of a police car in the background. There were two officers. One of them looked like James Callaghan, only he didn't have glasses. They hadn't seen me yet. I asked Katie to tell them I was getting dressed.

The decision to escape was not a conscious one. I just did it. I went to the kitchen, opened the door, sneaked into the garden and jumped over the fence, and then over the next one. While Katie was talking to the police, I was already out of her road and into the next.

★

The last day of November 1978. I was about to change my mind when I saw her turn the corner. She had been shopping, bags in her hands. She walked unhurriedly, taking her time. It made my blood boil. I had forbidden her to leave the house.

She slowed her steps, staring at a street musician, her back turned to me. I studied her profile. She was smiling. A surge of resentment rose inside me. Had I not told her that she was forbidden to go out, that she could not wear dresses that showed her legs? And here she was defying my rules, making fun of me.

I followed her. She stared at a shop window, obviously in no rush to go home. I thought she might be waiting to meet her lover but no such thing happened. When we approached our street, she tripped, dropping her purse. An old khaki thing I had never seen before. As she was picking it up, she noticed me behind her.

'Iskender . . .' she whispered. as if my name were a secret.

Iskender Toprak

The Stick and the Bundle

London, October 1978

Finding the Orator was more difficult than Iskender had thought. He visited several cafés, made a couple of phone calls, but got nowhere. It dawned on him how little he knew the man. All these months it had always been the Orator who had sent a message requesting a meeting and never the other way round. He had no idea where the Orator lived or what he did in his spare time. He remembered him saying he was a student at some polytechnic, but what exactly he studied was a mystery, like everything else.

But, through a friend of a friend, he did manage to find him, in a dingy martial arts studio on Brick Lane. He was surrounded by half a dozen young men in shorts, sitting close together on floor mats, like pigeons huddled under the gables. Some of them had stains of perspiration on their chests, towels around their necks. It looked as if they had just finished a hard session of exercise and had gathered to discuss something substantial before heading to the showers. When they saw Iskender approach, they fell quiet, eyeing him with a distrust they felt no need to hide.

'It's okay,' said the Orator with a wink at the others. 'I know him.'

Iskender didn't like the wink or the tone, but he greeted them all the same. A tilt of his head, the slightest curl of his lip and a short, 'Hey!'

Briskly, the Orator leaped to his feet and placed his right hand on his heart. '*Selamun aleykum*, brother. Would you like to join us?'

'No, thanks. I've . . . I need to be somewhere else. I came to say hi and return the tapes you gave me last time.'

Mumbling something inaudible to his friends, the Orator came forward. Iskender noticed how small the man was when stripped of his winter coat and sweaters. Narrow shoulders, bony wrists, slightly bowed legs.

'You didn't need to come all this way for that.'

'It's all right,' said Iskender, still not sure why he was there.

'You want to talk?'

'O . . . kay. A couple of minutes.'

The two walked to a quiet corner and sat down. Across from them sat an array of weightlifting equipment. They watched a short, thick-set man huff and puff under more weight than he could handle. A film of sweat on his face, red blotches on his cheeks, barely any strength left in his arms.

With a sideways glance at the Orator, Iskender murmured, 'Didn't know you work out. What do you do?'

'Oh, I do tae kwon do. I'm not much of a fighter, though. Not my thing, really. I'm a man of ideas.'

'Then why do you come here?'

'Because people like us ought to know how to defend ourselves. Did you hear what happened yesterday in North End? Skinheads, four of them. They attacked a Bengali shopkeeper. Four against one. Pretty equal, eh?'

'Hadn't heard about that one.'

'They pushed him down and shaved his head. They drew their idiotic symbols on his skull. The poor chap was so terrified he got sick. His wife cries all the time.' He paused for a breath. 'Well, at least you know how to defend yourself.'

Iskender nodded, though he wasn't sure if that was why he had started to box. He didn't do it in order to fight enemies, imaginary or real. He did it because, unlike many other sports that were staged and phoney, boxing was genuine, the true thing. Boxing was a one-to-one reflection of life. You were on your own in the ring. No team work. No substitutes waiting on the sidelines. Every man for himself. The good and the bad, the sublime and the base, the greed and the grace. It was all there. If you wanted to know a man's true character, all you had to do was watch him box.

The Orator said, 'You're a terrific boxer. A natural.'

'How do you know? You've never seen me.'

'I have, actually. I watched you twice on the sly. You don't dodge risky fights and your defence is pretty strong. It's almost like you know where the next punch is coming from. That's a rare talent, one you have to be born with.'

Not knowing whether to feel annoyed or proud, Iskender said nothing.

The Orator paused briefly, his eyes never leaving Iskender. 'Alex, there's something I've been meaning to ask you. Would you consider teaching us how to fight? The brothers could benefit from your know-how.'

Iskender exhaled, thinking. 'Dunno, man. I like to fight alone.'

All at once, the Orator's face was set in a frown. 'Look, I'm going to be honest with you. You're your own man. I can see that. No strings attached. That's the way you like it. But don't forget that great fighters are great inside and out. If you had stronger values you'd be invincible.'

'I don't wanna be invincible.'

'Then what do you want?' demanded the Orator, with absolute authority in his gaze, naked challenge in his tone.

Having never asked himself this question, Iskender had no answer in store.

'Why did you come here looking for me?' the Orator pressed. 'Because one part of you knows the truth. You need to belong somewhere. You need a purpose in life, a new direction. Join us.'

Iskender struggled to think of something to say that would let him off the hook, but nothing came. He unzipped his coat, pulling out the tapes he had borrowed.

'Did you listen to them?'

'Yeah.'

This elicited a grunt from the Orator. 'You never finished the booklets I gave you. None of them. And now the tapes – is that too much to ask?'

'Look, my brother and sister have the tape recorder all the time, okay? But I did listen to bits and pieces. There were a couple of things I enjoyed. Like the brotherhood part. One stick breaks easily but a bundle is unbreakable.'

'*But?*'

'But . . . I dunno, man. I guess I've too much going on right now. My girlfriend is in a jam. And . . . umm, I need to take care of some family matters.'

The Orator didn't comment. He knew Iskender was the type of boy who would tell more when asked less.

'What you said earlier struck a chord with me,' Iskender said. 'I mean, if your parents are in the wrong, you've got to stand up against them, right?'

'Yes, but don't get confused. What I meant was, if your parents don't know God, you've got to choose God over them. Because God is bigger than your parents. But beware. If you don't know God yourself and if you disobey your parents, you'll be floating in the air. No principles to hold you up, man.'

'Let's say, someone close to me . . . ' Iskender pulled his zip up to his chin. 'I mean, hypothetically, say, someone in my family is sinning. I'm trying to find out what my duty is.'

The Orator stiffened, sensing the gravity of the question. He scrutinized Iskender with brightened interest, only now noticing a nervous twitch at the corner of his mouth, and his fingernails, each chewed to the quick. He asked, 'Who, for instance?'

'Let's say, my mother.'

There was an uneasy pause before the Orator remarked, 'Well, talk to your father. It's his duty, more than yours. But if he is not in . . . then it's down to you. I'd never let my mother or sister or wife shame me.'

'But what can I do?' asked Iskender.

'I'm not going to tell you what to do unless you trust me fully. You understand what I'm saying? Come and join us, be part of something bigger, man. That's the right way. There's the answer to all your questions.'

'Umm, I'll think about it.'

'Yeah, go ahead, mull it over. But don't take too long. 'Cos something might happen while you're doing your thinking.'

★

That same evening Iskender stood by the gates of a club he had never visited before. He had anticipated this scene in his mind so many times that it felt curiously familiar. No sooner had he taken a step forward than he was stopped by a bodyguard twice his size. Slate-blue suit, mirrored sunglasses even though the sun had long gone from the skies, bald as an egg, a neck so short and thick that it looked as if his head had been mounted on his shoulders.

'How old are you, lad?'

'Old enough,' said Iskender, determined not to be intimidated.

'That's not an answer in my book.'

'I dunno which book that is, but I need to go in.'

More astonished than annoyed, the bodyguard took off his sunglasses. His eyes were too small and too close for his face. Impossible to read. 'Are you testing my patience, kid? Because I warn you, it's already spent.'

Iskender felt his cheeks heat up. The bodyguard could knock him out if he wanted to, and yet, somehow, he felt that the man was not as threatening as he seemed. *All bark and no bite.* It was only a hunch, but when it came to street fights his hunches were usually right.

'Well, I'm looking for my father. Is that a crime?'

A shadow of curiosity crossed the bodyguard's face. 'And does your father work here?'

'No. But he shags a woman who does.'

Sucking in a long, deep breath, the bodyguard said, 'Uh-hmm, and you were hoping to be introduced to this lady, I take it?'

'No, man! Why would I want that?'

'Just asking. How about your father, then? You've a bone to pick with him?'

'I'm not lookin' for trouble. I just need to talk to my old man, is all.'

The bodyguard put his sunglasses back on. 'Three minutes. Not a second more. You go inside, find your father and bring him out. If you're not back here in that time, I'll come inside and break your legs. Got it?'

'That's the ticket, man, thanks.'

As Iskender strode into the club, he thrust his hand into his pocket, feeling the glass flask there. It was a miracle the bodyguard hadn't searched him. Liquid acid. Practical and effective. All he needed to do was to aim it at her face. His father would not want to see her any more. Never again would any man desire her.

How many times had he imagined this moment? He would march into the club, which would be noisy, smoky, crowded and suffocating, and head to the bar to get himself a drink. Whisky probably. On the rocks. That would be the right choice. He would finish it in two gulps and then, his throat still burning, sneak backstage. He would stride along the narrow corridors that reeked of sweat and perfume. It wouldn't take him long to find her room. He would knock on the door that said *Roxana* but would not wait for an answer before going in.

'Who are you?' she would say. A trace of panic creeping into her voice. Her face would be heavily painted, her lips red as blood, her breasts showing through her robe.

I'm the son of the man you stole from his family.

That sentence changed each time Iskender envisaged the scene. Sometimes he replaced it with 'You don't know me but I know you too well.' At other times it would be 'I'm the one who should ask that question. Who do you think you are, to ruin our family?'

The woman's reaction would also vary. Mostly she would be embarrassed, apologetic. But sometimes she would make a scene, her nerves whittled to shreds. He imagined a stiletto hurled at the wall. A champagne glass shattered. Iskender had considered each option. If she were to get aggressive, hysterical, he would produce the bottle in his pocket. If she were remorseful, he would take it easy, giving her another chance.

At other times in the fantasy she would throw herself on the floor/chaise longue/sofa/carpet, tears of shame rolling down her cheeks. Among all the possible scenarios, this was Iskender's favourite.

'Oh, I didn't know he was married,' she would say, sobbing. 'I didn't know he had a family. He never told me.'

In this version Iskender would not take out the bottle. Instead he would console her. She would give her word never to see Adem again, and even when she turned old and grey, she would honour her promise.

His mind buzzing with such thoughts, Iskender scrutinized the club, and was surprised to see only a handful of people around, most of whom were staff. Too early for the punters. He walked to the bar, which was redolent with a musky-sweet aroma from hundreds of drinks over the years. A large, oval back-mirror with neon lights; a sleek, shiny, wooden countertop. Iskender allowed his finger to move along the scripts and symbols incised on the hard surface.

The bartender – an Afro-Caribbean man with tightly braided hair – was drying a glass. He inspected the customer with a wry glint in his eyes. 'How old are you?'

'Old enough,' said Iskender.

'Uh-hm, can I see your ID, Mr Old-enough?'

'Hey, if I'm here it means I'm old enough to be here. Otherwise that hulk at the entrance would never have let me in, right?'

'Nice try,' said the bartender. 'I'll give you a glass of water for that. Sparkling. No ice. And that's the most you'll be getting from me.'

Iskender sipped his water, and stood in front of the stage, observing the curtains on both sides. Was she back there? Should he go find her now? Again, he touched the bottle in his pocket. It felt both cold and warm under his fingers. He was still contemplating his next move, steeling himself for the encounter ahead, when he noticed the bodyguard looking for him. The man tapped his watch, unsmiling, unyielding. Iskender finished his water, thanked the bartender and shuffled out. Nothing was going as planned.

He waited on the pavement, his mind spinning. After what seemed like an eternity he noticed someone coming in his direction. His hair uncombed, his head lowered, his step apprehensive, as if he were afraid that his legs would give way. He didn't notice the boy as he passed by.

'Dad –'

Adem stopped and turned around. A smile bloomed on his face, easy and genuine, but it was quickly replaced by a darker expression. 'Iskender . . . has something happened to your brother or sister?'

'No. They're fine, really.'

For a moment Adem seemed relieved. But after relief came suspicion, and after suspicion, irritation. 'You shouldn't be here.'

This, too, was something Iskender had failed to anticipate. He had expected his father to be uncomfortable upon seeing him, perhaps unsettled, but anger was not in the picture. Iskender's face was impassive before he snapped. 'And neither should you.'

Adem's mouth turned down at the corners, his eyes blazing. 'Watch your mouth, lad. You can't talk to me like that.'

'I want you to come home, *Father*,' he said.

The insinuation was not lost on Adem. 'Go back to your mother before I break your bones.'

'What is it with my bones today? Everybody wants to break 'em.'

They stood in silence for awhile. Father and son retreated into their thoughts while holding each other's gaze, challenging the other to speak first. It was at that moment that an uncanny feeling overtook Adem, as though he were staring into a mirror, watching his younger self. His boy was like him but with more privileges, and none of the anxiety and passivity that had cost him dearly.

'I'll return when the time comes,' Adem said finally.

'And when will that be? When you get tired of that slut –'

The slap was immediate. Iskender seemed less bowled over by his father's reaction than by what had come out of his own mouth. He couldn't believe he had spoken like that. It was against everything in his upbringing.

Having witnessed the slap, the bodyguard angled towards them. 'Hey, you two. Take it easy or I'll ring the police.'

'It's o . . . kay,' mumbled Iskender as though to himself. There was an obscure look in his eyes, a sparkle that wasn't there before. Calmly, too calmly, he turned to his father and said, 'If you hit me again, I'll hit you back. My punch is stronger.'

Adem paled. He felt a pain in his chest so sharp that for a second he couldn't breathe. It wasn't only the shock, the sorrow and the shame of having his son insult him in front of strangers. There was something deeper, more painful. A belated recognition. Now he saw that this was what he himself should have done many years ago. When his own *baba* beat him, and kept doing so even after Adem had become taller than him, this is what he, too, should have done. It was an excruciating regret.

Taking a step towards Iskender, Adem slapped him again, harder. That was when the most frightening thing happened. Howling like a wounded animal, Iskender rammed himself into the wall of the club. He hit his forehead. Once, twice, three times. Thud, thud, thud.

Adem tried to control him, but to no avail. 'Don't touch me,' Iskender bellowed.

It was the bodyguard who pulled him away from the wall. But the need to hurt was so engulfing that Iskender couldn't stop. He sank his teeth into the guard's shoulder until he drew blood. He stomped on the man's foot, and shot his head back, hitting the bodyguard's chin with a loud dull thump. The man was expecting none of this. He lost his composure, and his face flashed crimson. He attacked back.

Adem tried to intervene. "No, no. Please, don't. He's my son.'

Other people clustered around. Customers, waiters, a few dancers. Among them was Roxana, watching the scene with wide eyes and a heavy heart.

When they were finally pulled apart, the bodyguard was trembling. 'I don't wanna see you two here again. You hear me? If I see you around I swear to God I'll hit you so hard you won't know what day it is.'

'Come on, let's go.' Adem pulled his son by the arm, gently but firmly.

They walked in silence for a few minutes, and once they were out of sight sat on the pavement under a streetlamp. Iskender's breath came in ragged puffs, as he tasted the blood in his mouth. 'Mother is seeing someone,' he said, bone-weary.

'What?'

'You heard me,' said Iskender. 'You need to return home and fix things.'

Adem took out a cigarette, lit it and offered it to his son. Seeing the surprise on Iskender's face, he said, 'Come on. I already know that you smoke.'

He lit another cigarette for himself. They smoked side by side. The night felt chilly, drab but full of possibilities. 'Does she love him?'

Iskender could not believe his ears. 'Dad, what are you saying?'

Adem put his hand on his son's knee. 'Look, I know you don't understand. Ten years ago, I would have been mad as hell. I would have done anything to stop it. But now I'm old enough to know I can't make your mother love me. She asked me several times for a divorce. I've ignored her request but it was the right thing to do.'

Hearing the word 'love' from his father's lips astonished Iskender. True, there had been times in the past when he had questioned how and why his parents had got together, but this was no longer about love. Adem was his father, the head of the family. Not a romantic teenager. 'But Father —'

'Listen, there was a headman once who told me that a man's love is a reflection of his character. I never understood what he meant, but now I know.' He let the smoke curl out of his nostrils. 'You think I'm not angry at your mother. I am. But I'm angrier with myself. We never loved each other. It was so wrong, our marriage. But I don't regret it because you were born, and Esma, and Yunus.'

Then something happened that Adem did not take seriously at the time, but that years later he would remember vividly, and always with a piercing regret. Iskender flicked his cigarette, watching its feeble light arc against the darkness surrounding it, and said, 'If you don't take care of this matter, then I will.'

The Rope

London, October 1978

Quickening her step, Pembe approached the cinema she knew so well by now. The click of her low heels against the pavement was steady, lulling. She did not look up or around, keeping her gaze focused on the ground, as if she were a child again and this was a game. If she did not see the world, perhaps the world would not see her.

She deliberately arrived late each time, reaching the cinema five or ten minutes after the film had started. It lessened the chances of their being seen together. Lately, though, she had grown a bit less cautious. On two occasions she had even walked with him on the street, once to buy some flowers, another time to listen to a street musician. She was still anxious, as always, but now there was an urge inside her, a voice dying to come out, to be heard. Having never experienced anything like this before, she didn't know what to do with this new audaciousness that was, and wasn't, a part of her.

A few threads from Pembe's grey coat caught in the door as she hurriedly pushed it open. She entered the building, inhaling the odour from filthy ashtrays, and the familiar smells from the refreshment bar, buttered popcorn, crisps and sweets. The swirls on the stained carpet made her dizzy if she stared at them for too long. She found it all strangely comforting. No sooner had she stepped into the foyer than a sense of lightness descended upon her. She felt calm, sheltered. The earth stopped moving, prompting her to do the same, and without a worry for the future she allowed the moment to surround her.

The young usher at the entrance to the auditorium checked her ticket, then opened the doors and signalled for her to follow him. The film had started. It was half dark inside, bathed in the silver light that bounced off the screen at each bright scene. As she followed the usher's torchlight, Pembe took a quick look round. There were ten or fifteen people inside, more than usual. For a fleeting second, she felt a tension that hadn't been there a moment ago.

Elias always sat in the same place. The middle row, the middle seat. Once someone else had occupied the seat, a glitch that had caused Pembe to go and sit next to a stranger. '*Hello, darling,*' the man had said, grinning. Horrified, Pembe had leaped to her feet and moved to the front row, where Elias was waiting for her, blissfully unaware.

Now, careful not to trip, Pembe passed by one empty row after another. She noticed an elderly couple holding hands, engrossed in the film. She tried to imagine Elias and herself in the same position, old, frail but still in love. Even the dream didn't feel real.

As she kept edging her way forward, in her distractedness, she did not notice the person sitting in the back row. He had hid himself, having slid down in his seat, his head tilted to the side, merely a shadow. He sat there in the darkness, watching, waiting.

The caramel torchlight stopped at row G. There in the middle, sitting on his own, his eyes shaded by an expectation he didn't allow himself to indulge, was Elias. Thanking the usher, Pembe glided into her seat, her breath quick. Elias turned, smiling. He reached out to her, his forefinger running along her fingertips, like a blind man recognizing his beloved from a touch. He squeezed her hand tenderly. She squeezed back. Over the course of these past months, they had mastered a language with lots of gestures and not many words. Slowly, he leaned forward and planted a kiss on the inside of her wrist, inhaling the smell of her skin. Pembe's heart pounded in her chest. She still didn't look at him. That, too, felt like a childhood game. If she didn't see him, he wouldn't be visible and if he weren't visible, perhaps he would never disappear.

Together they watched *The Good, the Bad and the Ugly*. She had not seen the film before. He had. It was their first film with sound. The week before, the cinema had finished its run of silent movies, and launched a new series of classic spaghetti Westerns. Having already agreed to meet there and being fond of the place, they had seen no reason to change plans. Besides, Elias assumed that the film, with its laconic characters and few words, would be equally easy for her to follow.

In just a few seconds, Pembe found herself drawn into the film. As Blondie, Tuco and Angel Eyes engaged in a maze of conflicts, inciting and dodging all kinds of danger, she watched the story unfold, taking sides. When the Bad inquired, 'If you work for a living, why do you kill yourself working?', she lowered her eyelids, considering the sentence until its meaning hit her fully. When the Bad scoffed at the Good, telling him that, in fact, they were not that different, she couldn't help but flinch. Lately she had begun to contemplate the meaning of good and bad as never before. It was her sister's letters that had compelled her. Her twin was the respectable one, virtuous and pure, unwavering. That left her as the Bad, the unchaste. But it had not always been like this. How fast things changed. Nothing was permanent, everything evolving in a constant flux.

When Tuco sat on a donkey with a noose around his neck, about to be hanged, a flash of dread crossed Pembe's face. She turned her head sideways. For a fraction of a second she thought she saw someone in the back row observing her, but when she checked again it was too dark to be sure. She then heard the Ugly say, 'People with ropes around their necks don't always hang.'

Pembe closed her eyes. For a sickening moment she was in a different place, a different time.

'Hey, are you all right, sweetheart? You seem to have drifted off,' Elias said in her ear, and added in a playful whisper, 'It's just a film.'

She nodded. It was only a film, she knew. In real life, people with ropes around their necks always hanged.

★

They were eight sisters, ages ranging from nine to twenty. The eldest of them was named Hediye, *a gift*. That was what she was, a present from the Creator, the firstborn, much treasured, even if a girl. She had a heart-shaped face, sharp nose, large almond eyes, grey like storm clouds. As the eldest in a family with many siblings and a meagre income, she spent her childhood playing with real babies instead of toys. Hediye was always cleaning, cooking, scrubbing, washing, feeding and rocking the younger ones. Her palms were hennaed, her wrists adorned with bracelets, fake gold, but nothing looked fake on her. Pembe did not remember hearing her complain even once, even though everyone else seemed to be whining all the time. Somehow Hediye had accepted her role, her unending responsibilities, ageing before her time, a girl-woman. Upon Naze's death she was her natural replacement, caring for them all, but especially for the twins, who were still young. When Berzo remarried, his daughters saw the woman as *Papa's wife*, but never as more than that, for their mother was none other than Hediye.

'I'll never get married,' she was fond of saying. 'I'll look after my sisters until all of them have tied the knot. I'll die a spinster.'

These words, heartening as they were for the twins to hear, did not turn out to be true. In the winter of 1957 Hediye started seeing someone. A medical man, *an inoculator*, appointed by the government to provide vaccines against tuberculosis, distrusted by most villagers, hated by all children. How it had all started, how they had met, twelve-year-old Pembe would never learn and the woman she was today could not construe.

Love was an illness, invigorating and uplifting, but a malady nonetheless. Suddenly Hediye was bolder than ever, indomitable. Even their stepmother seemed to fear her, unable to boss her around any longer, uncomfortable in her presence. For Hediye was resolute. The girl who had never had a moment for herself was now eager to make up for lost time. On a cloudless night, when the moon was a golden sickle in the sky, she eloped with this man whom she barely knew.

The next morning there was no one around to give inoculations. The children of the village rejoiced. The remaining vaccines were thrown into the Euphrates, erasing all traces of the stranger who had intruded into their lives, injected them with his ways and, in the end, stolen one of their number.

Pembe remembered the grief that engulfed the house, empty and heavy at once. It felt as if they were mourning a death. But Hediye was now worse than dead. No one asked about her, at least not aloud, her name deemed a profanity.

Their stepmother was particularly vindictive. 'May God burn you in hell!' she swore, seeing imaginary Hediyes everywhere. Suddenly everything that had been fomenting inside her – her shame at not being able to give a baby to a man who had married her solely to have a son; her agony at being as *barren as a desert*; and her resentment at having to take care of another woman's eight children – erupted into a sharp, sour fury at Hediye.

Berzo, however, was oddly silent. His eyes had sunk into their sockets. His head was low, brooding. He barely went to the tea house any more, sitting at home all day long, withdrawn and sulking, smoking cigarettes with an inch of ash dangling at the ends.

It was a harsh winter. Four months passed. One late afternoon in early spring, Hediye returned. She should have sent a message to see if her family were prepared to accept her. Instead she had taken a bus and come back, just like that. The medical man had turned out to be a coward. Even though he had promised to marry her, at the slightest opposition from his family, he had changed his mind, abandoning her in the big city on her own.

Hediye regretted what had happened. She was also frightened. But this was the only home she knew. She had no other place to go. Upon her arrival, finding the door open, she shuffled in. Neither Berzo nor his wife was in the house. But the twins were and the moment they saw Hediye they yelled in joy, clapping their hands, celebrating the return of their mother-sister. They ran rings round her, like planets orbiting the sun.

Yet Hediye was different. Insecure, reserved, tongue-tied. Drawing her knees together, keeping her eyes cast down, she sat on the edge of the divan; in her own house she was like a guest who wasn't sure of being welcome.

After a while their stepmother lumbered in, carrying a huge pile of fleece wool on her back. Her back had hunched, and her cheeks were flushed from the effort. She didn't notice Hediye at first. But she instantly detected the awkward silence in the room, and the twins' discomfort.

'What's going on? Did a cat come here and get your tongues?'

She had barely finished the sentence when she spotted the girl in the corner. The runaway. The bringer of shame. Dropping her load, the woman stood across from the girl, almost transfixed. Then she took a step forward and made a gesture with her lips as if spitting on the floor.

Hediye paled.

In the evening, when all the sisters were at home, nobody dared to speak to Hediye, lest they upset their stepmother. Nobody offered her tea or food. The sisters didn't eat much either. Several hours into this discomfort, Berzo appeared at the door. As soon as he walked in, they sensed that he already knew. He had heard the news and yet he had taken his time, listening to what the other men said. He had been in no haste to reach home.

Hediye sprang to her feet, running to kiss his hand, but her father held back.

'I have no sons,' he said loud enough for everyone to hear. 'God gave me none. I've never understood why He did that. Until today.'

The girls held their breaths, listening. Hediye's shoulders slouched.

'Now I know the reason,' Berzo said. 'If I had a son, I'd ask him to kill you and clean our family's good name. And your brother would go to gaol because of you. He would spend his life rotting amidst four walls.'

Hediye didn't weep, wail or ask for forgiveness. She kept her eyes glued to a spider on the windowsill and remained motionless, wordless.

Into the ensuing silence Berzo said, 'I never thought I'd say this but I'm glad I don't have a son.'

In the evening, as the sisters got ready to sleep on bedmats on the floor, they could hear their father and his wife arguing in the other room, though they could not make out the words. The girls, with their hair unbraided and dressed in thick flannel nightgowns, looked at Hediye, still perched on the divan. Quietly, Pembe stood up.

'Where are you going?' Jamila whispered.

'She must be hungry.'

'Are you mad? Papa and Stepma are not yet asleep. They'll find it out.'

With a shrug, Pembe tiptoed across the room into the kitchen and

266

came back with some bread, cheese and water. Under her sisters' eyes she carried them to Hediye, who accepted only the water.

The next morning Berzo had his breakfast later than usual. As he sipped his black tea and chewed his flat bread, the girls waited. 'I'm going to the tea house,' he said, without meeting anyone's eye.

Upon hearing this, Pembe felt a rush of panic. Their father had not entered the tea house since the day Hediye had run away. What had changed now to make him go there?

'What will I do with her under my roof?' their stepmother grumbled.

'You know what to do,' he said, and said no more.

Soon after, their stepmother, a grim look on her broad face, told them they would all have to leave. *A lot of work to do, carpets to weave.*

As her sisters put on their boots and coats, Pembe lingered behind, seized by a harrowing sense of dread. Something was happening and yet she could not pin it down. Shortly before they left the house, she saw her stepmother carry in the large, round, brass tray used for all their meals. The woman spread the dining cloth on the floor, set up the wooden base and balanced the tray on top. For a second Pembe thought she was serving Hediye some food. But an odd meal it would be. There were no plates. No water. No bread.

Hediye, in the meantime, did not budge. A statue of salt.

The last thing Pembe saw was a cauldron being brought in. Dying to know what was inside, she took a chance. 'I'm not feeling well. My throat is sore. Perhaps I should stay at home.'

The woman shook her head. 'Your father's orders. Nobody stays in the house.'

They went to a neighbour's and wove carpets all day. They knew the pattern by heart. Robin-egg blue, Persian-rose, periwinkle, cinnamon-brown. Pembe loved making colours. Red from henna, yellow from turmeric, brown from crushed walnut shells. As she soaked yarn in a bowl of honeydew, she confided in her twin.

'What do you mean she served her an empty cauldron?' asked Jamila, her eyes wide open.

'I swear she did,' whispered Pembe. 'Perhaps it wasn't empty. But it was peculiar. If there had been food inside, I would have seen steam, right? Or smelled something. Nothing!'

'Go back to work,' said Jamila, because she didn't know what else to say.

In the afternoon they swapped places. This time Pembe let Jamila prepare the dye while she wove. It was tiring. The muscles behind her eyes hurt, and her fingertips were sore. Parts of her body that she never thought about began to ache.

Secretly, Pembe included a motif in her carpet that wasn't part of the intended pattern. If anyone noticed it, and she was sure someone would, they would get upset. But she couldn't help it. It was a tiny mark, an *h*, as a reminder of her sister's name. When the carpet was finished, it would be sold to a local merchant, who would then sell it to a bigger merchant. From there the carpet would be carried to a smart shop in the Grand Bazaar in Istanbul. A tourist couple in the city for a few days would notice it in the window. They would buy it, even though it would cost them dear. The carpet would then be transported to Paris, Amsterdam or New York, wherever the couple lived, the letter *h* for ever concealed, but for ever alive all the same.

At dusk the family returned home – the seven sisters and their stepmother. As they neared the garden walls, a wave of nervousness surged through Pembe's body. She broke into a run. She had a bad feeling, less dread than fury, a mounting rage against no one but herself for not having acted earlier. About what, she didn't know.

It was she who found Hediye, her body limp like a rag doll, her neck broken, hanging from a brass hook in the ceiling, which had been used many times in the past for the hammocks in which babies were rocked to sleep.

She had hanged herself with the rope served to her in the cauldron.

★

The cowboy named Bad tried to smile, as a noose was pulled tightly around his neck. 'You're joking, Blondie,' he said, his voice breaking. 'You wouldn't . . . you wouldn't play a joke on me like that.'

Blondie squinted, and with a tilt of his head answered, 'It's no joke. It's a rope, Tuco.'

Clamping her lips tightly, Pembe realized she could not watch these scenes. She half stood up. 'I go now.'

'What? But why, my love?' Elias asked. 'Why are you leaving early today?'

'Yes, no . . . I go now.'

'Is it because of the film? You didn't like it?

'No . . . yes . . . I'm sorry.'

'Shall I come with you?'

'You stay, please.'

With that Pembe rose to her feet, leaving him without any explanation. As she walked hastily towards the exit and passed by the rows at the back, the person sitting there rubbed his temples to hide his face with his hands.

When the film was over and the lights went back on, Elias stood up with everyone else. He didn't know what to make of Pembe's sudden departure. He trudged to the foyer, his heart aching. Someone tapped him on his shoulder.

'Excuse me, do you have a light?'

A young lad, a teenager. Too young to be smoking. But it was none of his business to tell him that, and even if he did, he knew the boy wouldn't listen.

'Sorry, I don't smoke,' Elias said.

'Really?'

There was something in the teenager's stare and such awkwardness in his remark that Elias flinched. But before he could say another word, the boy gave a slight nod, and said, his tone hard and level, 'Well, have a good one.'

'Thanks. You too.'

Leaving the boy there, still watching him, Elias walked out through the double doors, his coat brushing the grey threads that Pembe had left there only an hour ago.

Sandstones

Abu Dhabi, November 1978

Only a week after the fight in front of the club, Roxana left Adem for another man – an Australian businessman with interests in the Gulf.

After losing her, a blanket of numbness fell over Adem, like night covering a valley of ghosts. Distracted and distant, he was here and nowhere, his mind drifting, his self-confidence dwindling. He did not know what the truth was any longer, and whether he had ever grasped it. His life had been a maze of mirrors, in each mirror he had seen a different reflection of himself, but which one of them was the real Adem, he couldn't tell. Despite everything, he did not return home. Nor could he stay in the flat he had shared with Roxana, which was, in fact, let in her name. Going to Tariq's house was not an option, unless Adem was willing to listen to him preach. So he sought refuge with his friend Bilal, who, though not sympathetic to his woes, was at least not dismissive of them.

Days passed with an excruciating slowness. There was a pain in his stomach, as if he had swallowed an iron weight that pressed down on the core of his body. Having little appetite, he skipped meals. He smoked three, often four packs of cigarettes a day. Asthma, his childhood illness, came back. As it became increasingly clear to everyone around him that he couldn't go on like this, Bilal tried to persuade him to return to his family.

'I can't do that,' Adem said. 'If I go back now, I'll leave again tomorrow.'

'But why are you running away from your own?'

'Why?' was a question Adem wasn't used to asking himself, or others for that matter. He knew how to deal with 'How?'(how to place biscuits in a box, how to operate a machine) and 'What?'(what to do at the roulette table, what to bet on), but 'Why?' was too abstract, and hardly fathomable.

Near by, a police siren went off and they were both distracted momentarily. When Adem started to speak again, his voice was solemn, his shoulders low. 'Look, I've been thinking this through. The Chinese will never let me off the hook. And my debt is not getting any smaller. I need to get out of here; this city is killing me.'

'Where are you gonna go?' asked a baffled Bilal.

'Actually, I was thinking of Abu Dhabi.' That was where Roxana had gone, but he wasn't going to tell this to his friend. Instead he said, 'I heard they're building a new city out there. Offices, apartment blocks, shopping malls . . . They're going to need workers. Thousands of them. Not only for a year or two, but for a long time.'

'Isn't it all desert down there? How do they build skyscrapers on soft sand?'

'Oh, the sand might not hold up, but the banknotes will.'

They mulled over every detail. How much money Adem would earn a month, how long it would take him to buy a Mercedes-Benz, honey-coloured and so well polished that you could watch the reflection of the clouds passing above on its bonnet, and how good it would feel when he came back to England a successful man laden down with gifts for his children. Between them they crafted a dream so vivid that a few days later Bilal was bewailing his own lot. 'Ah, if I didn't have a family and a bloody job in London, I'd come with you.'

'You can join me after. I'll write to you, give you my address.'

'The Arabs will treat you differently. It's not like you're second class there, you'll be their guest!' Bilal said.

A guest basking in the sun. Even the thought of it warmed Adem's heart. It had been eight years since he had come to London to work and yet he was still an outsider, an interloper. All the other immigrants he knew of had fared much better, and were happier, but not him. Even if there was a brighter future here, especially for the new generation, he was not part of it.

Surely, the Arabs would not be like the Brits and Abu Dhabi would not be London. No rain coming down in buckets, no pork sausages wrapped in glazed bacon as if to double the sin, no pint-sized kitchens in mouldy houses, no tomatoes without taste, no youngsters dyeing their hair purple and terrorizing the streets with their drunken madness. The Brits were always polite: they spat in your face so courteously that you expected them to hand you a handkerchief afterwards. You could not come to blows with an English gentleman, for he would hit you with faint praise. It took years to figure out when the English were complimenting you and when they were telling you that you had screwed up. With the Arabs, things would be more direct, more transparent. You would know that when someone said 'Welcome' they really meant it. Perhaps he would manage to bring the children over after a while. That would be nice.

Still, even as he fantasized about his life in sun-drenched Abu Dhabi, Adem knew the bit about the children joining him was a pipe dream. Esma was a Londoner through and through, and loved this country, *this civilization*. As for his younger son, what a special boy he was. *Such an old head on such young shoulders*, Pembe always said. Yunus was the wisest of all the Topraks, though he was weak in the face of love – a malady that ran in the family. And Iskender . . . it embarrassed Adem to recall their quarrel, but, more than that, to have to admit that he'd failed to live up to his son's expectations.

When you first became a father, you assumed your child was an extension of yourself. He gave you pride, and a sense of achievement and rootedness, until you came to realize, little by little, that a child was a being of his own making. He would keep to his own destiny, no matter how much you wished, prompted or forced him to follow in your footsteps. The moment Adem grasped this truth he couldn't help but feel cheated, beaten. This was not how he had behaved when he was a teenager. He had listened to his *baba*, always respectful, always obedient. If only he had known he had wings, and was of a different species, he, too, could have flown. But now it was too late. The freedom he had failed to secure from his father, his own child was now demanding from him.

Adem was done with London. Though mindful of the difficulty of leaving his children, he wished to go, though not for too long, of course; free as a feather, floating once again on a current stronger than he was. Abu Dhabi would be new. Abu Dhabi would raise his spirits. Once there he would find Roxana – everything in its own time. She would come back to him and he would accept her. The only problem was that he didn't have the resources for the trip. The old dilemma confronted him once again: in order to make money you had to have money first.

Upon the advice of Bilal, he went to see a man everyone called Mamut Baba. With a wispy goatee, dark slanting eyes that gleamed above high cheekbones, and a mouth set in a grim line, he was one of those people who radiated worldly power without being physically imposing. Born and raised in Bukhara, he had run away from the Soviets and spent many years in different parts of Europe, finally arriving in London. He spoke several languages and helped Uzbeks, Iranians, Turks, Arabs, Chinese, Mexicans and Portuguese . . . As long as he liked you, he helped you. Young people who couldn't find jobs, fathers whose daughters had eloped, families with bad blood between them, shopkeepers who couldn't pay their rent – they all went to Mamut Baba.

The room was full of men of every age, sitting on the carpeted floor, conversing in low tones. In the middle of the circle, with his back to the wall and an elegant fawn cape on his shoulders, sat Mamut Baba. His nine-year-old son – a wiry boy with dark eyebrows – was perched next to him, his gaze glued to a new handheld electronic game from America, his thumbs twiddling nonstop. From time to time a flush of excitement crossed the boy's face as he won or lost a game, and he would almost cry out, his lips closing around a ghost of a shout.

'Look at him,' Mamut Baba said blithely. 'At this age he is better with technology than I am. When a machine breaks in the house his mother asks him to repair it, not me.'

The men in the room listened, nodding and smiling when necessary.

'But that's the way it should be. Every generation must keep up with the technology of the day. We should not fall behind the times.'

'But . . .' Adem heard himself murmur and immediately fell quiet. The word had escaped him without thinking, almost like a sigh.

He noticed a gaunt, bearded man frown at him, annoyed that he had cut in while the master was speaking. Wriggling under the young man's stare, Adem lowered his face, not knowing that he had just set eyes on a friend of his son, the Orator, a prominent member of this circle.

In the meantime, Mamut Baba was glancing left and right, trying to see who had spoken up. 'What was that? I couldn't quite hear.'

Now feeling obliged to come forward, Adem cleared his throat. 'Uh-hmm, I'm sorry, I didn't mean to interrupt like that.'

'That's all right, my good man. Go ahead,' said Mamut Baba affably. 'Do tell us what you were thinking.'

'Well, I used to work at the United Biscuits Factory. The biscuits follow each other along the conveyor belt without an end,' Adem said, looking, despite himself, at the Orator, searching for a sign of encouragement where there was none. 'You do the same thing again and again, thousands of times. It numbs your brain. I was thinking these games our kids play, could all that repetition be good for them?'

Mamut Baba studied Adem with a new expression – a mixture of patience and tolerance. Then he embarked on a long speech about science and technology, which Adem found too abstract to follow. An hour later, as he was about to leave with everyone else, Mamut Baba asked him, and a few others, including the Orator, to stay for dinner.

The five of them sat on the carpet, circling a round, low table, and waited for their food to be served. It was then that Adem was able to bring up the subject.

'I need a loan to go to Abu Dhabi,' he said. 'When I've made enough money there, I'll return and pay you back.'

'How about your family?' Mamut Baba asked, as he tore a piece of bread.

'My son Iskender will take care of the house. He's a big boy.'

At the mention of the name the Orator eyed Adem with interest. *So this is the absent father the lad was talking about.* Just then the door opened, and a woman came into the room carrying a large tray crowded with plates. She was fully covered in a cinnamon-coloured *burqa* that exposed only her hands, and two dark eyes behind the slits in her veil. She served a creamy garbanzo soup in glass bowls, set the rice and lamb in the middle, distributed the flat breads, filled the water glasses, and disappeared.

'Does your wife wear the *hijab*?' Mamut Baba asked.

Adem felt tense, his stomach twisting into knots. Ever since Iskender had told him Pembe was seeing someone, he didn't want to hear a word about his wife, and was suspicious of anyone who referred to her in passing. 'Well, I've seen more veiled women in this neighbourhood than in Istanbul,' he offered. 'In my family, we don't have the habit.'

Mamut Baba drew himself up, saying, 'But if some day God grants you another marriage, consider a veiled wife. Their eyes see only their home.'

Breathing in deeply, Adem felt bile rising in his throat. He tried to swallow it, but failed. Was this an awful insinuation or just idle talk? Could people be casting aspersions about Pembe? The silence thickened, swelled.

'I must go. Thanks for the soup,' Adem said, rising to his feet.

Before anyone had a chance to stop him, and without a proper goodbye, he left the room. On the way out he passed by the kitchen, where Mamut Baba's wife and son were having dinner at a small table, the boy enjoying his food while fidgeting with his handheld game, breaking his own record.

★

Arriving in Abu Dhabi in November 1978, Adem became a construction worker. Over time, he would witness, admire and secretly dread the rise of buildings higher than anything he had seen before. In a city with a burning desire to transform and transfigure, he was a man who had only his past and no prospect of change.

The first few weeks were the hardest. Not only because the work was tough, but also because he had to abandon most, if not all, of his expectations. Of the fantasy he had shared with Bilal, the only thing that was real was the sun, hot and harsh on his skin. In the evenings, tired and covered in dust, he would return to the shed he shared with seven fellow workers. Men from different backgrounds, but lacking in similar qualities. On the odd occasion he had a free hour he searched for Roxana in every possible place he could think of – pacing up and down outside shopping malls, restaurants and boutiques.

One night he dreamed of Pembe, her hair loose and flowing. They entered a narrow corridor, walking hand in hand. When they finally reached the end, Adem realized, much to his horror, that Pembe had put on Roxana's frilly costume and was just about to go on stage, ready to dance in a strip club. He shouted with all his might to stop her, and, when that didn't help, he pulled her down off the stage. But the woman he held in his arms was Roxana – her face a mask of anger. He woke up to the realization that his shout had awakened the other men.

A few weeks into his new life and with still no trace of Roxana, Adem discovered a place that was to him what an oasis is to one lost in the desert. A makeshift gambling den that some workers had set up to win a quick buck and spice up the monotony. In an airless, dank flat, between forty to fifty men, swearing, shouting, smoking and praying in many languages, crammed together to watch a cock-fight. From time to time they would organize spider-fights and cricket-races, none of which Adem had seen before. But it was behind the wooden screens that the real wagering took place, and where he always headed.

All he had was what was left of the money Mamut Baba had sent via a courier two days after he had walked out of his house. He could have returned the money, but he hadn't. He didn't have much pride left and the need to leave London had weighed heavier than anything. Now he put aside his wages for his children and tossed the dice with Mamut Baba's cash. He played every night. Whereas others went slowly and took it easy, he pushed on. Most of them were amateurs, he could see that. The air was ripe with the anxiety of getting caught by the authorities – the fear of being deported. Many workers felt this tension, but, strangely, not Adem. Bolder than ever, braced by a wild impulse, he would wager, and then wager again. When the Mamut Baba money came to an end, he began to dip into his wages –

only dip, initially. Before long, he was betting his entire weekly pay in one night.

He bought himself an imitation Rolex, which he wore all the time. His walk wilted into a purposeless, languid stride. He took painkillers every day to help the throbbing in his chest that always worsened in the evenings. Perhaps like those cocks and spiders, he, too, was in a bloody fight, albeit with himself.

The landscape mesmerized him. He was astounded to discover that the desert was not a barren region, but rather a site of hidden beauties. Sometimes he would go hiking, relishing the feeling of his feet in the warm, liquid sand, carrying sandstones in his pockets. Oddly drawn to these feats of nature, he wondered how it was that they dissolved into dust, as if lacking an inner core. Increasingly, he came to liken himself to sandstones.

Someone told him that all these deserts had once been seas. If water could turn into solid earth, and ebb and flow no more, why couldn't man transform himself? Because, despite what they said in films, books and magazines, Adem had arrived at the conclusion that wherever you went in this world, one basic rule never changed: winners won all the time and losers kept losing.

Esma

London, November 1978

One placid evening, only weeks before the murder, my mother set the table. Three plates, three forks, three glasses. Lately dinners had become smaller, quieter. Although she had become accustomed to her husband's absence, it was harder for her to accept Iskender's frequent disappearances. She was more tired than tense. For the first time, I heard her complain about how difficult it was to make ends meet. She had raised us mostly on her own, but lately I suspected she wished there might be someone who could take care of her.

'Where's your brother?' she asked me, carrying a basket of bread from the kitchen.

'Which one?' I grumbled. 'If it's the older one, God knows where he is. Yunus, I believe, is busy taking up space in my room.'

'It's also *his* room.'

'All my friends have their own rooms, Mum. Their families respect their need for privacy.'

She arched an eyebrow. 'You're not an English girl.'

'Oh, come on. Our neighbours' daughters have their own rooms.'

'We are not our neighbours.'

'Mum, this is not fair. Iskender has his own room and he's only a year older than me. Why do you give such privileges to him just because he's a boy? You do this all the time.'

'Esma, that's enough! I'm not having this discussion again. Not now.'

Under my hurtful stare she marched purposefully towards my room, from which a strange noise was coming. I followed her petite form down the corridor, feeling like the ugly duckling behind the swan.

When she opened the door, she found her youngest child, her

baby, listening to the loudest, harshest music on earth. 'What're you doing?' my mother asked.

Yunus didn't look up at her. Or at me. Instead he kept his eyes on the carpet, as if fearful that his face would disclose something.

Curious, my mother retrieved the album from the floor and inspected it. There was a man on a horse, an eerie figure, and another person lying on the ground, being eaten by vultures. In a red frame above it, in capital letters, was written THE CLASH. Underneath there was another line: *Give 'Em Enough Rope*.

'What is this?'

'It's a band, Mum,' Yunus said. 'Music.'

'I know what music is,' she retorted. 'And it's not this boom-boom-boom.'

Yunus glanced up at me now. I rolled my eyes in sisterly solidarity.

My mother now pointed at the title of the album. 'What does this mean?'

'It means if people are too sad and there's no hope and if you give them some rope, they'll hang themselves.'

All the blood drained from my mother's face. 'Is this how you spend your time? You're ruining your brain with this poison.'

Yunus whined. 'It's just a –'

'No, it's terrible. Nobody should give anyone a rope! How can they teach such things?'

'Mum, please. You've got it wrong. They're not teaching –'

'I don't want my children to listen to such horrible things,' she exclaimed.

We had never seen her like this before, so distressed, so agitated. I said, 'Mother, it's a punk band. It's just their style. Nothing bad, believe me.'

Under our pleading eyes she stomped towards the wall and pulled the record player's plug out of the socket. The album stuttered as if choking and came to a stop.

'Why did you do that?' Yunus moaned.

She held his chin, forcing him to look her in the eye. 'Don't listen to dark things. Why are you running away from me? Don't you, too, change, please.'

Yunus grimaced. 'I'm not changing.'

Her expression softening, my mother hugged Yunus, and they stood in an embrace, warm and tight. She kissed the top of his head, inhaled the baby smell on his cheeks. Then my mother's eyes slid down to the gap between my brother's neck and his shirt to the skin below his nape.

'What's this splotch you got here?'

Instantly, Yunus straightened up. A trace of panic crossed his face as he tried to figure out what to say. It was too late. Besides, Yunus could never lie.

'It's a tattoo, Mum.'

'A what?'

I'd known about my brother's tattoo for a while now and butted in to help him. 'Don't worry Mum, it's –'

Ignoring me completely, she dragged him to the bathroom, despite his protests. She pulled off his cardigan, shirt and trousers, leaving him in his pants, and shoved his head under the shower. She scrubbed the back of his neck first with her hands, then with a sponge.

'Stop, Mum,' Yunus wailed. 'That hurts.'

'You should have thought about that before.'

Behind her, I made another attempt to interject. 'It's a tattoo, Mum. It doesn't wash off.'

She pushed my hand away, seized by a mad impulse, and kept on scrubbing. 'How long have you had it?' she asked.

I answered instead of him. 'Months,' I said with a bitterness I didn't know I had in me. 'You would have noticed it earlier, had you been paying us more attention.'

'What are you talking about?'

'You're always distracted,' I exclaimed. 'Your mind is so full there's no place there for us. I can't have a proper conversation with you any more. You're always telling me don't do this, don't do that. Nothing else.'

'That's not true, Esma,' she said doggedly and went back to scrubbing my brother's back. Minutes later, she accepted defeat. She threw down the sponge, her eyes blazing, and shouted at the boy, 'But why? Why did you go and stain yourself?"

'I didn't,' Yunus yelled back in tears, dripping like a little wet mouse. 'You did! I saw you with a man on the street. You're the one who's stained!'

No sooner had he uttered this than Yunus cupped his hands over his mouth. I looked at my brother, horrified, only now realizing this was the secret he'd been carrying. He stared back at me, his regret visible. Timidly, I turned to my mother. The expression I found on her face was one that I had never seen before. Her eyes were glassy, like marbles. She was crying.

A silence fell over the three of us. In that thick, awkward stillness only the water dared to move, softly trickling by.

That night in our room, after Yunus told me the whole story, I tossed and turned in bed, my mind a whirr. It was dark except for a sliver of moonlight streaming in through the window. In a little while I heard him whisper, 'Sister, are you asleep?'

'Nope.'

'Father has gone – do you think Mum will go as well?'

'No, you silly. She's not going anywhere, don't worry.'

Oddly, I was not upset at my mother. I was annoyed at her for other things, big and little; but, now that I realized she had another world of her own, or was trying to build one, against all the odds, something in me wanted to protect her. Suddenly, she had become, in my eyes, the snail in the bowl. I said, 'We need to make sure Iskender doesn't learn about this.'

Ink on Silk

London, November 1978

It was seven thirty in the evening. The end of a long day. Her hair tied into a careless knot, her back slightly aching, Pembe had been on her feet since early in the morning, but she didn't feel tired. She had told Rita she would stay behind to do the cleaning, though it wasn't her job, not really.

'You're an angel,' Rita said, kissing her on both cheeks. 'What would I do without you?'

She hadn't told her yet. She couldn't bring herself to inform her boss that she was leaving. She would not be coming to the Crystal Scissors tomorrow. Or the next day. She would write Rita a note. It was easier that way. She would excuse herself by saying that she was feeling unwell and needed to take some time off. Upon second thoughts, however, she decided to tell her the truth – or at least as much of it as possible. She owed this much to her friend. She would tell Rita that her elder son didn't want her to work any more.

Iskender was her beloved, a bit angry at times, a bit emotional, but a good lad. He had his reasons. Suddenly there was too much gossip around. Behind her back, beyond closed doors, in corner shops, cafés, kebab shops, launderettes and fishmongers', people had got wind that all was not as it should be in the Toprak household. Rumours spread faster than ink on a piece of silk. All her life Pembe had cleaned stains off clothes and carpets, but she did not know of any remedy for this kind of stain. *I will write to Rita. She will understand and yet she won't.*

Guilt was a bizarre emotion. It started with a single doubt, tiny as a head-louse. It settled on your skin, sucked your blood, laid its eggs everywhere. These days she felt guilty all the time. At work, at home, while cooking, shopping or praying, even in her sleep, guilt infested her soul.

As a child, more than a few times, she had been infected with lice. But the first time was the worst. She had always believed it was her twin who had passed it on to her, though Jamila claimed the opposite to be true. Their mother had kept them both in a hot tub for hours, scrubbing their scalps with a smelly lotion she had got from a healer. In the end, she managed to get rid of all the nits, but almost killed the girls in the process.

It had been more than an hour since everyone had left – the customers, the receptionist and the manicurist who came twice a week. Rita was planning to hire a *hairstylist* – a posh word. In England people treasured posh words. The labels they gave their food still astounded Pembe. *Tangy chicken with zesty, fluffy couscous*. She had seen it on the menu of a trendy restaurant where Elias had taken her. The first and only time they had gone out. She had never felt more uncomfortable in her life. She knew he was trying to find a place where they could talk without being seen by anyone. But that was impossible, wasn't it? Not only because everyone was everywhere, but also because of the ancient law of the universe: whatever you strive to avoid at all costs, you are bound to run into.

Over lunch she had mentioned to Elias that, where she was born, people would laugh if they heard you'd served a special guest couscous. It was a peasant dish. Not that her family were rich, but they knew the difference between a poor dish and a posh one.

In England things were topsy-turvy. The word *couscous*, though ordinary, was treated with reverence. Yet the word *shame*, though substantial, was taken quite lightly. When the English were disappointed about something, no matter how ephemeral or inconsequential, they exclaimed, 'Oh, what a shame!'

Pembe had told Elias all this to make him laugh, but he had stared at her with a sort of wistfulness, like he did from time to time, as if she reminded him of other, deeper, sadder things.

'So if you invited me over for dinner, you wouldn't serve me couscous?' Elias had mischievously asked.

'Of course not.'

She described the dishes she would set before him. First, there would be soup, because all food tasted better on a warm stomach.

Yoghurt soup with tarragon, mint and bulgar wheat, salad with pomegranate molasses, spicy roasted red-pepper *hummus*, lentil patties, Sultan's Delight* and, for a final touch, home-made *baklava*.

'I'd love to cook with you in the same kitchen, in *our* kitchen,' he had said.

It was one of those rare moments when they talked about their future together, allowing themselves to believe they had one.

*

A beauty salon might be a place to get a haircut and a blow dry, but, more than that, it was a place of words. The reason why some women went there so often was not because they had to change their hairstyle every other week. Many longed for a chat – words that resembled a meandering stream, content to simply flow. Now and again the customers needed someone who would listen to them and indulge them – treat them, in fact, like the princesses they had once read about in storybooks.

Not that Pembe was a great talker. But she was a remarkable listener. Having learned from growing up in a large family always to put other people first, she found listening came easily to her. Her customers blathered on about their expectations and frustrations. She knew the names of their husbands, children, pets and even annoying neighbours. When they made jokes she laughed at the right places. When they lambasted politicians, she grimaced with them. When they talked about a heartbreaking experience, her eyes watered as well. She did all of this with her limited vocabulary. Sometimes she missed some of the words, but never the essence.

The evening sun was long gone, and the street was already changing. The shops on both sides of the road had closed, the sounds of their steel shutters piercing the air. The shop that sold Indian saris, the Lebanese café, the *halal* meat butcher, the hippie place that smelled of incense and that other stuff, the local supermarket that had just started to sell rotisserie chickens . . . The people who worked or shopped in them were now on their way home.

* An elaborate meat dish with aubergine purée.

At eight thirty Pembe finished sweeping the floor, rinsing the brushes and washing the plastic bottles in which she mixed the hair dyes. Her hands were so used to scrubbing, wiping and polishing that she didn't think they would obey her if she ordered them not to toil. When there was nothing left to do, she grabbed her coat and hand-bag, and gave the salon one last glance.

'Bye-bye hairdryers,' she murmured. 'Bye rollers, scissors, bleaches . . .'

She had promised herself she wouldn't cry. Biting the inside of her mouth, she opened the door and stepped on to the street. A middle-aged couple kissed as they tottered by, looking quite tipsy. She tried not to stare but couldn't help it. Eight years had passed since she had come to this country and yet she was still not used to seeing people kiss in public. The woman noticed her, and pulled away from her lover, chuckling briefly, as if amused by Pembe's bashfulness.

Hurrying, Pembe locked the door and dropped the key through Rita's letterbox. She realized she had forgotten to write her a note but maybe it was better that way. There was no need to explain any-thing, and, even if she had tried, she didn't think she would succeed. Now she had to find Elias and tell him that from now on it would be more difficult for her to meet him.

The Encounter

London, 14 November 1978

That Tuesday at school, during the lunch-break, Iskender seemed psyched up, as always. Teasing, sneering, having fun. He ate his shepherd's pie listening to the idle chit-chat around him. The boys were talking about the next day's game. Chelsea against Moscow Dynamo.

Suddenly Arshad turned to Iskender. 'Hey, you gonna give me that puddin'?'

Iskender shook his head. 'Nn . . . not on yo . . . uuur . . . nn . . . neee . . . nelly! Fo . . . forr . . . gett . . . itt.'

The conversation hit a lull as everyone stopped and stared at him. They had never heard him stammer before. Or seen him blush. The moment came and went, and they resumed their banter, but Iskender's discomfort stayed.

In the classroom he kept his eyes glued to the collar of the student in front of him, unmoving. He remained like that until a crumpled paper landed on his desk. He took it, opened it. It was from Katie.

Maggie, Christine, Hilary. If boy, Tom.

Then came another ball of paper inquiring if he was all right. Iskender scribbled a short message to appease her curiosity and flung it back. Yet as soon as the lesson was over he grabbed his rucksack and walked out, even though he knew he would be in deep trouble for leaving without permission. After rambling around aimlessly for a while, feeling small and conspicuous in his uniform during school hours, he headed to the bus stop.

When the bus arrived, he went down the aisle without paying much attention to his surroundings. The thick, slightly fetid air entered him like a splinter of sadness. People were standing in clusters, although there were plenty of empty seats in the middle. Instantly he understood why. Sitting there all alone, talking to himself, was a tramp, a loony. His face unwashed, unshaven, his eyes raw red, he had taken his boots off and was massaging the soles of his filthy, callused feet as if they were the most precious things in the world. A stench like warm rubbish suffused the air.

On a whim, Iskender lurched towards the man and sat next to him. The tramp gawked at his companion with amusement, as if wondering what was wrong with him. Iskender noticed other people were staring at him too. He didn't mind. Now that he had started to stammer, he felt a bit mad himself.

When the bus made a lumbering turn, Iskender caught a glimpse of himself in the opposite window, his face pale and hollow. Though he had just turned sixteen he looked older. He remembered a comic book he had read in which a detective regularly ran into his future self. Perhaps that was what he was seeing now – a yet-to-come Iskender.

His thoughts went back to his stammering. He wondered if he had caught some kind of virus. His mother would know what to do; she would prepare herbal teas to soothe his throat and untangle his tongue. If she couldn't, she would write to Aunt Jamila. Didn't she always boast that her twin knew the secret language of herbs? Iskender sat back, feeling confident that he would be cured. His love for his mother kindled in his heart. *Uncle Tariq was full of nothing but crap*. How he wished he could find a time-machine and travel through the years back to his babyhood. Before Yunus. Before Esma. When it was only him and his mother wrapped in untainted love.

This, more or less, was his mood when the bus arrived at London Fields.

'Looks like somebody's in a hurry,' the loony announced in a chirpy tone to everyone in the bus, as if they were his friends.

Iskender felt the need to say something, and since he couldn't, he nodded in the man's direction.

'Tootle-oo! Don't keep Mummy waitin'.'

Upon hearing this Iskender felt a shiver down his spine. As he marched off into the bright day, the man's laughter still echoed in his brain. It was three thirty when he reached the house on Lavender Grove and rang the bell.

*

Elias was sitting alone in the living room, partly obscured by the half-closed curtains, when he heard footsteps outside the door.

'I want to know where you live,' he had said the week before, aware he was crossing some invisible line.

'Why?'

'My dear, you know where I live, my house, my plants, my work, but you are a mystery to me. When you're at home, away from me, I want to be able to imagine what you're doing. I need a picture in my mind, that's all.'

'A picture?' she asked, suddenly sounding forlorn.

'Yes, well, not like a photo. I mean, look, if I could just come and see – a few minutes would be enough. Nothing else. I will come like a cat, leave like a cat. No one will know. Just once. Is that possible?'

Biting at the inside of her mouth, she had murmured, 'But only five minutes. Then you go.'

That afternoon, when the children were at school, Elias walked into the house on Lavender Grove. As soon as he passed the threshold, he regretted the entire idea. He could see Pembe had not wanted to do this. The only reason she had yielded to the plan was to please him. She was so tense that the slightest sound sent a surge of panic through her. He felt terrible, not only for being there, but also for being in her life, and causing so much distress. He had wanted his love to create wonders, but perhaps it was only producing troubles. In order not to make her any more ill at ease than she already was, Elias kept his coat on, ready to leave at the slightest signal from her.

And yet the house itself was the insight into his beloved's existence that he so desperately craved. For this dim, tiny place, where Pembe spent so much time all by herself, was the reason why she so resembled the lonely ballerina in a wind-up music box. He saw the lace doilies on the coffee tables, shelves and armchairs; the embroidery she had crocheted, the dried peppers and aubergines she had lined up

on a string by the window to make *dolma*, and her scarlet slippers
with pompons. He took in the details, the colours. The entire place
was suffused with competing scents: home-made pastries, newly
washed clothes, a hint of cinnamon and rosewater. Everything was
new to Elias, and yet so much like the life his family had left behind
in Lebanon that it brought tears to his eyes.

When he was a boy Elias had spent a summer in Beirut with his
grandparents, sauntering by the gently rolling sea, the sand warm
and generous. Once, after a storm, he had come across a number of
deep-sea creatures that had been washed ashore. It had shocked him
to see these peculiar organisms so helplessly out of place. Over the
years, as he worked in numerous Western cities and observed the lives
of the first generation of immigrants, he would recall this scene.
They, too, were cut off from their natural environment. In their new
setting, they breathed uneasily, vulnerably, waiting for the ocean to
take them back or the beach to swallow their discomfort, help them
belong. Elias understood this emotion, for he had always thought of
himself as a man who lived on the shores of other cultures. Yet in one
fundamental way he differed from them. He could survive anywhere,
having no attachment to any particular piece of land.

Making his way towards the door, he thanked Pembe for letting
him in, and apologized for the anguish he had caused. She seemed
both relieved and saddened by his departure. 'Stay,' she said in the
quietest of voices. 'Drink tea. Then go.'

'Are you sure?'

There was a bronze samovar on the table with steam coming out
of it in puffs. Her hands shook so badly as she poured a glass that she
spilled some of the scalding tea on her crimson blouse.

'Oh, no,' Elias exclaimed. 'Did you burn yourself?'

Trying to keep her blouse away from her skin, she shook her head.
'It's okay. You drink here. I go change.'

He complied, waiting. He had barely finished his tea when someone rang the bell, a short ring, followed by another one, long and
persistent. Elias felt the sinews on his neck stiffen, and his fingers
tighten around the glass.

Dashing out of her bedroom, her white blouse wrongly buttoned,

Pembe looked at him, horrified. Her children weren't due back for another two and a half hours. Her neighbours were working, and didn't pop in just like that. Elias signalled to her that he would hide, though he had no idea how or where. They exchanged tense whispers. Then he crawled under the dining table, as though in a frightful dream, unable to believe this was really happening.

A second later a key was thrust into the lock. All the colour went from Pembe's face. Now she knew who it was at the door. Only one person had his own key.

The Cloak of Calmness

London, 1 December 1978

Elias was giving his air plant its monthly shower when he first heard about the murder. Air plants were peculiar beings, the enigma of the plant world. Absorbing moisture through the pores in their leaves, they survived without having any roots to transport nutrients such as water to them. Instead of being rooted in the soil, like all other flora, they latched on to all sorts of objects and grew almost in the air, the nomad-plants that they were. Elias kept his *Tillandsia* in a large conch shell on the kitchen worktop. When the house became too dry in the summer, he submerged the plant in water every ten days – *the bath*. But now that it was winter he made do with a bit of spraying every four weeks – *the shower*.

So immersed was Elias in his work that he did not hear the first knock. His doorbell had not been working properly since the last power-cut, and he had not found time to repair it. In a matter of seconds came another knock, louder. Curious as to who it could be at this early hour, he put the air plant in its place and dried his hands on a towel.

Pembe had come to his flat on four occasions, always timid and hurried, like a bird perching on a tree branch before finding the strength to fly off. Quiet and observant, she had sat on the leather sofa, the cat curling up on her lap. She had watched him work in the open kitchen, listening to him chattering on. Her smile was genuine, as was the discomfort in her eyes.

From the beginning she had struck him as a mass of contradictions. He could see how diffident she was, almost fragile, and yet underneath there was a resilient layer – a thread of courage, tenacious to the point of audacity, weaving in and out. It was all entangled. In her gaze he encountered the starry light he had witnessed in his mother's eyes as a child and had never seen in anyone else's again. Yet a permanent melancholy shadowed her, and it was, in part, this inexplicable sorrow that had pulled him towards her.

Since the day they had held hands at the cinema, watching *The Kid* together for the first time, he had craved to make love to her. He had longed to be intimate with her, away from all eyes, emptied of the rush and the guilt and the fear that she carried with her everywhere. But every time she had visited his flat, a strange sense of restraint had descended over him, a self-control he didn't know he was capable of exhibiting.

What he really wanted was to solve the riddle that she presented. But, more than that, Elias realized, he wished to make her happy. It sounded altruistic, almost noble, but he was aware that, in its essence, it was a selfish aspiration. He yearned for his love to work like a magic wand, transforming what it touched. If he loved her purely and profoundly enough, he could turn a Cinderella into a princess – beautiful, blissful and incandescent. And it was this desire to re-create her in a lighter, freer mould that both intrigued and thrilled him.

In some ways she was, and acted, like a young maiden. She would hold hands, and allow him to steal kisses, put her head on his chest and rejoice in the warmth of his body against hers, but she never dared go further than that. He had intuited quickly that any attempt to move beyond that line would make her utterly uncomfortable, and induce a huge amount of guilt. She was already feeling mortified: a married woman with three children getting involved in clandestine meetings with an older man. Several times she had confessed to him she would like to get a divorce and so might her husband, but she did not want to upset her children, especially the youngest one, who was still too small. Her physical inaccessibility, far from putting him off, had drawn him even closer. And so, much to his own surprise, he had accepted her as she was.

All too suddenly, sex resembled a dessert kept to the end of a long meal. Delightful and exquisite, no doubt, but not the main course, and not at all impossible to skip when it came to it. They were only at the starters now. Elias didn't know how long they could go on like this, and he was in no rush to find out. There was something oddly sexy about refraining from sex. He laughed at himself for making such a discovery at his age, precisely when he thought he was too old to discover anything new.

'God is testing us,' she said to him once. 'You think we pass?'

'I'm not interested in God's tests. I want to face my own challenges.'

She didn't like to hear him speak like that. She wanted them both to be hopeful and faithful – traits he had lost long ago, if he had ever possessed them. Ever since he was a young man he had managed without pleading for anything from a higher force, consistently sinful, if sin it was. Still, Elias decided not to talk about his reasons for agnosticism. He didn't want to break Pembe's heart – or her God's.

Nonetheless, deep in his soul, Elias was certain that some day, perhaps not so distant, their fingertips would meet, as if on their own accord and that would be the beginning of a new phase in their lives. They could then look into each other's eyes, earnest and alive, comfortable in their nakedness. There would be no more qualms. No more shame. Love would be enough, and everything else would follow. She would come to him, free and light. He would help her to raise her children, be present whenever they needed him. He would love and be loved, and the hole in his soul would finally be mended.

Now as he strode down the corridor to answer the door, Elias couldn't help but wonder if it could be Pembe visiting him. It wasn't her habit to appear out of the blue, but she could have decided to surprise him. When he unlatched the door, however, he was disappointed to see a stranger there. A teenage girl. Flared jeans, wide-sleeved russet shirt, a creamy silk scarf around her neck. Hair parted in the middle with loose curls on both sides, a broad forehead and a protruding chin.

'I am looking for Elias,' the girl said.

'Yes, how can I help you?' he answered, his smile cautious.

'So it was you?' The question was so unexpected, and sounded so menacing, that he was unable to conceal how it troubled him. She said, 'My mother . . .'

'Excuse me?'

The girl raised her head, without quite meeting his gaze, aware that he was scrutinizing her. 'My mother is dead.'

She turned aside, ready to leave. He grabbed her elbow, a bit too harshly, his panic kicking in.

'What are you talking about? Who are you?' he asked, his voice darting unsteadily, and in the same breath he said, 'Who is your mother?'

Only now did he notice that she'd been crying.

'Don't you know who I'm talking about?' she said reproachfully.

He was beginning to. 'I . . . I don't understand. But when . . . how?'

'My brother stabbed her. Because of your affair.'

His eyes grew wide, and all the blood drained from his face. It took another silent beat of his heart before it could receive what his mind had already processed. He let go of her arm, in his need to lean against the wall.

'You've brought us nothing but shame,' she said. 'I hope you're satisfied now.'

Elias began to sense how much she had loved her mother and yet also envied, begrudged and possessed her, all at once. But he had no words with which to console her or himself. He opened and shut his mouth, like a goldfish in a bowl.

'We don't want to see you around. Don't come to her funeral and don't try to involve yourself any further. Just leave us alone. Got it?'

The question was too painful to be left unanswered and he nodded his head. 'Yes,' he said. Then again, 'Yes.'

He watched her scurry down the steps, without looking back. A part of him still refused to believe her. *The girl must have invented this awful lie in the hope of saving her parents' marriage.* Children did such things all the time. There was nothing to be alarmed about. Everything would be clear in a matter of hours.

Finding an excuse not to go to work, Elias stayed in his flat that afternoon, waiting for Pembe to come round and comfort him. He drank quite a bit, slept poorly and woke up with a taste in his mouth like rust. First thing in the morning he fetched the newspapers. It was there. On the front page. *Boy Murdered Mother for Honour*. He blinked at the words, seeing and recognizing each one of them but refusing to grasp their meaning as a whole.

★

Elias had first noticed that a teenager was following him when he was in his local Indian shop, buying mango pickles. Spicy and tasty, they went well with various dishes, and he was planning to serve them with marinated rabbit. He had no sooner grabbed a jar than he felt an odd discomfort, sensing someone's gaze on him. Instinctively, he turned his head, and the boy was there, outside the shop window, staring at him over a pile of cans and boxes. There was animosity in his face, but also something akin to curiosity. A flicker of interest flashed in his eyes, like a spark that leaped from burning coals.

Elias left the shop, glancing left and right, determined to talk to the boy should he find him waiting out there. But when he stepped on to the pavement there was no one. He must have been looking for someone else, he assumed. No need to become paranoid. Elias chose to believe this, even though he had recognized the boy: he had approached Elias for a light in the cinema and he bore a striking resemblance to Pembe. Two days later he spotted him again, smoking in front of Cleo's. When he walked out of the restaurant later that night, prepared for the worst, the boy had once again vanished into thin air.

And so it went. Over the next few weeks the boy followed Elias at different hours of the day, appearing and vanishing, like a phantasm that had lost its way. Not once did he try to hide himself, though he kept enough of a distance to take to his heels if necessary. Elias never mentioned these encounters to Pembe, which, he now realized, was a big mistake.

★

Several times Elias was tempted to go to the hospital nearest Pembe's house or the morgue, but his worry about the scene that might erupt should he come across her relatives or neighbours stopped him cold. He wished to have a private talk with her daughter again, but even if he could find the right words, he didn't expect to be welcomed. The girl had made that very clear. He thought about going to the police but believed he had nothing to tell them.

He spent the next days mostly in his kitchen, wearing the same clothes, his hair unwashed and lifeless. He prepared sauces and soups, bright red, rich orange and creamy white, none of which would be served to anyone. Inside him the rage, the self-reproach and the sorrow made a concoction of their own. It was his fault that things had reached this point; it was all his doing. How could he have failed to see it coming? How could he have been so naive?

The papers said that Iskender Toprak, the prime suspect, was on the loose. Elias waited for him to appear at his door, ready to face him. Instead of Iskender, however, Scotland Yard appeared. They asked him too many questions. Took pictures of his house, gathered detailed information about his work, quizzed him endlessly about his *relationship with the deceased*.

When they finally left, Elias drew the curtains and lit a candle, which he watched burn until it was but a stub. Meanwhile he put on a record by Fairuz, her powerful voice penetrating into every crevice of the flat, changing the air like a gust of wind. When she started singing 'Sakan al-Layl', he collapsed, crying.

The night is calm, and in the cloak of calmness are hidden dreams . . .

All these years, he had deluded himself into thinking that he could not spend a day away from Cleo's; his answer to the exhaustion brought on by working hard had been to work even harder. But for the next three weeks he confined himself to his home, barely going out. His staff kept ringing him, asking when he was coming back. When they sensed the depth of his pain, though not exactly the cause, they insisted that he take some time off. A month later Elias put his second chef in charge of the restaurant. Having relieved himself of his duties, he slipped into a dreamlike state in which he was surprised to find that even the most urgent tasks were not that urgent any more.

Early in 1979, after testifying in court and having nothing else to do, prove or confess, he did something he never thought he would do. He packed two suitcases and distributed the rest of his belongings among his employees. The ageing, Persian cat he gave to Annabel, who was delighted to have her back. Then he bought a ticket, one-way, and returned to Montreal.

The Watch

Abu Dhabi, March 1982

One morning, just after dawn, Adem walked to the construction site where he worked. The night guard – a hefty Pakistani with big, black eyes – was surprised to see him, but also content to have some company.

'You're early,' the guard said.

'I couldn't sleep.'

The man smiled knowingly, and said, 'You must have missed your wife. Send her some money. When wife is happy, you are happy.'

Adem cast around for a reply that would be in agreement with the remark but not disrespectful of Pembe's soul. All he came up with was a curt nod. He watched the guard's eyes shine like dark jewels, wondering if it was true that putting a few drops of lemon in your eyes made them brighter.

Adem placed a cigarette between his lips and offered one to the guard. For a while they smoked in silence, each of them lost in his own thoughts. Adem dredged up a time when he – as a young man in Istanbul – would gather cigarette butts from the streets to eke out one final drag. Once he had found half a cigarette with a lipstick mark on the pavement. He was doubly mystified by the discovery: amazed that someone would dispose of a fag that was only partly finished, and amazed that a woman could smoke on the street.

When he arrived in London, he had grown used to the sight of women puffing away in public, and the first time Roxana shared a cigarette with him he had been elated by the intimacy of the moment.

'Here, take it,' he said, holding out the almost-full pack.

'You are giving it to me?' the man asked.

'Yes, a present for my brother.'

The night guard beamed, displaying a set of milk-white teeth.

Could that be lemon juice too, Adem thought. Pity he had never tried that. The English had rather poor teeth. He should have told them about lemon juice.

Suddenly overhead came the noise of hundreds of wings, as a flock of migratory birds passed above them as if they were a single body. They might have flown all the way down from Istanbul. Or perhaps they had come from London and been spotted by one of his children – Esma leaving a bookshop with newly bought books, or Yunus writing graffiti on the walls with those punk friends of his, or Iskender, in prison, looking out of a prison window, watching the drizzle hit the courtyard – but no, he still found it painful to think about his eldest son and the terrible place where he had ended up. Adem blamed himself. He held himself responsible less for the things he had done than for those he hadn't been able to. He thought, with a dawning comprehension, that he had always played truant in life, always been absent, always fearful of being swallowed by the earth.

Catching the Pakistani's eye, Adem smiled ruefully. There was a rare innocence in the night guard's face – a quality he had not come across in a long while – and he felt close to this man, as if they shared a common loss. Had they met at a different time, he would have asked him what his story was. He would have liked to see the pictures of his wife and children, for the man had given Adem the impression of being the sort of person who would carry his family's photos with him everywhere, even into the makeshift hut where he watched the night alone.

Perhaps Adem, too, would have shown the night guard a photo of his children – Iskender and Esma holding baby Yunus in their arms, half proud half perplexed, still in their early years in England, their clothes slightly tatty but their expressions already adjusting to their new country. Adem also had a photo of Pembe taken on the day they had left Istanbul, but he wouldn't allow anyone to see it, not even himself.

Rising to his feet, he pointed at the site, and said, 'If you don't mind, I've some thinking to do in there.'

The night guard shrugged. 'Fine, but don't mull over too much,' he said and tapped his head. 'No good for the brain.'

Adem trudged along, his feet crunching upon the gravel path. Just as he was about to enter the building, which looked almost spectral in the metallic blue of morning light, the guard came running after him, waving a yellow object in his hand.

'Hey, wait. You forgot to put on a helmet.'

'Oh, yes, the helmet. Thanks, brother.'

He put it on, gave a mock soldier's salute and walked in.

★

When Adem was eight years old – or was it nine, he could never be sure – his mother had taken him for a stroll, just the two of them. He felt privileged, as it was he – and not any of his brothers – who had been specially chosen to accompany her.

They walked hand in hand. It was a radiant autumn day, but it felt like spring. They took a *dolmush* to the train station. The boy was mesmerized by the sight of the trains – their smells, their sounds, their grandeur. There was a man waiting for them, smoking behind a pillar, half hidden. He had waxed back his dark hair, making his wide forehead and bushy eyebrows stand out, and was smoking a cigarette. How long had he been standing there? What was his name? How did he know his mother? He never would learn the answers.

When the man saw the woman approach, a slow, confident smile etched its way across his face – until he noticed the boy.

'The child . . .' he said.

'I couldn't leave him behind,' she said. 'Please.'

'We've talked about this, Aisha. I told you.'

He looked fed up, and in a hurry. His eyes darted from the woman's face to the train, and from the train to the big, round clock.

'He's my youngest,' she said, deadpan. 'He needs a mother.'

The man tossed his cigarette on to the floor and stepped on it, as if he were squashing a cockroach. Then he raised his head and stared into the woman's eyes. 'I told you already, I'm not going to bring up another man's child. Leave him with his father. That's better for everyone.'

Gently, she put her hand on her son's shoulder. 'Darling, go and ask someone what time it is.'

'What? But . . .'

'I said go and ask,' Aisha repeated.

When the boy came back – having learned that it was twenty past eleven – he found the man fulminating and his mother gazing at her feet, saying nothing.

'We won't be able to take the next train,' the man remarked. 'There's another one at three o'clock. Come back then. Alone.'

On the way out they held hands again, he and his mother. They whisked out of the station into the drizzle, which was so light they didn't need to seek shelter. Buying two *simits** from a vendor near by, they sat there on the stairs. The child fed half of his *simit* to the pigeons, while his mother watched with unseeing eyes.

'Who was that man, Mama?'

'Just a friend.'

'I didn't like him,' he said, his lip quivering. He hadn't yet decided whether to start crying.

Aisha pulled him to her and ruffled his hair. 'I don't like him much either,' she said.

Despite the relief he felt on hearing this, the boy knew something was wrong. It was so wrong that even when he ran in circles to scare away the pigeons, sweating inside his thick jacket, his mother did not scold him. Even when he stepped in the muddy puddles, his shoes making a squeaky sound as water seeped into them and his toes began to freeze, his mother remained silent.

'I want to come with you.'

'Oh, do you?' she asked.

'Yes, Mama. I want you to take me with you. Promise?'

Suddenly Aisha was serious. 'Yes, my little love,' she said.

'No,' the boy corrected. 'You have to say my *big* love.'

*

Adem entered the freight lift and pressed the top button: twenty-two. After that he had to take the stairs to the twenty-seventh floor.

* Bagels with sesame seeds.

From there you could not go any further, as there was barely a construction frame, just a skeleton of iron bars. When complete, it was going to be one of the tallest buildings in Abu Dhabi.

When he reached the top, he pulled a bag of cement close to the edge and sat on it, his mouth dry, his hands shaking in the way they always seemed to these days. But the view was perfect, flooded with light. Better than the view that the rich had from their penthouse apartments and smart offices. Diagonally across from him was a famous hotel with ornate balconies and an elaborate façade. For a second he imagined that someone was watching him – a feeling that left as quickly as it had come.

As he sat there observing the clouds drift by, his legs dangling over the frame, he tried to guess the first time their *baba* had heard the gossip about their mother. Odd though it was, he couldn't recall any scenes from his childhood in which it was clear that his dad actually *knew*. Nor could he think of anyone who might have besmirched Aisha's name, though he reckoned that quite a few had. Was it a neighbour? Was it the *halal* butcher around the corner – letting it slip while he was preparing the lamb chops? Or was it a complete stranger sitting next to him in the tea house, pretending to be a friend while his mouth spewed spite and slander? Innuendo travelled faster than light. *What a thing to do to a good man like you*, they would say, offering fake solace, thriving on other people's unhappiness.

The story had repeated itself through years, through generations. Recently, a Turkish worker had arrived who knew of Iskender's crime and the reason behind it. If the man had a loose tongue, which Adem was sure he had, the rumour would spread here as well. He would see in the eyes of his co-workers the sinister gleam he had come to recognize – pity, derision, curiosity. But it didn't matter. As of this moment, Adem decided, nothing mattered any more. He was a shadow of the man he had once been, and no one could possibly hurt a shadow.

Far in the distance the horizon was covered in an orange-crimson streak of light, vivid and dazzling. Under this hazed glow the world seemed strangely still and strangely wise. Adem sat there admiring

the daybreak, the distant buildings aflame against the placid landscape. It was as if the sky had slit open to reveal another universe, and
everyone and everything was painted with God's brush.

★

That afternoon, at three p.m., Adem's mother did not go back to the
train station. Instead, she grabbed her son's hands and together they
went to the outskirts of the city. They trekked up a hill, battling
against the wind, ignoring the signposts along the way, all of which
said NO TRESPASSING. It was forbidden to get this close to the dam,
and yet they did. No one saw or stopped them. They sat on the
embankment, the waters glistening mysteriously down below.

'You see, I'm not leaving you,' Aisha said. 'Are you happy?'

The boy said he was, but his teeth were chattering and his lips had
turned a pale blue, although it was not that cold. There was a handkerchief in his hand, which he twisted and twisted into a knot he
then couldn't untie.

'Let's go home,' he heard himself plead, his breath wheezing. 'I
want to go.'

'What's at home?' she snapped. Her voice, as thick as the humid
air, was the voice of a stranger. Then, as if ashamed of her reaction,
she put her finger to her lips and added, softly, 'Quiet.'

As if prompted by her request, everything fell silent. The cicadas
in the trees, the crickets in the field, the lorries on the road far away
and even Istanbul with its perpetual hum and drone . . . The world
came to a stop. Everyone and everything abided by her wish. It was a
game they were playing. Adem felt special, grown-up. His mother
was sharing a secret not with his brothers, but with him.

'Mum . . .'

'Hmmm?'

'Where are we going?'

'Sweetie, we talked about this before.'

'I forgot.'

'We're going to a lovely place where there're lots of toffee apples.'

'But if I eat too many, my teeth will rot.'

'Don't worry. You may eat as many as you want.'

302

Adem attempted to show a flicker of joy, but his eyes remained confused, troubled. He didn't like the change of tone. Mothers should fuss and scold, sweets should decay teeth or upset tummies. He had a feeling lately that nobody was doing their duty properly.

Aisha sighed, sensing her son's unease in the way a barn owl perceives the slightest movement in the dark. She said, with her eyes cast down, 'Where we're going nobody gets sick. Your teeth will be just fine and my head won't hurt any more. Isn't that great?'

Then why are you crying? he wanted to ask but couldn't. The thin, ticklish warmth of her embrace was both tender and painful. As he hugged her back, the boy could feel the heat of the sun on her body. There was in her breath – beneath her usual warm, sweet smell – a sour odour of something in decay. He touched a bruise on her right cheek, just under the eye, which had been barely noticeable when they left the house. But her make-up had washed off, causing the mark to stick out in its green-blue ugliness, darker towards the centre.

Gripped by a fear unlike any he had experienced before, Adem clutched his mother's hand, his fingertips cold and pale against her skin. Together they approached the edge, dragging their shadows along. Her lips were moving non-stop, and he knew she was praying. Just as she was about to thrust her body forward, taking him with her, he panicked and, reflexively, jerked himself to one side. His hand slipped out of hers as swiftly as a dagger comes out of its sheath. This sudden move confused everything, causing her momentarily to lose her balance, if not her determination. Aisha fell, but instead of plummeting forward down into the waters below, she tumbled sideways, rolling down the slope. She dropped a few yards, the nettles and stones cutting her face; her bottom lip split open.

'Mama, are you all right?' he shouted from above.

She was fine, and yet not fine at all. They went back home and never said a word about this to anyone.

Two years later, unable to take it any longer, Aisha abandoned them. One morning she was gone, her coat no longer on the hanger, and a tattered suitcase missing from under the bed. Adem refused to believe she had left without taking him, and, in order to assure himself that this wasn't the case, he opened her dressing-table drawer several times a day, checking for her silver hand mirror and hair-brush. As long as they were there, she would come back. When people gossiped – inside and outside the house – he listened to the ugly remarks they made, but he never mentioned to anyone, especially to Baba (the Drunk One) that she had tried to kill both herself and him. Nor did he disclose anything about the man he had seen at the station – the man, he now understood, with whom his mother had run away.

*

The night before in the dusky flat on the edge of the desert, Adem had gambled again and lost – an amount so large he could never pay it back, no matter how many extra shifts he worked. Now as he wiped his eyes he sniffed in surprise at the teardrops on his hand. He didn't know he was crying. But it wasn't exactly sorrow that he felt. A deep indifference washed over him, an acceptance of the things he could not change – including himself.

He took off his watch and put it aside, careful not to break it. If it were a real Rolex he would have liked to leave it to one of his sons, probably to Yunus. But he didn't want to bequeath to any son of his a fake gift. He only hoped that the night guard would be the one to find it.

***

Shrewsbury Prison, 1991

The next morning at dawn Zeeshan wakes me up to meditate. Unlike other days I don't grumble. We sit cross-legged on the floor, facing each other. He beams. I wonder where he gets his zip from.

'Clear your mind,' he says, like he always does. 'Air pollution no good for cities. Brain pollution no good for humans.'

For ten minutes we sit in silence. This is an exercise he taught me last month. I'm supposed to not think anything, which I can never manage. Sure enough, my mind starts zigzagging and soon it's a witches' coven in there. I'm worried about the mysterious visitor. I cannot stop running through possible candidates. Uncle Tariq, the Orator, my old buddy

Arshad . . . I don't want to see any of them. I blame them all for making me the person I was. And yet they are all free, enjoying their life, while I am here burning.

So the meditation doesn't work. It never does. But Zeeshan doesn't look put out. He never does.

'Iskender, when you think of others, all energy inside you goes to them. You have nothing left for yourself.'

In Zeeshan's world there are invisible networks in space that connect people, incidents and places. Through these tubes we send things to one another. Like a crazy science-fiction film.

'Human heart like cooker. We produce heat, we make energy, every day. But when we accuse others, when we say terrible things, inner energy goes elsewhere. Our heart becomes cold.'

Zeeshan says, 'Always better to look within. Leave other people to themselves. Every bitterness is heavy bag. Why carry? You are hot-air balloon. Tell me, you want to go up or down? Let go of anger, hurt. Drop the sacks.

'There are two arcs in the universe. One is ascent, the other is descent. Every human being is constantly moving. Some go down, some go up. If you want to climb, start criticizing yourself. A man who cannot see his faults can never heal.'

There have been many times since the day Zeeshan showed up in my cell when I wanted to punch him in the face or just tell him to shut up. Strangely, I can't. I must have a high tolerance threshold for this bloke. I listen to his twaddle, on and on, sometimes amused, sometimes half convinced. So when I hear what he says next, I even listen to that.

'When visitor comes from past, promise Zeeshan you don't go banana.'

I laugh. 'Ba-na-nas.'

'Yes, yes. No quarrel with anyone. You are working on yourself, don't forget? You are a gem, but you have rough edges, very rough. Have to labour on your heart, like workman.'

He is very confusing to me, this man. In the same breath he manages to call me a cooker, a hot-air balloon and a construction worker. Then I hear myself say, 'I'm not a gem, Zeeshan. Unlike you, I've committed a crime, a big one.'

Eyes closed, Zeeshan exhales. A long, deep wheeze that reminds me of my father's asthma attacks. 'Many people in this world go down. But few

of them fall all the way down. At the end of arc of descent, you know
what is there?'

'No.'

'Hell,' he says. 'You have been there. Ah, your soul is in flames. But it
has to be. Because you did terrible thing. You have to burn. Afterwards you
start to work your way up. Arc of ascent. You know what is at the end of it?'

'Heaven?' I offer.

'Yes, when we love and when we are loved, when we free of harmful
energy, we get close to heaven. Every day one small step. I cannot
promise you can achieve. But we try, Alex. We work.'

That same week I walk to the visitors' room not knowing what to
expect. Officer McLaughlin is there. He doesn't look at me, but it doesn't
take a wild leap of imagination to guess that he wants to watch the
spectacle, should there be one.

Then I see him. It is Yunus. My kid brother whom I haven't seen in
years. Since the day I was banged up he has come to see me just twice.
Once, right after the trial. We didn't speak a word. He just sat, looking at
his hands. He came back a year later. Again no words. Then he stopped
coming.

He is a grown man. Medium height, slender, quite handsome. As
much as he has changed, his eyes are the same. Soft, kind, heavily
lashed. The eyes of a boy in love with a punk girl.

'Hi, mate.'

'Hello, brother,' he says.

We stare at each other. I avert my eyes first. It was easier for me to face
Esma. She hates me. Plain and clear. Every now and then she would
come here to vent her anger. She would say all sorts of things to my face
and no doubt behind my back too. And yet she never made me feel half
as guilty as I do now. In Yunus's eyes there is something I cannot stand:
the need to understand. He is still looking for an explanation. He still
believes human beings are good and something bad must have overcome
me for such a horrible thing to have happened.

'How's your music going?'

'Great,' he says keenly. 'My first album just came out. I brought you
one but they took it. They said they'll pass it to you.'

'Yeah, don't worry about that,' I say. I know I will never get that album. 'Why are you here, Yunus? Don't get me wrong. I'm happy to see you. It's just . . . I'm surprised.'

He hesitates. A shadow crosses his face. 'You'll be out soon,' he says. 'I need to know what your plans are.'

My plans? It sounds so lame. So boy-scoutish. But this is my little brother. I'm not going to break his heart. And I promised Zeeshan that I'd start to climb, whatever that means.

'My plan is to find a decent job. Pay my way. Live a quiet life. If Katie is prepared to be reasonable, it'd be nice to catch up with my son.' I wait a beat. 'And spend more time with you and Esma. If you want me back.'

Yunus straightens his back, looks at me squarely. 'I've been wondering whether or not to tell you this and I decided not to. All these years, I didn't. And neither did Esma. We had an agreement. But now I'm not taking any chances.'

I chuckle, unsmiling. 'Hey, stop talking in riddles. I don't know what you're on about.'

He takes a deep breath. 'I was a kid when you killed Mum. I couldn't stop you. If you harm her again it'll be different. I'm not a kid any more. I'll fight you.'

For a second I fear my brother has lost his mind. I've seen it happen before. Men in the loonies' wing, out of their minds with grief.

'Yunus, what are you sayin'?'

'I'm saying I love Mum and I won't let you hurt her again.'

'Brother, Mama is . . .'

'No, I haven't finished yet,' he interjects loudly. Officer McLaughlin looks our way with a glint in his eyes. The drama he has been hoping for is about to begin.

Then Yunus drops his voice to a whisper, so low and gruff that afterwards I'm not entirely sure I heard him right.

'Iskender, listen to me,' he says. 'Mum is alive.'

Iskender Toprak

Mirror Image

London, 30 November 1978

Yunus raised his head from his breakfast plate, smiling at the two women on the sofa. A miracle had happened. His aunt Jamila had come to London. It had been three years since the boy had last seen her. Before that, they had visited her occasionally, summers mostly, encounters so brief and intense that it had left them almost dizzy. For the last three years, however, the family had stopped travelling, holidays having become an expense they could no longer afford. Now, after much mutual longing, the sisters were under the same roof again: Pink Destiny and Enough Beauty.

Sitting back, Yunus searched for the differences between the mirror-image twins, as if he were playing a game of odd-one out. Pembe was left-handed, Jamila right-handed. Pembe had a dimple on her right cheek, Jamila a dimple on her left. Pembe's mole on her face was to the right of her forehead while Jamila's was located on the other side. Their cowlicks grew in opposite directions. Overall Jamila was half an inch taller, her limbs a tad longer, her fingers slightly bonier.

'What else, Mum?' Yunus asked.

'Well, actually, there is one more difference. You've forgotten the most important one.'

Yunus barged in, 'Really? What is it?'

The answer came from Jamila. 'Our hearts beat on opposite sides.'

'What do you mean?'

They had a condition rarely seen in twins. Pembe's heart beat on the left side of her body, while Jamila's heart was situated on the right.

'Wow,' Yunus exclaimed.

Seeing their excitement, Pembe laughed, feeling lighter, and somehow more complete, than she had in a long while.

None of them paid much attention to the fact that Jamila had been unable to greet two other members of the family: Adem, who had left London for Abu Dhabi, and Iskender, who had come home the night before after everyone was asleep and gone out before Pembe had had a chance to tell him his aunt was there. They were planning to surprise him that evening.

Yunus begged his mother to let him stay at home. He was not feeling very well, he said, *sore throat, feeling very poorly*. Pembe knew that even if there were some truth in that, he was stretching it very far, but such was her joy to be next to her twin that she let her son skip lessons for a day.

As they sipped their teas by the window, they began to speak in Kurdish, which effectively excluded Yunus from the conversation. Pembe confided to Jamila that somehow people had got wind of her affair with Elias. There was tittle-tattle, bad-mouthing. It had reached Iskender's ears. He didn't look at her face any more, she whispered. Iskender had forbidden her to go to work, and, when that was not enough, had barred her from leaving the house. She explained all this with a forced smile, so that Yunus couldn't sense how fretful she was.

Jamila said, 'We'll solve this, God willing. Let me talk to my nephew.'

Then, as if the exchange she had envisaged had, in fact, already happened, she smiled gaily. 'Tell you what, why don't I go out and do the shopping today?'

She would choose fresh vegetables, get good bread and find the best herbs. She didn't speak a word of English, but if Yunus, whose throat suddenly seemed on the mend, could lend a hand that wouldn't be a problem.

Yunus, thrilled to spend time with his aunt, seized the opportunity. 'Yes, yes, Mum, let me go!'

'But don't be late,' was all that Pembe said.

It was a day like any other. Only better. The 30th of November, a Thursday. Just as Jamila and Yunus were putting on their shoes and coats, Pembe stopped them.

'Oh, wait a sec!'

She fished a lipstick out of her bag, a deep plum, and painted her sister's lips, which were dry and pale from years of sun, wind and neglect. Then in one move she pulled the headscarf off her twin's head. Jamila's thick hair fell on her shoulders in a cascade of sepia and brown.

'You look prettier like this.'

Jamila hesitated. In the narrow mirror in the corridor, she caught a glimpse of herself. This new dress, this new hair, this new her made her uneasy. Standing beside her, Yunus urged in Turkish, 'Come on, Auntie. You look terrific.'

She yielded. 'If you say so.'

Smiling, Pembe gave some banknotes to her sister and a fistful of change to Yunus. Then she kissed them both. 'Don't forget to buy cardamom. We're having meat tonight. And I need it for the coffee.'

Thus they left the house. Jamila and Yunus, delighted with each other's company. She tried to speak Kurdish to him and was disappointed to see he didn't grasp anything at all. Both of them being poor in Turkish, they conversed little, holding hands, enjoying themselves. As happy as Yunus was to be with her, after two hours of shopping he saw an opportunity to peel away on the journey home. He had other things to do, more important things, having run into Tobiko on the street.

The punks were planning to retake their old house. Finally the big day had arrived. At midnight the crew, having mustered their forces, were going to launch the long-awaited comeback. Using crowbars to get behind the hoardings surrounding the Victorian house, they would reoccupy the place with their sleeping bags and ammunition. The next morning the entire neighbourhood would wake up to their presence, and if the council sent along its *troopers*, they would chase them away with stones and bottles.

Seeing how agitated Tobiko was, Yunus asked his aunt if it was okay for him to hang out a little bit with his friend. They were nearly home anyway, he said, and they had bought everything on the list.

'Are you sure your mother would say okay?' Jamila asked.

It sounded less like a question than like a light reprimand, and Yunus assured her, 'I'll catch up with you in a jiffy, I promise.'

Nodding, Jamila grabbed the bags and headed in the direction Yunus had shown her. Along the way she stopped a few times: to listen to a street musician, to stare at a mural on a wall, to glance in shop windows, marvelling at the array of things on sale. Such was her distraction, and her sense of awe and wonder at being in a city this strange, that she did not notice that someone had started to follow her.

Lemon Tree

London, 30 November 1978

Pembe was in the kitchen, humming an old Kurdish love song, 'Susan Susie', which had a melancholy that weighed down the spirits of the singer, as most old Kurdish love songs tended to. She was, however, far from forlorn. Though her mind was in a whirl and her heart ached for Elias, Pembe couldn't help but feel a sense of bliss. Her sister's presence had renewed her faith in life and given her fresh hope. A few months ago she had written a letter to Adem, explaining to him that they needed to separate for good. He had never responded. Now she would find a lawyer. Adem would be sad but not surprised. It might even come as a relief that it was she, and not he, taking the first step. No doubt it would be much harder to convince Iskender, but perhaps she could make him understand. She would tell him no more lies, only the truth. Things would be different from now on. Pembe didn't know how, but she trusted that it would be so.

Having formed a plan, she set about preparing a lemon-meringue pie – a recipe she had learned from Elias. She was hoping to surprise Jamila with this luscious treat. When they were girls, they used to love nibbling salted lemons, and even had a rhyme for it: *Sour plus sour equals sweet.* Their elder sisters could never manage this, their faces crumpling at each attempt. Yet the twins could eat five lemons in one sitting, and their favourite jams were always the sour-sweet ones.

There did not seem to be much left of Jamila's old appetite, though. She had arrived in London the day before, and since then she had eaten little, said little about herself. She had changed, her sister. Her eyes were shadowed with dark circles, her smile was hesitant, almost apologetic. But the changes were so subtle that only Pembe had noticed them. The children were amazed to observe how identical their mother and their aunt still were. Once Jamila had shed her rough woollen garments and put on one of Pembe's dresses, combing her hair the same way – towards the front of her head where it naturally broke – they were impossible to tell apart.

When she had finished whisking the eggs and sugar to a thick foam, Pembe turned on the oven. Elias had advised her to add a generous amount of grated lemon. Pembe always kept the lemons, oranges and limes in a bamboo basket on the balcony. In the past she had tried to grow lemon trees, but each time they were killed off by sudden frosts.

Still humming the same song, Pembe scurried out on to the balcony. Inadvertently her eyes slid beneath the steel railing towards the street below. Something held her gaze. A second later she saw her twin enter Lavender Grove, carrying a number of bags. Pembe craned her neck over the railing and waved. Her sister didn't notice at first.

'Jamila . . . Look up! Here!'

Jamila lifted her gaze towards the balcony, a placid expression on her face. Pembe broke into a smile. There was, beneath her sister's solemn countenance and dignified bearing, something of her childhood naivety, as delicate as mist. She couldn't help but be envious of how eye-catching her twin was. For, although they were similar, they were not the same. Charm came to Jamila naturally, the way a bee homed in on a flower. Jamila was brimming with life and light, full of grit and composure, Pembe thought, unlike herself.

'I'm making a dessert for you!'

'What?' Jamila asked, distracted by a passing car.

'I am –' Pembe stopped, having just noticed Iskender walking up the road.

For a second or two Pembe watched her elder son trail behind her sister. Iskender's eyes had narrowed into slits; his jaw was tight, his lips moving incessantly, as if quarrelling with himself.

She couldn't figure out what was going on. Even when she saw him lunge towards Jamila, even when she noticed the knife in his hand, even when he blocked her sister's way and uttered words that could only have amounted to steeling himself against any doubts, what was taking place in front of her eyes continued to make no sense. But then suddenly the curtain that was clouding her vision lifted, and she saw the full truth, the full danger. She felt the air go out of her. Still clutching the lemons, she flew from the balcony to the living room, through the corridor, out the door, into the street.

Pembe ran. She was eight feet away when she saw her son stab her sister. Iskender swung the knife sloppily and hastily, as though he wanted to get it over with at once and go on his way. The blade drew a half-circle in the air, entering Jamila's flesh on the right side of her thorax. Behind them a strangled sound came from Pembe. She knew instantly, she knew in her bones, that the knife had gone into her twin's heart.

Iskender took a step back, paused for an instant, frowning at the knife in his hand. For a moment he seemed confused, as though he didn't know what he had done, as if he had been a puppet dancing to the pull of strings and was only now waking up. With a jolt he threw the knife aside and sprinted in the opposite direction.

Pembe could hear someone scream. A piercing howl in the wind. It would be another minute before she realized the sound was coming from her. She couldn't budge, for she had no body. She had no substance. She was only a voice. Her entire being was reduced – or magnified – to a cry that gave way to new ones in spirals, independent of her will, spinning, swirling, melting into an endless echo.

Her eyes wide open, her stomach churning, Pembe stumbled towards her sister. The contents of the bags were scattered on the street. Bread rolls, cheese, green apples, a pot of basil, a pack of cardamom.

Like a sleepwalker, Pembe cuddled her twin. She kissed Jamila's face – her forehead, her cheekbones, the soft hollow in front of her neck. She checked her pulse, but it was muted and her body felt limp, already losing warmth. All the sparkle was drained from her face, except for her lips, which were now the colour of her wound. Pembe began to shiver, as if life were bleeding out of her too. A pool of blood so dark it was almost black widened and thickened on the ground. She heard hurried footsteps, hushed tones. The siren of an ambulance turning the corner. Slamming car doors, police radios. She staggered away from her twin's body, the tarmac hard against her slippers.

Half a minute later an elderly woman, a kind-hearted Albanian neighbour, approached the street from the other end, having just noticed the commotion. Puzzled and fearful, she dived towards the body on the ground. She fell on her knees, shrieking, wailing.

'Oh, poor thing! What happened to you? Pembe, dear!'

Further down the street gooseflesh had broken out all over Pembe's body. Hearing herself being mourned was uncanny and chilling, but, in an odd way, it helped her to disconnect herself from her surroundings. She neither stopped nor glanced back. Her arms folded over her chest, her head lowered as if walking against a strong wind, she floated through the crowd like the ghost she already felt she was.

*

For the rest of the day Pembe roamed the streets, seeing parts of East London she had never been in before. She knew she couldn't go back home or to Elias when Iskender was out there somewhere, unrestrained. It was surely only a matter of time before her son realized his mistake and came back to find her. Such was her fear that she wasn't able to grieve for her sister. She became increasingly apprehensive, as if anxiety were a substance, a liquid that filled her up little by little.

Several times she had to stop and take deep breaths to steady herself. Her feet drew concentric circles around the Crystal Scissors, until she came to a stop opposite the entrance. She had left her work without an explanation. She had put the keys through the letterbox and called it quits. Now, hiding behind a Royal Mail van, she watched the flamboyant profile of Rita through the window. There were two customers inside and someone who must be the new apprentice – a young Asian woman with hair the colour of an aubergine.

Pembe sneaked into the area behind the salon, where they dried the towels, smocks and aprons. If she was lucky she would find something to wear. Her blouse was stained with blood, which she had been hiding by keeping her arms crossed and her shoulders hunched. Funny how those she passed had failed to notice. Or perhaps they simply had preferred not to see. She opened the back gate, crept in and stopped.

Swaying from side to side in time to the music playing in the salon, a piece of chewing gum in her mouth, the apprentice was coming to collect the towels off the line. It was too late to go back and there was no place to take cover. Pembe found herself gaping at this stranger, who now was gaping at her.

'Sorry,' Pembe said, her cheeks growing hot. She lunged forward, grabbed a smock and scurried away.

'Hey, what're you doin'?' the assistant yelled. 'Thief! Thief!'

But Pembe was already gone.

Over the next few hours she kept wandering, the setting sun a tepid caress on the back of her neck. She had nowhere to go. If she went to the police, they would interrogate her. Unable to understand the language, she would fail to answer their questions, and perhaps end up being held responsible.

She couldn't seek refuge in a neighbour's house either. Who would want to take the risk? Besides, she didn't know whether Iskender had acted alone or been guided by others. If so, who else was involved? Was Tariq in on this? How about her husband? Had the two brothers convinced Iskender, her sultan, the apple of her eye, to kill his own flesh and blood? Her head was throbbing. She couldn't trust anyone, except Elias. The thought of him sent a shudder down her spine. This was it. She would not see him again. It was a good thing that Iskender didn't know where Elias lived or worked, she thought. As long as she stayed away from him, Elias would be fine. It was better that he came to believe her dead.

Guilt, that sneaky serpent that had been feeding inside her chest for months, growing stockier each day, had now emerged in all its ugly grandeur and was gnawing at her soul. She blamed herself and herself only. It was her love affair with Elias that had brought on this calamity. How could she bear to see him again? The truth was that even then, even there, Pembe was trying to excuse Iskender. She longed to see her other two children. What would they do when they found out that their aunt was dead and their mother had gone missing? What would the police tell them and what would they, in turn, say to the police?

When darkness fell, Pembe plodded back to her neighbourhood, though she knew it was dangerous. Hiding herself as best as she could, she arrived in Lavender Grove. In the spot where Jamila had died only hours ago, there was now a silhouette that had been drawn with white chalk. The site was cordoned off and a few people were smoking near by, commenting. Unable to get any closer, she decided to vanish.

That night Pembe found a litter-strewn corner in front of a Barclays bank and curled up there, wincing each time a car went past. She used a public toilet, begged some water and food from a restaurant owner and cried herself to sleep.

'Wake up! Get up, you slag!' A homeless man was towering beside her. Tall and beer-bellied, with a swollen face, bushy eyebrows, missing teeth. 'Bloody hell! What d'you think you're doin' in my place?'

Pembe bolted in panic, her lips quivering. 'I . . . I'm sorry.' She caught his smell in the air. A mixture of wine, tobacco, mothballs and urine. The man tottered towards her with intent. Pembe dodged him and ran for it.

'Hey, come back, little birdie! Why're you so afraid?'

The tramp watched her hurtle down the road until she disappeared around the corner. Sniggering as if sharing a joke with himself, he settled himself in the corner that was still warm, sighed as he took off his boots and began to nurse his feet absent-mindedly.

Esma

London, 1 December 1978

There was too much food in the kitchen – in cauldrons and stewpots brimful with delicacies, wafting heavy, pungent smells; casseroles, pastries and desserts were on the worktop, on the table, on the chairs, on the floor. I didn't know who was going to eat it all, now that there was only me and Yunus. But the mourners kept coming, and they brought their food, determined to feed us. In the living room there were women of all ages sitting side by side. Some were old neighbours; some were people I knew only vaguely; and some I was seeing for the first time. With each new group of visitors, Aunt Meral, as the host, stood up, welcomed them, cried with them. Yunus and I were sitting in one corner, both there and not there – like two somnolent fish in an otherwise empty aquarium. Everyone approached us, stared at us, studied us, tapping the glass wall that separated us from them, and then waited for us to react. We saw them and we heard them, but we didn't feel anything, numb to their words of consolation. Our minds were busy solving a riddle of which only we were aware.

'Esma, it's all my fault,' said Yunus, his voice brittle.

'What do you mean?'

'I left Auntie alone . . .'

I held his hand, hugged him. 'It was Iskender who did this, not you, *canim*.'

'But if it was Aunt Jamila in the ambulance, where is Mum?'

'That's what I'm wondering myself.'

In less than an hour we would learn the answer. Around midday the door opened again, and a new guest walked in, clad in bright green from head to toe, including a feathery hat. The mourners gawked at her sparkling accessories, painted nails, strange ways, speechless.

I, however, was delighted to see her. 'Oh, Rita . . .' I said, as I ran to her in tears.

The two of us sat together at the kitchen table away from prying eyes.

'My mother isn't dead,' I whispered.

She nodded.

'Is she with you?'

Another nod.

Rita said that early in the morning, when she had gone to open the salon, she found her old co-worker sleeping on the doorstep. She asked her what had happened but got little from her. She took her into the room at the back, served her tea and biscuits, pulled the shutters down, gave the apprentice the day off and declared the place closed. She then helped my mother to wash her face and clean herself.

'Can you keep her safe for a few days?' I asked. 'Until we figure this out.'

Rita shook her head. Her boyfriend would never allow her to bring my mother home, and, even if he did, she wasn't sure he could be trusted with such a secret.

'There's one more thing,' Rita said. She handed me a piece of paper with Elias's name and address. 'You have to tell him that your mum is dead. Pembe thinks it's better this way.'

There was no other exchange. I walked her to the door. Playing her role to the hilt, Rita gave me a tearful hug before she left, 'I'm sorry, love. Your ma was so dear to me.'

★

After sunset Yunus and I entered the Crystal Scissors through the back door, holding hands. For as long as I live I'll never forget the moment we ran into her arms, sobbing and laughing all at once. She looked so shaken, her face sunken, dark rings around her eyes.

Yunus's head rested on Mum's bosom, as he moaned, 'It's all my fault. I left Aunt Jamila alone. I was talking to my friends, I let her walk back on her own.'

Mum kissed him. Then she kissed me, whispering, 'Did you talk to him?'

I briefly told her about my visit to Elias. She listened, slumped and drained, as if in some half-dream.

'They're saying awful things about you,' Yunus interjected. 'We don't talk to them any more.'

That's how my mother learned that the entire neighbourhood was abuzz with gossip. Some people accused her of bringing disgrace to the family and provoking her son into choosing such a dark path.

I stared daggers at my brother. 'There's going to be a funeral in a day. Aunt Meral is organizing everything.'

It was then that Yunus grabbed my mother's arm and patted it with authority. 'Don't worry. I know where to take you. There is one place in London where you'll be totally safe and no one will hand you over to the police.'

And that's how my mother, Pembe Kader Toprak, thirty-three years old, and deceased according to official records, began to live in a dilapidated squat in Hackney, occupied by a group of punk rockers.

The Cleaning

London, 5 December 1978

Pembe sat propped up in bed, her face a mask of exhaustion. Wrapping her arms around her bent knees, she locked her fingers together. There was a tightening in her chest, a mounting ache, as if something were pressing against her ribs. Breathing was an effort. Swallowing hurt.

She listened to the sounds in the old Victorian house, which was now drenched in darkness, and smelled the faint acrid tang in the air. Dust, sweat, musty furniture, damp laundry, grubby sheets, empty bottles, full ashtrays. Being in a room where several people slept on the floor side by side brought back memories of her childhood. She recalled how she and her seven sisters would slumber the night away, spooning round one another, seeking each other's warmth. No matter how many blankets there were, she would wake up in the middle of the night chilly and uncovered. Pulling the nearest blanket over her head, she would wrap herself as best as she could, thus leaving another sister exposed.

Now Pembe looked past the sleeping youths at the bleak nothingness beyond the window, feeling a kind of listlessness she had never experienced before. An hour passed by. Maybe more. She had no way of knowing. After a while her eyes caught the first glow of light on the horizon. Shafts of crimson, sharp as arrows. Dawn was breaking above the London skyline. A bitter dread rose in her throat. Soon they would all be awake. Eating, joking, smoking. Though they had agreed to shelter her, and though they did their best not to disturb her, the punks couldn't help asking questions, unable to grasp what was going on.

Most squatters loved to sleep in late, but, given the current uncertainty with the council, they were being extra vigilant, fully aware that the halcyon days of lie-ins were a thing of the past. Thus around eight a.m. everyone was awake, groping for yesterday's clothes, lighting the first cigarette of the day, elbowing one another out of the way at the one chipped sink. Even Iggy Pop, who slept with homemade earplugs, was up and about.

In the kitchen Tobiko was watching Pembe make pancakes for an army. She struggled to find something to say but only came up with, 'Wow, this smells good.'

Pembe gave her a faint smile. Her hands kept working, fast and focused, her mind miles away. A few minutes later she handed Tobiko a large plate topped with pancakes. 'Go . . . eat . . .' she said.

Tobiko hesitated. 'How about you?'

'I eat later.'

'You know we love your son,' Tobiko said out of the blue. 'He's like our mascot. And uh-hmm . . . I don't quite know what the problem is, but Yunus mentioned it was a bit hush-hush and you had to hide for a while. Whatever it is, you're welcome to stay here for as long as you want.'

Pembe felt a rush of compassion for Tobiko so profound that her eyes welled up. She hugged the young woman, who wasn't expecting this, but who instantly hugged her back. The moment was broken by Iggy Pop, shouting at the top of his lungs the *agora*. 'Oi, we're starving in here. People want food!'

Smiling, Tobiko took the plate and scurried inside.

Alone in the kitchen, Pembe grabbed a tattered broom and began to sweep the floor. If she didn't do what she always did, she feared she would lose her mind. Thus, in the ensuing hours, she scrubbed, swept, dusted, mopped and polished the entire squat under the bewildered eyes of the residents. Such was her frenzy all day long that no one dared to make fun or to tell her to stop. And it must have been contagious, for a few people offered to help, using mops and makeshift brooms to join in with her madness. Soon, however, they gave up, tired and bored.

Come the evening she was still working, and the punks were still tiptoeing around behind her, watching this woman from another culture, another language, another story, constantly cry and clean, cry and clean.

***

Just three months before my release an old woman in intensive care at a local hospital opens her eyes. She complains of thirst, and a pain in her back. But other than that she seems perfectly fine. When she is ready to talk they ask her about the man who stole her handbag and assaulted her with a broken bottle one chilly day. She describes him. Her memory is in mint condition. And the description in no way matches Zeeshan. Still not convinced, they show her a mugshot of my cellmate. She says it isn't him. They take Zeeshan and make her look at him through a two-way mirror. She says it isn't him. The court decides to have the case reopened.

'You must be over the moon,' I say. 'You'll be a free man soon.'

'Zeeshan free man already,' he says. 'No need to go to moon.'

'You'll be much missed, man.'

He looks crestfallen, swallows hard. 'I go out and think about you,' he says. 'You were my best student.'

'And you, a bad liar.'

He chuckles, his shoulders hopping. 'Don't forget to do your homework.'

'What homework?'

Then he tells me.

The morning Zeeshan is set to leave we meditate together for the last time. Unlike other days, I don't take the mick. I don't protest. I sit cross-legged on the hard floor, looking at him. And, for the first time, I manage to keep my mind still, even if only for a short while.

The same evening, with Zeeshan gone, I lie on my bunk, thinking. It sits heavily with me, his absence. Last time I felt like this Trippy was dead. But I try to finish what he asked me to do. My homework. It's the hardest thing I've ever done. My assignment is to write a letter to my mother and hand it to her when I'm out of here.

A pen in my hand, I scrawl different letters on different days. A few of them seem so-so, but there is so much missing, and most of them are pretty lame. I rip them to pieces, start again, getting nowhere. Every day I scribble something, just as I promised Zeeshan. I meditate a bit too.

Officer McLaughlin comes and goes; there is no love lost between us, but we're not at each other's throats. Not any more.

Then I compose something that somehow seems less dreadful than the others. And this time I decide to keep it. Zeeshan instructed me to copy my letter on to a blank page each day, until I've memorized it, and that is what I do next.

Dear Mother,

I'm not going to send this letter. I'll bring it myself, inshallah, and give it to you, because it's easier to write the contents than to say them. This year I had my eyes opened. I had this daft cellmate. Daft in a good way. You would have liked him. His name was Zeeshan. Good bloke, helped me a lot. I understand this better now that he's gone. Too bad, we always appreciate what we have after we lose it.

If I could be sixteen years old again, I'd never do the things that I did to cause so much pain. To you, my sister, my brother, my poor aunt. I cannot change the past. Not a single moment of it. Zeeshan says I can improve myself now. Even of that I'm not sure. But if you'd accept me into your life again, if you could find it in your heart to forgive me, what a blessing it'd be to once more be your son.

Iskender Toprak

Esma

London, 12 September 1992

Saturday morning. I am preparing breakfast in our newly fitted kitchen. It has cost us an arm and a leg, more than we could afford. But my husband has insisted on getting the latest of everything. It is his present to me on our eighth anniversary. Espresso-coloured units, maple floorboards, a posh American refrigerator, a whole-fruit juicer, no need to chop, so practical. *Sleek, serene and practical*. That is what it said in the brochure.

I scrape the eggs with a spatula, watching the well-cooked bits at the bottom come to the top, like fragments from the past surfacing into the present. It is not easy to make scrambled eggs when your mind isn't on the job. You have to have the right timing to achieve a good result, and my timing, I suppose, is never right. I might have a problem with the notion of time in general. I can neither let go of yesterday, nor focus on tomorrow. Of the girl with big ideas and coruscating words not much is left today. When I think of the bright-eyed me, which I do often, I cannot help feeling betrayed, though by no one other than myself.

My daughters are sitting at the table, chirping on about the presenters of *Blue Peter*, their favourite programme. As usual, they hold opposing views. I listen to them but my brain is a kite. It flutters every which way in the wind.

'Mum, can you please tell your other daughter to shut up?' bellows Layla.

'Uh-hmm, yes,' I say, taking the pan off the heat. The eggs are not exactly ready yet, but I don't want them to overcook. Not again.

'Mum!!!' Jamila exclaims.

'Sorry, dear, what did you say?' I ask, but it is too late. When I turn back I find one of them beaming, triumphant, the other upset.

It is my husband who runs to my rescue. 'Leave your mum alone. She's got a lot on her mind today.'

'Why?' asks Layla.

'We've talked about this,' says Nadir amiably. 'Your uncle is coming to meet us. Your mother hasn't seen him for a long time.'

'Oh,' says Layla, though there is no trace of surprise on her face.

I notice Jamila watching her father intently, a glint of defiance flickering in her eyes, dark and almond, so different from the eyes of the woman for whom she was named. Suddenly she says, 'Are you two lying to us?'

My hand, dishing up the eggs, stops in mid-air. I listen to the ensuing silence, unable to break it.

Nadir is calm, composed, as always. 'That's not a nice word to use when talking to your parents, darling. Or to anyone else.'

'Sooorry,' Jamila says in a singsong voice.

'All right, now tell me what did you mean by that?'

Relishing the attention, Jamila purses her lips playfully. 'Well . . . I don't think Uncle Iskender works in Alaska. I think . . .' She scans the table as if hoping to find a clue in there. 'He's a Russian spy.'

'In your dreams!' Layla butts in.

'It's true. He drops bombs on icebergs.'

'He does not!'

'Yes, he does!'

I put a few slices of tomato and a leaf of basil on each plate and carry the dishes to the table, wondering if things would have been easier had my older brother been a spy working for the Russians, testing bombs at the North Pole.

Later, when the girls have gone to get ready for a birthday party, Nadir wraps his arms around me, tilting his head sideways. I look at him squarely, taking him in. The way he squeezes his eyes into a tender squint, the smile lines on his cheeks, the fine wrinkles on his forehead. His hair, thick and bushy, is growing upwards, defying gravity, refusing to cover his ears. There are a few grey streaks at the temples, hinting at his age. He is sixteen years older than me. Exactly the same age difference that was between Elias and my mother. A coincidence, of course, I always remind myself.

I love him and yet it didn't start out as love. We both knew at the beginning I wasn't devoted to him in the way he was to me. Deep in my heart I concocted a mixture of feelings for him: respect, fondness, admiration and, especially, gratitude for pulling me out of the sludge in which I was wallowing. You sometimes hear people say that being with their partners has turned them into 'a better person'. You hear it, and you don't quite believe it, unless it happens to you.

After the last day of November 1978, our family thawed like a snowman under a scorching sun. Suddenly all that was left of our previous life was a grey pile of slush. What had once seemed solid and steadfast quickly became elusive, undependable. Yunus and I lived with Uncle Tariq and Aunt Meral for a while, and, though they were neither unkind nor ungenerous to us, I hated every second of it. I never forgave them for spreading dirt about my mother in the weeks before the murder, and even as I stayed under their roof, ate their food and wore the clothes they bought for me, they were at the top of the list of people I loathed. At first Father sent us cards, gifts and money from Abu Dhabi, though this became more sporadic over the years, until eventually all contact dried up. My uncle and aunt kept his suicide from us as long as they could. Covering, marring, distorting the truth. And I should know, because here I am doing the same thing to my children now. It's a family tradition, shrouding the truth in veils, burying it deep within the stagnation of everyday life, so that after a while it cannot be reached, even in your imagination.

My memory of those years is a shifting ground, a quicksand of hurt and despair. Having tumbled into it, I found only anger could pull me out, and so it has been for some time. Early days of Mrs Thatcher, huge changes under way. England fast moving away from all that it had been, a behemoth waking from a sluggish winter dream. My exam marks were high, always. The Department of Education showed a special interest in our case, and both Yunus and I were transferred to a boarding school in Sussex. That helped a bit, the distance. But I held on to my rage without realizing that it wasn't getting me anywhere. I was drowning in my resentments. After boarding school I went to Queen Mary College, where I read English. Then I met Nadir.

He is a man of science, a scholar who believes in universal certainties and objective truths. Born in Gaza, raised in a Palestinian refugee camp, he left his motherland for England at the age of nineteen thanks to a relative who generously supported his education. Shortly after the Beatles released *Yellow Submarine*, Nixon was inaugurated as president and Arafat became the chairman of the PLO, Nadir arrived in Manchester, taciturn and timid but faithful. He then pursued a career that was as far from politics as possible: molecular biology. While the world spun faster in a whirl of conflict, he retreated into his laboratory, neat, methodical and controllable, to study the morphology of cells.

His kith and kin are still in Gaza. I have met them several times. A large family. Warm, proud, curious, garrulous. I observed my husband amidst his relatives, cynically searching for signs of change in his character, a swing that would bring out the core beneath the veneer of decorum. But Nadir is the same gentle soul everywhere and with everyone. He never acts on a whim or an impulse. He likes to process, to *cogitate*, a favourite word of his. He is never in a hurry. His motto in life: *Still waters run deep*. No wonder he and Yunus get along so well.

'You all right?' he asks me.

I nod. To be alone. That is all I want right now. To take my coat and walk out the door, leaving everything as it is, untouched, the leftovers on the plates, the crumbs on the tablecloth, the stains on the mugs, the pieces of my past.

'It's going to be a long day, is all.'

'Don't worry about us,' he says. 'I'll pick up the monsters from the party. You ought to spend time with him alone.'

I listen to my husband's accent. The guttural sounds, Arabic tinges.

'But that's exactly what I fear, having time with Iskender.'

Nadir cups my cheeks in his hands, planting a kiss on my lips. 'Darling, it's going to be o-kay.'

For a fleeting moment I wish he wasn't so considerate, so caring. Nadir is the kind of man who, in the face of aggression, physical or verbal, will avoid confrontation at all costs. If anyone does him wrong, as a co-worker at the university once did, he will accept the situation and even hold himself responsible. It suddenly dawns on me that, knowingly or not, I have married the exact opposite of my elder brother.

'I dunno,' I say. 'Maybe I shouldn't go. My uncle might show up. Or some of his old cronies.'

Nadir arches an eyebrow. He can see it coming back, my bitterness. He seems to be choosing his words carefully. 'You should go to see him. If he hasn't changed a bit, if he's the same man as before, you don't need him in your life. But you ought to go and be sure.' Then he pronounces four words that will ring in my ears all day long: 'He is your brother.'

'What am I gonna tell the girls when he's here? Hello, darlings, this is your uncle whom you've never met. Why? Well, because he was in prison. Why? Umm, because, you see, he killed your —'

'You don't need to explain anything to them. Not yet.'

My eyes water, and when I speak my voice comes out strained. 'You and Yunus always want things to be simple and easy. But the world is so complicated. Everything is complicated.'

Nadir's mouth puckers as he dotingly mimics my tone. 'Forget the world. *Make the most of what we yet may spend,/ Before we too into dust descend.*'

I laugh, despite myself. 'Is that Khayyam again?'

'Omar Khayyam it is.'

This man of tender words and uplifting poems. This man who is honest, dependable and righteous sometimes to the point of a naivety that drives me crazy. This man who believes that honour has got to do with people's hearts rather than their bedrooms. I try to imagine what he sees in me, how it is that he still loves me. Unable to come up with an answer, I murmur, 'I'd better go and get ready.'

'All right, darling.'

Once I thought I was cut out for important things, worthy struggles, life-sized ideals. I would become a writer as well as a human-rights activist. I would travel to different parts of the world to campaign for the oppressed and the abused. J. B. Ono — the renowned author of novels in which no one was ever fooled by love. Once I wished to be the centre of the world, but then I came to accept that I was only one of the many characters in a story, and not even a major character at that.

I wrote for a while, once I finished my A-levels, hard though it is to remember now. At university my results were good, my essays inventive, and there were people who believed in me, but something had changed irreversibly. I had lost faith in myself. Like a plant that looks vibrant in the shop but mysteriously droops after it is brought home, my wish to become a novelist wilted as soon as I was out of my familiar environment.

After that I didn't write. Other than letters, lots and lots of letters. I wrote to Shrewsbury regularly, and to Yunus, whenever we were apart. I also corresponded with Elias (with whom I got in touch) and with Roxana (who got in touch with me), and they each helped me, in their own way, to find the missing pieces of the jigsaw puzzle. And I wrote to my mother, twice a week for the next twelve years.

Then, last summer, after my mother passed away, I started to write down the story of her life. I worked day and night, as if frightened that if I stopped, even for a moment, I would lose the urge, or the urge would lose me, and everything would crumble. The things I described were so personal that some parts hurt, while others latched on to something inside me. Still, shortly after the manuscript was completed I was seized by a sense of estrangement. It wasn't mine, this story.

The past is a trunk in the loft, crammed with scraps, some valuable, but many entirely useless. Although I'd prefer to keep it closed, the slightest breeze throws it open, and, before I know it, all the contents have flown everywhere. I put them back. One by one. The memories, the bad and the good. Yet the trunk always snaps open again when I least expect it.

The pregnancy was more of an accident than something planned. When I found out, I was shocked, terrified and euphoric, all at once. And upon learning that it was twin girls, I cried for a good hour, feeling, once again, that my life, whatever I chose to do with it, was merely a link in a chain of stories. During those nine months my body was remoulded, as if made of clay. So, I hoped, would be my soul. Now my daughters are seven years old. Layla, with hair like the black satin of the night, and Jamila, named after her late great-aunt, though she doesn't know why.

Upstairs in my bedroom I hear the phone ring and my husband pick it up. I have a hunch it is Yunus – the boy named after the most reluctant prophet. Lately my younger brother and my husband have been ringing each other daily. A manly camaraderie. I know they are conspiring about me, and my wretched moods. They see me as a time bomb, constantly ticking, ready to explode, and they, always collected and rational, are trying to figure out how to defuse me. I picture myself as a suspicious package on the road, and Yunus and Nadir as bomb-disposal experts, dressed in flameproof suits and helmets, approaching me circumspectly.

'Darling, Yunus wants to talk to you.'

I pick up the phone, wait for my husband to hang up on his end, and say, as blithely as I can manage, 'Hi, my dear.'

'Esma, love. How are you feeling today?'

Why is everyone asking me how I feel? 'Jolly good,' I blurt out. 'How about yourself? How's the weather over there?'

He ignores my banality and goes to the heart of the matter. 'Good. When are you going to pick him up?'

In the background I can hear the band rehearsing. The piano, the guitars, the *ney*. My brother has a concert in Amsterdam tonight. A glitzy cultural event. Prince Claus is expected to attend.

'I'm leaving in an hour.'

'Look, umm . . . I know this isn't easy. I feel terrible letting you down. I wish I could be there.'

'That's okay. You've got things to do.'

I catch a tinge of tartness in my voice. If Yunus, too, has detected it, he doesn't let on. 'You know what I was thinking about this morning: that day when I went to visit him. He was happy to hear she was alive. He was . . . so touched. It's such a pity he couldn't have seen her and asked her forgiveness.'

I roll my eyes. 'Ah, her forgiveness . . .'

'It could have happened,' he insists. 'It would have been nice if he could have kissed her hand, and asked her blessing.'

'Oh, please, give me a break.'

There is a heavy silence and I'm beginning to suspect that the line has gone dead when I hear Yunus say, 'I think he's suffered enough.'

I close my eyes, feeling my blood boil inside my veins. 'How can you say that? There is no way he has suffered enough. He's a selfish man who killed our aunt and he'll die a selfish man.'

'He was a boy.'

'He was not a boy! It had nothing to do with his age. Now *you* were a boy. You didn't do what he did. It was his personality.'

'But he was the eldest,' Yunus says. 'You were always going on about being treated differently because you were a girl, and I found it tough to be the youngest child. But did you ever consider that maybe it was harder on Iskender?'

'Yeah, being a sultan can't have been easy.'

He sighs. 'Listen, sister, I gotta go. I'd be there if I could. We'll talk when I get back. We'll figure this out. Together. Like we have always done. Okay?'

Not quite trusting my voice, I bob my head, as if Yunus can see me. After I hang up I go to the bathroom to wash my face and put on some make-up. I begrudge Yunus for being able to forgive and forget, and I begrudge Iskender for what he has taken from us: a normal childhood. That comforting sense of security, love and continuity you get from your family before you grow up and plunge into the big world with its real miseries. I was fifteen years old when Iskender lost his head. After that, ordinary life as I knew it was shattered and a steady ache made its home in my heart. For my mother it was even worse.

In murdering one, Iskender has killed many.

★

I drive to Shrewsbury, past well-kept lawns and rolling green pastures. Time slows down. My mind drifts back to Yunus. He is becoming pretty famous, my little brother. Nadir tells me his students know his music and love it. I am proud of him. And, at those moments when I'm honest with myself, I am also envious. I wonder if it is another one of God's games that I, the so-called creative one, have ended up with a middling, domestic life, while Yunus, the calm and composed one, is following his dreams around the world. I suppose it never ends, this sibling rivalry. You compete for your parents' love, even when they are no longer there.

When I reach Shrewsbury Prison, I wait outside the building, surprised that no one else is around. No Uncle Tariq. No Aunt Meral. No neighbours, friends, relatives. Where are they? Iskender's old chums haven't shown up either. Has everyone forgotten about him?

An hour passes. There is a creeping chill in the air, muting all sound, and I feel a bit thirsty. Had I had gone into the building, the officers would, in all likelihood, have offered me some water, if not a cup of tea. I would have asked them what to expect, and perhaps learned a few new things about Iskender. But then he would emerge, and we would have to hug or shake hands in front of everyone. I'd rather wait here, outside.

Finally, the double gates open. Under this light, wearing a pair of jeans and a corduroy jacket, he looks so different from the last time I saw him. He has taken care of himself, seems fit and wiry. His gait has changed. He doesn't push his shoulders back and crane his head the way he used to do. After taking a few steps forward, he stops and gazes at the cold, overcast sky, just as I imagined he would.

Then he notices me. My face, a blank. He moves slowly, giving me time to go back to the car park, start the engine and leave should I want. When he approaches, I take a step forward, my hands thrust into my pockets.

'Hello, Esma,' he says.

Suddenly I am upset with Nadir, and Yunus, and all the spirits in the world for convincing me to come here. But I try to push the dark thoughts away. 'Hello to you, brother.' I pronounce the last word with some emphasis.

'I wasn't expecting to see you.'

'Oh, I didn't think I'd come myself.'

'Well, I'm glad you did,' he says.

In the car I feel the need to say something to fill the empty space between us. 'I thought Uncle Tariq would be here.'

'He was planning to be. I told him not to come.'

I tighten my grip on the wheel. 'Really? That's interesting.'

Iskender leans back, doesn't comment. 'How are the girls? And Nadir?'

I tell him the girls are acting in a school musical this term. Layla will be a Singing Fish, but we don't know yet which kind. It will be a haddock probably, though she'd much prefer to be a dolphin. My younger has been given the part of the Fisherman's Wife, a nasty, greedy character, but quite a central one. So there is a bit of competition going on in the house at the moment. Singing Fish versus Fisherman's Wife.

I tell him all this without mentioning Jamila's name, though he knows, of course. 'They are both excited,' I conclude.

'Great kids,' he says, smiling.

The silence that follows is disconcerting. I put on the ABBA cassette I have brought with me, but somehow dread pressing the play button.

'Do you want a cigarette?'

Iskender shakes his head. 'I quit a while ago.'

'You did?' I study him out of the corner of my eye. 'So, if you don't mind my asking, what will you do now?'

'I'd like to see my son as soon as possible.'

I don't mention that Katie phoned me a few days before. She has settled in Brighton. Married to a clairvoyant. A man who reads palms and claims to see the future, though I doubt whether he has prophesied the release from prison of her rather notorious ex-boyfriend. They have three children together. As we chatted on the phone, I couldn't help but suspect she still cared for my brother, and perhaps even loved him a bit.

As if he has read my mind, Iskender asks softly, 'How is Katie doing?'

'Happily married.'

If that hurts, he doesn't let it show. 'That's fantastic. I'm happy for her.'

Does he really mean it?

'It was kind of you to come to pick me up,' he says. 'I won't be staying long, though. I'll find a place. And a job. There are Good Samaritans who help people like me. Then . . .' He pauses. 'I'd like to go to visit Mum.'

There is anticipation after his words, hovering in the air like steam wafting off Mum's *boreks*. I change gear, accelerate and say, thickly, 'She died.'

He turns a blank stare on me. 'But . . . but Yunus told me –'

'I know what he told you. It was the truth.' I wipe my eye. 'Six months ago, she passed away.'

'Alone?'

'Alone.'

I don't tell him how it happened. I'll do that later.

'I was . . . I was going to ki . . . ss her hand,' he says, and I detect a slight stutter in his speech. 'I was hoping she would agree to see me.'

'I'm sure she would have,' I say, because it is true. 'I have her letters with me. You'll read some of them, you'll see she always asked about you.'

Iskender drops his head, studying his wrists as if there are still handcuffs around them. He turns to the window and sighs, his breath fogging the glass. He rolls down the window and pops his head out, breathing hard. Then he takes a piece of paper out of his pocket and lets it go into the wind.

'One more thing,' I say, when he rolls up the window again. 'Nadir . . . My husband, he doesn't know.'

'What do you mean?'

'Only Yunus and I. And now you, of course. No one else in the family knew Mum was alive and no one else ever should.'

It was our oath, Yunus's and mine. When we understood that everyone had confused Aunt Jamila with my mother, we swore on the Qur'an that we would never reveal the truth to anyone. Not to our father. Not to Uncle Tariq. Not to Aunt Meral. Not to Elias. Not even to our spouses if and when we got married. Only the two of us would bear the secret.

'Then why did you tell me?'

'It was Yunus's idea, not mine. He thought it was time for you to know. He hoped that the two of you would meet, reconcile. He wanted you to prepare yourself, I guess.'

We pass by a sleepy village without coming across a single soul. The afternoon is drawing to a close, and the world feels complete and

334

content. At a red light, he turns aside and meets my eye. 'You live with too many secrets, sister.'

'Speaking of which,' I say, opening the glove box, 'can you take that out?'

Slowly, he fetches the object at which I am pointing. A book. On Alaska.

'You've an hour and a half to learn everything there is to know about Alaska. That's where I told my daughters you've been all this time, working.'

Smiling dolefully, Iskender begins to peruse the book. Snowy mountains, grizzly bears, salmon dancing in cold fresh waters. Suddenly, it doesn't look like a bad place to be, not bad at all. Alaska.

Dream within a Dream

A Place near the River Euphrates, May 1991

Opening the chest, she took out the prayer rug and stood listening to the sounds of the valley. That was another thing about living there. As long as the wind blew northwards, it would carry the calls to prayer from the mosque in the village far below; but when the wind changed direction she was no longer able to figure out what time it was. The clock she had brought with her from London had stopped working and was waiting in a corner, like an ancient, withered face too tired to talk. But she needed to know the hour to pray, for she had so much to tell God.

Perhaps it was her age that was making her more observant, though she was far from being old, only in her mid forties. Or perhaps it was simply because there were too many ghosts in her life now, too many to grieve for. Every day she asked God to help her twin find peace in heaven, as that surely was where Jamila would have gone. Somewhere in that prayer she included Hediye, the mother-sister whom she remembered not as the mass of swollen, purple flesh hanging from the ceiling but as the jovial young girl she once had been. She also prayed for her husband, contemplating all that they had, and had not, given to each other. Then she prayed for her long-deceased parents. If she still had any energy left, she mentioned the three village centenarians who had recently breathed their last, one after the other.

Once she had paid her respects to the dead, she moved on to the living. She started with her granddaughters in rainy London, whom she knew from pictures only. She asked for guidance *for my headstrong daughter and that caring husband of hers.* This was followed by an elaborate prayer for Yunus (and sometimes for his band), that he might excel and soar high without being seduced by the trinkets of fame. Next she took a minute to pray for Elias, that he might be well, healthy and content, and find a person to love, if he hadn't already. Then came the longest prayer of all, for Iskender. *Her sultan, her lion, the apple of her eye.*

There were times when she wondered if she had done the right thing by coming back. But the serenity that wrapped around her like a shawl every morning at dawn was confirmation enough. Living such a solitary life could be only a short step to insanity. She tried to keep herself balanced by expressing thanks to God for everything He had both given and denied her. It was harder to go mad when you were thankful.

The early days in England now seemed as distant to her as a dream within a dream. The first time she took a big red bus, the children still little by her side and Yunus yet to be born. She would never forget the excitement of seeing the Queen's palace through the steamed-up windows and the Queen's soldiers, sober and serious on high horses. A sense of loneliness had washed over her upon arriving in Hackney, with its rain-soaked streets, adjoining brick houses and thimble-sized gardens. The house her husband had found was shabby and in need of paint, but she didn't mind, being used to making a home in small spaces. What she couldn't adjust to, however, was the weather. The rain. The gloom. The clouds always a tint of some obscure colour. Growing up by the Euphrates had inured her to harsh winters and harsher summers, but she didn't adapt easily to waking up to a permanently overcast sky. Yet she loved going to the market on Ridley Road, watching the people rummaging for bargains, the street buzzing with purposeful activity, like a beehive. It was nothing like the bazaars in Istanbul, though it was throbbing with life, and that she cherished. One could come across so many different people with skins of all shades of brown, white and black, from places that were, to her, only names on a blurry map.

It wasn't things such as the traffic coming at her from the left or the drivers sitting on the opposite side of the car that startled her so much as the way Londoners carried themselves. The starchiness of old ladies, the brazenness of the youth, the freedom of housewives, the kind of confidence she never had and never thought she would obtain. She would watch the women in their T-shirts with their nipples showing, their hair iridescent in the sun, and marvel at how they wore their femininity like a gown. Couples kissing on the streets, smoking, drinking, debating. Never had she seen people so keen to lead their lives out in public. The villagers of her childhood had not been the most loquacious types, and she herself had always retained a reticent nature. To her, England was a nation of words, and she tried hard to crack the hidden meanings, the in-jokes, the irony.

But it was the birds that amazed her the most in big cities – confined to gaps and holes, mostly invisible, except when they were crowding and jostling against one another for a handful of grain or when they dropped dead on the pavements. The birds of the Euphrates were not like that. Perhaps there weren't very many species, surely not as many as in the London Zoo, but they were free – and welcomed.

In London she would be dismayed to see windowsills with prickly needles cemented on to them, like a porcupine's bristles, to prevent the birds from perching and soiling the place. It reminded her of the garden walls with embedded shards of glass that she had observed in Istanbul. It was to keep the thieves away, she was told. Even the thought of it had made her cringe. Whoever lived in those houses did not only want to stop trespassers but also wished them to cut their bare hands or feet. Windowsills with needles, garden walls with glass – she didn't like either of them. Or what the city life did to people, bit by bit.

*

After the murder, Pembe stayed in the squat for several months. Yunus and Esma took turns visiting her, always watchful, always on guard not to breathe a word to their uncle and aunt. By then Iskender had been arrested and put in gaol, but Pembe was still confused as to whether to come forward or not. Initially, she had feared the squatters would find out why she was in hiding, but the fact that they barely read the newspapers, let alone listened to local gossip, worked in her favour. Not that they didn't sense trouble, but they imagined that it related to the Home Office. Being against all sorts of authority, they were happy to shield her, even after they discovered the real reason for her stay. Yunus asked them to help his mother change her appearance and they jumped at the opportunity. They cut Pembe's hair and dyed it a soft ginger colour, *like an Irish lassie's*. With a pair of big, round glasses and wearing jeans, she was unrecognizable.

Nonetheless, try as she might, Pembe would not have made it through the darkness of those days had it not been for the help of her twin. One midnight in the squat, as she was sitting by the window, staring into an emptiness only she could see, she noticed a form in the garden, listless but wakeful at the same time. It was her sister. Jamila neither approached nor shared a word, but the sight of her was enough to send a bolt of tremendous joy through Pembe. The moment was swiftly curtailed: the apparition dissolved in the air like a drop of milk in water. But the experience somehow assured Pembe that her twin was not in pain and the place she had migrated to was not unbearable. After that day, the same ghost would from time to time appear, commuting between Pembe and Iskender in prison.

Shortly before Yunus and Esma began boarding school in Sussex, Pembe decided to leave. She had realized, with a deeper surge of understanding, that she had completed her time in England and had to go back. To the Euphrates, to the place where she was born, for, unlike Elias, she was no air plant and needed to embrace her roots. Yunus and Esma supported the plan, provided that they could pay visits in the summer.

They still had the Amber Concubine, which Jamila had brought with her in the hollowed-out heel of her shoe and which she asked her sister to keep safe for her. None of them had the foggiest idea about its worth or how to sell it. In the end it was Mrs Powell who came to their rescue, with the Captain, much to the disquiet of Yunus. The diamond was sold, while Mrs Powell helped to arrange Pembe's trip. She also made sure that some money was put aside in a bank for Yunus and Esma. With the rest of the money the punks threw parties so wild that they would be the talk of Hackney for months to come. The only detail that escaped Pembe, when the deal was done in Hatton Garden, was that the diamond could be given or taken as a gift, but never put up for sale. She hadn't been informed about the curse, but, even if she had been, she would still have gone ahead with the plan. Pembe, the woman with endless superstitions, was tired of her fears.

When Pembe went to her sister's hut in the valley, she wasn't overly dismayed by the wreck she found. The passage of time, the four winds, the bandits and general neglect had partly ruined the peaceful hideaway that Jamila had created.

The peasants were thrilled to have the Virgin Midwife back, though they would never understand why she refused to attend births. But they helped her to clean and to fix her hut. The region had become a dangerous place, however. There were Kurdish insurgents fighting against the government and soldiers patrolling day and night. In the middle of all this Pembe remained, replacing her twin. There were times when she dodged danger, but she never mentioned this in her letters. She wrote only about good things.

She had promised her children the move would be temporary, that she would stay a while and then return, a new woman, but once she walked into her sister's house and started putting things in order, Pembe knew she wouldn't be leaving in a hurry.

Esma

They say you begin to understand your mum when you become a mother yourself, but for me it was Pembe's letters that helped me to get to know her better.

She wrote to me regularly, openly, telling me more about herself than she ever had to my face. Getting a blue airmail envelope from her became indispensable to me, a cherished weekly routine. I would make myself tea, sit at the kitchen table and read, once, then many times, knowing that she was well and thriving.

My dear daughter, the light of my life, in this world and the next,

I think about you all the time. Please don't stop visiting your brother. Forgive, Esma. Try. I know how hard it is, but you must. Make sure he understands he's not alone. We are never alone. I pray to Allah that He sends him a companion, someone who has compassion for his fellow human beings and knows how ignorant they are but still loves them anyway. I pray every day that He finds this person and sends him to prison to accompany Iskender.

Don't frown, my love. Don't say that I am being biased towards him even now. Can you choose one finger over the other? That's how it is for a mother. You cannot favour among your children. Iskender, Yunus and you are equally and so dear to me.

These days it is harder than before to send out post. Don't worry if you don't hear from me for some time. I had a most peaceful dream yesterday. I was here and there in Queen's London at the same time. It was raining, except it was a strange rain of colours so vivid it was like watching fireworks without any fire. I woke up and thought, but it is true. I am there with you. Always.

Your loving mother, Pembe

It was the last letter I received from her: the one I have read so many times that the paper is slightly tattered around the edges, and carries fingerprints all over it, mine on top of hers, like storylines that intersect and diverge.

Later on, when I managed to travel to Turkey, the villagers told me in detail how it had happened. They assured me she had not suffered, not the least bit. A virus. The disease began with a skin rash around the neck and arms, patches of pink, nothing particularly alarming. Before long, the patient started to shiver and to sweat, and, if it went untreated at this stage, a high fever would follow, a comatose sleep that weakened the lungs so fast that many couldn't wake up. It had emerged late in the spring of 1992, passing from animals to humans, and killed half-a-dozen people in a month – then it disappeared as if it had never been. She had probably contracted it when she paid a visit to her village, Mala Çar Bayan, to get provisions, and had accepted the offer of tea from a woman who wanted to show her the carpets she had woven in her youth. The woman's six-year-old son was carrying the virus, though nobody knew this at the time. The child survived; my mother didn't.

It was only when her letters ceased to come that I understood she had died for the second and last time.

Acknowledgements

I would like to thank David Rogers for reading an early draft and offering valuable suggestions.

Thanks to my agent, Elizabeth Sheinkman, for her encouragement and for being her lovely self. Special thanks to my two wonderful editors, Paul Slovak and Venetia Butterfield, for their insightful notes and scrupulous attention to detail, and to Donna Poppy for her unique contribution.

My greatest thanks go to Zelda and Zahir, who, when asked at school what mothers typically did at home, answered 'They sign books'; and to Eyup, husband, beloved, nexus of patience and wisdom.

I am also grateful to the women, East and West, who have shared their personal stories with me, as well as their silences.

Elif Shafak
www.elifshafak.com (http://www.elifshafak.com)